ANTOINETTE IN THE DARK

TRAPPED BY HER OWN FANTASIES, INTRIGUE, AND DESIRES

EUNICE SCHOFIELD

Publishing Services provided by Paper Raven Books LLC
Printed in the United States of America
First Printing, 2023

Paperback ISBN 979-8-9887047-0-6
Hardback ISBN 979-8-9887047-1-3

DEDICATION

To my quirky family:

James, for holding the fort with Herculean strength and unequaled patience and poise, so that I can chase after my dream. And, of course, my kids: Daphne, Joey, and Aaron and Andrew (the twins). These four are the most enthusiastic cheerleaders a person could ever have. They would cheer me off a cliff, if that's what I wanted to do. I love you guys, to the moon and back!

CHAPTER 1

NIGHTMARE ON ORCHARD LANE

*"I'm just a whisper of smoke, I'm all that's
left of two hearts on fire, That once burned
out of control, You took my body and soul,
I'm just a ghost in this house"*
- "Ghost in This House," song written by
Hugh Prestwood

An awoke from a heavy and troubled sleep. Something was terribly wrong. Her heart was jumping out of her chest, her mouth full of cotton, and her throat scraped with sandpaper.

Her head pounded. She felt lightheaded and out of sorts. An scanned the perimeter of her bedroom, trying to assess what in the world was happening. She identified the boxes she had been packing last night, neatly stacked by the far wall, just as she'd left them.

Like a tsunami, memories came flooding, saturating every fiber in her body—nearly twenty-five years of tears and laughter, joy and sorrow. She could hear the pitter-patter of little feet running down the hallway, the happy giggling and squeals the girls made. She could still smell the sweet aroma of chocolate chip cookies baking in the kitchen oven… so many Thanksgiving dinners and Easter egg hunts, so many Christmas trees decorated and Halloween pumpkins carved.

Her sobs came in little gasps that turned into great big gulps. The sound both startled and angered her. She had slipped so deep inside her own thoughts that she hadn't realized she was crying. She wanted the pain to stop.

Sitting up on her queen-sized bed, surrounded by her favorite oversized blankets and fluffy pillows, An swiped at her hot tears and suddenly became aware of swirls of colored light—like strobe lighting splashing blue and red across her walls and ceiling.

What the heck? She frowned in confusion as she climbed out of bed and walked to one of the two bedroom windows facing the neighbors to the left of her house. She looked down at a flurry of activity below on her normally quiet lane. An rubbed her eyes with both heels of the palms of her hands and then pinched her arm, just to be sure she wasn't dreaming.

Not sure what she was witnessing, she reached for her hair tie on the nightstand and used it to secure the thick folds of dark hair—now with a silver strand here and there—away from her face.

Feeling a gnawing need to be comforted, An hugged herself tightly, as she continued to scan the street below, blinking furiously to better focus. She could see various rescue trucks and police cruisers strewn about. People milled around, quizzical looks stamped on their faces. The room felt colder than usual for October in Northern Virginia. She shivered.

Crossing to the other side of her bed, An stuffed her feet into her worn slippers and picked up her robe, which had been faithfully hanging on one of the bedposts at the foot of her bed. She put it on, cinching the belt tightly around her waist. She had lost a bit of weight lately, and her robe hung loosely around her small frame.

Walking back to the window, An muttered under her breath, "What has happened?" Her headache had worsened, as if her head was being squeezed in a vise. She decided to make her way downstairs to look out the library window, which might give her a slightly better angle to the scene outside.

Moving as quickly as she dared in the dim gray of daybreak, An turned light switches on as she made her way along the upstairs hallway, then down the flight of stairs, turning right when the stairs split into two directions, past the powder room, and into the library. She was mindful not to let her gaze linger too long on the moving boxes dotting every corner of the home.

How was it that she was in this place in time, carefully stowing away her entire life in these cardboard boxes? Not wanting to dwell on those thoughts, she argued with her mind to stay focused on deciphering the meaning of the lights and commotion outside. This way she kept her memories at bay, the memories of sunnier days when she actually enjoyed getting out of bed to face each new dawn.

She reached the large windows in the library, pulled the heavy drapes aside, and poked her head through, peeking out anxiously. An ambulance pulled away just then, its lights flashing in the haze of predawn. No sirens, she noted. A fire truck made a U-turn and followed the ambulance out of the lane. Its shiny red coat glowed ominously as it went past her house. OWENSVILLE, VIRGINIA FIRE DEPARTMENT was printed on its side. There were still two police cruisers and a number of unidentified cars left on the street.

Some neighbors huddled nearby, looking on with glazed, stunned eyes. Most were in pajamas and robes. An turned to look at the clock above the mantle. It was just 6:09 on a Saturday morning, or was it Sunday? Her mind was so clouded lately. It was Saturday, she concluded.

She decided then she would brew a strong pot of coffee. *Coffee and chocolate, dark chocolate to be precise, are the two addictions I don't ever want to give up!* An smiled at her own thoughts as she followed the length of the downstairs hallway toward her cozy kitchen in the back of the house. A nice hot cup of black coffee would obliterate her headache and clear her head. She was still foggy from sleep, and her stomach felt sour. It was most likely the effects of all the turmoil in her life right now, although whatever was happening out there was adding to her physical discomfort. Not knowing what was going on right outside her front door filled her with uncertainty and anxiousness.

In her kitchen, An felt some of the anxiety lifting. This was her sanctuary, the place where ideas took form, dreams came to life, and so many nighttime conversations kept the lights above burning into the dark. It was a bright and cheery space with white cabinets and white tiles and sky-blue walls. A few years back, mostly in an attempt to have a common project they could work on together, An and Brad had upgraded the kitchen and added all new, stainless-steel appliances.

The kitchen extended into a sunroom boasting a bay of windows spanning all three walls. From there, a door led outside to a patio and another one of An's most favorite places: her garden. Here she had spent hours each day, lost in her tomato vines and basil plants, azalea and raspberry bushes. Her mint leaves went into her homemade sweet tea and salads, and her parsley into her jasmine rice dish. Her roses and gardenias decorated many dinner tables.

Farther out, on the perimeter of her yard, she and Brad had planted flowering dogwood and redbud trees. Crawling on the back wall of the house, trumpet vine grew wild and unchecked.

Out of an ornate green-and-peach-striped canister on her countertop, An spooned Starbucks robust morning blend coffee—freshly ground as of the previous night—into the coffee machine basket. Her mind wandered again into nostalgic territory. She touched the cabinet above her head, thinking how she had stripped and painted these herself. She sighed.

Time was running out; she really needed to get working on thinning down the contents of these cabinets. The thoughts made her head begin to pound harder, so she shuffled them to the back of her head. *Coffee! Just make some coffee, An,* she told herself. *One thing at a time, one day at a time.* The bitter, hot liquid would go down nicely right now, warming her inside and out. She needed that warmth badly.

A rattling sound startled An, and she turned toward the patio door. A light drizzle had begun to fall. Yellow, orange, and rust-colored leaves swirled about, hitting the panes of glass like fingernails lightly rapping and scratching. The wind was picking up speed too. That must have been what she heard, just the wind jiggling the door handle. She inhaled and exhaled slowly letting her breath out, trying to calm her jarred nerves.

Her hands were trembling a little. "It's okay," she told herself out loud. "Everything's going to be just fine. Focus, focus…"

Once she had the pot on, she walked back, this time through the dining room with its Amish-made oak table and corner hutches—more remnants of her previous life. The dining room led into the living room that opened into a foyer area. In the living room, she absent-mindedly fluffed the pillows on the couch and looked around to be sure all was as she had left it.

Then she walked across the spacious room and back to the library. The nine-foot ceiling dwarfed An as she made her way across the room. Back to the library windows again, An noted that the neighbors had pretty much vanished from sight. Probably back in their own comfortable homes, hungry for warmth and dry clothes. Only one police car and a dark sedan remained. She strained to see what else she could see.

Whatever had happened seemed to be not at the house right next to her but the next one over. She didn't know those people well at all, but she knew they were a couple about the same age as she and Brad, in their late forties or early fifties. She was pretty sure there had been kids living in the home at some point, but not anymore, as far as she knew. The wife was a recluse who neighbors saw only from behind the safety of her windows. But the husband liked working in his yard, planting things and tending to his flowerbeds. At times, in the evenings, he could be found smoking a cigar on the front porch. Their yard was beautifully manicured. She knew what the man looked like but wasn't sure she could identify the woman.

Movement at the corner of her eyes pulled her out of her reverie. Someone in a dark hooded jacket had come out of the shaded area between the houses and was briskly walking across the lawn toward An's own home. It looked like a woman, but it could also have been a small man. Something about that walk was familiar, but she couldn't place it. Her heart began to pound in her chest, and she became oddly agitated.

Who is that? Why is someone walking toward my home, and what could she want? She flattened herself against the wall between the windows, closed her eyes, and willed this morning away—along with whoever that figure might be. Heck, she willed the last five years or so of her life away, maybe more, maybe all of it... back to her birth. Clean slate. Do-over.

But she also wanted some of her old life back; she wanted normalcy. She longed to be a wife and a mother again. She should have tried harder, she should have fought tougher, she should have loved deeper... *Oh, Lord, too many ifs, too many should haves!*

Life didn't always give you what you want, and it didn't allow you to keep certain things and discard others at will. The events that had taken place could not be undone.

There was frantic knocking at her front door.

An jumped, and her eyes popped back open. She tried to steady her nerves as she walked to the front door and tentatively opened it, sneaking a look. She came face-to-face with a petite woman holding the hood of her jacket with both hands to shield her face from the wind and rain outside. The wind was howling like a wounded creature now. It was probably safe to assume that the sun would not be showing its face any time soon. It seemed apropos considering the mood outside and how An was feeling inside.

The woman gave An a flimsy smile.

"Hi there!" she said, much too cheery for the somber mood, although her voice cracked a little, betraying her attempt at happiness. She was trying to appear and sound calm, but there was a palpable current of urgency and panic in her demeanor. "An? I'm so sorry to barge in like this, but we have to talk about what's happened at the Spencers' home."

An opened her mouth to speak, but no sound materialized. She felt utterly confused. This whole morning was like a bad dream she could not escape.

"You know me?" she finally managed to say.

"I'm not sure, but I think we know each other. I'm Angela—Angie for short. Lisa assured me you would know me. But I don't have a lot of time to explain—"

"How do we know each other?" An interrupted. Her confusion was building momentum. This woman was familiar, but An had no recollection of ever meeting her. What in the world was going on? "I don't know you, and frankly, you are scaring me a little," An mumbled as she took a step backward. The front door slammed open against the door stopper, leaves swirled into the foyer, and fat raindrops pelted her face.

Don't let her in! she thought. *Keep her out!*

"No, no, no, don't be scared," Angie pleaded, palms up. "Please. Listen, those investigators surely are coming to talk to you about what happened. A woman died this morning, and I need you to help me get to the bottom of it. For Lisa, she's the one asking. Pleading, please, An!"

"What? Oh my God!" An muttered, now absolutely befuddled. "Whodiedwhathappened? The Spencers? Lisa? Lisa died?" Her voice quivered a little, and her right hand flew to her throat in an automatic response. Her heart pounded faster in her chest as an eerie sense of déjà vu engulfed her.

"We were good friends a long time ago," Angie continued, talking fast now. "I hadn't heard from her in a very long time, until late last night, when she called me out of the blue. She said by dawn she would probably be dead. I believe she was right. The police will likely want to talk to everyone on Orchard Lane, including you." Angie's words tumbled out like a slap to An's face.

Angie quickly glimpsed behind herself, making sure no one was coming yet or listening to her rant.

"But I didn't see or hear anything? I don't know anything? I don't understand? How did she know…" An let her words trail when she noticed that she had started speaking in question marks. She had a habit of doing that when she was nervous or uncomfortable.

"An, please listen to me. Listen! She called me in the middle of the night, probably hours before she died. She told me to come to you, that together we can make a difference. We can make sense of this." Angie was now talking in a loud whisper and still making very little sense to An. "I think something strange is going on. I need to know what happened. I need your help to get answers. Do you understand? An, we need to work together. I need your help!"

"But why me? Can't you ask the police? What about her husband? Or her other neighbors? I don't know anything." An's voice cracked and splintered at the end. She wanted no part of whatever this was.

"No! No, I can't. You are it. Lisa said you. I don't understand it either right now. I'm going on instinct here. I think you need to go talk to her husband; he will trust you. You both have gardening in common. He will open up to you." Angie kept throwing furtive looks behind her as she spoke. She appeared scared, getting a little wild-eyed. "I don't want the police to know what we are up to. They will think we're meddling in police business. Of course, we're not, not really. In fact, we may be able to help. I just need to get to the truth. Lisa needs us. I'll never have peace of mind if we don't get to the bottom of what happened to her."

"But are you positive something has happened to her, and do you really think her husband had something to do with it?" An asked, trying to think this through with a splash of logic. She was confused and distressed, but something about this woman made her want to listen, to understand, to help. Maybe it was the panic in her voice, maybe it was the fact that she was so familiar, maybe it was the intrigue of it all. She was compelled to listen even though she wanted to be left alone.

An had a bad feeling about all of this. This was a matter for the police. She was no Kinsey Millhone, even if that was her teenage idol in her beloved Sue Grafton novels.

"I really don't know… I hope not, but I have to try to figure it out. Will you help me?" Angie pleaded.

"How?"

"Bring the man a plate of your famous raisin-oatmeal cookies or a casserole or something. Befriend him. Get him to open up, to talk to you. Can you go today? The sooner, the better."

"I don't know… I'll try?" An told her. "It just seems so weird. Um… He may not want to see me. He doesn't know me, and this is a sensitive time… Wait, how do you know so much anyhow? About them, about me?"

An stared at Angie. Her face flushed hot, yet a cold sensation ran through her veins. An's heart pounded in her chest.

"Lisa told me. Okay, look, I have to go now, but I will be back," Angie said as she turned to leave. An watched her speed walk down her front lawn lined with azalea bushes, across the driveway, then disappear toward the mouth of Orchard Lane—in the opposite direction of the Spencer home.

Angie had appeared like a mirage and then vanished like a ghost. Leaves and rain were gathering by the front stoop, tracking into the small foyer, so An closed the door and stood there, both frozen and shaken by the exchange she had just had with this woman, Angie. *Did this conversation even happen at all?* An wondered. It was so strange that it seemed surreal. *And how did Angie know about my raisin-oatmeal cookies? How did Lisa?* But An didn't have time to ponder that at the moment. Other things were front and center in her mind.

If Angie is to be believed, a woman is dead! A neighbor! Oh. My. God! An was frightened and confused; she had a gazillion questions and no answers. She couldn't make heads nor tails out of any of this. She needed her coffee, pronto! She gathered up some leaves on the tiled floor by the door and walked back to the kitchen to get her much-needed cup of java.

Discarding the leaves in the trash can, An reached for her oversized coffee mug in one of the cabinets. But before she could pour her cup of coffee, there was more rapping at the front door. With a long sigh, she shuffled back to the foyer to open the door once more. This time two strangers stood on her stoop under the overcast, wet sky, their clothes looking crumpled. One was a man and the other a woman. Almost certainly, these were the detectives Angie predicted would be coming. *This is a heck of a morning!*

"Good morning," said the man, extending his hand for a shake and offering An a dazzling smile. "I'm Detective Connor, and this here is my partner, Detective Conrad. We're with the Owensville Sheriff's Office, ma'am. May we come in, out of the rain, and talk to you for a few minutes?"

An accepted his handshake, which was strong and reassuring and somehow put her at ease. Shaking her head yes, An motioned them in. Detective Connor thanked her with another brilliant smile and walked past into the spacious foyer. Detective Conrad followed but did not offer her hand for a shake. They were both drenched.

"Let me get you some towels to dry off," An said, as she unceremoniously walked toward the powder room at the foot of the stairs, without waiting for a response.

She returned with two towels, which she handed to the detectives. As they dried off, An took the opportunity to ask, "What has happened, Detectives? It looked like something major going on out there."

"Indeed, something major has happened, ma'am," Detective Connor told her. "We need to ask you some questions about it."

The detectives had followed An into the living room where they let their gazes wander around the spacious area. An motioned them to the couch. "Would you like to sit? Could I get you some coffee?" An asked the detectives.

"That would be great!" Detective Connor said and looked to his partner, who shook her head yes.

"Okay, let me get that," An told them and disappeared toward the kitchen.

As she walked down the hallway to the back of the house, An thought about how they both looked to be in their mid to late-thirties. He had pale blue eyes, short blond hair, cropped in a military style, a day or two of a beard shadow on his angular jaw. He was on the short side, maybe five-five, with broad shoulders. There was nothing special about the man's very forgettable face, but when his smile lit up his face, the world around disappeared, and An found she wanted to give him her total and absolute attention.

The woman, on the other hand, was tall by comparison, a good three or four inches taller than Connor.

She was very thin, with almond-shaped brown eyes and dark hair that had been pulled back into a short and severe ponytail. An noted that the woman detective—Conrad—had not offered a smile, but instead had a perpetual frown creasing her forehead. *That frown is going to turn into unattractive wrinkles later on,* An thought of the woman's pinched face.

Once An had carefully loaded up everything, she gingerly made her way back with three coffee-filled mugs on a tray, which she placed on the coffee table. She had also brought the sugar bowl and a few creamer pouches.

Detective Connor was sitting on the large couch. An sat across from him on one of the oversized chairs, coffee mug in hand. Detective Conrad reached for her coffee as well and sipped it black. She remained standing, pacing a little.

Actually, now that An was noticing the pair more carefully, they reminded her of Popeye The Sailor Man and Olive Oyl. She smiled at them in an attempt to stifle the laughter in her throat.

She turned her attention to watch Detective Connor add three heaping spoons of sugar to his coffee. *Wow!*

Then he asked her, "What did you see, Miss… um, sorry, I didn't get your name. For the record, can you give us your full name, please?"

Setting down her mug on the coffee table, Detective Conrad quickly pulled out a small flip-type notebook from her side pocket, revealing a gun strapped to her side. A pen materialized from her pocket, and she was poised to write.

"I'm sorry, where are my manners?" An apologized. "It's Antoinette Goode… no, no, that's not right," she stumbled. "Sorry, my divorce was finalized recently, and I am back to my maiden name, Antoinette Jordan." An lowered her gaze, trying to hide her discomfort and her emotions from the detectives, who were both quizzically watching her.

Detective Connor was the first to speak again. "Ms. Jordan… Antoinette. Can I call you by your first name?"

"Actually, I go by An, just A-N."

"That's different. A. N. Hm, you're not Vietnamese, are you?" asked Detective Connor, taking a casual tone, searching her face.

"What? No, no, I'm not."

"I dated a Vietnamese woman for a long time. I think An—A. N.—is a Vietnamese name. Names fascinate me!"

"Oh. It might be a Chinese surname. But maybe it's Vietnamese. I don't know. I have my younger brother to blame for my nickname. He went by CJ, which is his first and middle name initials. When he was little, he couldn't pronounce my name, so my parents started referring to me by A to help him out. Then it turned into my initials too, A-N, eventually becoming An. It just stuck," An explained to the detectives.

"Interesting," said Detective Connor. "So, now I'm curious. What is your brother's name, and what is your middle name? Like I said, names fascinate me."

"Oh. Well, CJ is short for Carson Jasper. And I'm Antoinette Nina, my two grandmothers. CJ was named after our two grandfathers," An replied.

"Very cool names," Detective Connor told her, slowly nodding his head in the affirmative. "And I definitely like the whole familial thing; it makes the names even more interesting."

Detective Conrad was wandering around the room again, looking at pictures and examining objects, fingering this knickknack or that trinket. She picked up a picture perched on the console table behind the couch.

The photo had captured An and Brad standing on the boardwalk at Rehoboth Beach, Delaware. The blinding white sand and crystal-blue ocean created the perfect backdrop. An was holding her hair away from her face, the wind blowing it every which way. She wore a flimsy, gauzy purple dress. They both had dark shades covering their eyes, but their smiles were luminous. Brad had his arms possessively around An's shoulders, and she was leaning into him. They looked young and happy.

An had been distracted by the sight of Detective Conrad holding that picture and hadn't heard Detective Connor.

"An, is everything okay?" he asked.

"Yes, yes, I… I was distracted. That's all. I need to pack the photos. Sorry, what were you saying?"

"Peace."

"Um… what?" Confused, An stared at Detective Connor. She found him to be young, pleasant, and just a tad on the odd side. But, hey, there was nothing wrong with being odd. People probably thought she was odd too. She had never cared what anyone thought of her and totally embraced her oddness. He seemed to embrace his as well.

"Your name means peace," explained Detective Connor. Then he moved on to the topic at hand. "Did you know the family living at 32 Orchard Lane? Analise and Benjamin Spencer?" he asked.

"Analise?" An had to think about the name. She knew the woman as Lisa, but Analise must be her legal name. "No, I only knew them by sight. I did go to a cookout at their home once, many years ago, now that I think of it. I haven't seen the woman face-to-face in a long time, so I'm not even sure I would know her if I saw her out and about. The man works outside a lot." An's voice trailed off because she wasn't sure what she was supposed to say or what she should reveal to the detectives.

"That's strange, that you didn't know them, don't you think? This seems like a friendly kind of neighborhood. How long have you lived here, An?"

"About twenty-five years. And no, I don't think it's strange. I mean, they keep to themselves, seem really private. And I guess I kind of keep to myself too." An felt awkward. Maybe she should have done better, been friendlier, and acted more neighborly. But everybody always seemed too busy for idle chitchat, and the last few years had turned An into a husk of herself. She was too consumed with her own issues to befriend and socialize with her neighbors.

"Well, the Spencers have been on Orchard Lane for nearly a decade. I find it odd you didn't know them. Didn't you ever question why Analise Spencer was rarely seen outside? Right? You said you hadn't seen her in a while. How long was she, uh, 'out of sight?'" Detective Connor was smiling as he said these words. It bothered An, both what his words implied and the smile. His words sounded accusatory, and that smile that seemed welcoming a few minutes ago now made her think of news reporters who often told horrid stories with big smiles pasted on their faces—just out of place.

"I used to see her coming and going, I suppose to work and when running errands on weekends. But after the first few years, I saw her less and less. I don't remember seeing her at all the last two or three years, maybe more. I don't know. I don't really recall."

"Hmm…" was all Detective Connor could muster on the topic. He was frowning a little—perhaps a habit he had caught from Detective Conrad? His lips pursed, and he moved them from side to side, as if swishing mouthwash.

An lowered her gaze, feeling a twinge of guilt. "Is it relevant, Detective, that she was out of sight? What happened to her?" An asked the second question in a near-whisper.

"I simply find it curious, An, just curious… She expired under suspicious circumstances, actually. Sometime between midnight last night, when her husband claims he heard her in the bathroom upstairs, and four this morning, when he called 911 saying she was unresponsive." Detective Connor explained all this to An, while closely watching her reaction through narrowed eyes.

Detective Conrad had stopped her perusing and was watching An too, eyebrows raised. It was as if they were anxiously holding their collective breath in great anticipation of her reaction to the news.

An's hands involuntarily flew to her throat. She gulped audibly, then whispered, "Oh, my gosh! She died? How?"

An was genuinely perturbed, although she had already known that Lisa was probably dead from Angie's earlier visit. She still found it hard to believe someone so young and so close to her in age and proximity was gone. Just like that, death came for you in the middle of the night and snatched you away. *Life is tragic*, she thought. *And it sucks to no end.*

"It's too early in the investigation to know exactly what happened, so at this point, everyone is a potential suspect, as far as we're concerned," Detective Connor said.

"Everyone? Well, I was asleep!" An exclaimed indignantly. "And I'm guessing so were most of the other neighbors. I didn't see or hear anything! I don't know anything about it! And I don't see how I can help you?" Her voice was an octave higher. Tears were stinging her eyes. This had been the strangest of mornings. An was exhausted already, at not quite eight o'clock in the morning.

She took a deep breath and seemed to deflate, lowering her gaze to stare at the dark liquid in her cup, like a reflective black hole between her fingers. Detective Connor continued to watch her intently.

Detective Conrad had wandered into the library and was admiring the collection of books on the built-in shelves that took up most of the wall space in that room. Brad had labored for months, working on those shelves. She remembered being angry with him for taking so long to complete the project—an entire year! She had been so anxious to display her Dean Koontz and Sue Grafton novels, among her many other beloved books. But she should have been more patient, knowing how many of Brad's home improvements involved an inordinate amount of research, planning, and dreaming before they took any material shape. He never did anything on impulse.

"You never really know what you really know now, do you?" Detective Connor said ominously. An snapped out of her thoughts to look at him. She was puzzled by his riddle but decided to just let it go. Maybe she would ponder it later.

"Is that your husband?" Detective Conrad asked, pointing at the Rehoboth Beach photo. Her voice was surprisingly soft and gentle. She had walked back into the living room. An looked up, a little surprised by the change in topic and the fact that Detective Conrad had spoken at last.

"Yes, that's Brad. Bradley Goode, if you need it for the record," An replied, a bit of sarcasm in her tone. "We were vacationing in Rehoboth Beach, just a few short years before everything fell apart and went to crap." An was quiet then, her hands clasped tighter around her mug on her lap in front of her. She quickly lowered her gaze again. She didn't want to open that can of worms and wasn't sure why those words tumbled out of her mouth in the first place. "It was a difficult divorce," An quickly said as a way of explanation. She didn't want them delving into her personal life any more than necessary. She hoped that would be the end of that conversation.

"I see," said Detective Conrad, and she left it at that. She picked up another picture, this one showcasing two young girls about eight or nine. They were wearing matching blue jeans and pink tops and had their arms draped over each others' shoulders, bright smiles on their pretty faces. The younger one had short blondish-red hair, and the other had long dark hair. They were standing in front of An's house. It looked like summertime. Big pots of various shades and shapes could be seen behind them, full of loud, bursting color.

"Are these your children?" Olive Oyl asked.

"Yes… my stepdaughters, Lynne and Erica." An looked away quickly, trying to hide the sadness and the fact that she had referred to Detective Conrad as Olive Oyl in her thoughts. An turned back to Detective Connor. "Sorry, were you saying something?"

"So, you were asleep all night and heard nothing, saw nothing?" asked Connor.

"That's right," replied An. She was tired and getting a little annoyed, both at the detectives and at the maddening headache that persisted. Plus, she hadn't even finished her first morning coffee yet. The aroma permeated the whole house, making her crave more of it. *Yep, I'm a coffee junkie, and I don't apologize for it either*, she thought to herself.

"When was the last time you saw Mr. Spencer?" Connor asked her.

"Oh, maybe a week or two ago?" An said pensively, thinking maybe there was another, more recent time, but she couldn't recall. "He was out decorating the steps with pumpkins and mums. It was a weekend, and I needed to get out of the house for some fresh air, so I went on a short walk. I walked past his house and around the cul-de-sac. I saw him and waved."

"Did he seem… normal?" Detective Connor asked. Detective Conrad had put the picture down and was attuned to the conversation now, her pen poised for more note-taking.

"I guess. He waved back. Like I said I don't really know them. I'm not sure what normal would look like for them," An answered. She definitely wasn't liking Detective Connor anymore. His grin seemed almost to mock her. It was unnerving.

She tugged down on the neck of her nightgown, feeling hot and clammy. *What kind of name is that anyway? Isn't it a first name? Does the man have two first names for a name?* "Detective, the lane dead-ends at the Spencers' house, so I don't really have much occasion to go past their home? Have you talked to other neighbors? They might be a bit more helpful?" An noticed she was talking in question marks again.

"We certainly will," said Detective Connor. "We've taken up too much of your time, ma'am. Do you have any other questions, Kim?" He turned to look at his partner.

An looked at Kim—Kim, not Olive Oyl. She wondered what Popeye the Sailor Man's first name was. They seemed to be communicating with their eyes. An smiled to herself, thinking how the detectives made a cute couple. In an odd sort of way. *Nothing wrong with odd*, she reminded herself.

"Not at the moment," said Detective Conrad. Then, directing her gaze to An, she said, "But if you think of anything that might be important, Ms. Jordan, will you call us?"

Detective Connor stepped in and pulled a business card from his pocket. He handed it to An, who studied his card between her fingers. Daniel M. Connor. *Nice, strong name*, she thought. She wondered what the M stood for.

Both detectives began walking toward the front door. Detective Connor looked back at An and asked, "When was the last time you saw your ex-husband? Does he still live here, or does he come around? Do you know his whereabouts?"

Didn't they teach them at detective school to ask one question at a time? An wondered, but instead answered, "I saw him a few days ago at the courthouse when our divorce was finalized. And, yes, he stops by regularly, to check on things—check on me," An said. "He's always been a little controlling. Plus, we're trying to divvy up the last of our possessions and such..." An let her words trail off. She was again annoyed at herself for revealing more about her personal life. It was none of their business, and she didn't want to talk about herself. So why in the world was she letting these nuggets of information slip? She mentally sighed and rolled her eyes, irritated at herself.

Detective Connor cocked his head to the right, pursing his lips, swishing them from side to side again. "Hmm," he said. "And how long were you married to him?"

"We were married twenty-five years, as long as we've been in this house," An answered in a whisper, wondering why it was any of his concern.

"That's a long time. What happened? Did you two *drift apart?*" Detective Connor prodded, putting emphasis on the 'drift apart.' His partner listened and watched as if she was holding her breath.

"I loved him," An said, defiantly making eye contact. "I was committed to the point of destruction. It turns out he was just using me and had other motives. But there were many happy years, many happy moments. Though some memories can't be erased. I've tried."

"You're right, so right... Here's a piece of advice, An. Maybe it'll help you. You can take it or leave it. It's your choice. This is off the record now. I think you're a beautiful woman, and you seem like a nice person. Take a stand and move on with your life. Don't look back. Whatever happened, your husband probably doesn't deserve you, your tears, or your guilt." He was halfway out the door when he turned again. "Oh, and we may want to talk to Bradley at some point too. Feel free to let him know."

An didn't respond. She was speechless, not knowing how she should react. Great, she divulged too much when she should have shut her mouth, and now that she should respond, nothing came to mind. She was an enigma to herself sometimes.

Why would they need to talk to Brad, anyhow? He didn't live here anymore.

After they left, An stood still for a long time, feeling sorry for herself. Then she was angry, wondering about the gall of that man. How dare he? Her guilt? What did he know about her anyway? It wasn't just about Brad. It wasn't just that she was a divorced woman, another one among millions.

It was the way it happened. It was about how she lost everything in degrees. Everything, including herself. She was left naked and void of all that was hers.

It was all that Brad stole from her.

For many years, things cracked, splintered, and then just crumbled to pieces. She clutched at the remnants of her life like a drowning rat, and tried desperately to weave back together the frayed edges that were slowly, then rapidly, coming undone. But at the end of that valiant—and very stupid—fight, she lost it all, each loss cutting deeper than the previous. Her home, her job, her husband, her children, her happiness, her purpose… Like a flicker of smoke, an entire life, full of memories and promise—gone.

Just like that. Years and years of building, bulldozed. Just. Like. That.

That was to mention nothing of the evil that they had birthed together. She couldn't hold that thought simultaneously with the other memories. It was simply unbearable.

She had been Mrs. Antoinette Goode for so long; she didn't recognize Antoinette Jordan. She would recreate herself eventually, but the way it all happened was the most devastating of all, and she wasn't sure how to reconcile with that part of it.

Lisa Spencer suddenly came to mind. An had a faint recollection of a curvy and attractive woman with a shy smile and shoulder-length, honey-brown hair. Who was she? What was her story? Detective Connor had said "suspicious circumstances." Was her life crushed too? To the point she took her own life? Or was it snuffed out by someone or something else?

An walked back to her bright kitchen and took comfort from the wonderful aroma of fresh brewed coffee. She closed her eyes and breathed in deeply, anticipating that bittersweet liquid traveling down her throat, warming her entire body. She poured herself a second cup of much-needed coffee.

Then she took a deep breath and opened some cupboards, taking inventory of its contents.

"Raisin-oatmeal cookies!" she said out loud, doing a pretty good imitation of a cheerful voice. "Mr. Benjamin Spencer is going to love my home-baked cookies." She smiled dreamily. Then she became serious and still again, thinking. Had she brought her oatmeal-raisin cookies to that long-ago barbeque at the Spencers'? Was that how Lisa knew? The memory eluded her.

An had always enjoyed being in her kitchen, engulfed in the various aromas, filled with the sounds of cooking and baking. For her, this was therapeutic. She decided she would make a chicken casserole as well. Why not? She needed some therapy. She went through the shelves in her pantry to be sure she had all the ingredients. She knew she had chicken breasts in the freezer. The recipe also called for condensed chicken soup and cornmeal stuffing. Yep, she had that.

She mentally noted that she had enough raisins, old-fashioned oats, and plenty of flour for her cookies too. She walked over to the fridge and found the remaining ingredients, including sour cream. She checked the expiration date on the bottom. It was good to go. She hadn't been grocery shopping for a while, but her kitchen was always well stocked, so it didn't really surprise her that she didn't have to make a special trip to the supermarket before embarking on her cooking and baking venture for Benjamin Spencer.

Raisin-oatmeal cookies had always been Brad's favorite. He especially seemed fond of his wife's recipe, which made An feel good. "Mom's are good, but not delicious like yours!" He would giggle as he'd say those words, his mouth full of the yummy crumbs. "Don't tell her I said so." He would wink at her mischievously. He bragged to random people about his "wife's amazing cookies from scratch!" She smiled, reminiscing and savoring the memory. Once he had told one of her coworkers at a Christmas party that he had married her for her amazing skills in the kitchen, especially her raisin-oatmeal cookies!

An chuckled at the memory. She loved hearing Brad refer to her as *my wife* or *woman of mine.*

They were married for nearly two-and-a-half decades! She marveled at the thought. With the exception of a few hiccups, the first three years or so were wondrous. It had truly been a fairy-tale marriage. She thought she had captured her knight in shining armor, her soul mate, the love of her life. And friends and family commented about how he gazed at her with adoring eyes, how he doted on her and worshiped her. Their life together back then had been simply beautiful.

An clutched at her chest as her breath caught. She was still incredulous at the memory of her beautiful life that was lost to the horror that followed. Her eyes filled with tears, and her heart felt as if it would burst.

She didn't quite know why it hurt so badly now. The loss had been a long and complicated one; it had occurred in increments, not all at once. But when the divorce was final, the realization of everything hit her like a ton of bricks. The dull ache over the years suddenly became pure agony, the reality of it like a punch in the gut. *Why was this last time different?* she thought. After all the years of looking the other way, why couldn't she avert her eyes this time? She knew the answer, but she had to keep that memory separate, always separate. Knowing didn't give her back the life she had envisioned, the life she had dreamed about, the life she so desperately wanted the entire span of her existence.

Even though she had to keep things compartmentalized in order to keep her sanity, An knew some things with clarity. It wasn't losing Brad, it wasn't the lost life they had shared, it wasn't even the loss of her girls that tore at her; it was the illusion—the dream—of the perfect life that seemed possible and within reach but never truly was.

It was easier to mourn for those things that had shape and substance in the physical world: the husband, the home, the children. It was easier to understand those losses. The dream, the desire, the need for the life in her mind, however, could not be seen, could not be touched, was never even born so how, then, should she mourn its loss?

Somehow, though, back in the material world of the senses, the prospect of making a casserole and baking a few cookies for this man who just hours ago lost his wife gave An a sliver of hope and a smidgen of purpose. She had a mission! Her cooking and planning would hopefully lift her spirits, and the thought of meeting and talking to Benjamin Spencer made her smile.

She wasn't sure exactly what was happening to her and why she felt this sudden glimmer of hope, like an awakening, deep within her. But she held on to that feeling. She was going to put this "mission" ahead of her pain and her inner fog. She was going to look outward instead of inward. *Funny,* she thought, *someone else's loss and tragedy is strangely bringing me hope. What a strange morning this has been!*

CHAPTER 2
NEW BEGINNINGS: 1989

"Love bears all things, believes all things, hopes all things, endures all things."

         - 1 Corinthians 12:4-8

"Beginnings are sudden, but also insidious. They creep up on you sideways, they keep to the shadows, they lurk unrecognized. Then, later, they spring."

     - Margaret Atwood, *The Blind Assassin*

An didn't have a whole lot of vivid recollections about her childhood. It had been comfortable but not brimming with love and joy. It had been sparsely dotted with good memories and laughter, but short on touch and affection. Her parents were older by the time An and her brother, CJ, came along. Together their parents had owned a baked goods business, which they had single-handedly built from the ground up. The business grew nationally, distributing to all fifty states, and eventually even internationally to a few select countries. Their brand of pastries became well recognized worldwide.

Growing up, An remembered her parents—especially their mother, Juliet—being consumed with the business to the point of excluding their children and family life. Growing up in poverty on the hills of Preston County, West Virginia, Juliet had passionately vowed to never go hungry again. "So help me God, as long as I live," she would state emphatically whenever one of her children asked her why she had to work all the time.

Their days were lived around the business schedule and the customers' needs. Some Christmases, there might be a tree and decorations; some Thanksgivings, there might be a turkey baking in the oven. Other times, holidays were just another day. There was little consistency and no real traditions to hold the family together. But An's parents were good providers, and deep down, they were salt-of-the-earth, good people. Their father, Harrison, was a bit softer than Juliet—at least that's how it appeared. Save for his wife's fears and pressure to make more money to feed the family, Harrison would most likely have stayed home more often, indulged in more vices, planned more vacations, and engaged his children a bit more.

"Children don't feed and clothe themselves, HC. The bills aren't going to magically get paid either," his wife would admonish. "If we don't work, we don't eat, you crazy fool!"

"Relax, woman! I work from sunup to sundown. We have many trusted employees. We are doing better than just fine," Harrison would bellow in his deep, booming voice. Then the giant of a man would turn to wink at the kids or whistle as he skip-walked away, doing a little jig he liked to do to make them laugh. Better to ignore or downplay his wife's concerns, better to act foolish than to face her deepest, darkest fears. They had all glimpsed her inner monster once or twice and knew it was better to steer clear of that black hole. An knew their father loved their mother with all his heart and would do anything for her, but none of them were equipped to face the sadness and the demons that haunted her.

Both An and CJ had the opportunity of a good college education, they always had a nice home, and they had or did things their contemporaries had or did. Although lacking some emotional nourishment, they were fairly stocked in material comforts. Not that their parents lavished them with things—that wasn't their way—but still, they allowed their children some luxuries that made their lives comfortable.

But An longed for more, dreamed of more, and hungered for something meaningful. There had to be more to life, right? There must be or should be more. She wanted the closeness, the love and nurturing, the traditions, the family gathered together at Thanksgiving and Christmas. She knew that once she had her own family, it would be different. She would make sure of it. She and her husband, along with their troop of beautiful, well-behaved, pretty children, would drink eggnog as they weaved strings of homemade popcorn around the floor-to-ceiling, live pine tree at Christmas.

At Thanksgiving, hordes of people—the kids, grandkids, neighbors, and friends—would gather around their table for a turkey feast like no other. They would carve pumpkins in October and hunt for egg treasures in April. In February, they would decorate the house with pink and red hearts. In July they would travel to Rehoboth Beach, or maybe the Jersey shore or the Carolinas, to soak in the warm rays of golden sun, build sandcastles, and swim in the vast ocean. In January, the whole family would ski down the slopes of nearby Massanutten or Wintergreen. Afterwards, they would drink hot cocoa with marshmallows swimming on top, while sitting by the fireplace in one of the chalets.

Yep, she would create special memories for the entire family—memories they could all hold near and dear the length of their lives. She would take a million pictures to memorialize their time together and create unforgettable scrapbooks they would view together years later. Her family would be close. Her family would have heart. Her family would be a real family, not a pretend one.

But before starting the family of her dreams, An had to get her education underway. After much thought, she had settled on James Madison University. George Mason had been her second choice, but it was too close to home, and she felt she needed the space to spread her wings a bit. She considered William and Mary, too, but thought that might be a little remote from home. She had always loved the Shenandoah Valley area. Harrisonburg was perfect with the mountains in the near horizon and a nice homey atmosphere. Not too large but not too small either. It was a perfect setting for An.

The Shenandoah Valley, cradled by the Allegheny on one side and the Appalachian mountain range on the other, created the perfect oasis for An. She loved to hike, she loved nature, and she loved the raw, natural beauty. She felt right at home in historic Cantrell Avenue and soaked in the energy and the feel of the place. She fit in and belonged here, as if this space was created with her specifically in mind.

In the summer of 1986, An, with her parents' help, moved into a studio apartment in a brick building with white awnings right on Franklin Street, in Harrisonburg, Virginia within walking distance to campus. As she prepared to begin her psychology degree at James Madison University, she found everything she needed to make this her home for the next four years, including a part-time job at a popular coffee shop in quaint Town Square. Although her parents would pay for everything and she didn't really need to work for money, An wanted a venue to force her to get out, meet new people, and immerse herself in the community and culture of the area—a little extra cash was welcomed too, of course.

Her senior year in high school, her parents had bought her a reliable, used Honda Civic, which she now used to go home for a visit about once a month. Sometimes she drove into nearby towns or ventured to the mountain trails. She loved the freedom of getting in her little car and just driving and exploring unknown territory. She would put all the windows down and let the fresh air invade her space and fill her lungs. She marveled at the beauty that took her breath away and dreamed of one day having a little getaway cottage in the foothills of these mountains. Sometimes, she would bring her backpack along and trek through the woods, hiking and inspecting more up close and personally the nooks and crannies of this wilderness.

An enjoyed her trips back home, but for the most part, she stayed in Harrisonburg, quietly living life, making new friends, taking her weekend excursions, and studying. The party life didn't appeal to her, and she was never a night owl. On occasion, she went out for a beer or found herself at a frat house party wondering what the heck she was doing there, noticing little else but the sticky, grimy floors, and feeling like her eardrums would rupture at any moment. That scene simply wasn't her.

Halfway through An's studies, CJ began his own college experience at George Mason University, pursuing an English degree, which made sense to An. CJ loved to read and write and all things literary. In high school he had won many writing contests, was named the class poet, and had been the editor of his school paper, *The Battlefield News*. He had a brilliant mind, she thought, combined with a genuine sensitivity for his fellow human beings.

She stayed in touch with her brother, missing him every day, and experiencing the distance in her heart. Growing up, CJ was her one consistency, the one person who always had her back and was always there. But CJ led the life of a distant introvert, and An never truly felt she knew the real CJ. His life was probably similar to hers on the surface, but on totally different tracks, and he often seemed mysterious to her.

Her parents lurked in the periphery of their lives, providing the essentials, but emotionally passive. Yet, despite the relationship with their parents being truncated—at least from An's perspective—there was love; there was respect and appreciation toward each other.

Despite her feelings that her family had some serious shortcomings, An could not imagine life without these people. The older she got, the better she understood that there was more to all of them, and so much more to their intricate relationships. She began looking deeper than the surface, through the lens of maturity. She clung to the few family memories that peppered her life, savoring each and every activity, each and every moment of togetherness. She had resolved that once college was behind her, she would do better about getting to know her parents and brother. She was going to be a better daughter and sister.

When it came to romance, An had dated on and off all through high school and college. Boys liked her and found her attractive, maybe a little off-limits, but refreshingly different. What was not to like about her creamy complexion, the dark folds of hair that fell to her waist, and her penetrating hazel eyes? But things never seemed to progress to a serious level, to An's chagrin. Although she longed to start that large family that she always dreamed of creating and nurturing, she just didn't seem to be able to develop a meaningful and long-lasting relationship with a guy.

She thought she was a pretty good girlfriend, always attentive and accommodating. She would write cute notes and decorate them with hearts to be handed to the guy she was dating. She bought small gifts to express her feelings. She even cooked a meal or two. She understood and didn't complain if they couldn't pay for dinner out or if they had to cancel a date. An was attentive, doting, considerate, and unselfish to the guy she was dating.

But soon she realized maybe she was just a little too accommodating and understanding because most of the guys she dated eventually drifted off to someone else's arms.

Someone else more willing to enjoy the physical aspects of dating… maybe. A girl who lived a little more on the edge, who didn't study so much or crave solitary walks in the woods… perhaps. Someone more exciting, more worldly, more spur of the moment… who knew? She felt utterly inept and awkward at the whole dating and relationship thing.

An had decided early on that she would not share her body with just any guy. He would have to be pretty special, or they would wait for the honeymoon. She wasn't quite sure where she got the notion or how she had become such a goody-two-shoes or such a Pollyanna—she was often accused of being these by many who knew her. But it wasn't that she was trying to be good, or virginal, or whatever. It was simply and unapologetically who she was.

She remembered once asking CJ, "Why don't boys like me enough to stick around? You're a guy. What's wrong with me, from a guy's perspective?"

"You're too nice," he had replied without hesitation. "And you're probably too serious and too intense. Lighten up some!"

Geez! This, from the most serious, non-smiling, non-joking guy that ever lived! Go figure, An thought. She had pondered her brother's observations long and hard, however. Although she wanted to change in order to potentially attract her future husband, she decided she was who she was—that would have to be good enough.

If the guy was truly the right one, and if he was going to be *the one*, then he needed to appreciate and love her for the unadventurous nerd she truly was, right? She didn't want to pretend to be someone else. She wouldn't even know how to begin.

By the time An started her senior year in college, she had resigned herself to the fact that she might have to wait longer than expected to unearth Mr. Right. She might just end up having kids in her forties like her mom. It pained her a little, knowing that her plans would have to take a different course, that the life of her dreams would have to be put on pause for now, but she figured it was more important to find the right person than to try to rush into something, or force herself into a relationship. So, she went about her somewhat solitary, ho-hum life, and devoted most of her time to finishing up her studies and finding a solid and rewarding job after college.

Little did she know that Mr. Right might just be lurking around the next corner.

It had been a busy morning at the coffee shop one Saturday in December. Christmas was fast approaching, and people were out in droves, searching for that perfect gift. An was in deep thought about nothing in particular, just scattered items on her to-do list. The crowd had finally thinned right before lunchtime. An was wiping the countertop, breathing a sigh of relief for now, trying to enjoy the temporary lull before the next wave of customers.

She was a little preoccupied with an upcoming exam, but figured she'd ace it like always.

Out of nowhere An began humming a tune she had picked up somewhere but didn't remember what it was or where she had heard it.

"It must've been love, but it's over now... I lost it somehow... make-believing..." She sang the lyrics that she recalled and hummed the rest under her breath. She wished she remembered all the words. For her, music was all about the words; it literally had to speak to her. A catchy tune was good, but the words were pure magic, building narratives, weaving stories that took her elsewhere in the vast landscape of her mind.

She was startled out of her thoughts by a clearing of the throat, followed by a deep, but pleasant voice.

"That had to be the best cup of coffee I've had in a long time, and the entertainment is quite lovely too!"

An jumped, dropping her rag and knocking down the broom that had been propped up against the counter. She looked up, and there he was.

She gave a whistle inside her thoughts—at least she hoped it hadn't leaked out. He was like a picture straight out of a magazine. *A movie star?* she wondered. He had a neat afro with shiny beads in it. She had always been impressed by people with straight, dazzling white teeth. And, boy, he had that in spades! *I'm in love*, she thought.

He had dark brown eyes that seemed to miss absolutely nothing. His hands were stuffed in the pockets of his jeans, and he was wearing a fuzzy gray-and-red scarf around his neck. It complimented his black sweater nicely. In fact, the whole package was all around very complimentary. He was so pleasant to look at that she simply stared for a moment, grinning from ear to ear, before finding her voice.

"Hey, I mean, hi! My mom says hay is for cows." An chuckled, but it came out more like a snort. "I'm so glad you enjoyed the coffee. Coffee is our business, you know? And we have pastries, pies, you name it, to go with the coffee, of course. Did you happen to have some? The pastries, I mean. The apple strudel is by far my favorite…"

Gosh, I'm sooo rambling. You're a disaster, An, she admonished herself as she stopped to take a breath.

She gave herself a mental slap upside the head to stop the babbling. She bit down on her lower lip to try to stop her heart from thumping so loud. Her cheeks were burning. She gave him an apologetic smile and offered her trembling hand.

"I'm An," she told him. *And Doofus is my other name. Geez!*

"Hi there, An! It's good to meet you. My friends call me Jimmy." Their gazes held for an enormous second as they stood shaking hands.

His handshake was firm and warm, not one of those limp, clammy ones. They continued shaking hands and looking at each other, neither noticing their two right hands were getting well acquainted.

"I like your singing and humming too… and your pretty face," Jimmy said, smiling, goo-goo-gah-gah spelled out across his face.

Her cheeks burned hotter, and she mumbled, "Wow!" *Wow? What the hell, An*, she admonished herself again. This was getting old.

Finding her voice, An said, "I don't think I've ever seen you around. Are you just passing through?"

An hoped and prayed, crossing her fingers and her toes—she'd have crossed her tail too if she had one—that he would say he lived in the area, or had just moved to the area, or maybe was within a short driving distance… or even willing to relocate.

"Oh, I've been all over the place the last two years, but I guess North Carolina is home right now. I have family in Northern Virginia, though. That's where I'm headed for the holidays. How 'bout you?"

An sighed, a little deflated and hugely disappointed. *North Carolina? Really, God?*

She tried to look at the positives though. "My parents and my brother live in Nova too! I guess we have that in common," An managed to say, with as much cheer in her voice as she could muster, to mask the disappointment.

"I'm a senior at James Madison, so I guess I call here home for now."

"Well, An, I plan on staying in Harrisonburg for another day or two, so maybe I'll see you around?"

"I would love that!" An blurted before catching herself. *That sounded not desperate at all!* She rolled her eyes at herself.

An's enthusiasm was bubbling over unchecked. She wished she could keep it under control, but she wanted more than anything to see this beautiful creature again. She had to see him again, she was meant to see him, she was sure of it. Right? I mean, why else would God put him directly in her path, or her work as it were?

"Tell you what," Jimmy said with a thoughtful look in his eyes, his lips pursed. "Are you slaving around this place for the rest of the day, or are you free for… say, dinner? Tonight?"

An cleared her throat, too excited for words, smiling from ear to ear. "I'm off at four o'clock today. I have to go home and study a little for a big final exam, but I can definitely have dinner with you this evening, sir!"

Sir? Oh, Lord, what is wrong with me! She laughed, trying to steady her nerves and mask her awkwardness. But, if truth be told, what she really wanted to say was, *I'm available ALL day for you and let's go now!*

"How about seven?" Jimmy asked. "Would that give you enough time? Can you recommend a nice place, or should I just pick you up and we can decide then?"

"How about we meet back here, in the parking lot? I can suggest a few places."

They parted shortly after that, but An couldn't stop thinking about Jimmy. She hoped he would come back, and she hoped he was a nice guy and not a psychopathic ax murderer or serial killer or something. That gave her pause. What if he *was* some psycho? She had just made a date with a guy she had never seen before; not a single soul knew where they were meeting or going tonight. This was so irresponsible and so unlike her.

She had never accepted a date from a total stranger, and she was a little shocked by her behavior, but what the heck! She was getting a tad desperate for her knight in shining armor to materialize, and frankly, this guy fit the bill so far.

Although a little scared, and a lot nervous, An felt mostly excited about the prospect of spending more time with this man and getting to know him. North Carolina, huh? Well, North Carolina wasn't all that far away from Virginia, although it was a big state. But, if he was Mr. Right, they would make it work. If he did have bad intentions, well, to hell with it. She was going to see him again and that was that.

An had a hard time concentrating on studying and finally succumbed to daydreaming about Jimmy. She had always done well in school anyhow, and currently held a 3.8 grade point average. Maybe CJ was right. She just needed to lighten up a little—and that's what she was doing, right?

She rummaged through her closet until she found three possible outfits and laid them out on her bed. She ended up trying probably every article of clothing she had at the apartment before picking her first choice to begin with, a form-fitting, maroon-colored dress with long sleeves and velvet trim around the cuffs, the square neckline, and the hem. It left quite a bit of her creamy chest exposed. Daring, but she liked the way it looked on her. This had actually been one of her mom's discarded outfits that An had claimed as her own. An had been waiting for a special occasion, maybe a Christmas party, to wear it. *Is it too dressy? Nah! It's what I want to wear for Jimmy.*

She spent a considerable amount of time on her hair and makeup. She let her luscious waves freely bounce a little past her shoulder blades—a recent cut made her hair look even shinier and thicker—and went with ruby-red lipstick that matched the red tones of her dress. Like the dress, the tube of lipstick was one of her mother's discarded items. She wore her knee-high black boots and carefully placed tiny gold hoops on her ears—a birthday gift from CJ a few years back.

After examining herself in the full-length mirror one last time, she was ready to go. With ten gazillion butterflies fluttering their tiny wings in the pit of her stomach, An put her coat on, picked up her shoulder bag, and went out to find Jimmy with his dimpled pearly-white smile.

They ended up going to a small, family-owned restaurant she was fond of that served Italian-style food. After meeting in the parking lot of the coffee shop and talking for an hour that seemed to fly by as if it were only five minutes, they agreed that they both loved pasta and cannoli, so it was an easy decision. They ordered food and ate, but aside from the warm, crispy bread they dipped in a mixture of olive oil, grated Parmesan, and red pepper flakes, An could never remember what exactly it was either one of them ordered or ate that night. It was all a delectable blur in her mind.

They talked about everything under the sun and moon. They laughed easily and held hands without even noticing at first. An learned that Jimmy had graduated with honors from a Christian university in Charlotte, North Carolina and that he planned to become a minister. She was fascinated by this revelation and figured it was yet another exciting and somewhat mysterious facet to Jimmy's personality and character. He seemed enthralled by her as well and thought psychology was a fitting area of study for her. She was happy to realize that with each passing moment, he seemed more interesting and totally normal. Not an ax murderer after all. *Oh, sweet Baby Jesus, let him be The One*, she thought.

An and Jimmy happily concluded that they both liked music and dancing—in fact, they both liked jazz. The friendly waitress told them about a hole-in-the-wall place on Warsaw and Main that played jazz and had a cozy dance floor. They walked into Sly Cat's muted semi-darkness. Cigar smoke and a sultry tune immediately greeted them. An felt at home. Her father enjoyed a cigar now and then while listening to bluesy tunes by artists in line with Bessie Smith and Duke Ellington, two of his most beloved artists.

There weren't too many memories that captured An and Harrison together, and that was one reason An remembered the cigars and music her father enjoyed so poignantly. She could recall every detail of the few encounters with the utmost precision: the swirls of smoke that would escape her father's lips in little circles that widened and dissipated as they climbed high toward the heavens, and her every fiber quavered with the sad notes from his record player.

An swayed from side to side now, and Jimmy seized the opportunity, instantly twirling An to face him. He grasped her by the waist, pulling her close to him. She interlaced her arms around his neck, on her tippy toes to reach him. Their heartbeats joined the sultry beat of the music, and they swayed on the speck of a dance floor, bodies touching and sensing, minds understanding the need and desire inside. An kept her eyes closed, feeling her surroundings rather than seeing. Jimmy's arms were strong yet gentle. When he put his cheek next to hers, she felt the prickling of desire in the back of her neck and up and down her spine. This was definitely a new feeling.

The night was over in a blur of enthusiastic conversation and laughter. Fresh memories of the dancing and their closeness made An dizzy. By the time Jimmy dropped An back to her car, it was the middle of the night—early morning to be more precise. They remained in his car to keep the chill at bay, sitting in silence for a while, holding hands, reliving the night in the privacy of their individual thoughts. It felt so good to just sit next to him and bask in his warm, radiant energy.

Oh, and he smelled so amazing, a combination of sweet apple pie with vanilla ice cream on top, and a hint of musky citrus and spice. He was smart and good-looking and the embodiment of everything she had ever dreamed of in a man. She felt at home with Jimmy. The problem was that he was almost too good to be true, like a fleeting dream. *Is that really a problem? Nah!* she concluded after a nanosecond. She would take the fleeting dream and gobble it right up—savor it in its entirety.

At the end of that long silence, An turned to Jimmy with a smile, thinking of saying goodnight and thanking him for a magical time. At that very moment, he had stilled his nerves enough to turn and kiss her. He reached behind her graceful neck and pulled her to him, leaning in for a soft, probing kiss. They lingered, enjoying the feel of their lips joined together, tasting each other's sweetness, smelling each other's scent. An lifted her right hand to caress his face with the backs of her fingers. She hoped to memorize every line and curve, every story etched on that gorgeous face. Yes, the notion of love at first sight was, indeed, a living, breathing fact. An was sure of it.

Jimmy held her face with both of his hands, then burrowed his fingers in her hair, as he brought her closer for a deeper kiss this time. For nearly an hour, they were lost in their kisses and caresses, not wanting to let go and oblivious to the chill outside. An had never been with a man, but she felt sure that if he had asked her, she would give in and let him have his way with her. She blushed at the thought, but she was totally lost in the moment, in his touch, in the love and thrill she felt. She was sure there wasn't enough oxygen reaching her lungs with her breath catching in her throat. Words fell short of doing justice to how awesome it felt to be near Jimmy, how totally perfect and comfortable it was.

The Christmas lights framing the coffee shop's window twinkled happily in the night. But then the Closed light sign on the door made a zapping sound, forcing both An and Jimmy to lift their gazes and temporarily come to their senses. They made plans to see each other the next day and reluctantly discussed why it was time to part ways. He never asked to follow her to her apartment, and she didn't offer either, although she had desperately wanted him to ask. She most likely would have chickened out, but the want was—without a single doubt—there.

Once the blood started flowing back into her brain, she had told him how she needed to study for her Monday exam, and so they called it a night. They would get together for dinner the next day. This time they'd meet a little earlier in order to have more time together. But, Monday morning, An had to get back to her studies, and Jimmy was scheduled to hit the road, heading for Manassas. They talked about the possibility of seeing each other at Christmas in Northern Virginia.

He had explained how he was staying with some friends—a married couple with two young children—in the outskirts of town, and he wanted to get back there before the sun came up, so he made sure she was safely seated in her car, then got back in his own vehicle and pulled away with a wave. From her rearview mirror she watched him disappear into the distance.

An always remembered that weekend as special, magical, and dreamy. Sunday had been a repeat of the previous day. They had opted for juicy burgers and fries for dinner, then stopped at a small, barely known café for coffee and dessert. She adored blondies, and he had never even had one.

"What exactly are these things?" he had asked her, then said, "Sounds like a white version of a brownie," once she had explained.

"It is!" she told him. "How did you live this long without eating one?" They had laughed about his obvious description as they shared one, with a huge scoop of vanilla ice cream on top. An had closed her eyes, chewing slowly and deliberately, a permanent smile on her face as Jimmy watched with delight, his fork poised to dig into the chocolaty, gooey mess.

They talked for an eternity, oblivious to their surroundings and the passing of time. *Ugh, that pesky Time again, always getting in the way of things, muddling and meddling with the enjoyment of happy moments that end too quickly.*

An learned that Jimmy's parents were in Chicago, Illinois, where they lived, and the entire family spent most Christmases together. However, this year, his parents were spending Christmas in Los Angeles to meet their new granddaughter. Jimmy's brother and his wife had recently welcomed their first child into the world. Jimmy would be spending Christmas with his two older sisters and their families in Virginia. He also had many aunts and uncles, and a bunch of cousins in the area. He was looking forward to seeing everybody.

"As a child, I grew tired of all the family gathering, the noise and commotion," Jimmy confided in her. "I wanted to get away from the hubbub and distraction. All that eating and interacting was tiresome." He laughed.

An listened with joy and anticipation because this was what she had always dreamed a family should be. She envied Jimmy and wondered how he could have found it all boring.

"But now I live for it. I miss it and am nostalgic for it. I can't wait to see everybody," he told her. "I wish we weren't so dispersed. Family is everything."

An agreed wholeheartedly with Jimmy. She was due to head to the Northern Virginia area herself in a few days, once finals were over, to spend Christmas there with her own parents and CJ.

An and Jimmy did end up at her apartment at the end of that second night, but the intense physical longing of the previous night was now replaced by a quiet affection for each other, tinged with sadness in the anticipation of their separation. This time the need was for touching skin on skin, not exploring each other's chemistry. They held each other close, stretched out on her couch, enjoying the silence that cradled them both, thinking about the miles that would soon come between them.

They soothed themselves with plans for Christmas in Northern Virginia and eventually had to extricate themselves from the embrace and move forward on two separate tracks that would hopefully lead them back to the same destination. With one last long and deep kiss at the door, they said their goodbyes. The endless kisses and caresses and the mountain of memories they had created in their short time together would have to tide them over until their next rendezvous.

An went to bed that night smiling at the promise of this fledgling love she had stumbled upon, out of thin air it seemed. Her entire being hummed with happy thoughts and visions of a future yet to be painted in permanent strokes, although the outlined sketch seemed quite promising. With her mind full of images of Jimmy and their time spent together, An fell into a deep dreamless sleep, a smile etched on her lips.

He had been worth the wait.

CHAPTER 3

THE SPY NEXT DOOR

"Every man is surrounded by a neighborhood of voluntary spies."

        - Jane Austen

"Mystery creates wonder, and wonder is the basis of man's desire to understand."

        - Neil Armstrong

An was on pins and needles, anticipating meeting Benjamin Spencer. She hummed to herself as she cooked. The batter for her raisin-oatmeal cookies was resting to the side, awaiting its bake time in the oven. She would do that last so the cookies would still be warm and chewy when they reached the Spencer home.

The chicken breasts had been cubed and were stir-frying along with the chopped onions and minced garlic. The stuffing was also cooked and waiting its destiny atop the chicken mixture. Next, she would add the frozen peas, condensed chicken soup, and the sour cream. Pour that into a glass baking dish, top it with the cornmeal stuffing, and dot it with butter before baking. The smell of onions and garlic sauteed in olive oil was probably one of her favorite aromas. It lingered in the air, making her smile. "Mm-mm, good!" she announced to the room. Her stomach growled in response.

Once her cooking and baking were under control, she went upstairs to shower and dress. As she was undressing, she eyed the jet tub in the corner. It had been so long since she had enjoyed a nice soak in it. It just sat there, accumulating dust and cobwebs. She remembered how excited she and Brad had been when they had it installed. They talked about filling it with bubble bath and scented bath salts. They would sit across from each other, sipping wine and reading to one another. Candles would glow all around them. But like so many of her dreams, that one never materialized. They had used the tub a time or two, but it was always hurried. After a while, it became a point of contention. She complained that they never used it, and what was the point in having it? He would give her the cold shoulder and go on to do something else—just to show her he was in control and she really didn't matter.

Toward the end, when they were attempting to mend the relationship with the aid of marriage counseling, one of the counselors had suggested they have a romantic night, just the two of them. An had suggested the tub, and Brad agreed, albeit with a hint of petulance in his tone. That night, after a home-cooked meal, An had filled the tub, poured her favorite bath salt into it, added some bubbles, and then brought a bottle of wine and two wine goblets upstairs. Brad had said he wanted to check something on his computer and would be up shortly.

An had soaked for an hour, which seemed like an eternity to her. She had drunk her glass of wine, then his, then emptied the bottle, guzzling straight from it—and she didn't even like red wine that well. Finally, as she was about to turn into a giant prune, she had stepped out and dried herself off, tears stinging her eyes. She had put her nightgown on and climbed into bed alone.

She didn't know why that episode had come to mind. She just wanted to put it all behind her once and for all. She decided to rinse off the tub and take a bubble bath. Why not? Soon, she would have to give up this house, too, and all its amenities and memories. But, while here, she would enjoy it. She knew she didn't have any wine in the house, but she went downstairs while the tub was filling and got herself a tall glass of ginger ale. She added a few cubes of ice, some fresh-squeezed lemon juice, and a sprig of her homegrown mint leaves. She took her concoction upstairs and into the soaking tub with her. The jets, the aromatic oils, and the hot water all combined to help her muscles relax, and soon she was feeling oozy and limp. She closed her eyes, savoring the moment.

She was startled out of her light sleep by the ringing of the telephone. She realized she had been soaking for thirty minutes, judging by the oversized clock on the wall opposite the tub, and it was time to get out anyhow. She jumped out, making a splash, and grabbed her extra-large terry cloth bath towel that had been lying on the tub stoop. She ran to get the phone on her bedside table, leaving little puddles along the way.

"Hello?"

"An, honey, how have you been?" It was Cristina, the neighbor across the street, house number 31.

"Hey, Tina! I'm good. You? Everything okay?" An asked the question, while wrapping the towel tighter around her, a frown forming on her forehead. She hadn't heard from Tina in a really long time. Why was she calling now, out of the blue?

"Fine. Everything's fine. Did you hear about the Spencers? Did the detectives come by to ask questions?"

"Yeah, I heard, and yes, the detectives were here. I'm actually thinking about stopping by the Spencer home to offer my condolences."

"Are you crazy?" Tina blurted out. "What if he was involved? People are crazy these days, you know. Don't you watch the news or ID TV?"

"I don't think he had anything to do with it. She may have been sick, or maybe it was an accidental thing.

We just don't know. Besides, even if he was the culprit, I don't think he will off me on his doorstep." An chuckled.

"That's not what the detectives think, and none of this is humorous to me. You be careful, Missy," Tina said with concern. "I wish you would rethink the whole idea." Tina tried in vain to dissuade An.

"What do the detectives think? What did they say to you?" An asked.

"Well, they didn't come right out and say it, but it was implied, you know. I mean, everyone knows it's usually the husband who done it, anyway." Tina did love watching those investigative shows. An thought maybe she was relying too much on stuff she watched on TV. Lisa Spencer was obviously a recluse, and likely suffering from depression or mental illness, and had committed suicide. Period. The end. *C'est la vie.*

"Have you talked to any of the other neighbors? What are they saying?" An pressed on, curious to hear others' perspectives. Tina was the neighborhood busybody, who knew everybody and everything going on, although her imagination kind of got the better of her sometimes.

"Well, they—like me—think there was something fishy going on in that house, and Benjamin Spencer is just a strange duck. Lisa Spencer rarely left the house, and this went on for years. No one came to visit, except maybe the kids now and then. Suddenly, last week, there's a flurry of activity there, and then wham! She's dead!"

"Well, being strange doesn't make you a murderer, right? And what flurry of activity?" An asked, curious about this previously unknown piece of information.

"No, being strange doesn't necessarily make you kill your wife, but it makes his behavior a little suspect to me. Well, get this," Tina dropped her voice into a conspiratorial tone, "last week, Maddie—the new mutt we got—was sick, and I was up in the middle of the night cleaning up her puke, and I noticed lights outside. I peeked out the window and saw a strange car pull up to their house, and a man and woman went in, kinda hurriedly. Plus, I talked to both Josephine Michaels and Kate—you know them, they live in that first house as you come in the lane. They both reported seeing strange cars in and out of the Spencers' driveway last week, at odd hours."

"Interesting," An replied. Indeed, this was an interesting development. Who were all these people, and why were they in and out of the Spencer home?

"Plus," Tina continued, "Benjamin Spencer was gone a lot, even overnight sometimes. Makes one wonder where he went and why. What was he up to?"

"Did you tell all this to the detectives?"

"Well, yeah! You can't hide important clues like that from the police. It wouldn't surprise me if they come to arrest him in the next day or two."

"Well, I have to get some clothes on before I freeze my butt off, but I'll call you or stop by soon," An said, ready to end the call.

"I've been talking to you this whole time while you are standing there naked? Girrrl!"

An chuckled and promised to be careful and they said goodbye. She sure missed her friend's easygoing banter, but frankly, An had been a little surprised Cristina called. They hadn't talked in a very long time. Tina and her husband, Ed, had been close friends of An and Brad. But once divorce became a probable route for the marriage, Tina and Ed seemed awkward around the Goodes and began putting distance between them. They stood them up on card nights and gave lame excuses when it was their turn to host. Apparently, a suspicious death in the neighborhood had a way of bringing people back together, forcing dialogue between old friends. An was sure the entire neighborhood was aglow with gossip and the buzz of speculation. She really wanted to pick Tina's brain a little more… soon.

An took an inordinate amount of time getting ready. She felt like she was going on a date, trying various clothes, mixing and matching this article and that. In the end, she wore a very flattering pair of stretchy black slacks that showed off her trim figure. She chose a mustard-yellow sweater that seemed ideal for this time of year. Her hair was as thick and wavy as it had been back in her college days. Her friend, Sarah, often told her how jealous she was of her wavy, thick mane. And An would often reply, "Well, I envy your gorgeous, sexy legs, so there! We each have our assets, don't we?"

An chose her comfortable ankle boots to finish off the outfit. Although the temperature wasn't really cold out and the rain had broken, the wind was still whipping around, so she put on a lined vest and a fuzzy scarf, both stored in the downstairs hall closet. Thank goodness she hadn't yet boxed her clothes! After carefully packing the food, she began her short walk to the Spencer home.

It felt good to get out of the house. The lane was deserted, but Josephine—who lived right next door to Cristina—was getting out of her station wagon with bags of groceries. An waved. It was nearing supper time, and most people were probably arriving home from their errands or excursions and getting ready to eat dinner. She walked briskly, trying to keep her hair from blowing in her face. *So much for getting every strand just right and using hairspray!*

The Spencer home was on her right. She turned to unlatch the white picket gate by reaching in on the other side. It was a pretty home with a brick front, bright and cheery blue shutters, and dormers on the top floor. There were planters of flowers on all the windows, as well as potted mums and other fall flowers on the deep porch.

She had always loved that porch—extending the entire front of the house and boasting four white pillars, two on each side. It was so grand-looking and so Southern. The Spencers had placed two rocking chairs on the right side of the porch, with a small round table in between. On the opposite side, there was a two-seater glider. *So nice and cozy*, An thought. She could picture herself on that glider, all wrapped up in a warm blanket, her feet out in front of her as she lazily swung forward and backwards.

There were potted flowers, some bordered with green, carefully placed to create an attractive and inviting atmosphere. Interspersed with the purples and yellows were brighter splotches of orange and reds—mostly from the mums An had seen Benjamin Spencer placing on the steps to the porch. She was impressed with the flower arrangements and the care that had obviously been put into the creation of this colorful arrangement. Everything looked serene and untouched by the tragedy that had occurred last night and into the wee hours of this morning, and the subsequent traipsing of the police and first responders.

An walked up the stone path leading to the front door, then up the steps, and as she was poised to knock, she felt suddenly nervous and awkward. She wanted to turn around and run. *This was silly and intrusive,* she thought. In the driveway, she noticed an extra car she didn't recognize. *Oh, God! He has guests. Maybe his children are here, and I'm imposing on their time of grieving.* But she was here, and it would be even sillier to just turn and bolt. She opened the glass storm door and knocked gently, three times. She wondered why people rapped three times when they knocked—there must be a reason. No one answered after a few seconds, so she knocked again, this time a little more forcefully.

Nothing.

She began to turn away, relieved that no one answered, but as she reached the top step, the door suddenly opened. She turned and came face-to-face with Benjamin Spencer.

His shirt was crumpled, and sleep still lingered in his eyes.

"Hi!" he said, tugging at his shirt. He offered a weak smile and a tentative wave.

"Hi, Mr. Spencer? I'm An from a couple doors down there." She pointed toward her house. "I wanted to stop by just to offer my condolences and see how you are holding up?" An pulled down nervously on her scarf with her free hand.

"An? Yes, right. The white house, right?" he asked. "Please, just call me Benjamin, or Ben. My family calls me Ben. Did you want to come in?"

"Well, I don't want to impose, but I brought you a casserole and some cookies?" There it was again. Her discomfort turning statements into questions. She mentally smacked herself upside the head and again told herself to cut it out. *Pronto! Geez!*

Benjamin—Ben—didn't seem to notice. He was very cordial and even better-looking, she noticed, once she got up close. He had piercing dark eyes and a shiny bald head. Below his bottom lip, he had grown a jazz spot. His skin was smooth and the color of café Americano.

"Please, come in and sit for a minute," he said, stepping aside to make room for her. She hesitated but walked in. The house was very warm. She entered a roomy but cozy foyer; two benches on either side of the door held lots of colored pillows. Straight ahead, there was a round table with a large mirror above it. To the right was a dining room and to the left a living room. He led her into the living room.

"You have a beautiful home," she blurted, still feeling a little uncomfortable being here, probably intruding. *Besides, just this morning, a dead woman was found in one of these rooms!* She shivered.

"Thank you, but most of it was my wife's doing." His eyes clouded over, and he winced as he said this. He seemed sad.

"I brought these for you," she said, holding up the bag she was holding. "I'm sorry if I'm intruding."

"Oh, my, I really appreciate it. No, intrude away, please. I can use some company." He took the bag from her and walked across the way to the dining room to place the bag on the table. "That is very nice of you," he continued. "I haven't been able to eat much today, but my daughters are here—they went out to get some dinner actually—and they've been taking good care of me… and everything else." He ended with a sigh, put his hands in his jean pockets and looked down. *Was this a man mourning the loss of his wife or a man subconsciously hiding something?* An pondered.

"Please, sit," he said to An, indicating one of the sofa chairs in the room.

There were two fabric love seats facing each other, with a coffee table in the middle. One had a pillow and blanket on it. An assumed it was where Ben had been resting, so she chose the other seat. Ben sat down across from her.

"Excuse the mess," he said, moving the blanket and pillow to one side. "I was just stretching out for a minute. It's been a heck of a day, as you can imagine." An nodded. It had been a heck of a day for her too.

"Are you okay, Mr… um, Ben? I mean as well as you can be under the circumstances? Do you need anything? Some of the neighbors are concerned?"

"Well, my daughters live about four hours away, but they were on their way as soon as I called. My son is in the military and overseas right now. He and his wife will most likely get here in a day or two. It wasn't a shock to us. Lisa had been sick for a while and battling a lot of demons, you see."

Demons? An cocked her head to the right, puzzled by the comment. "Oh, I'm sorry. I didn't realize she had been ill?" *Gosh, I did it again! There it was, that stupid question mark at the end of my sentence, again!* "I know I've been an awful neighbor—dealing with my own personal issues? But if there is anything I can do for you and your family, please… what was wrong with Lisa, if you don't mind me asking?" She mentally rolled her eyes. *I guess I'm just going to talk in question marks to this guy, and that is that.*

"She has always been sickly with one ailment or another, but depression was the boogeyman she battled daily, in recent years especially. Well, she took matters into her own hands… that was Lisa… But, look, she's at peace now, I'm sure of it." He attempted a smile, but his eyes had that hooded, sad look again.

"Did you love her?" An blurted this out, surprising herself. *What is wrong with me? That is so darn blunt and rude.*

"Did I love my wife?" Ben looked at her quizzically. "Yeah, I love my wife." Now he looked indignant.

"Well, I mean, couples drift apart sometimes, lead different lives?" An tried to explain, noticing that pesky question mark again.

"I see," Ben said and then was quiet for a long minute. An waited for his response, watching his face.

There seemed to be a lot of emotions going on within him. An found him difficult to read.

"I think you're asking me if I loved my wife in a romantic way, or if I was still passionate with her. The answer is no. I loved her. I will always love her. We had a long history together, and children—three of them, triplets. Did you know that?"

"No, actually, I didn't. For some reason, I thought you had two girls?"

"Yeah, a boy too. Anyhow, back to your question." Ben paused, appearing to be searching for the right words. "The romance and passion faded away a while ago. I assume most people who have been together for a long time like we were are like that. Part of it was her illness, too, and how she felt about herself." Ben took a deep breath and looked at An with fresh eyes. "Are you always this intense? You have me pondering all sorts of things now."

"No," An said. "I'm not always this forward. I..." Suddenly, there were voices outside, and the front door flew open. Two dark-haired women came in, holding bags and packages. They turned to face Ben and An. An's mouth flew open in astonishment. She stared. The women looked to be in their mid to late twenties. They were wearing matching boots and matching jackets, matching everything! Their hair was the same length and the same style and the same color. Their faces were almost identical. An hadn't realized people did this anymore: siblings dressing alike, even if they were twins—triplets—and especially not as adults. *Does the brother dress alike too?* she wondered. It was cute in a way, but An was taken aback.

Ben stood up then. "Charlotte, Savannah, this is one of my neighbors, An. She stopped by to pay her respects, and she brought some food." He turned to An then. "My daughters. And I should have told you they like dressing alike—all the time." Ben rolled his eyes at his own statement. "Your expression was priceless." He smiled, a little amused. An and the younger women exchanged hellos. An gave a nervous laugh, and the women chuckled too. They were probably used to this type of reaction.

"I must have known about you, but I don't remember ever meeting you two," An told the women. "You are both stunning, though."

"Oh, we were already away at college…" the one named Savannah started.

"…when Mom and Dad decided to move back here," the other, Charlotte, concluded.

An blinked. They even shared sentences. *Fascinating!*

"Well, I don't want to take up any more of your time? I should go," An said. "It was so nice to meet y'all, and please call on me if there is anything at all I can do?" She was rambling now. It was time to just get the heck out of Dodge. She stumbled toward the door, thinking, *once a klutz, always a klutz.*

Ben followed behind her to the door and thanked her again. By now the sun was barely peeking over the horizon, and the wind was still whistling and whispering conspiratorially. An wrapped her scarf around her neck and head and speed-walked home. Her head was beginning to spin again, that pesky headache returning.

The detectives had said the Spencers lived on Orchard Lane for about a decade, yet An had never interacted with the Spencer girls, and frankly, she didn't recollect ever seeing the boy either. Surely, they had visited, even if they were college students. In fact, she had never heard Tina—who seemed to know everybody—talk about the Spencer children before today. *How odd!* She racked her brain, trying to think if she saw pictures of Lisa or the kids in the home, but she realized there were none. In fact, there were no pictures at all. That was strange too. The home was immaculate, and beautifully decorated, as if by a professional. Ben had referred to his wife's battle with demons. *What the heck was that? Strange choice of words, for sure.*

An felt exhausted by the time she closed her front door behind her. She immediately kicked her boots off, flinging them in front of her. She removed her vest and scarf, carelessly throwing them on the living room couch as she went. She climbed the stairs to her room to change into pajamas. She needed to get out more. She decided she would make chamomile tea, sip it slowly, and then go to bed.

She looked at her bedside clock. *Geez, it isn't even 7:00 o'clock yet!* Maybe she would have a bite to eat and read or watch television and then go to bed. But she felt so tired, unusually so. This emotional rollercoaster was getting the best of her. She went back downstairs, sat down on the chaise lounge in the library, pulled the wooly blanket she kept on the back of the chaise over her, and fell fast asleep.

She woke up in the middle of the night, dry-mouthed and disoriented. She was having a nightmare or something. She looked around trying to distinguish her surroundings. Was she home? Where was she? The room was spinning, and she thought she saw bursts of light and voices whispering. Her eyes popped wide open then. Her heart was pounding, and she was frightened.

Something felt… wrong somehow. She tried to stand up but was too weak. *Should have eaten something,* she thought. *Why didn't I eat?* She fell back down on the chaise. She looked around, trying to focus. Everything looked normal, everything was where it needed to be, everything was as it should be. So, why did she have this foreboding sense of things being askew?

When An awoke again with the sun streaming through the windows, she had a horrible crick in her neck, which made it difficult to move her head without moving her entire body. The house was chilly despite the sunshine beating on the windowpanes. She looked up at the mantle clock. *It is almost eight!* She was surprised she had slept so long. Then she remembered the strange dream she had. Or had she been awake? In any event, it had been a weird experience. She shivered, trying to erase it from her mind.

Her head was pounding again—two mornings in a row. She had to get up and get some coffee going.

Once her pot of coffee was brewing, she went upstairs to shower and dress. If her headache persisted, she would take an Advil, even though she hated medicating herself. She spent a luxurious twenty minutes under the hot needles of the showerhead. She lathered up her hair twice, enjoying the steam, the smell of vanilla and citrus, and the hot water beating and kneading her muscles. When she stepped out of the shower, she was feeling better, and ready for her coffee, but the telephone was impatiently ringing off the hook. She rushed over to her nightstand to answer it.

"An? It's Angie. Did you know your telephone number is listed? I hope you don't mind me calling so early, but I have a crazy day ahead. Can you meet me in an hour?"

CHAPTER 4
SMOKE CASTLES: 1989

"Maybe it's like becoming one with the cigar. You lose yourself in it; everything fades away: your worries, your problems, your thoughts. They fade into the smoke, and the cigar and you are at peace."

        - Raul Julia

"A cigar numbs sorrow and fills the solitary hours with a million gracious images."

        - George Sand

Growing up, An's dad, Harrison, seemed larger than life in her eyes. Perhaps because he was such an enigma to her, or perhaps because the memories were so few and far between, she filled in the gaps with fantasies of her own making. In An's mind, he was a rock the entire family could stand on, an anchor that kept them tethered in place through life's tempests. He reeked of Old Spice and cigars—An loved it.

To this day, either of those scents would send An into a tizzy of fond memories, transporting her back in time to the days he was still with them. He smiled easily, and he could always muster up a story or two, usually about his wife, whom he called Jules: her beauty, her gentleness, her compassion, her skills as a homemaker, and as a savvy businesswoman. An and CJ would listen and believe, starry-eyed and expectant, even if the stories appeared to laugh in the face of their reality.

Harrison stood over six feet tall with broad shoulders and a vast chest. An and CJ looked up at his invincibility and were awed by his strength, his power, his wisdom. He seemed to know all of life's puzzlements, and he would always be there to bolster them if need be. Boy, the shock when An found out he was human after all and, in fact, he was a flawed human to boot.

Harrison had met Jules for the first time in 1942 when she was just fifteen—looking twenty—and living in utter poverty in the boondocks of Preston County, West Virginia. He was twenty and on his way to France to fight the Germans. He made a stop in Garrett County, Maryland only long enough to see some old friends who were spending time ice fishing in the picturesque Deep Creek Lake area, right on the Maryland-West Virginia line.

Sitting on the bed of his friend's beat-up Ford pickup truck, thinking of mischief, while his friend—who was twenty-one—went inside the corner store to buy some beer, Harrison spotted Jules walking.

"There she was," Harrison would intone, dreamily. "Intense violet-blue eyes, long blonde hair like a halo around her heart-shaped face. She had this shy smile and all-around cuteness, wrapped in this killer body. Wowee, she was quite the looker!"

"Pop!" An had exclaimed, her cheeks growing hot with embarrassment the first time Harrison referred to Juliet in a sexual way. He had chuckled and told her she'd understand one day.

Somehow, despite the age gap, they started up a conversation and exchanged addresses. He asked her if he could write to her from whatever battlefield or hellhole he was going to end up fighting the enemy from.

They stayed in touch through the years, Jules marrying someone else in the meantime, but that union being short-lived. Harrison always knew she was the one and that they would get to one another traveling crooked lines, but eventually, they would end up in the right place and at the right moment. He was right. It took five years for them to see each other again. Harrison paid Jules a visit in her hometown of Terra Alta and convinced her to go to Virginia with him to meet his parents. She never looked back and never returned home either. They got married the following year, and the rest was history, as they said.

But their marriage wasn't made in heaven by any means. In fact, Juliet left numerous times. The only things that kept her coming back were the successful baking business they had started together with one old family recipe from Juliet's grandmother, and the little house Juliet had wanted so badly that Harrison had bought for her—with the white picket fence and all. That fence was an important feature to her, and Harrison had built one for her with his own bare hands.

When she announced she never wanted kids, well, Harrison had lost it. He had always wanted a big family, being an only child and all. But Juliet claimed kids had ruined all of the lives of her friends. She was not about to give up her body, her time, and herself to a bunch of crying, snot-nosed, needy, clingy babies.

But they patched things up like they always did and kept on going. The business grew, keeping them both occupied. Harrison never gave up hope that one day they would have a family. Then in 1968 An came along. Harrison would say that Jules was a little slow to warm up, but he was in love the first time he laid eyes on An—and Juliet fell in love, too, he would explain to An… eventually. Two years later, CJ—Carson Jasper—made his entrance into the world as an underweight, premature baby, but "cute as a button," Harrison would intone.

Harrison so idolized his wife that it was difficult to reconcile the fact that he was unfaithful. The first time An heard about it and actually understood its implications, she was about ten years old. They were arguing in their bedroom—they never had words in front of An and CJ, and their arguments were always in hushed, stifled tones. But this time An had her ear up against the door, straining to hear.

Through what sounded like gritted teeth, Juliet spat out, "Well, if you want it so badly, why don't you go get it from that whore of yours!"

An jumped back, furiously blinking as if she had been jabbed in the eye with a red-hot piece of sharp iron.

Sitting at the breakfast table one morning, An found herself alone with her pop. It was Saturday, and her mother was at her favorite spot: work. CJ had spent the night at a friend's house and wasn't expected back until that afternoon.

"Pop, who's your whore?" An blurted out innocently. Harrison choked on his coffee, and his paper slid to the floor. He coughed until his face turned crimson and his eyes bulged and watered.

"Where in tarnation did you hear such an ugly word, girl?" he finally cried out.

"Ma?" An whispered tentatively, head bowed, tears stinging her eyelids. Harrison didn't get angry often, but when he did, he looked demonic and scary to An—like now. An wasn't expecting it this time though, and instantly regretted the question. She had known the word she uttered was a bad word, but Pop always told her that she could ask him anything, talk to him about everything, and she shouldn't bother Ma too much.

So, she had asked. Lesson learned: there were always exceptions to the words *anything* and *everything* in the adult world.

He rubbed his eyes with the heels of both palms and sighed deeply, obviously trying to calm his nerves.

"Okay, okay, little lady," he said. An waited patiently to hear his wisdom. "Life can be complicated and confusing, understand?" he said knowingly. Then he further clarified matters by saying, "One day I'll tell you all about it, but for today, let's just say that grownups are aliens from another planet, and those that get married are out of their noggins." An looked at him with her face all scrunched up in confusion.

"Uh-huh… Gotcha, Pop," An said, not getting it at all. That day An came to the realization for the first time that Pop was flawed, and for sure one of his character weaknesses was that he was inept at explaining and clarifying adult matters. But the enigma of him only made him appear more mysterious and more omnipotent in An's mind.

Years later, An did learn about her father's "whore." It was 1963, business was booming, and they hired a secretary to help with paperwork at the bakery. She was young and pretty, and her husband had recently died in a motorcycle accident, leaving her with a six-year-old son and a three-year-old daughter to raise on her own. Harrison had taken pity on her and took her out shopping on occasion and helped her around the house sometimes. Harrison and Juliet's relationship had grown a little tepid by this time.

Juliet did not want children, and Harrison was desperate for a family of his own. They butted heads about it often. This woman not only offered Harrison love and warmth, but her children became the surrogate family he craved. Juliet found out about it eventually and nonchalantly gave her blessing, saying she understood and was fine with it.

But every now and then Juliet acted insecure or angry about it, like a jilted lover. Eventually, it became a competition of sorts, and that's how An always believed she had come about. Yet Harrison's double life continued for decades, even after Juliet conceded to having children. His affair became a secret everyone came to know, kept tightly wrapped but loosely veiled.

When Harrison had gotten sick and died so suddenly, An's world turned upside down. Through all the craziness and tumultuousness that was their relationship, Juliet did not know how to live without Harrison. For An and CJ, they had lost their rudder and were without direction. Up until then, An had never conceived of a time when her pop would not be there, reassuring them with his occasional tales and lighting their way with his humor. Maybe he hadn't been there as often as he should have been, but he had been there when it counted.

How could he be snatched away like that? An's life was just starting. She wasn't even done with college, no husband in sight, no children yet, no big accomplishment… how was it possible that she would have to go through the rest of her life without her pop? Who would be proudly snapping photos as An accepted her college degree? Who would walk her down the aisle on her wedding day? Who would praise her for her first job? Who would give her advice when buying her first car or home? Who would her children call Pappy?

When An arrived home the day Harrison died, she made a beeline to his bathroom cabinet and doused herself with half of a bottle of his Old Spice. Then she found one of his Cohibas in his locked humidor on his desktop—the key had been in its usual hiding place. Those Cohibas from Havana had always been his favorite. He had a friend that brought them into the country in a diplomatic pouch. Harrison had confided in An once that he hated skirting the law but hated smoking lesser cigars more. An had wondered if the allure and the mystique of smoking smuggled cigars added to the experience. They had chuckled together then as the haze of smoke danced around their heads. Harrison's eyes had half closed with a faint smile on his lips, savoring something in his memory.

An cut the tip of the Cohiba and carefully lit it like she had watched her dad do so many times; making small circles with the flame so it would light evenly. She sat on his big, squeaky leather chair. Then she put her feet up on the desk and crossed her legs at the ankles, just like he did. An slowly and deliberately puffed, mentally saluting the old man. She blew the smoke out, watching it swirl around her, mingling with the scent of Old Spice. She closed her eyes and inhaled her pop's smells. It made her smile to think of him like this, in his glory, so at peace with the universe.

An's anguished sobs were done waiting for her to open the gates to the depths of her soul and release them. The cigar was half spent, and the room was spinning. She ran to her room, slammed the door for good measure, sank to her knees, and got busy yelling at God. Her strangled cries collided with her choked words, spittle flying every which way, tears spilling unchecked, her arms flailing madly.

"Why, God, why? It's not fair! You're a mean, despicable God! Give him back to me! Give! Him! Back!" She screamed until her voice cracked and her throat was a burning mess.

After wrapping up finals her senior year of college, An arrived in her hometown of Fairfax on a crisp December afternoon, only days before Christmas. She hadn't seen Jimmy in nearly two weeks, but he had called her most nights at her apartment. An had been preoccupied with her exams and the travel home. Jimmy had been distracted by family gatherings and obligations. They were looking forward to seeing each other at a local mall to do some Christmas shopping, get a quick bite to eat, and catch up on the events of the past week.

An was on pins and needles with excitement. She couldn't wait to see Jimmy at last, driving as fast as she dared. Normally, she enjoyed the pristine mountain views and the quiet hum of her tires on the pavement. Once she hit Interstate 66 East, she knew home was near, and it was only a matter of time before she would see CJ's smiling face. But, on this day, An's mind was elsewhere: Jimmy.

She drove straight to their meeting place. An could see Jimmy pacing at the entrance to the mall as she walked briskly toward him. He saw her too and began half walking and half jogging toward her. They reached each other, embracing for what seemed like an eternity. Just holding on for dear life.

When they finally let go, it was only to gaze into each other's eyes, searching, questioning, reassuring.

"How have you been?" Jimmy asked, studying her face and tracing her lips with his fingertips, then pulling her away to size her up. "You look thinner, but quite the sight for sore eyes!"

"I've been too busy to eat much," she chuckled. "Just living on coffee lately." She smiled up at him, her arms encircling his waist. "I've missed you so, so much."

"Me too. You have no idea," he told her, his voice husky with emotion.

They didn't have a lot of time as An's parents and brother expected An home for dinner on her first night back from school. They had decided they would exchange early Christmas gifts and would try to see each other on Christmas Eve if they could somehow sneak away from family obligations. They walked around while holding hands and catching up. Every few steps, they would stop to kiss and gaze at each other, awed at how their separate paths in life had somehow crisscrossed at the perfect moment, and all the stars in the universe had lined up just so.

There was a little Christian store An adored because it was full of books and cute little trinkets. An bought Jimmy a Bible there. A King James version, leather-bound in shades of gray and black. Inside it, she inscribed, *"To my dearest friend, Jimmy. May love and happiness find you wherever you go. Love, An. Christmas 1989."*

Jimmy had brought An's gift with him, a small box wrapped in shiny gold foil, with a tiny red bow on top. It was a gold pendant with a thin gold chain and a heart, holding within it three rubies the size of pinheads. He put it around her neck and told her, "Think of me whenever you touch this heart. I will always be with you no matter where we travel in life."

They shared Cinnabons at the mall kiosk as their time together came to an end much too quickly. Again, cruel Time would not linger a minute longer, not even for two young lovebirds. They kissed and parted ways after making tentative plans for their next meeting.

An's drive home was a blur of happy thoughts. She parked in front of the large brick home and noticed CJ's car there too. She assumed Ma's and Pop's were both in the garage. The air was chilly and breezy as she made her way from her car to her doorsteps. She held the collar of her coat up over her ears to keep the cold at bay. A dusting of snow swirled around her ankles. Her things would have to wait in the car until she could get CJ to help.

An was impatient and too cold to meander around to the back door, so she headed straight for the imposing front door, unlocking it as quickly as she could make her fingers work. She clumsily stumbled in, slamming the door shut and calling, "Ma? Pop? CJ? I'm hooome!"

She could see lights burning in the back of the house: the area of the kitchen and sunroom. But the living room, library, Pop's office, and dining room were all in the shadows of pre-dusk as she crossed them to get to the other end of the house. The sun had dipped on the horizon, and evening darkness stood poised to completely reign. The air was frigid inside too.

"Where are you guys?" she called out as she went, puzzled at the silence that greeted her. They had said dinner at home, An was positive of that. *Stuck at work yet again*, she thought, disappointment gripping her.

She finally reached the sunroom, the very last room on that floor, past the spacious, open kitchen to the left and a short but wide hallway connecting the dining room, sunroom, and kitchen. She slowed her steps, trying to understand the scene unfolding before her. Her mother sat on the wicker sofa with CJ next to her, his arms around her neck and his head buried in her shoulder. She sat very erect and stiff, arms limp on her sides, unseeing, staring eyes. She looked haggard and old, her eyes rimmed in red and puffy. CJ's face was half buried in her hair and half hidden by shadows. He seemed to be sobbing.

"What has happened?" An whispered. "Where's Pop?"

CJ moved then, seeming to come out of his stupor to acknowledge his sister. He got up, walking toward An with arms outstretched, ready to embrace her.

"An," he said in a voice full of emotions and not quite his own. "Pop is in a coma. Doctors don't have much hope."

"Wait, what? When? How? Why?" An blurted, confused, scared out of her wits, and beginning to feel the cold tentacles of tragedy squeezing her heart. Her mind was racing in crazy circles. "What do you mean, 'doctors don't have much hope?' What's that supposed to be?"

CJ crushed her against him, trying to stifle her questions. He didn't have the answers she needed, and he was clearly scared too. He tried to explain how their father had collapsed at work. He had been battling a nasty and persistent cold for weeks. He was taken to the emergency room, where he was examined and doctors thought pneumonia had settled in his lungs. Harrison was notorious for not taking care of himself despite Juliet's nagging. The business, playing golf, eating expensive cuts of steak, or smoking his cigars always took precedence over his health. Juliet and CJ had been at the hospital with Harrison but had come home to gather some items for him and to wait for An to arrive.

An approached her mother, worried at the blank look on her pale face.

"Ma? It's me, An." An glanced over at CJ with a frown. "What the hell is wrong with her?" she asked in a near shriek.

"She's in shock or something," CJ responded. "I don't really know."

Juliet made a whimpering noise, and An got on her knees in front of her mother, holding her cold hands in between her own. "Ma, you need to snap out of it so we can all go see Pop." Juliet stirred, finally focusing on An.

"What am I going to do?" she whispered with a sigh, directing her question at An, who had absolutely no clue what any of them were going to do.

At the hospital, Juliet was inconsolable, one minute lashing out at An and CJ, the next screaming at the nurses. "How could this have happened? He was fine just this very morning!"

Doctors tried to explain how systemic infections of any kind could be deadly; Harrison wasn't responding to antibiotics, and sepsis had caused the coma. They all knew he was no young buck anymore, and he wasn't the best at taking care of himself.

But Juliet didn't want to hear this doctor gobbledygook. She didn't want the medical gibberish. She just wanted her husband back the way he was that morning. She would not leave Harrison's side that entire night. She cried and pleaded with God, and the powers that be, and anybody who would listen, for mercy. "I can't live without him!" she wailed. "He's half of me. I'm half of him."

An had never before experienced her mother in this shape, so out of control, out of her element, a different creature altogether. Juliet was a broken woman. Her whole life, An had seen her mother as a solid pillar, all business, dealing with one work-related crisis or another—nothing ever seemed to ruffle her feathers. Even when she was angry or upset, she never seemed distraught, always composed and dignified even when she was delivering sharp words or stinging actions.

When it came to their relationship, An couldn't even remember her parents ever kissing or holding hands. Then again, she rarely heard them fight either, unless it was work-related and behind closed doors. All emotions were taboo in her home, especially for her mother. Yet here she was, falling apart in public, and shedding big, fat tears—tears! Who knew Ma was capable of tears? Who knew Ma had such deep emotions?

An watched, a little detached, maybe in shock herself. Their family life was lacking, yet An had never been gripped by this type of numbing grief. The emotions churning in her right now were alien to her, and her capacity to manage the events unfolding before her was shrunken and shriveled.

In vain, An tried to console her mother. By her father's side, she awkwardly held his hand at a loss for words. Was he even there anymore? Could he sense her, hear her, see her at all? The regrets came fast and furious, coursing through her thoughts. She had assumed he would always be there, that time was boundless and endless.

While lamenting that her father wasn't around enough and the family was short on love and affection, she had overlooked her part in it. She, too, was a link in the circle that was her family. What she did or didn't do affected the whole. Always dreaming and scheming about her own future family, An hadn't been present in this family—something she was quick to accuse her parents of doing. She scolded herself for being just as much to blame as her parents for not keeping the family alive. She became consumed with guilt and shame, knowing full well that time had run out for amends.

She realized that all the conversations she had hoped one day to have with Harrison were void and null; all her questions for him would forever be question marks in her mind. Gathering understanding about the true Harrison Carson Jordan from the man himself would no longer be within her grasp. He would forever be a muzzled story wrapped in mystery to her. Plus, the hope for a better, closer relationship with her father was now crushed.

In her heart she knew he was already gone from this reality, but still she talked. She told him she wished she had tried harder to spend time with him, to understand him, to love him. She told him she regretted that they never went to a ballgame together; never sat on the sand at the beach, side by side, letting the waves wash over their feet; never sat at the dinner table playing chess and talking about the minutiae of life like two old friends.

"Thank you for taking care of me, Pop. Thank you for loving me. Thank you for sharing some of your cigar time with me."

Her words sounded hollow and superficial to her own ears. She wasn't sure what to say or how to grieve for this man she called Pop. She didn't know how to feel. Later the paralyzing sadness would come, then the rolling anger, but for now, mostly, she was reacting to the regret of everything that could have been and never would be.

For two days, the three sat at the hospital with Harrison. When it was finally over and Harrison had permanently lost his grip on this life, An went home feeling exhausted, confused, and scared. CJ's face seemed to reflect her own emotions, and her mother's was a blank mask—Juliet's tears spent and emotions now buried deep.

Time had warped, and An wasn't sure of the hours and days she had lost. It wasn't until she played the phone messages a few days after returning home from the hospital that she realized Christmas Eve had come and gone and so had Christmas Day. Life as she knew it was no more. There were a number of messages from Jimmy. He would be returning to North Carolina soon, he said. She could not focus on that right now. Jimmy seemed like a figment of her imagination at this point. Her life seemed too tangled to comb through. She didn't want to think or process anything at all. Not even Jimmy.

She walked back to her bedroom, finding a glimmer of comfort there: the white-painted furniture and the bright-colored wall hangings, the sheer white curtains and apple-green shaggy rug on the side of her bed, the black-and-white checkered bedspread… she felt an acute sense of deja vu as she got on her knees and began to pray.

She rarely prayed and didn't remember going to church with her parents, ever. There had been an older black lady named Brenda, whom they called Aunt Kitty, who took them to her church sometimes. Aunt Kitty had been an employee and friend of An's parents. An closed her eyes, hoping to find some inspiration, some way to communicate with a God she had never met or personally known.

"Give us comfort, God," she whispered. "Help us all heal. Get us through this." This conversation with God felt very similar to the one she had had with her father at the hospital. It was strange and foreign, but her guilt and her regrets propelled her to speak the words. "I don't know you, but know you are somewhere in me, around me, with me. I hope, anyhow. I need you."

An fell silent afterwards. God never said a word back to her that she heard, but she felt a blanket of comfort enfold her, warming her down to her very core. She got back in bed, pulled the comforter around her, and let sleep overtake her. She slept better than she had in days—a peaceful, undisturbed sleep that gave her the illusion that she was whole again.

The next morning An awoke refreshed and ready to face the day. She hadn't seen Ma or CJ. Their bedroom doors had been closed so she let them be. The large rooms were dark and quiet as if in mourning too. She put a pot of strong coffee on and went back up to shower and get dressed. She even put on a little mascara and lip gloss. She dressed in jeans and a hunter-green sweater with shimmery beads, in honor of the Christmas they had missed. She drank a cup of coffee and ate half of a cinnamon-raisin bagel—she found a whole bag in the freezer—and was ready to look in on her mother and brother.

She found Juliet sitting at her vanity table staring at the mirror with glassy eyes. Her nose was red; her eyes were red-rimmed. She looked like Rudolph with red eyeliner. The thought almost made An chuckle out loud, which would not have been appropriate. Juliet's tears were probably totally dried up by now. Her white hair—when had it turned totally white?—was disheveled, and her hands rested on her lap.

"Ma? I made some coffee. I know you like coffee." She waited for Juliet to make some movement, some utterance, an acknowledgement.

Nothing.

A little distressed about her mother's nonverbal condition, An went to find CJ. After a couple knocks, he came out, already dressed in jeans, a light blue dress shirt with the sleeves rolled up to the elbows, and an oatmeal-colored wool vest. He usually wore dark colors, so this outfit was definitely an improvement—an attempt at cheerfulness. He was barely twenty, but she could see his hair already prematurely thinning on the crown of his head. *Poor guy*, she thought. He looked ten years older than his actual age. She realized he carried a lot of stress and pressure on his young shoulders. He had always felt responsible for taking care of Juliet and Harrison in a way An had never done.

With her voice cracking a little, she said, "Ma is not well."

"I know," he responded. "I'm not sure what to do. Should we call her doctor?"

Ignoring his question, An said, "He was only seventy-two, CJ. That's not old in this day and age. How could this happen? I thought we had all the time in the world." An's voice and words were anguished but laced with anger too.

She looked at her brother, their eyes meeting and locking. She saw fear and concern in his deep blue eyes.

"I'll take over the business," he said, almost to himself.

"What about your school?" An asked, alarmed.

"You're too close to being done to quit now, An," CJ said. "You finish school, and I'll take care of the business for the time being."

"You're barely twenty!" An exclaimed. "Do you even know anything about running a business… of any sort?"

"I can learn. I know enough. Ma is in no condition…" His voice cracked, and his eyes were shiny with tears.

"Is Ma going to be okay?" An asked no one in particular. They were standing at her bedroom door now, looking in. She just sat there. Her age showed in the wrinkles on her pale face and her hair that had turned completely white overnight. *Where had she gone?* An wondered. *Who was this woman, really?*

"I don't know," CJ answered. "I really don't know."

CHAPTER 5

FAREWELL TO YESTERDAY: 1989

"Grief is like a marathon in reverse... instead of the last half being the hardest, the first half is when you experience the most agony."

- Zoe Clark-Coates

"It's not so much the goodbye that hurts, but the flashbacks that follow."

- Unknown

An and CJ had managed to make the funeral arrangements as best they could. Some of the trusted employees of the company had come to the rescue. There were no other family members to notify and no one to call for assistance or direction. Aunt Kitty had started her transition many years ago. The fifteen or so local workers were all they had in the way of family, and they were all virtual strangers to An and CJ.

The family attorney informed them that Harrison's will was simple: everything had been left to Juliet. There was a Buy-Sell Agreement in place that spelled out what would be done with the business in the event of Harrison's or Juliet's death. Insurance vehicles had been set up as well to protect everyone. With Juliet in no shape to run the business, CJ and An would take over the day-to-day operations. Certain key employees had also been named to step in and assume various responsibilities.

Harrison's service and funeral consisted of a small gathering. He would never have approved of a big crowd. He often joked about wanting a party when he died, no crying and definitely no wearing gloomy black. An's high school best friend, Peggy, came to pay her condolences. Her two close friends from James Madison, Sarah and Maria, also came. CJ had a handful of friends who showed up to support him and whisper heartfelt condolences as well.

Juliet was a shadow of herself. Her white hair hung loosely, blowing around her shoulders, looking lackluster. Her face had an unhealthy pallor. She had not had the energy or the desire to put any makeup on her pale complexion. An had hastily dabbed a coat of pink lip gloss on her mother's pale-white lips on the way to the service when she realized how ghostly Juliet looked.

An wore a gray pantsuit with a midnight-blue short-sleeved sweater underneath her jacket. Her mom wore a long, dark blue dress that covered any vestiges of skin, other than her hands and face. She had wanted to wear black, but An had reminded her of Harrison's wish. CJ looked very dapper—and so mature—in his black suit, crisp white shirt, and black-purple-gray striped tie. He was the only one allowed the black outfit since he didn't own any other color of suit. In fact, most of his clothes were dark-colored, to An's chagrin.

"You're young. Why don't you have bright happy colors in your closet, CJ?" she had asked him, a little annoyed. "We're going shopping, very soon. You're getting purple, yellow, red, fuchsia, orange… all kinds of happy colors in your wardrobe," she told him without fanfare.

He knew better than to argue so he raised his eyebrows in question and simply said, "Fuchsia?"

After the service and funeral, the family gathered at their home. Juliet had been clutching a small handheld mirror "her HC" had given her when they were first married. It said *To My Beautiful Jules* on the back of it.

"He always called me that," she whispered. An smiled at the memory, and because her mother had uttered a few words.

The early January sun was already making its westward descent. The handful of people still present huddled in small groups in the various shadows of the library and living room in the front part of the home. The two rooms were separated only by an archway, so it was a large, open area that could easily accommodate a lot of people. An and Juliet were sitting in silence, side by side, on the spacious living room couch when the doorbell bonged. No one budged, so after a few heartbeats, Peggy shuffled to the door in bare stockinged feet—unaccustomed to heels, she had discarded them in a corner somewhere.

There were some whispers at the door, and then the group appeared. Juliet didn't outwardly react, but An couldn't help letting out a small gasp through her slightly parted lips, eyes wide in disbelief, when she saw *her*. Standing there, regal as always, accompanied by her now-adult children, was *Pop's Whore!*

Jill—funny that her name was so similar to Jules—was poised and beautiful as ever. The years had been kind to her. Where she had been a pretty woman in her youth, she was striking now in her late fifties. Her shoulder-length red hair was wavy and brushed away from her face to reveal creamy skin that was still firm and supple—totally unblemished and unwrinkled—except for a few freckles. Her cheeks were naturally rosy, her lips painted in a deep matte peach-colored lipstick, outlined by a darker shade of peach. Her emerald eyes were hooded by dark-mascaraed lashes.

Although she had put on some weight over the years, it actually agreed with her, giving her a curvy and appealing suppleness. She wore a pink-and-black checkered dress donning an empire waist traced with black piping and boasting a black bow in the center. The square neckline was low, showing a vast cleavage that made all the men in the room blush and stare, and all the women blush and glare.

On her hands, she had long black gloves that went past her elbows. To complete the outfit, a small black purse dangled from her left elbow and, on her feet, black heels to match. She had already removed her short black fur coat, which she clutched on her right hip. She strode right out of the pages of a 50s fashion magazine with that outfit. Somehow, it all worked for her. She looked fresh and stunning—quite the contrast from Juliet.

Jill walked right in, no fanfare, not an ounce of restraint. Her two children were close behind her, a little on the tentative side, looking uncomfortable, maybe even scared. They clearly did not want to be in this place but were appeasing their mother. The girl—now an adult woman, probably in her thirties—wore an attractive and modest gray-and-black flowered dress underneath an unbuttoned, long, dark-colored wool coat. Her face was mostly hidden under her red hair that cascaded down to her waist. She was carrying a casserole wrapped in foil, so she mumbled, "Hello," and kept walking with Peggy toward the dining room area where the food had been laid out. The boy—now man—stood awkwardly behind his mother, wearing khaki pants, a hunter-green dress shirt, and a stylish brown, hip-length leather jacket. He was attractive, in a movie star, pretty-boy way. He looked a lot like Jill, with the green eyes, fiery-red hair, and freckles.

Locking eyes with Juliet on the couch, Jill had stopped mid-stride to make an exaggerated sad face, arms outstretched, saying, "Oh, Jules, honey. May I come in and sit?" Since she was already inside, the question seemed a little silly and redundant to An, but there it was.

An felt her mother stiffen beside her. Juliet simply gave Jill a little nod, then grabbed An, pulling her toward her so she could whisper in her ear, "Feed them and send them away. Quickly."

An looked at her mother as if to say *how rude!* She had no intention of doing anything of the sort. Plus, she was curious about Jill—always had been, always would be, most likely. She said nothing to her mother as she continued to stare expectantly at Jill, marveling at her beauty and her spunk.

As the other woman reached the couch where Juliet sat, An jumped up as if her rear end had been scalded, allowing room for Jill to sit next to Juliet. Since Juliet had not reacted to Jill's outstretched arms, Jill quickly filled the spot, sitting next to Juliet, smiling at An as she landed with an *oomph!*

"Thank you," she said to An, then, turning her attention to Juliet, "I'm so sorry to hear the news. I debated coming, but felt it was the proper thing to do. Thanks to the staff who let me know."

Juliet pulled away a little, making no attempt at eye contact or friendliness. Then as if she had resolved to do something, she turned to Jill, looking her up and down, disdain at the corners of her pale lips. The room was in total hush; everyone there could have easily heard a pin drop.

"Please, do stay a bit and help yourself to a bite to eat in the dining room. Your children too, of course." Juliet said the words softly, enunciating each word purposefully.

Jill smiled at this and tried again to hold Juliet's hand. Once more, Juliet pulled away.

"But before you do that, just answer me this," Juliet continued. "Why exactly did you find it *proper* to come here, to *my* home?"

Juliet's tone had gone from tepid to frigid in a split second. Everyone seemed to be watching in freeze mode, unblinking, stuck in mid-sentence, mid-bite, mid-breath. An was now standing next to Pretty Boy, and she audibly gulped, noticing the icicles in her mother's voice. *Oh, boy, this may not turn out well.*

"I loved him too, and I wanted to pay my respects to you, and to remember him in his space, his home..." Jill answered. She composed herself by shifting in her seat before continuing.

"Yes, and *his* family," Juliet interrupted, hissing the words like venom directed at Jill.

"He loved me too, you know. He thought of my kids and me as family. He would have wanted me to come. He would have wanted us to get along."

"I think you misunderstand, Jill," Juliet informed the other woman. "I loved my husband deeply. I tolerated a lot of his shenanigans because I understood him more than anyone on this earth. I knew his deepest needs and desires. But he is now gone, and I no longer have to play the charade. I don't have to understand or accept his actions and behavior any longer. That includes you. It's no concern of mine at this point what you think he would have wanted." Juliet emphasized the last word.

Jill winced at Juliet's words, blinking her eyes several times. An had winced too, thinking, *Ouch!* Yet she couldn't help smiling at her mother's outrage. CJ was unreadable as he stared at the spectacle taking place before them, but knowing CJ, he would have wanted the women to be cordial to each other and maintain the peace. The other guests were still gathered in the background watching and listening with curious trepidation at this tennis match of words between the two women. No one else dared to move or say a word.

Jill looked at Juliet with sadness clouding her pretty features now. Despite Jill's nonchalant attitude, Juliet's verbal onslaught had apparently cut her deeply.

Although dissimilar in most ways, the women did have hurt feelings in common. An knew Juliet's own words must have hurt her as much as they had hurt Jill in that moment because it shone a bright light on that dirty little secret. And now, here they were, the two women sitting side by side, the secret shamelessly in the open in front of all those people. There was nowhere to hide. No way to ignore the issue.

Although Juliet had sounded strong and sure of herself while spewing her litany, it seemed to have weighed her down and tired her out.

Jill didn't stay long after the words were spoken and the hurt inflicted. CJ, ever the peacemaker, had come to the rescue. Offering his arm to Jill, he had asked her to please come to the dining room and eat something. Jill looked relieved and grateful as she took his arm, smiling pretty again. As they walked away, CJ turned to An to ask her to take their mother upstairs. She needed her rest.

Eventually, everyone left. Peggy was spending the night with the family, so she remained. While Juliet lay in bed upstairs, CJ, Peggy, and An cleaned up, in silence at first. Then they slowly added words to their actions.

"I can't believe she had the audacity to come here… now, on this day," Peggy said as she pulled the bursting trash bag out of the trash can with a grunt.

"Well, Pop pretty much gave her that right," CJ said in answer. "She was like a second wife to him." He stacked up the dishes he had finished drying and walked them into the adjacent dining room.

"Pop was always such a puzzle to me," An said as she propped the broom against the kitchen counter and pulled her long hair away from her face, fanning herself.

CJ had returned to the kitchen, and the three stood there for a second, looking backwards in time, each lost in their own memories. When An began walking toward the sunroom, the other two followed.

"I don't know if I ever mentioned this to either of you," An began, as she made her way to one of the windows, pressing herself against its coolness. The three stood huddled close together now, fogging up the window, as they looked at their own reflections and the backyard beyond.

"It was senior year in high school, just before my eighteenth birthday, April, I think, because the weather was warming up and flowers were beginning to bloom all over the place. I was at the bakery helping out with some marketing stuff when Pop suddenly announced he was going out for a while. He grabbed his sport coat, and, stuffing a cigar into his pocket, he was already halfway to the door.

"'We have this marketing project to tend to, HC. Where could you possibly be going that's more important than this right now?' Ma had belted out, all dramatic, the way she did sometimes when it came to work-related stuff. She had grabbed two big stacks of mail and held them up in each hand to make her point."

An paused with a faraway look in her eyes that told CJ and Peggy she was reliving it, frame by frame. They watched her reflection in silence, soaking in the images she was bringing to life.

"Pop said he just needed fresh air and he'd be back a little later when he could focus better. I had gotten my own car the previous summer and was itching to drive it as much as I could; driving was still a novelty to me. Plus I was so curious about Pop, so I resolved to sneak after him, get in my car, and follow him. I just had to know where he was going so urgently, daring to go against Ma's wishes… I had to know.

"Looking back now, I should have known exactly where he was going and who he was seeing. Actually, I kinda knew, but I guess I hoped I was wrong. The telltale signs were there, but up until that point, the whole issue of Jill was something I instinctively knew I needed to keep tightly wrapped and tucked away. I hadn't wanted to think about her. It was the whole loyalty thing to Ma, I suppose. But on this day, I just had to know. Something inside me changed, and I had to know." While An paused to take a deep sigh, CJ and Peggy seemed to be holding their collective breath, almost in a trance.

An continued with her recollection. "So I got in my car and followed him out onto Route 66 and all the way to Gainesville, all the while wondering, imagining where she might live. At that point, I was no longer kidding myself. I knew he was going to her. To my surprise, Pop had meandered around a few back streets and pulled up in front of this pretty little house with a white picket fence. I couldn't believe it! I had seen pictures of the house. I knew this house. It was Ma and Pop's very first home, the one he had practically built himself.

"I hadn't realized up until that day that he had kept it when he and Ma bought and moved into the big new house in Fairfax right before I was born. All these years, he had kept it! He parked right in front of the house and hopped out with a new pep to his step. I kept on driving past the house and parked on the side street."

An stopped to take a deep breath and compose her thoughts. She shook her head slowly from side to side. The others continued to stare at her reflection quietly, anticipating the ending.

"You know, for a minute, I truly expected—no, not expected. I wished. I wished and hoped that he had kept the house for himself, just for his lonely escapes when Ma got to be too much. The house sat on a decent-size corner lot. Looking through the bushes, I had a good, unobstructed view of the patio out back while keeping myself pretty well concealed. The fence on that side of the house was taller than the front, so all I had to do was bend down and look through the wooden slats. The yard was simply gorgeous, so beautiful with amazing blooms for early spring. The flower beds were already exploding with color. I think that's when my love of flowers and gardening began—that day. It was just so pretty and so peaceful… a slice of paradise, really.

"I couldn't identify the flowers by name then, but later, I recognized red tulips, purple and dark pink bluebells, grape hyacinth, crocuses… She had turned that place into a heavenly oasis. The white wrought-iron outdoor furniture was beautiful and feminine… a little koi pond, a bird bath… it was all so gorgeous and perfect and calming. I can still see it all in my mind, like a picture permanently etched there."

An paused again, her eyes dreamy, a faint smile twisting her lips upward.

"Then I heard them," she continued. "I heard them before I could see them, their voices and laughter. They walked outside, arms around each other. Pop had his cigar between his lips, and she had a fringed white shawl around her shoulders. They walked outside to sit while Pop smoked his cigar. Their chatter and laughter was contagious. It made me smile even though I wanted to cry or pound something. 'How dare he do that to Ma?' I thought. How dare he! And to keep that special little house for her! Did Ma even know?"

An apparently had come to the end of her story because the silence stretched on while they stood there by the window. She placed her palms against the cool glass pane. It felt good, cooling the indignation that had risen up and out of her at that moment.

"Ma knew, An. She knew all of it." CJ finally broke the silence. "First of all, Pop was never good at concealment and lies; second, he never stopped punishing Ma for *forcing* him into another woman's arms when she refused to give him a child." CJ had indicated quotation marks around the word "forcing" by bracketing with his fingers as he said it.

"By the time Ma had come around and agreed to kids, I believe Pop had fallen in love with Jill and her kids, and being with her was too darn comfortable and accommodating to give up."

"But I thought you guys had said that they broke up at some point." Peggy had found her voice to make a contribution to the conversation.

"Nah, that was only for short bursts of time. I don't think he could bring himself to do it, permanently, even if he tried," CJ informed her. "Whenever he traveled for work, he took her. I don't know how he did it, but he was just able to keep the two families as if they were in two separate universes. He compartmentalized everything."

"Yeah," Peggy said. "Whenever I was around, he seemed so loving toward your mother with his words, always saying sweet things to her and joking around, being jolly and funny. I liked your dad a lot. I don't see how there was room for another woman!" Peggy looked An's way to be sure she hadn't said something too upsetting. An was shaking her head slowly in agreement.

"We all loved him," An said. "I could never figure him out. I hated that he had another family, and he wasn't always pleasant to be around; he could be moody, but I still loved him. He was my pop. There is no one like him, and never will be."

CJ and Peggy agreed in silence, heads shaking in unison.

An had wanted to call and at least leave a farewell message for Jimmy at his sister's home. Somehow, she couldn't muster up the courage or the will. She wasn't sure why she felt she had to keep Jimmy at arm's length. Although she treasured the memories and a part of her wanted and needed Jimmy in a bad way, there was this unexplained anger that uncoiled and sprang up in her whenever the mere thought of seeing him came to mind. It was as if she blamed their love and happiness for causing her father's death.

Intellectually, she knew that wasn't the case, but the guilt and shame of finding happiness while her mother wallowed in sorrow and her family fell apart ruled over the rational part of her brain. Although her heart was breaking, she felt an overwhelming need to keep him away, far away. She simply could not face happiness while living and sleeping with this sadness that enveloped her. The two simply could not—and should not—coexist. And somehow Jimmy knew all this because he never attempted to contact her. He simply faded away.

An busied herself with other thoughts and business that had to be tackled. Two days after the funeral, An and CJ managed to go through the finances, with minimal help from Juliet, who seemed to be in a perpetual catatonic state, barely talking, eating, or sleeping. An was worried. Her mother did not look well. An took an extra week off from school to help Juliet and her brother. CJ spent as much time as possible at the office trying to get a sense of the business and reassuring the employees as best he could. There was so much he didn't know about running a business. There were two separate businesses, really: the office personnel that actually managed and oversaw the entire operation, and then there were the hands-on people who created it all and made everything happen.

In the beginning, when it had started with a fleeting dream, it was just Juliet and Harrison and an oven in their own kitchen—and Juliet's Grandma Nina's custard-in-a-pastry-cup recipe, which they called "crisp 'n pudding." From that, they eventually had opened up a little pastry shop that became popular beyond their dreams.

People drove from places near and far, sometimes waiting in line, for a taste of the flaky cup containing the smooth custard, baked to perfection, and dusted with cinnamon and powdered sugar. The little bakery grew to become an icon of Main Street, Fairfax. Later on, Juliet and Harrison went on to purchase the entire building, renovating the historic structure, which turned into their headquarters. To this day, the original "Crisp 'n Pudding" store was located on the bottom, while the main operation of the business was conducted on the top floor.

CJ hadn't anticipated how much of his time, his energy, and his skills the business was going to take. He had hoped to continue his studies part-time, taking classes on the weekends and in the summertime. With the help of the seasoned and trusted employees of the company, he thought he could actually pull it off. Plus, they were hopeful that Juliet would eventually come out of her self-induced cocoon of despair and take over the business reins once more.

An felt horrible leaving CJ behind to take care of Juliet and the family business alone, but she realized CJ was right, wise beyond his years. She only had a semester left. It would not make sense to drop out at this point or put things on hold. With a heavy heart, she loaded up her car and began the two-hour trip back to school.

Every day, she had thought of Jimmy and prayed that he was healthy and happy. She had checked her answering machine at her apartment to no avail. There were no messages from Jimmy. All she had were the memories of their short love affair to remind her that their encounter had been real.

She could close her eyes and feel his hands tugging at her hair and caressing her cheeks. She could taste his lips and feel the heat of his body next to her. She missed him terribly and wished she could be with him. *Someday. Maybe someday, if it's meant to be,* she told herself. Her gold heart pendant had been her constant companion. She never took it off, not even to sleep or shower. It was the most bizarre thing she had ever felt up until that point. She missed Jimmy, and she longed for him, yet she hated him and hoped he would stay just a fond memory in her mind. It was a dichotomy of warring emotions inside her.

To forget, An occupied herself with school and worrying about CJ dealing with the family business and their mother's debilitating condition all by himself. Juliet had simply stopped caring, CJ had shared with An during one of their telephone conversations. She had told CJ that she wished to die to be with her HC. There was nothing to live for any longer. She didn't even care about the business, something that had been her life and her passion for as long as An could remember.

Juliet had sat home in front of the television set the last few days before An returned to school, watching soap operas and eating pies: pecan pies, apple pies, blueberry pies, lemon meringue pies, rhubarb pies... so many pies! Who knew there were so many different flavors! It's the only thing that kept Juliet going. She would leave the house only to find and buy her pies. Her hypertension had worsened, and her diabetes was out of control, her doctor had told CJ when he managed to have the doctor make a house call. Juliet didn't care. She would sit with a fork and a pie on her lap and devour the sweet morsels like a starving animal.

CJ was terrified but didn't know what to do to help her. When An was home for a short few days for spring break, she, too, attempted to cajole her mother to take her medicine and try to get better. Nothing helped.

By the time May rolled around and An was finally done with school—having missed the graduation ceremony altogether to rush back to CJ and Juliet—she arrived home to find a mother she barely recognized. Juliet hardly even bathed or showered anymore. She was committing suicide in a strange and bizarre way, but suicide nonetheless. Her sixty-seven-year-old frame simply could not survive this avalanche of inactivity combined with the huge amounts of ingested sugars. She had completely stopped taking her medications, refusing to comply with her doctors' instructions and her children's pleas. CJ and An watched helplessly.

"We need some kind of intervention," An told CJ one day. "She's going to die!"

"She'll do it one way or another, An. She doesn't want to live; she's done with this life. I don't think we can stop her," was CJ's response. "She's a grown woman; maybe we should let her be."

CHAPTER 6

BROKEN WINGS

"Give sorrow words; the grief that does not speak knits up the o-er wrought heart and bids it break."
- William Shakespeare, *Macbeth*
"Some secrets never leave us alone."
- *Secret Justice,* Chapter 34

It took An a second or so holding the phone to gather her wits about her. She remembered the previous morning—Angie coming to her door, speaking in hushed tones, asking for An's help to gather information and intelligence about Lisa Spencer's unexpected and somewhat suspicious death.

"Angie, right. Hi!" An managed to say into the receiver. "Has something happened? Where should we meet?"

"I have some business your way and thought I might see if you've gone over to see our friend, Benjamin Spencer, and if you have any insights. I also wanted to give you a little more background on the situation, maybe put our heads together and see what we come up with."

"Oh, okay," An said, eyes squinting and lips pursed. She felt so strange about this Angie person. On the one hand, Angie gave her the heebie-jeebies. On the other, Angie was like a mysterious but good light force beckoning to An. She couldn't resist the intrigue and the need to know more, understand more, about Angie and her purpose. An assumed there was a purpose for Angie coming into her life. There must be a purpose for what was happening, even if An couldn't yet see the big picture. She was trying to remain patient, hopeful that enlightenment would come in time.

"There's a quaint little bookstore on Jacob Street, called 'My Time.' Do you know it?"

"Yes, I do! I've been there. They have a wonderful selection of books, plus really good coffee and pastries in the back."

"That's it!" Angie exclaimed. "Can you be there in about an hour then?"

"Sure," An said, already dreaming about getting a new book, sipping some of their strong coffee, and maybe even sampling one of their croissants—hot and buttery, with apricot preserves perhaps. Okay, she sold herself on the idea. With a smile on her face, she went about getting dressed and ready to go out.

Angie was already there when An arrived. Making a beeline to the back of the bookstore, An tried to decide if she wanted a croissant, or if she wanted to try something different this time. She remembered a very nice selection of various delectable pastries. There were only four small, round tables in the place, and Angie had selected the one furthest away from the glass pastry counter, in the shadowed corner. No one else was there so they would have the place to themselves. The two women made eye contact almost immediately.

"Hi!" said Angie, lifting her cup of coffee in a salute.

"Well, I see you already got yourself a cup, huh?"

"Yeah, I got here sooner than expected, but go ahead and get your coffee. I think I'm going to get one of those apple turnovers."

They each headed to the counter from different directions, coming together in the middle. An noted that Angie was dressed very professionally in an attractive maroon-colored skirt suit, an off-white silk blouse peeking from underneath her buttoned-up jacket. She had wavy dark hair that fell to her shoulders. Her eyes were light brown, the color of caramel.

"You look lovely," An said to Angie.

"So do you!" Angie said, smiling at An, in turn admiring her lovely hair and makeup so perfectly in place.

"What do you do for work?" An asked.

"Oh, a little of this, a little of that, mostly real estate." Angie looked away and did not seem interested in elaborating, so An said nothing more on the topic. An turned her full attention to the yummy baked goods on the other side of the glass. Unable to decide on a single pastry, she ended up getting her croissant, plus a chocolate danish for later at home. Angie got the apple turnover she had been eyeing.

When they finally sat back down, An took a sip of her coffee, savoring its rich bitterness, then said to Angie, "I did go to the Spencer home yesterday to offer my condolences, and I have to say they are a really nice bunch. My first impression is that Ben Spencer probably had nothing to do with whatever happened to his wife."

Angie smiled. "Well, the girls must have been there. They are very pretty and very charming young women. As far as *Ben* is concerned." She emphasized the name Ben and paused for effect. "And by the way, I've never been comfortable calling him that. I never quite figured him out. In all the years I knew Lisa, Benjamin and I never warmed up to each other."

"How long did you know them and under what circumstance?" An was curious to know.

"Well, Lisa and I knew one another our entire lives! I moved away, then she moved, but we always managed to stay in touch one way or another. There were times we were extremely close and then there were times we didn't hear from each other for months, years even. She always was a loner, but in the last ten years or so, it became pronouncedly worse."

"Before or after she moved to Orchard Lane?" An wanted to know.

"I suppose about the time she moved there. At least she was able to hold a job until a year or so after moving to Orchard Lane."

"Ben said she battled demons and was depressed. Is that true?"

"We all have our demons, An," Angie said, then took a long sip of her coffee, eyeing her from behind the rim of her cup before continuing. "Lisa was very much an introvert. She did have bouts of depression from a young age, and she went through some troubled times." She paused again for a bite of her pastry, looking pensive, her eyes staring at something past An.

"But demons?" Angie said. "Maybe so. Life seemed to wear her down. She was acutely sensitive, so things affected her deeply. I, on the other hand, was more of an extrovert and dealt with issues in a more outward way. I'm not known for being the most tactful or thoughtful person, so I guess we balanced each other's personalities fairly well. Probably one of the reasons we stayed friends for so long."

An had been listening quietly, trying to piece together what Ben had said about his wife with what Angie was saying now.

"Was she a sad person?" An asked.

"She brooded a little. She was highly intelligent and easily grasped problems at a level most of us don't get. She wanted to fix things, but intuitively understood her limitations, so I guess it made her frustrated as well as sad sometimes. Did Benjamin describe her as sad, soulful, moody?" Angie rolled her eyes as she said this.

"I suppose yes. Was there something that made her particularly brooding or sad, though?" An wanted to see if Angie knew more. Ben seemed to be holding something from her, something that had made Lisa sad.

Angie sighed and looked past An again, seeming to struggle with something. It made An's skin crawl with goosebumps.

Then as if making up her mind, Angie said, "Yeah, when she lost Baby Lilly. She was the last child they had, a good ten years after the triplets. Lilly only lived a few hours. It was gut-wrenchingly sad." There were tears in Angie's eyes. She bowed her head in an attempt to compose herself. An reached out to touch Angie's hand on the table. Her fingernails were long and well-manicured, painted a shiny, dusty-rose color.

"With everything that you've said, and everything that you know about Lisa, don't you find it very plausible that she took her own life?" An asked Angie. *Lisa had battled depression her whole life, she was sorrowful after losing her youngest child, she had become a recluse…* It seemed to An it was very possible life had become too much of a burden, one Lisa Spencer simply could no longer shoulder.

Angie seemed to give that question a decent amount of consideration. "I can see how you might come to that conclusion," she said. "But Lisa was so sensitive and so thoughtful. She's the type that would have been devastated by the thought of how taking her own life would affect her kids and Benjamin. She was also very gentle; she couldn't hurt a fly. To have done something to herself and then wait all day long to die… Impossible! I don't see her doing it."

"What do you mean?" An said, puzzled by what Angie had just disclosed. "What do you mean she 'waited all day long to die?' Where did you hear that?"

"It could have been by some type of threat or coercion," Angie said, appearing to not have heard An's question. "I don't know, An. I'm really only speculating."

An pondered that one, intently staring at Angie and feeling unsettled and a little scared with this conversation. "A threat? Coercion? You seem to know a lot about it. Have you talked to the police? I have Detective Connor and Detective Conrad's information in my bag. We should call them. Right now!"

"No, not yet," Angie said calmly.

"Then tell me more about what you know. If you want my help, I need more, Angie."

"Okay," Angie said with a sigh. "The police will eventually get around to me anyhow. The phone record will show my number. Lisa had been in contact with me the night she died— late, maybe midnight or after, multiple times."

"Why didn't you contact the police? Why didn't—"

"Let me finish," Angie told An, raising her right hand to silence her.

"Lisa wasn't making a lot of sense, kinda rambling. She explained that she was tired and just needed sleep. I told her it was late and that she should just go to bed and call me in the morning. She said, 'No, I'll probably be dead by then.'"

"Oh, my God, Angie!" An clutched her throat. "You should have called for help."

"I told her I was going to hang up and call the police, that she was scaring me. But she just pleaded with me not to. She said everything would be okay, that she was just in a funk. She hung up then, saying she would call back."

"Did she?"

"Not for a while. I became frantic with worry and called her, hoping Ben wouldn't answer. I was so conflicted. On the one hand, I wanted him to be there to help her if she needed help, but on the other hand, I worried that he might be the cause for her distress. There was no answer."

"Then what?" An was on pins and needles. Her left eye began to twitch, and her heart raced a mile a minute.

Angie sighed audibly, gulped, and continued, "I was getting ready to leave to make the two-hour drive to Lisa when the phone rang again. It was her! I was so relieved. But she sounded too calm, too distant… I should have gone to her immediately, but she kept reassuring me everything would be okay."

"Did she say anything else more revealing? What about the waiting all day comment you made? Wha—"

Angie cut her off again, putting her arm up. "Shhh, listen! She said she was so very tired. Again, I said, 'Go to bed, Lisa. Get some rest.' She said, 'I've been waiting all day long for sleep, to just lay my head down and find peace so I don't have to deal with anything anymore.'"

"Didn't that seem like a strange comment? What did you tell her?"

"Well, I assumed at the time that she was going through one of her depressions and was just talking. I didn't take it literally!" Angie said with indignation in her voice. "It wasn't until later after I had pondered it a little that I realized something was horribly amiss."

"So, then what? How did I come up in conversation?"

"I asked her if anyone was there with her. She said yes. I asked her if Ben was there. She said she didn't want to discuss Ben. I asked her if she wanted me to come there. She said absolutely not, that it would cause problems. I said, 'Well, if you don't want me to call the police or come there, how can I help? What do you need me to do?'"

"Good. What did she tell you?"

"She said, 'If you want to help, get together with An Goode. She lives a couple doors down at 28 Orchard Lane.' I was quite puzzled. I started asking questions, and she told me not to question things, to just listen. She said, very emphatically, that together, we held the key to helping her. I asked about Benjamin, and she said, 'Yes, Ben has information. Have An talk to him, though; he won't tell *you* anything.'"

"Wow." An sat back on her chair. She had been on the edge of the seat, trying to soak in every syllable. This puzzle was growing more intricate by the minute.

"I told Lisa that I didn't get it. I didn't even know you. She said, 'No, you two have met before. She bakes these amazing raisin-oatmeal cookies.'"

"That was it?"

"Pretty much. I tried asking more questions, but she said she was really tired. She promised to call back and then hung up. A couple hours went by and nothing so I had tried calling her back, but no one answered. I tried just going to bed but couldn't sleep a wink. I finally decided to make the drive to her house and scan the neighborhood. See what I could see.

"By the time I got to Orchard Lane, I saw the commotion and knew something had happened—something terrible.

I don't really know why, but I just didn't want to face the police or Ben. The conversations with Lisa kept replaying in my head. Something just wasn't adding up. I decided to walk through the wooded area behind the houses to get to your house. I'm not sure why Lisa asked me to come to you but for whatever reason she wanted us together; she wanted us to find answers together."

"Uh-huh," was all An could muster as her mind raced, trying to make sense of all this. Her fingertips felt cold, so she began rubbing them on her lap, under the table. She wasn't sure what to believe. Despite Angie professing to not getting along with Ben, An thought there was more to her sneakiness. If she was so worried about her friend, why didn't she just go inside when she saw the commotion and sensed something foreboding was taking place? She had been, after all, Lisa's good friend at one point. They had remained in contact for many years, albeit on and off. Why not go in the home and find out what had happened, and maybe aid the police? An was suspicious. Something was definitely fishy with this entire sordid story.

"I know a lot of this doesn't make sense. But I need your help. I need you to be my eyes and ears since you're so close to it all, and I can't really talk to Benjamin," Angie pleaded. When An remained silent, she continued, "You should know that Benjamin and I had very few words after Lilly died. Emotions were raw that day in the hospital.

We both said things we shouldn't have, and we practically became enemies after that."

An wondered if there was more to this story, much more. Angie continued her explanation in an attempt to convince An to keep helping her.

"I was at the home on Orchard Street only a handful of times. Normally, I tried to avoid Benjamin. One time for a barbeque when they had first moved in, one time when Benjamin was out of town… Don't get me wrong. We were all good friends at one point. I guess I blamed him for what was happening to Lisa. The more distant and introverted she became, the more I hated him. When Baby Lilly died, I blamed him for that too. I was so angry with him I couldn't see straight."

Angie had paused, trembling a little. An watched and listened intently, mesmerized. She had hoped Angie would finally get to the crux of the problem, and at last she was getting somewhere.

"Why do you think you have so much anger toward Ben? It seems to me Lisa had some part in what was happening to her, and Baby Lilly was not something anyone could have controlled or changed. It was just God's will."

Angie popped the last piece of apple turnover in her mouth, took her last sip of—now cold—coffee, and dabbed her mouth daintily with her napkin. She seemed to consider An's words carefully.

"I felt Benjamin had been the catalyst to all the transformation. He changed her, or caused her to change, in dramatic and permanent ways. I felt she was disappearing from me and the rest of the world because of him. He was never happy with her being who she was. He had to mold her to fit his own needs, his own purpose."

"But you still haven't told me how exactly he did this or how it is his fault she changed. We all change, don't we? No one *makes* us," An told her. "It's normal, human, evolution. It's life!"

"Don't you see?" Angie eyed An, incredulous. "She went on diets for him, she changed her hair color for him, she dressed the way he liked, she went to places she could not care less about only for him, she even changed her politics because of him… my God, she practically erased her true self just to please him!

"She's not here because of him! If she couldn't be who he wanted her to be, then she felt she was nobody!" Angie concluded, breathing through her clenched teeth. Her eyes were wild with fury.

The women stared at one another, Angie still fuming. Trying to wrap her brain around what Angie had told her, An sat in a quiet stupor. *This is powerful stuff,* she thought. So many unanswered questions, and now there were more unanswered questions. This conversation had cast more doubt instead of clarifying things.

"I'm so confused," An said.

"I don't understand a lot of what's happened either. I'm trying to do the right thing, that's all. Will you still help me? Just keep talking to Benjamin. I think he may have useful information," Angie said.

"I don't know… I feel deceitful. That's not my nature."

"You're too good, An," Angie told her. "You need to grow some teeth and bare them every now and then, or you'll get swallowed up like Lisa."

An stared at Angie, unable to respond. Her ears pricked.

"Listen, I have to go. We've been here for more than an hour already," Angie said. "But I'll be in touch again soon. I promise. Hang in there, An."

"Wait!" An said, feeling frantic. "I feel like I need to ask more questions. I need more. How do you think we met, and why did Lisa single me out? Please, just stay a while longer."

Angie laughed a throaty, husky laugh. It was so contagious, An wanted to laugh too. "Wasn't it at that barbeque?" Angie answered her. "I can't remember either."

"Why did she want me involved, though?" An complained.

"It's a no-brainer to me. I think Lisa recognized that you are gutsy, perceptive, loyal to a fault—even if you don't believe you are those things anymore. Plus, you live two doors away."

"Well, you and Lisa sure seem to know me better than I know you guys." An blew out a sigh, seeming deflated. She felt suddenly bone-weary. This conversation had taken a lot out of her.

Angie was buttoning her coat. She picked up her purse, slung it over her left shoulder, and came to stand by An. She put a hand on her shoulder. "You'll be okay. I promise. Even if nothing comes of your visits to Benjamin, maybe you will find a friend in him. Who knows? He's not my cup of tea, but maybe he's yours. You're right; it is possible Lisa took her own life. At least I hope you will gather some insightful information that will tell us more accurately her frame of mind."

She started walking away, her heels clicking. "Thank you, An!" She half-turned to blow An an air kiss and was gone.

An waved a limp hand. She finished her croissant without really tasting it. Her coffee was now lukewarm, so she left it. She picked up her things and decided to look for a good book before leaving. *Why not?* She was already here. At least books made sense to her; they were chock-full of organized information that revealed the answers to every question posed. And books—more than ever now—kept her going, kept her sane, and filled her empty world.

An's drive home was a blur. She rushed through her door, vaguely hearing a familiar voice calling in greeting from outside, "Hi, An!"

"Hey!" She waved, not sure who she was waving to. Sounded like Tina. The ringing in her head was getting louder. She squeezed her eyes shut once she was inside. She kicked her boots off, threw her coat on the couch, and numbly walked to her favorite seat—the chaise lounge in the library. After the kitchen, this was probably her next most favorite place in the house. There were dozens of pictures scattered about, smiling faces, happy places… Memories, so many memories scattered all over the place. She yawned, her eyes already drooping.

Lynne… Erica… memories.

Melancholy wrapped itself tightly around An like an old familiar blanket. On the mantle, Lynne and Erica smiled down at her, in various poses and different ages. Her favorite wedding-day photo had been in the center, but recently, An had moved it to one of the bookshelves, not so prominent now. At some point soon, she would box it up for good and stow it away for the next voyage of her life.

She looked for it now, admiring it from where she sat. Her dress was simple but elegant: no frills, no shiny beads, no poof, just a long, form-fitting white dress that flared at the bottom with a short trailing train. She wore a crown of pink-and-white tiny rosebuds attached to a thin veil that fell and settled on her shoulders. Underneath, her hair spilled down in waves to her shoulder blades. Next to her, Brad smiled from ear to ear, wearing a black tuxedo. The girls were standing in front of them, wearing pretty pale pink dresses in shiny satin, little crowns of baby's breath on their tiny heads.

Here, her favorite books surrounded her. *Ah, books, where I could lose myself traveling to unknown exotic places, or try on alter egos for the right fit.* In the early days, she and Brad used to read to each other all the time—mostly, she read to him. In bed on weekend mornings or on car trips. Sometimes he would make her stop reading so they could analyze a character or rewrite a scene. She didn't like sad endings and argued that all books should have good endings since life was already tragic enough. Brad would tease her about being a silly dreamer and a hopeless romantic. "My mom already gave me that speech, thank you very much!" she told him once. "She used to tell me that I was a dreamer, and dreamers don't go far in life."

They had been lying in bed. Brad had gotten quiet before saying to her in a husky voice, "Come here." An had cuddled up to him, feeling tears stinging her eyes. "You will always be my beautiful, intelligent dreamer, and the sky's the limit as far as what you can do." She loved him for saying that. So long ago, yet forever etched in her memory. That was many moons ago when he still loved her, or at least pretended to love her, feigning caring. At that moment truth and fiction colluded to confuse her, and she could no longer discern what had been real and what had been an illusion.

An let her thoughts take flight. She thought of Lisa and her lost baby girl. She thought of all the times she and Brad had tried to get pregnant, then the miscarriages, the tears, the agony. The sense of loss was so intense, so sharp, she could hardly breathe. She felt the sorrow and sadness once more for all of her lost babies, lost possibilities. Her broken heart was cracking and ripping apart all over again. She knew exactly what Lisa Spencer had experienced because she had lived it, over and over. And she understood, completely, the piece of death within that followed each loss.

Later that day, after waking up from her short nap, An decided to do some more packing. She was in the library carefully boxing some of her books when she heard light rapping at her door—three times, of course. She smiled and walked to her front door. Peering out the side glass panel, she saw Benjamin Spencer. There was a chill in the air, but the sun was shining bright. An opened the door and shielded her eyes with her hand. Smiling at Ben, she said, "Well, hello there!"

Ben looked even more handsome than the previous day. His face was freshly shaven, save for that little soul patch on his chin. He held up her bag from the day before. She smiled as she took the bag from him.

"I wanted to bring your containers back," he said. "And I wanted to thank you for stopping by." He paused, hands in the pockets of his jeans, looking down at the ground. "You were a spot of shimmering light in an otherwise very somber, dark day."

"Come on in, Ben. Please," she said, still smiling at him.

"Okay," he said, eagerly stepping inside and looking around with curiosity. "Wow, this is really nice! Looks like you have Lisa's eye for decorating."

"Thank you!" An said with a chuckle. "Come on back in the kitchen? We can put some coffee or tea on?"

"That would be super," said Ben, as he followed her to the back of the house. "I love the coziness yet elegance of your decorating. Very tasteful. I can't believe I've never set foot in your house before."

"My husband—soon to be ex-husband—and I did most of the work. I love it, too, and it was such a joy working on it?" An sounded animated and enthused. They had reached the kitchen. "Here, have a seat anywhere you like?" she said to him. She noticed she had started speaking in question marks again. She made a conscious mental note to watch those squiggly things at the ends of her sentences.

"It's very nice what the two of you did. By the way, those oatmeal-raisin cookies were amazing! And the casserole was one of the best meals I've had in a long time. So tasty and homey. Thank you."

"Oh, you're very welcome. I think I get my love of baking from my mother. Sit, sit…" She pointed to the table and chairs. "Do you prefer coffee, or tea? I can also make hot cocoa…?"

"Oh, I like them all," said Ben. "But, please, just tea would be great."

"No problem!" An said cheerfully. Smiling, she went about making the tea and getting the cups ready. "Do you like crackers and cheese? I have some really good aged Parmesan?"

"Super, but don't go to any extra trouble for me, really."

"Oh, no trouble. I live for this stuff. I appreciate you stopping by and giving me the opportunity to *entertain*." An had emphasized the word *entertain*, and they chuckled at it.

"I guess you're moving?" Ben asked rhetorically, indicating two moving boxes stacked up in the kitchen.

"Yes, unfortunately. This place is too big for me now that my divorce is final… and the kids have moved on…"

"Sorry to hear that, and just when I'm getting to know you. Maybe something will change your mind. You never know."

An laughed. "Well, 'you never know' is right," she said. "Anything can happen, especially since I don't even have a for-sale sign up in front of my house yet. I just like planning well in advance, and it gives me something to keep my mind occupied, as well as an incentive to clear out. I'll probably look for an apartment and hope to move out in the next few months."

Ben listened intently as An spoke, shaking his head up and down, eyes focused on her. "I had heard rumors through the neighborhood grapevine about you and your husband, but I didn't realize the divorce was underway and things are now permanent, it sounds like."

"It's been headed that way for years… Yeah…" An let her words trail. She was doing her best not to fall apart. *What the heck!* An pondered. *Why these stupid emotions rupturing everywhere? The divorce had been in the making for forever, so why can I not just move on with it already? These stupid up-and-down emotions are getting old.*

"What happened?" Ben asked. "If you don't mind me asking."

"Oh, it's such a long and complicated story. I wouldn't know where or how to begin. Everything just added up. I had overlooked so many things and brushed away so many signs. Typical of me, you know?" An was visibly uncomfortable with this line of conversation, fidgeting with the collar of her sweater and making very little eye contact with Ben.

"I know it must be difficult, but I'm a good listener most of the time. I don't mind listening," Ben told her in a soft and gentle voice.

"Would you look at me?" she said. She had spilled some water on the counter while trying to fill the teapot. She wiped it, a little too vigorously. "Pathetic," she said. "I'm making a mess while you're the one needing a listening ear, and here I am babbling about myself."

"It helps me to focus on something else. Truly, I don't mind," he told her, trying to encourage her to continue talking.

An was silent for a second, before sighing audibly. Making up her mind about opening up to Ben, she said, "I don't miss him, per se. I mean, we had been together for so long, it was comfortable. We had both gotten so complacent about each other, and we took each other for granted? But I just assumed we would keep working at it, and things would eventually get better? I'm such a stupid optimist, you know? I didn't know about his secret life… I didn't know much of anything and ignored a lot. My choosing ignorance, it hurt others I love. But I made my bed, so I should just lie in it, right? There is no one else to blame."

She turned away from Ben, feeling ashamed for saying so much, but the need to talk, to get it out of her system, was so intense. Like a caustic poison trapped for too long, it all wanted to bubble up to the surface and gush out. She didn't want to let it all escape, but she knew that if she was going to survive, she would have to expel all that garbage at some point. Some of it had come out during counseling, but it had been a long time since she had had a session.

The shame of it all was strangling her.

She busied herself with arranging the crackers and slicing the Parmesan. Ben remained quiet, perhaps trying to give her time to compose herself. She must have seemed so lonely, so vulnerable.

"So many secrets," she continued in a cracked voice, her eyes now unfocused and haunted. "So much evil. How did he keep them stashed away so carefully, so callously?" she mumbled. "Did you and your wife talk about stuff?" An asked Ben the question, intending to divert the conversation away from her. She wanted the focus elsewhere so she could arrange her thoughts and feelings. Plus, she could only relive the past in tiny bites of memory so that her mind wouldn't completely shatter.

"Oh, yeah, a lot," Ben told her. "Not at the end, though, I'm sorry to say. Lisa had shut herself away, including from me. But for many years, before and after we were married, we had some very powerful discussions about all kinds of things. It was one of the major strengths of our relationship."

"Brad and I did, too, early on. I miss what we had. I miss being a wife, a mom, knowing my role in life? But I didn't ponder a lot of it until it was all lost to me and unspeakable things revealed to me. How does all that end? How can people build and build—a home, kids, traditions, everything—and then lose it all? What's the point?" An's voice was brimming with emotion as she talked.

"All good and valid questions," Ben said. "I don't have adequate answers, unfortunately. And it sounds like a rough go for you. I hope you will be able to talk about all of it someday." He was silent for a moment. An brought the crackers and cheese to the table on a narrow, long, silver-plated tray. Then she worked on the tea and accoutrements: delicate china cups and saucers, a pot of hot water, little sugar cubes, lemon slices, and honey. When everything was set, she joined Ben at the table. She sat down at the head of the table, to his left.

Ben had been watching her intently as she moved fluidly in her kitchen. *Can he see me?* An wondered. *Can he see what I'm feeling? Even with my eyes averted, can he sense my sadness?*

"I never imagined my life like this. I dreamed of lots of kids, grandkids, the house alive with laughter and people and activity?" She shook her head vigorously. "It makes me so deeply sad. Yet I am relieved that the sham is over, and he is gone. But I still wish it had turned out different."

Ben put his hand on her shoulder. It felt warm and comforting to An.

"What is it like to lose your spouse the way you did, Ben?" Again, An felt the need to move away from her personal painful memories so she could catch her breath and regain a modicum of control.

"I suppose it's not very different from the way you lost your spouse. The sense of loss, I think, is very similar. We had love and a beautiful family. We also had our share of problems. Then we grew apart. We were often miserable but had unexpected slivers of sunshine… and now she's gone. Very much like your story."

"But the way she was taken from you… Doesn't that add to the loss? Doesn't it change everything, that she was ripped from you without your control or say so?"

"It makes it extra trying, I suppose. It's tragic. She was still young, and the road ahead was full of possibility. But that was her choice. I don't agree with it; I even think it was a selfish act. But I respect her decision."

"Was it?" An asked, without thinking or even realizing the implication her question was about to pose. "Was it her decision?" She searched Ben's face for something, some clue that he had something—or nothing—to do with Lisa's death, some inkling of guilt or innocence.

"She didn't have help ending her life," he said earnestly. "None that I'm aware of, certainly not at the hands of someone else—other than her demons, her guilt, her desperation, her sadness... Do those things count? Can those things murder a person?"

An seemed to ponder that for a moment before speaking. "Yeah, sure. I believe they can. Those things probably get away with murder every day. There's no law against them and no prison for them."

They were both silent again, eyes locked and searching. *He looks sad and lost,* she thought. Then she asked, "Does it bother you that some people may speculate you had a hand in her death?" Her heart began thumping. She held her breath, waiting for his answer. *Have I gone too far?*

"No," he said simply, breaking eye contact with An to sip his tea. He didn't seem offended by her comment. "Lisa killed herself, plain and simple. I had nothing to do with it. I believe she had been thinking about it for a long time. It was well planned and calculated, from what I could see. Then she executed it flawlessly. She got all her business taken care of: her will, her insurance policies, her burial wishes, all of it!"

He took a deep breath, looking down at his folded hands on the table. His eyes filled with tears as he looked back up at An.

"It's so like her," he said plaintively. "Despite her sadness, her depression, and ultimately not being able to leave the house, she was always in control. She always took matters into her own hands. She was stronger than any of us gave her credit for."

"Was there a note?" An asked. "Did she leave instructions, a letter of explanation? As to why she did it?"

"No, not necessary," he said. "She did her nails for God's sake!" His voice cracked a little, and there was something akin to anger in his eyes. "She colored her hair and put makeup on and got dressed up! Aren't those clues enough of her intentions?"

An expelled a long breath through her mouth. "Wow!" She said. "I hadn't realized… Wow! How did she do it, Ben?" An asked this question in a near whisper. "You mentioned she was ill. Was she on pain medicine? Was that it?"

"She was foaming at the mouth when I found her." He began sobbing quietly, his large hands covering his face. "Bottles of her pills scattered… The room reeked of bleach or some kind of cleaning chemicals," he told her while trying to control the sobs that made his chest rise and fall sharply.

"Bleach?" An questioned, horror in her voice. "Why bleach?"

"Oh, God, it was so terrible!" Ben mumbled. "I don't know… Maybe she drank it? Was she cleaning? I don't know for sure… I just didn't understand her like I thought I did. How could I let it happen?" His voice was anguished and his face wet with tears.

An scraped her chair as she stood, coming to put her arms around Ben, trying to comfort him, finding all this fascinating and sad and confusing. She would need time to process it all. Why were the police convinced it was a suspicious death? What did they know or find? Was Ben covering something? Did he know more?

Eventually, Ben wiped his face by blotting it on his shirtsleeves. "I'm sure a crying man is not an attractive sight," he said finally.

"It's fine. I'm so sorry, Ben," An told him. "I had no idea about all that. My God!"

She took a different approach, after a stretch of silence. "You don't suppose the police really suspect you had something to do with it, do you?"

Ben cleared his throat and leaned back away from the table. "Oh, they asked all sorts of questions. I'm sure they are looking at me as a *person of interest*. After all, I'm the husband. But in time they will exonerate me because I had nothing to do with it. I wasn't even in town that entire day. I'm sure that was part of Lisa's careful planning too. I think she began taking the pills, or whatever, earlier in the day and waited."

An was taken aback by this comment. It seemed almost verbatim what Angie had said. She blinked several times, trying to clear her head. *What am I missing here?*

She decided to go at it with yet another probing question. "Well, I'm sure they'll do toxicology tests as part of the autopsy, or whatever other tests to figure it all out… Where were you that day, Ben?" An asked him.

Ben chuckled. "Wow, you are full of questions, aren't you, Miss Junior Detective?"

An winced. "Sorry," she apologized. "We should be talking about more pleasant things, like your kids maybe?" An hoped she hadn't pushed too far and wedged distrust between them.

He acted as if he hadn't heard her last statement and went on to explain, "I've been in the medical field most of my career, starting out as a paramedic. Lately, I'm doing mostly consulting work. I have a few out-of-state clients. The day Lisa died, I had flown to Florida to see a client. I had planned it weeks in advance, so Lisa knew very well where I would be all day. I didn't return until late that night."

This seemed to agree with what the detectives had said and what Tina had confirmed.

"One last thing and then we'll change the subject," An said. "Are you worried about anything you are engaged in, some activity the police might use against you?"

"Such as? I'm not sure what you're getting at," Ben told her.

"Well, I dunno… like an affair, maybe? Clandestine work-related stuff?"

Ben sucked in his breath, then blew it out, looking up at the ceiling. *This doesn't look good,* An thought. He took a deep breath and sat up straight in his chair, interlacing his hands behind his head.

"You are quite perceptive," he told her. "Unfortunately, I just can't talk about that right now," he finally said. "But, suffice it to say, there have been some, ah… some marital indiscretions?"

"Whaaat?" An was beyond shocked. Her jaw had dropped, and her eyes were as big as her tea set saucer. "What are you admitting to?" she asked incredulously. She honestly had not expected him to confess to anything like an affair; she had simply been grasping at straws, hoping for something illuminating to come out.

He laughed. She liked the sound of it. It was better than the tears. He rubbed his face.

"It wasn't just on my part either," he began. "But that's a long and complicated story left for another visit." He took the time to sip some of his tea, his large hands looking comic holding the delicate teacup. He struggled to get his grip just right, using his thumb, index finger, and middle finger. He popped a cracker and slice of cheese in his mouth, crunching and chewing. He seemed to be buying time.

"Okay, okay," she said, chuckling nervously. "I'll just have to wait to hear all about it. I will try to be very patient, but don't be surprised if I show up at your house in a few hours, pulling my hair out of my head, unable to contain the suspense." They both laughed heartily at that. It felt good to An to be laughing again. It kept the tears at bay, at least temporarily.

Ben cleared his throat and searched An's face. "Didn't you ever have an affair or think about having one?" he asked her, after a long pause.

"No, I honestly never did have an affair. But maybe I thought about it?" She scrunched up her face, squinting her eyes and biting down on her lower lip. "I think women need a good reason for infidelity, like they have to be pushed into it. Either they feel unloved, or ignored, or are bored, which act as motivation to fall into someone else's arms. I felt some of those things, but I just chose to deal with it in a different way. Men, on the other hand, sometimes do it out of sheer spur-of-the-moment opportunity, I think. The opportunity is there, and it just feels good, so it happens. Or, maybe chasing someone other than their spouse is exciting to them?"

"Yeah, well, I can tell you Lisa did it in part out of loneliness but in part to spite me because I did it to her first. That's my take."

"Why did *you* do it?" An asked him.

"Oof, loaded question! And one that's not so easy to answer because the reason was multidimensional. I'm not sure I understand it myself. I felt neglected and unappreciated. Lisa had pretty much checked out. I also felt unaccepted, like an outsider in my own home. For a little while, my affair gave me the attention and acceptance I craved. It validated me."

An was riveted by Ben's revelation. She focused on him and his words with an intense frown on her otherwise smooth forehead. She marveled at his openness and honesty even as she recoiled a little bit that he had chosen to commit adultery. *Wow, people never cease to amaze me!*

"That's an interesting insight. From what you've told me so far, I can see how you might have felt a lack of attention from Lisa, but not accepted? How were you unaccepted?"

"Now we're getting into some dicey territory," he told her. "In part it had to do with race, which is a sticky subject. I never truly felt accepted by her or her family. Yes, they all loved me; yes, they embraced me as one of their own, but there was always this unspoken ghost of a thing that clung to all of us: I *wasn't* the same as them. They knew it, I knew it, and we all pretended not to see it. The proverbial elephant in the room."

Ben paused for effect. An let him have the silence he needed to compose his thoughts and feelings before continuing.

"There was always this tiptoeing around issues that made me feel different despite their reassurances that I was part of the family. No matter how I tried to fit in or how they tried to show me I was one of them, I simply wasn't. At times I felt inferior somehow, like I was an aberration, a freak of nature that she—the pious, generous one—*chose* to love."

An was at a loss for adequate words. "That's a stunning revelation. I… I don't know how to respond. I never thought of it like that." She stumbled to say the right thing. "How should Lisa have treated you or behaved so that you would feel accepted then?"

"For starters, the centuries of enslavement and racism would have to be erased off the face of the planet," he told her, his eyes aglow with some strong emotion that made his entire body visibly vibrate.

"But that's not possible. It's already a done deal, in the past," she answered by stating the obvious.

Ben laughed heartily at that. "Yes," he said. "I'll cede you that point. The thing is I wanted Lisa to see me, including my color. She told me over and over that her love for me—and I know with certainty that she did love me, no doubt there—was blind to my skin color.

"Initially, I found that phrase to be endearing, reassuring. Over time, it bothered me deeply, and it alienated me from Lisa, I think. I wanted her to *see* my color, accept it, and love me for it. See what I'm saying? Can you see the difference?"

"So, you wanted to be acknowledged and *seen* as you are? And be loved for those things that make you, well, you. We all want that!"

He smiled at her. "Sorta," he said. "We all want it, but some get it without asking for it."

They were silent, eyes locked, minds churning, understanding on the periphery of their grasp.

"How did we get into this depressing conversation anyhow?" Ben finally broke the silence. "Gosh! My daughters are probably ready to call a search party to come look for me."

"Oh, geez, your daughters!" An exclaimed, both hands cupping her face. "You should go. But I'll tell you what—you have stretched my world today, Ben. My perception of you is different, which makes my understanding of the world bigger and better. Thank you… I really like you, Ben."

"I like you too, An," Ben told her with a little chuckle. "I'm sorry you have suffered so much because you seem like an amazing woman."

An blushed a little and smiled back at him, suddenly gripped by a strong connection to this man. She hoped this was the beginning of a wonderful friendship and prayed that he had nothing to do with his wife's death.

Ben smiled too. "Well, you're right. I should probably get back home… but before I go, it looks like we will have a service for Lisa at the end of next week. It will be a celebration of her life, nothing too sad or sappy, I hope."

"Oh, okay," An said in a quiet voice.

"We wanted to give my son, and others from out of town, plenty of time to make it. Lisa wanted to be cremated anyhow, so we have a little extra time. Will you come?"

"Of course, of course," An told him. "And if there is anything I can do to help, please let me know. I have the time these days."

"I might just take you up on that," Ben said. "I know it got heavy there for a minute, but I *really* enjoyed talking to you. And thank you for not making fun of my silly tears."

"Not at all," An told him. "Tears are never silly and usually necessary. It clears the vision."

They both got up and stared at one another for a second. Then Ben pulled An to him and squished her with a bear hug. She hugged back, patting his back.

"I've enjoyed your company, An. Thank you. I needed this."

"Me too. Let's do it again soon," An said, meaning it. "Oh, one more thing before you go," An blurted as they reached the front door. Then regretting it, she said, "Never mind. I should stop with the prying questions."

"No, no, go ahead. Now I'm curious about what other crazy insights you want to know about my life." He looked at her with an amused smile.

"Well, you mentioned insurance. I was wondering—I mean, it occurred to me…" An couldn't find a tactful way to finish her sentence.

"You're wondering if there was an insurance policy that benefits me from Lisa's death?"

"Is there?" An asked, sheepishly.

"Yes, An, actually there is," Ben said after a short pause. "And it's a substantial amount. I'm the sole beneficiary."

He opened the door and walked out then, leaving An to ponder this last implication. She had one more question she never got to ask. Had she been to his home before and brought her raisin-oatmeal cookies?

An had a hard time going back to her packing once Ben had left. The sun was low on the horizon, and the house felt cold and sterile—so empty and quiet. In these dark rooms, her mind was ablaze from talking to Ben. On impulse, she walked around turning all the light switches on in the house, downstairs and upstairs, all the lamps too for good measure. Then she turned some music on, all to keep the loneliness and the sadness at arm's length.

A long time ago, she remembered enjoying singing and dancing to the radio. *What did I used to listen to? 98.7? 97.1 Wash FM, that was it!* She began humming some long-ago tune. In the library now, her memories floating around her head, she placed her left hand on her stomach and her right hand lifted up in the air to meet her imaginary partner's hand. She began swaying to the music, eyes closed.

CHAPTER 7

ECHOES OF NOSTALGIA: 1991

"She was a girl who knew how to be happy even when she was sad. And that's important—you know?"

> \- Marilyn Monroe

"Sometimes things fall apart so that better things can fall together."

> \- Marilyn Monroe

Lord, Juliet was such a beautiful soul! But it was hard to penetrate her façade of bravado, strength, and control and see the gentle, kind, and nurturing woman she started out being—at least according to An's dad anyhow. Life has a way of doing that to some people, placing them in an armor of steel and hardening their soft edges. Not An. Life's experiences had pretty much ended up turning her into a big bowl of Jell-O.

An admired her mother's strength and perseverance, but growing up, she had longed for Juliet's touch, just a soft look or a hint of a smile, anything that revealed that tender side of her. Once when An was about twelve, she had complimented her ma on her new coat. Juliet's eyes grew misty, and she gave An's arm a squeeze. Oh, how An had treasured that moment and savored it—such a rarity she still remembered nearly four decades later. It was all the reassurance An needed to know that the gentle, nurturing mother she so longed for did exist inside the woman she called 'Ma.'

So it was disconcerting to An, to say the least, when Juliet lost her grip on that armor suit of hers and slipped right out of it when Harrison died. What was left of her was unrecognizable to An and CJ; she was not the soft-spoken and gentle young girl residing in Pop's stories, and she was no longer the shrewd businesswoman everyone had come to know either. All the pieces of her crumpled in a heap before An. Juliet's eyes turned inward, perhaps looking at the memories she and Harrison had shared, and all that could have been and never was, but now time had run out.

Juliet wallowed in her self-pity and sadness, a sorrow so deep there was no way to the surface for a gulp of fresh air. She plopped herself in front of the television set, her eyes unseeing, her lips sealed shut, except to eat the pies. In the week that An was home after Harrison had died,

Juliet left the house only to buy her pies. Her hair grew stringy and oily, her jeans soiled and smelly. An's beautiful, glamorous-looking, Marilyn Monroe look-alike mother was no more.

An tried everything to stop her from carrying out this slow suicidal ploy of hers. She sang Loretta Lynn songs to Juliet, read Virginia Woolf poetry to her, stroked her cheeks, prayed with her. An tried looking at old family photos and reminiscing about their few family excursions. She begged and pleaded with her mother to live. She told her they would see a therapist together to help them deal with their loss, that they could visit Pop's grave and talk to him every day. But absolutely nothing worked. Juliet told An that life was dead to her and nothing appealed to her anymore. She was done.

"BUT I'M NOT DONE WITH YOU!" An screamed, out of her mind with fury. "I've just begun with you. Ma, pleeease," she cried, her voice husky with emotion and tears. "I want to see a movie with you! I want hugs and kisses! I want to cook a seven-course meal with you! I want to watch sunsets and sunrises! I want you at my wedding! I want my children to know their grandmother! I want your love and encouragement and advice and I want Christmas and Thanksgiving dinners and I want you to live!" An stopped, breathless. Her entire being shook from head to toe. Her face felt hot and wet with tears, but her fingers were icicles as she looked at her mother's pale, sunken face, waiting for a reaction.

There was none.

"Remember that cruise we all took to Europe a long time ago? Let's do that again—Ma, look at me!"

Juliet slowly turned her eyes on An and very softly said, "I don't have the strength. You do it without me."

"I love you, Ma," An said in a near whisper. "I want to hear you say you love me too. Ma. Mama, say it. Please say it."

But no words of love were uttered from Juliet to An that day. No other words were uttered, period. The image of their European summer vacation played out in An's mind: Juliet's red lipstick, her skin so bronze, her golden hair shimmering in the sunlight. She had smiled as she backed into the waves, her feet sinking in the wet sand.

"Come on, come on, An! This feels divine! Let's ride the waves."

An had never seen her mother so happy, so alive, so dazzling. An had only been thirteen then. Her dad and brother had come running behind her, squealing with delight as they met the crashing waves. An had smiled too then, beginning to run toward Juliet.

"Wait for me, guys!"

Back in the living room with Juliet, An's heart shattered and splintered into a million little pieces, her ears going deaf, her words mute. For all intents and purposes, this day marked the day An buried her mother. Juliet's light dimmed to pinpricks in her eyes, and her smile forever faded. Her expression was simply a memory, a mask plastered on for the outside world. Inside her, emptiness reigned without her HC.

An sank down at her mother's feet and cried bitter tears until CJ got home and pulled her away.

"Go back to school, An," he said calmly. "Why agonize over what you have no control over?"

"How could I ever leave you alone to deal with all this? I can't!" An shrieked at him.

"Yes, you can. Your future is wrapped up in your studies, and you only have a semester to go. You can't change the course of things, An. This is a script that has been written and played out long before us. Just accept it."

"Who are you?" An had said with awe. "When did you become such a sage?"

He smiled his toothy-white smile—so like Harrison's—and then crushed An against his chest. An could hear his heart beating fast and furious, the beginning of a sob rising up in his throat. He smelled of fresh linen laundry detergent and Dial. And he had grown so tall! How had An missed that? She had to get on her tippy toes then to hug him back, her arms encircling his twig of a neck.

An closed her eyes to better hold on to this moment, as Little Brother continued his spiel, saying without ceremony, "My education, on the other hand, is going nowhere. I'm aimless and indecisive, and the best place for me right now is learning the family business." At barely twenty he was already an old, wise Confucius.

"Trust me," he continued, "you have some catching up to do, but I know you can do it. Go finish your education and then come home, and we'll pick up where you left off. It'll all work out somehow."

He pulled An away so they could study each other's faces. Their gazes locked, and in that moment, they understood what needed to be done, and no other words were necessary. The siblings embraced again and stood like that for a long time, knowing they had each other—always had, always would.

Juliet held on until the end of that summer and then succumbed before the leaves had even started to turn golden. She was finally at peace, hopefully with her HC. An and CJ buried their other parent only nine months after saying goodbye to their pop. An was confused by her feelings about her mother's passing. She was conflicted, feeling sadness and regret for a mother-daughter closeness she only shared with her mother in bursts. She had never understood Juliet and never grew to know her deepest thoughts and desires—not in a meaningful way.

The sense of loss was a crushing, suffocating, devastating one, yet not as intense as when she lost her pop. There was relief too, this time. Perhaps she had gotten acquainted with the sense of loss and was more accepting now, and more mature. The relationship with her mother had been an obligatory and superficial one at times, yet the love was always percolating on the surface of their everyday lives. The tears flooded her. The loss cut deep. But the reality was that life eventually fell back into pace with the new normalcy. A chapter had closed, and life would still go on unconcerned and unabashed. It was just the cycle of things.

"Why is this happening to us, CJ?" An had asked her brother the day of their mother's funeral. "It's too soon, too soon for yet another loss," she had whimpered. "I can't stand the barrage of emotions. Why would God do this?"

CJ had pondered the question. "Don't you believe there's another realm, a better place, a heaven if you will? Where we will all meet again someday?"

"Nope. I really don't. I think we slip into a deep sleep… forever. Period. The end. That's it. Bye-bye."

"No, An, you need to believe. You need to trust that there is more!" CJ was adamant, his words so fervent.

"But why? Why do I *have* to believe?"

"Well, for starters, it helps you live a fuller, happier life, without the fear of the unknown shackling you, freezing you in place. You can't truly appreciate this life if you think there's nothing else.

"Look at it this way. You get to the finish line of a race, and there's… nothing. You give birth to a child and hold him in your arms, and there's… nothing. That would stink! Everything that happens is for *something*!"

"Wouldn't that mean I would appreciate life more if I think I only have this one life?" An argued.

"No, An. What would you be living for then? It would make you despondent. Why give a crap about anything if it's only for nothing, only a long, dark, forever sleep at the end?"

"Alright. You're way too smart and too deep for me, Little Brother. Go away. You're making my head hurt," An told him, kiddingly.

The next few months had rumbled past at the speed of lightning. CJ had done quite well holding the business together, and once he had turned twenty-one, they decided he would take over as president of the enterprise. An helped out whenever he needed her, mostly with the marketing and accounting side of business. She found she was good at it and thoroughly enjoyed it. The business was thriving at a steady pace, solidly holding its own, which allowed An to not feel like she needed to hover.

She felt she had to create some space in her mind to ponder the rest of her life. Maybe she should go back to school for an accounting degree, she considered. She had been applying for jobs related to her major, although nothing interesting had crossed her radar.

Their parents' will was simple and didn't do much in the way of impeding the siblings from divvying up the money and property in a way they saw fit. Their parents must have known there wouldn't be contention among the two. An and CJ had sold the family home and had disposed of most of its contents by the time a year rolled around.

Between the proceeds from the home, a number of insurance policies, and the business, An and CJ felt pretty good about their financial situation and future. They agreed that CJ would retain the majority share of the business, and An would keep the vacation home in Rehoboth Beach. She adored the beach and loved the little bungalow she remembered going to with her parents—and later her friends—on a few occasions.

An wasn't sure what she was going to do next. Finding a career was at the top of her list, but other than that, what? What was life all about? What exactly was her purpose in life? In May she would turn twenty-four years old, and her future looked… well, empty and shallow. Maybe she would buy a little house somewhere—a fixer-upper. She could get busy working on it. But that didn't quite appeal to her. She had always envisioned doing something like that with a partner—a husband. Maybe she would go back to school and get her master's degree? But, then again, not just yet. She was burned out from school.

Thoughts of Jimmy suddenly flooded her senses. Closing her eyes, she could see his image, hear his voice, taste his lips, feel his touch. *What is he up to?* she wondered as her thoughts strayed to that weekend so long ago, it seemed. Why did he never try to call or look for her? Did he still have the Bible she had given him, like she still wore his pendant every day? He had vanished from her world like a whisper of smoke.

It was mid-October again, and An was still in Northern Virginia, now renting a small apartment in Vienna, trying to decide what to do with the rest of her life. A year had flown by since her mother passed away, and the second Christmas without Pop was avalanching in her direction. Winter was fast approaching, and soon it would be Halloween and Thanksgiving again. *There will be no pumpkin carvings or large turkey dinner this time either,* An thought sadly. She felt aimless and hollow.

Although the weather was cooling, the day was sunny. It was the middle of the week, hump day. Trying to move away from the family business and build her own career apart from it, An had just finished another interview for an office management position for a small psychologists' office in the Tyson's Corner area and was feeling unsettled.

The interview had gone well, but so had many others, and she still had not found what she was looking for. Working with CJ in the family bakery business was rewarding enough, but she didn't want to do that for the rest of her life. She felt there was something more she should be doing with her time and talents, but what that something should be eluded her right now. It was the middle of the day, and the thought of going back to her small apartment was too depressing.

The building where she had interviewed was architecturally interesting to the eye: lots of windows and curves, beautiful grounds with a darling courtyard. There were benches and walking paths, greenery and plenty of full-grown trees, potted flowers still with color in bloom here and there. The lower floor boasted a small café with delicious aromas wafting out into the courtyard. She noticed there was also a small field with a playground behind the building, containing more benches and winding walking paths. A couple of people were walking their dogs or jogging. She decided she would take a stroll.

She found a pair of old canvas shoes in her car and put them on even though she was wearing a long, black pencil-thin skirt with a matching jacket and pantyhose. *What the heck!* The sun felt good on her head and shoulders as she began her walk. There was a light breeze carrying a hint of the earthy smell of heather and freshly cut grass. Birds were chirping, and she could hear a dog barking somewhere in the not-too-far distance. She closed her eyes for just a second, to fully take in all the scents and sounds around her. Her arms went up like a scarecrow, head thrown back. She didn't have a care in the world at that moment.

"I love this place and this time of year too," a deep male voice boomed.

Jarred out of her reverie, An jumped and opened her eyes, feeling a little embarrassed. She had been taking in small breaths through her nose and out of her mouth. *Plus, those old canvas shoes with pantyhose and a skirt? Geez, Louise!* She must have been a strange sight. A tall man was standing in front of her, an amused smile on his face. He had such intense dark blue eyes. A large black-and-tan dog was by his side; it looked like a German Shepherd.

"Hi there!" An chimed. "I'm sorry. I must have gotten a little carried away. It's so beautiful out today!"

"Oh, no, don't apologize. I love nature too, and so does Gunner here." He looked down at the dog, who had patiently sat on his tail and was panting while looking at her with an amused smile plastered on his face (at least that's what she thought), his big brown eyes a little guarded.

"He's beautiful!" An exclaimed.

"Thank you! He's been well-trained," the man said. "Part of his training is that he needs his daily walks, without exception."

"Are you his trainer then?" An asked, her smile getting wider by the minute. She liked this guy. He had a nice open face. He seemed so confident and strong. His shoulders stooped a little—probably from his height, well over six feet tall, she imagined. She noticed his hands were large and strong-looking. Most people looked at the eyes or the smile as a telling first impression of someone. An liked to look at the hands; they normally spoke to her about the person.

"Yep, sure am! His owner and his trainer," he said with pride in his voice. "I work here in the building, and I am fortunate enough to be able to bring him to work with me. He's still a pup."

"Aww, he's adorable! And, look at him, such a well-mannered and gorgeous pup at that!" An said. That compliment made the man smile. His teeth were a little crowded and crooked, but it was a nice friendly smile nonetheless. The dog perked up, standing up to wag his tail at her. "Well, I just interviewed for a job here, so maybe we'll be work neighbors!" An said, laughing a little.

"That would be awesome!" The man moved the dog leash to his other hand and offered his outstretched right hand to An. "I'm Brad."

"Hi, Brad, I'm An! Good to know you."

They smiled at each other, eyes locking. "Don't let me keep you from your walk, An. I have to head back, but hopefully, I will be seeing you around. I work at the gun shop on the first level if you ever want to look me up, but I'm out here with Gunner a lot." Brad explained all this as he was starting to walk away from An, twisting forward and backward, getting tangled in the leash. He waved by wagging his fingers.

"Okay, it was nice to meet you, Brad!" An yelled back and waved, turning to walk in the other direction. The image of Jimmy flashed through her mind. She tried swatting it away. It had been almost two years since she and Jimmy had met and then parted ways, and then never heard from each other again. She fingered the heart pendant she kept draped around her neck day and night. Jimmy was miles away and probably had forgotten all about her a long time ago. It was time to move on.

Life goes on, she thought. *The sun is shining on me, and I can still experience all the vibrant sights and smells around me—without Ma, without Pop... without Jimmy.*

CHAPTER 8

THIS THING CALLED LIFE: 1991

*"Love bears all things, believes all things,
hopes all things, endures all things."*
> \- First Corinthians 12:4-8

*"Dearly beloved, we are gathered here today
to get through this thing called life."*
> \- Prince, "Let's Go Crazy"

Later that week, An heard back from the psychologists' office, where she had applied for a job, hoping to get a career underway. They had finalized their interview process and wanted to offer the position to An. She was excited to finally have a job—and the money was better than she expected. They had rewritten the job description and wanted her to take on more responsibility, which was a-okay with her.

She accepted, thanked the personnel manager who had called, and hung up the phone.

"Woohoo!" she screamed as she did a little dance in her nearly empty apartment. "I have a job, I have a job!" she sang, throwing her hip to the right and to the left, one hand on her waist and the other up in the air, her wrist doing little circles. Her first real job ever! Now she needed to work on a husband and a couple children, and maybe some nice household items.

Her apartment was surprisingly large for the price and for a single person. She had brought the furniture from her college apartment, but that simply included her bedroom set, a couch and TV, and a small table with four chairs for the kitchen. She inherited two corner hutches with glass doors from her parents. She had placed those, along with the kitchen table and chairs, in the spacious kitchen-dining room combination. She also had inherited an old, round table with claw feet, and sides that could be left up or down, from her parents.

She had her TV on top of that in the living room, along with her college apartment couch. She had bought two bookcases, which were already filled with her beloved books. Those stood on one wall in the living room. Other than the books, little else had been unpacked. Most of her clothes were still in suitcases and boxes. Her heart just wasn't in it. But now that she had a job, she had to at least sort through her wardrobe and find a home for her clothes.

It was now Wednesday, and she was due to start the following Monday. She turned the radio on and got busy working on the apartment, humming and dancing to the catchy tunes. A Prince song came on, and she turned the volume up, starting a new dance, this time thrusting her hips forward, then shimmying her buttocks.

"Don't have to be rich to be my girl, don't have to be cool to rule my world… I just want your extra time and your… kiss," An sang into her knuckled hand acting as a microphone, her eyes closed and lips puckered.

When a slow, sad song came on, she stopped dancing and singing and fingered the heart pendant hugging her neck. It seemed like eons ago that Jimmy had given her the gold chain. She removed it from her neck, tears threatening to spill at any moment. It was time to put it away. Brad's face flashed before her. She would likely see him at her new place of employment. A faint smile formed as she thought of Brad, replacing the sadness in her. A new day awaited its dawning. She was ready for it.

That Monday, An started her new job, and she saw Brad again. This time he looked very dapper in a dark suit, salmon-colored shirt and a striped tie. No Gunner. An was on her lunch break and had gone downstairs to the little café. She had ordered a turkey melt sandwich on rye and was waiting at one of the tables in the back when Brad walked in.

"Hey, Kathy! Hey, Gina!" He waved hellos to the women behind the counter.

"Hey, handsome!" one of the women said. She leaned across the counter, cleavage spilling out. "You look good enough to eat!" she said in a singsong voice, a smile as big as the River Nile, winking at him with her long fake lashes. They continued talking as Brad put his order in, and An tried to look out the window, pretending not to be paying attention, a little embarrassed for that Gina chick, the one with the watermelon bosoms. She also had green streaks in her hair, long nails painted bright red, and hot-pink lipstick. *How was he not distracted by all that?*

A short while later, Brad spotted her and made a beeline to An's table. "Hey, you! We met the other day, remember?" He stood across from her and, pointing at the empty chair, said, "May I?"

"Yeah, yeah, sure!" she said. "We met at the park a couple weeks ago when I interviewed for the psychologists' office on the fourth floor. They hired me!"

"Well, I'll be darned! I figured they would. So now, we're work neighbors!" He smiled big at her. She was impressed he remembered her comment. "An, right?" Now she was even more impressed. He actually remembered her name!

"I'm impressed!" An exclaimed. "You remember me! And you're Brad, right? You have a pup named Gunner."

"Wow! My turn to be impressed. You are beautiful and smart, with an awesome memory!"

An blushed and lowered her gaze, feeling beautiful and smart indeed under his unrelenting gaze. He sat across from her, eyes glued to her, smiling across the way. He seemed to see right into her soul. She squirmed a little and then spoke, more to break the silence than anything else.

"You look very professional in a suit today," she said.

"Oh, yeah, I had a court appearance this morning."

"Everything okay?" An didn't want to prod, but she already knew the answer. She had overheard the conversation while he and Gina were flirting at the counter.

"You probably heard me telling the ladies here my divorce was final today. See, the ring is gone!" He pointed at his left-hand ring finger.

"Well, you sure don't seem too broken up about it. Bad marriage? What happened?"

They were interrupted by one of the women—Kathy, thank goodness, no distracting cleavage peeking out at them—who brought their sandwiches and drinks and set them on the table.

"Anything else for you guys?" she asked.

"Thanks, Kathy! I think I'm good," Brad said. An said she was good too, as she anticipated Brad's answer to her earlier question with bated breath. Brad opened his bottle of water and took a sip. An opened her ginger ale and took a swig, the bubbly liquid burning her throat and making her eyes water. Brad unwrapped his sandwich carefully, methodically. It seemed he was pondering her question, buying time.

He finally cleared his throat, then said, "Yes, bad marriage. We were happy the first year. Then she had a miscarriage and was never the same. She became despondent, then angry, then sad, then unstable."

An was at a loss for words. She didn't expect this very personal, in-depth explanation. "Oh. Um, how long were you married?" she finally managed to say.

Brad had taken a bite of his sandwich and put a finger up to indicate that he needed a minute. He chewed slowly and deliberately, then finally answered, "Almost seven years—would have been seven years next month, actually. We were high school sweethearts, got married a couple years after high school. Then she lost her dad, then the miscarriage, then a baby… It was too overwhelming, I think."

An choked on her bite of grilled turkey-and-cheese sandwich. Once she had stopped coughing and composed herself, she said, "You have a child?"

"Two!" he said. "Lynne is five, and Erica turned three years old last month—my baby girls!" He smiled, shaking his head from side to side, obviously a proud daddy.

She was floored by that revelation. She expected him to have a dog, maybe a roommate. She was definitely not expecting him to be a husband and a dad. He looked so young! She kicked herself for not noticing a ring that day in the park. She was normally very observant about these things. She composed herself as best she could, trying to stifle her surprise.

"Aw, they are just babies. I love kids. Do you have pictures?"

Brad pulled out his wallet and scraped his chair back to move it right next to her. He smelled clean but a very subdued scent, something like Ivory soap maybe. With their heads nearly touching, Brad flipped through the photos of the girls in a plastic photo holder, explaining each picture in detail.

"And this one was Christmas last year. Lynne had just turned five—she was almost a Christmas baby. This year, they will both appreciate all the presents better."

"They are beautiful!" An told Brad. "Is this your ex-wife?" An asked, looking at a pretty blonde holding an infant wrapped in pink. She was very thin and petite, with sad, distant eyes. Brad nodded his head, then quickly put the pictures away.

An and Brad finished their lunch and headed back to their respective offices to continue their workday. They told each other they would bring lunch from home the next day and eat in the park behind the building. Brad would bring Gunner.

The two met at the park the rest of the week for lunch. Brad shared his German spaetzle with An, and they were delicious.

"How do you make these?" she asked in awe. "You actually cook?"

He laughed at her comment. "Yeah, I cook. And love it!"

"What's that hint of sweet I taste?"

"Oh, that's probably the nutmeg."

"You'll have to share your recipe. It's so good."

Brad smiled. "It's really simple. It's just flour, eggs, milk, a pinch of salt and pepper, and nutmeg. I use a spoon and fork to dribble small amounts at a time into hot broth. Once cooked, you can stir fry the spaetzle with whatever you like or whatever you have on hand. This time, I stir-fried them with fresh onions, garlic, broccoli, and sliced-up German sausage."

"Yum!" An said. She was impressed daily with Brad, and she was baffled and intrigued by him too. The day before she had learned he was an avid hunter. He promised to share some venison with her next time he caught a deer. She wasn't sure how she felt about eating Bambi, but she was intrigued. He managed a gun shop and claimed to be proficient with all sorts of guns and gun accessories. Again, she was intrigued. Now he was sharing recipes with her. He was a blend of macho and domestic, quite the paradox.

She also learned that Brad was trying to get full custody of his two girls. He claimed his ex-wife was unstable and unable to care for them. Brad's mother, Agnes, had made a commitment to help care for them, but she had a full-time job so it would be challenging. He seemed to easily open up to An, which she liked. She had been told she was a good listener and easy to talk to, and it was a boost to her ego. She enjoyed listening to other people, and she was eager to try to help. But Brad seemed to be a complicated man with complicated issues; she wasn't sure she had the skills or tools to help. She would have to call CJ or Peggy or both soon, to get some advice and insights.

Brad told An he was taking the girls to his dad's house in Ohio over the weekend. He confided that he was taking a friend with him too—a female friend. An felt a slight twinge of jealousy, which she casually brushed aside, annoyed at herself for feeling it. He explained that he had many friends, some of the opposite sex. They had been walking the trail side by side as they talked. Gunner was with them, being the perfect companion, alert to any slight noise or movement, but staying put and keeping pace with Brad and An. Suddenly, Brad stopped and turned to face An. He was only inches from her. His body heat seemed to emanate from him, wafting into her personal space.

Almost in a whisper, he said, "I wish it was you coming with us."

It caught her off guard. She stood very still, looking up at him unblinking. He reached down and very gently pulled a strand of hair that had fallen across her face, tucking it behind her left ear. Then he traced her face with his finger, starting at her forehead down to her chin, where he lingered. He gently lifted her face toward him and bent down to softly kiss her on the lips, just a feather of a kiss. She closed her eyes, trembling at the touch. Then, in the blink of an eye, they had pulled away and began walking again—this time in silence. It was a fleeting moment in time. The kiss ended as abruptly as it had started. An wasn't sure what to make of what had just happened, but she was smiling.

"Will you come with us next time, An?" Brad asked, breaking the silence at last.

"Sure," she said, touching her lips. It was all happening so fast. They had been talking for less than two weeks at lunchtime, he was freshly divorced, and already, he had kissed her, and there was talk of a car trip together… with his children! Plus, his life seemed so full and chaotic. Was it a bad omen? Look what happened with Jimmy. In the span of one weekend, she had fallen head over heels, and then it was all over with. Done. History.

But An brushed all the clutter and cobwebs aside in her mind. She had totally enjoyed their conversations, even though they had been intense at times, and she was becoming more and more fond of Brad. She felt as if she was the only woman in the entire world he had ever noticed, ever touched like that. She felt pretty. She felt smart. She felt needed and wanted. It was a wonderful feeling, and it made her want to please him and make him happy forever. *Wow, forever! That was a powerful word,* she thought.

Brad was gone Monday and Tuesday of the following week—her third week at her new job. An missed him more than she was willing to admit. Lunchtime just wasn't the same without him. She had spent the weekend working on organizing and cleaning her apartment. It was starting to look and feel very homey. She experimented with cooking and baking too. She even tried Brad's spaetzle recipe. She used canned chicken and vegetable soup as her broth to cook the noodles. It tasted so good that she left the spaetzle in the soup and added some northern beans—her favorite! All she had were stale crackers to go with it, but she decided that next time, she would have to get fresh bread. She might even try baking the bread herself!

She called her brother and told him about Brad and her feelings for him. Very uncharacteristically of CJ, he told her, in no uncertain terms, that she needed to run from the relationship and not get more caught up in the chaos that seemed to be Brad's life, at least at the moment. She was puzzled by this and a little disappointed.

"An, you're not even twenty-four! You've had to deal with some awful tragedies recently. Your emotions are probably really scattered right now. You're trying to take on too much, too soon. Don't!"

But what CJ didn't realize was that An was already too involved, too wrapped up in Brad's world. She was already falling in love, blind and deaf to reason. Brad was good-looking and smart. He was a good husband and father; he was a good person. After all, he had a dog, and two beautiful little girls he seemed to adore. She hadn't expected her family to come in the form of a ready-made one, but she would gladly take it. She wanted children to fill her life with their smiles and giggles; she wanted life to begin already. She wanted a husband and a beautiful home. She was ready! Her brother would just have to come around, and he would, once he met Brad and his charm.

Next, An called Peggy, her friend for as long as she could remember and a constant voice of cool, calm reason. Although Peggy was happy for An, and sounded supportive and positive about the relationship developing, she cautioned An to take it slow, rein it in, get to know Brad better.

An reassured Peggy she would not rush things. She pondered the conversations with CJ and Peggy but came to the conclusion that ultimately, it would be her and Brad's decision to make, even if it was just the two of them against the entire world! She threw caution to the wind. After all, she had always known what she wanted, and here it was. No way was she turning her back on it.

She could hardly wait for Wednesday when Brad was due back to work. They had not yet exchanged phone numbers, which meant she had not talked to him at all since Friday. She was having Brad withdrawals. Although she liked the fact that she missed him, it also disturbed her a little, especially after her phone conversations with CJ and Peggy. The feelings were coming on so strong and in such rapid succession, they scared her just a tad. She wondered if having lost both parents and the upheaval in her life in the past couple of years was, indeed, contributing to her dependence and her feelings for Brad.

She waited and waited on Wednesday, but Brad never showed up at lunchtime. With only about fifteen minutes to spare before she had to return to work, she decided to find his office. She could see Brad behind the counter when she walked in the gun store. He appeared distracted as he answered a customer's question. When he was done, he looked up and waved at An.

"Hey, beautiful!" he said, but something seemed off. She told him she wanted to make sure everything was okay and that she had missed his company at lunch. They agreed they would meet the next day in the courtyard and eat together.

It wasn't until that Friday when Brad finally opened up to An and told her what was bothering him. It was cold out, and they had decided to stay inside the café for lunch. They opted for hot soup and sandwiches instead of eating what they had brought from home, which was nothing too appetizing—just a hodgepodge of leftovers. Brad was quiet and serious, but he reached across the table to hold An's hands in his, inspecting her long nails—no nail polish. She hated nail polish.

Then, without warning, he pushed his chair back and leaned across the table to kiss her on the lips. An looked in the direction of the counter, expecting Miss Cleavage to be spying on them. It baffled An, this out-of-the-blue, unexpected kiss. For the last few days, Brad had been aloof and distant; then, without warning, he was warm and loving. *What did this dichotomy mean?*

An was pulled away from her thoughts when he said, "I'm sorry. I haven't been myself lately." Then he went on to tell her that while he was at his family's house in Ohio, his ex-wife, Alison, had learned somehow where he was and got upset that he had taken the girls out of state and that he was there with a female friend. She had actually driven to Brad's father's house to confront him and had an "episode," as he called it.

According to Brad, she was out of control and deranged and tried to run him over with her car. He was considering a restraining order against her, and he was pretty sure he could use this to his advantage on the child custody case.

An's head was spinning. She wasn't sure what to say or how to comfort him. It sounded like a bad situation. She had this fleeting thought that she should run away from this whole thing, as CJ had so strongly suggested. But the way Brad was looking at her now with those beautiful blue eyes of his just melted her heart. She couldn't desert him, not now when he seemed to be in distress about all this.

"What can I do?" she finally managed to say. "How can I help?"

"Just be there for me… please?" he pleaded. She nodded her head and grabbed his hands in hers this time, bringing his big knuckles to her lips and tenderly kissing them. No other words were needed. Their soup and sandwiches arrived, and they went about the business of eating their lunch. Brad's smile changed just then, like he knew something others didn't, An thought. But she chose to see Brad's smile as one of love and adoration, nothing more.

Things progressed quickly from that point on. An kept brushing aside her brother's words of advice and her friend's concern. She was a woman on a mission, and two young girls' lives depended on it. Brad needed her, wanted her, loved her. Didn't he? He professed so with his endearing words; he proved so with his actions. Didn't he? She believed it with all her heart and was prepared to pay any amount of sacrifice to see it through.

Because Brad had given up his marital home—a two-bedroom rental house nearby—and was staying with his mother, he came to An's apartment on Saturday morning. There, they had a good-sized apartment all to themselves, with all the privacy they needed. Gunner and the girls were with Agnes, in her home in Warrenton. An wasn't well versed on her culinary skills, but Brad seemed to like everything she cooked for him. She made an onion-and-tomato omelet and sprinkled it with freshly grated Parmesan—her favorite cheese in the whole world. She made toast and cut up fresh fruit to go with it: berries, oranges, and bananas. He loved it!

They talked and ate and watched old movies until early evening. They realized they both liked Hitchcock, and An happened to own a large collection of Hitchcock videos; her little DVD player got quite the workout that weekend. Late that evening, he decided he wanted to take her out somewhere nice. They went to a local steakhouse and had the best aged steaks, prepared to perfect deliciousness—rare for him and medium for her.

An's face was glowing and rosy from the excitement of being with Brad. The hours just melted away. That night, without pre-planning, without ever talking about it, they made love for the first time. It was slow and tender, and Brad was gentle and considerate, knowing that for An, it was the very first time, ever. She had never felt so loved and cared for, never so wanted, needed, and desired. He made her feel as if she was the only one he had ever loved and made love to like this. He caressed her and held her afterwards. He kissed her eyelids and brushed her long hair away from her face to look deep into her eyes. "You are so special," he said. "I would die for you."

She believed, unconditionally, every syllable he uttered.

An was happy beyond words. She laid her head down on his chest then and cried blissful tears. He rocked her in his arms, shushing her and kissing the top of her head. When she awoke the next morning, he had been up already, and the apartment was trilling and singing with the smell of freshly brewed coffee and the sun streaming through the living room windows.

Brad was sitting at the kitchen table sipping coffee and reading the paper, as if he had always been there, always belonged there. He sent her back to bed as soon as she appeared in the doorway. A few minutes later, he arrived in the bedroom with a hot mug of coffee for her and bagels slathered with cream cheese for both of them. They ate in bed together and then picked up where they had left off the night before.

This time, the lovemaking was more daring, more intense, more probing, especially for An. She was sure then that she had at last lassoed her knight in shining armor, the man of her girlhood daydreams. As she lay in his arms, feeling cozy and content, she knew that she had completely fallen in love, and there was no going back. Ever! There was no doubt in her mind she would one day be Mrs. Bradley Emerson Goode.

Nothing was happenstance, An felt. This moment was meant to be. She marveled at how Brad seemed to be all-knowing, so confident, so strong. His actions and decisions seemed so well planned and coordinated. She felt clumsy compared to him.

Who was this man that dazzled her like this? Who was he really?

Brad stroked An's hair then, looking past her. She looked up at him. Bringing his gaze back to An, Brad smiled dreamily as he kissed the top of her head. An placed her head down on his chest, listening to his heart beating. She felt her eyelids droop, noticing their clothes scattered about, the sunlight shining from the outside in.

Dazzling.

Everything was so beautiful, so perfect. It was as if a higher power had planned it all so precisely.

At this very moment in time, who could have predicted the ending to this romance? Neither An nor Brad had an inkling about the other's private thoughts. If they did, the outcome would have been altered. No doubt about it.

CHAPTER 9

THE GATHERING: 1990

"Only where children gather is there any real chance of fun."

> \- Mignon McLaughlin

For the next few weeks, An and Brad were inseparable. They met for breakfast before work most mornings, shared their lunch hour practically every day, spent most weekends together, and devoted the bulk of their free time to each other. It was time for An to meet Brad's girls and Brad's mom. Brad had actually shared a lot about his mom with An. Agnes and Brad's dad, Donald, had divorced a few years back. Donald kept the family home in Ohio, since Agnes wanted to move back to Virginia to be near Brad.

It was an amicable divorce, which was rare. They had been married for nearly thirty years, had led separate lives for most of that time, and there came a point when they each wanted to pursue other interests and other relationships, so they came to a mutual agreement. They still took vacations together with Brad and the girls, enjoyed family time as a unit, and had become better friends now than when they were married.

The family home in Ohio was actually a working farm Don still ran and operated. Don employed a number of people who lived on the property. His elderly mother lived with him also, and so did his daughter, Brad's sister, and her two children. According to Brad, it was a wild and crazy place, but he enjoyed visiting and liked the idea of the girls growing up with an understanding of farm life.

There was a babbling creek on the side of the main house, an inground pool for the kids in the backyard, and farm animals everywhere: cows, horses, goats, and chickens. Not to mention the other wild critters, such as deer, foxes, snakes, and even a bear or two at times. Brad couldn't wait to take An to the farm to introduce her to everyone. An, pretty much a city girl her entire life, was apprehensive about the visit. Snakes gave her the willies. And bears? Nuh-uh, no way! No way did she ever want to encounter one. She was fortunate to never have encountered anything other than an occasional deer or squirrel in the hikes during her college days.

It was the weekend before Thanksgiving. Brad wanted An to meet the girls before then so that she could join them for the Thanksgiving feast and not feel out of place and awkward. In fact, the Ohio clan was supposed to be there, too, and Brad didn't want An meeting the girls with a house full of people. Brad had spent Saturday night with An, and Sunday morning they headed over to Warrenton. Most of Saturday into Sunday morning, An had fought her jitters. She hoped the girls would like her. Brad had reassured her they would absolutely love her, but she was still nervous.

"My mom will love you. The girls will love you; you are just a lovable person. Don't worry." Brad had tried to reassure her over and over.

The day before, they had gone out, and An had picked out some outfits and toys for the girls. Then they had baked chocolate chip cookies to bring—according to Brad, it was the girls' very favorite thing to eat in the entire universe.

They held hands on the way to see the girls. Brad kept squeezing An's hand and kissing her fingers. She watched his profile, loving him more every day. Agnes's house was small but cute, resembling a tiny German chalet from a distance. Brad's mom hadn't expected Brad and the girls to be living there when she had her home built. Brad had explained that they only had two bedrooms, but there was a finished basement with an extra bedroom and bath—that's where Brad slept—but the laundry room was down there too, so it got noisy at times. In the past, Brad's mom had rented that space for a little extra cash.

There was a natural wood fence surrounding the house and stepping stones with names and dates on them leading up to the front door. An was wondering what those meant just as she heard Brad say, "They're names of pets that have gone on to heaven, and the dates they died."

"Oh," An said. "There are so many!"

"This is the country, sweetheart. Here everyone has pets, lots of them."

An had never had pets growing up, except for a fish. "I had a goldfish once," she told him. "CJ had a pair of cockatiels!"

Brad laughed, squeezing her and kissing the top of her head. "You will have other pets," he reassured her.

The front door burst open before they reached it.

"There you are, my loves!" A short, wiry woman stormed out, arms flailing. Her voice was penetrating, very high-pitched, like Mickey Mouse. An wanted to giggle but held back. *Nerves, perhaps?*

Agnes was wearing a large-brimmed white hat and lime-green gardening gloves. To complete the outfit, she wore faded, baggy blue jeans and a long-sleeved navy-blue T-shirt. Her face was weathered with leathery wrinkles, and silver strands of hair poked from under her hat. She approached An like a hurricane, pulling her roughly into her pillowy bosom and giving her a bear hug, roughly smacking her back multiple times. An suppressed a cough, lurching into Agnes a little. *Geez, this is a lovely encounter,* she thought. She prayed she'd go home in one piece. Brad had not warned her about anything like this.

"Daddy, Daddy!" A tiny voice, followed by a little person with dark hair flying behind her, trailed Mickey Mouse, The Hurricane. Lynne just about knocked her grandmother to the ground as she flew past and ran to Brad. *Must be a family trait,* An was thinking, as Lynne flashed past her and flung herself into her father's arms.

"Hey, Punkin!" he said, scooping her up in his arms and lifting her high up in the air.

"Weeee!" She giggled and shrieked, arms out like a little airplane. That gleeful little laugh was the most beautiful sound An had ever heard, prettier than the chirping of birds on a beautiful sunny spring day out in one of her walks.

Agnes grabbed An and pulled her to her chest again, hugging her and swaying from side to side. "An, darlin', I'm Agnes, but feel free to call me Mama. Everyone else does."

"It's great to finally meet you, Ag… Mama!" An felt strange calling her that. She was about to offer her hand, then pulled back. *Handshakes are probably not cool here. This is a hugging and kissing kind of place,* An thought.

She felt a tug on her sweater and looked down to see little Erica. And, oh my, she was even more beautiful in person: eyes like shiny little sapphires; freckles dotting her pale skin; long, reddish-blonde hair streaming down her back. She was a little porcelain doll! She had on blue jeans and a red polka-dotted shirt. Her right thumb was in her mouth, and she was carrying a pink baby blanket with little brown monkeys swinging across the fuzzy fabric. The blanket was dragging across the ground. An bent down so she and Erica were eye to eye.

"I Er-qua," she said. An giggled, already deep in love with this little person.

"Hi, Erica, I'm An."

Erica put her tiny hand in An's and smiled, suddenly shy. Lynne was talking a mile a minute with her dad. Brad looked over at An, smiling from ear to ear.

Agnes couldn't seem to stand not having anything to do, so she waved her arms, saying, "Come on, come on, loves! Let's go inside."

They began walking in. Brad whispered something to Lynne, and she suddenly appeared shy and demure, lowering her gaze to study the ground. But after a split second of thinking about what her dad had said, she ran over to An and hugged her legs.

"Hi, An. I'm Lynne," she said.

An looked back at Brad, smiling and thinking her heart was just about to burst with happiness. She bent down and hugged Lynne back, giving Brad the chance to steal little Erica, scooping her in his arms. It was Erica's turn to giggle and squeal with delight. They walked into the house and into a large living-room-dining-room combination, with the kitchen visible in the back and a hallway to the right.

An's jaw dropped at the sight. The place was surely the site of a natural disaster! There were *things* everywhere! Toys on the carpet, clothes piled up on couches and chairs, even a garden rake standing guard by the kitchen sliding door! *Agnes lives here,* An told herself. *That's all the explanation needed.* Brad had not prepared her for this either. *Oh my goodness!*

An closed her mouth and turned to Brad, who was saying just then, "Aren't they the cutest things ever?"

"Oh my gosh, absolutely they are!" An responded, thinking she was on cloud nine right now and temporarily forgetting about the chaos around her. She could totally see them being a family. Plus, they would add a couple more little ones to the brood. The longing hit her so intensely, she almost blurted out, 'Let's get married right now and be a family!'

"Sit down, An, stay a while," Agnes said in her Mickey Mouse voice. An looked around, wondering where people sat and stayed a while here. There were books, newspapers, clothes, toys… a potted plant? All atop anything that resembled a sitting place. She eyed a pile of newspapers on top of what looked like an oversized chair with cushions poking out. She lowered herself to sit, felt movement, and a fat black cat went scurrying off to the side. After the initial startle, An sighed under her breath and plopped herself down on top of the newspapers, trying not to think about what else might be under the pile.

"I was out back cleaning the gutters and picking up the yard a bit," Agnes was saying. An looked out through a glass sliding door, where the backyard could be seen. She saw two dogs bouncing around and peeking into the room every now and then. Plus, Gunner was there too, peering in behind the other dogs.

"That's Kimby—the yellow lab—and the black-and-white mutt is Shor-Shor," Agnes explained when she noticed An looking out.

"They are… um… exuberant," An said, unsure as to how she'd feel about having a couple dogs slobbering and pawing all over her. As she was pondering this, she felt something rubbing up against her. Suddenly startled again, she jumped, then looked down. Both Agnes and Brad started laughing. An stared down at a fluffy gray kitten, purring and rubbing himself on her pants leg. He seemed very friendly and appeared to be harmless and much friendlier than the annoyed black one. But she was afraid to touch him.

"Does he scratch or bite?" she asked, alarm clear in her shaky voice.

Even little Erica laughed at An then. "You should have seen your face, honey," Brad laughed.

Lynne bent down and picked up the kitten. "She's a girl, and she's just a baby," Lynne said. "See? Do you want to pet her? Her name is MeMe."

An reached out to pet the kitten with hands that were trembling ever so slightly. "Nice kitty, nice little kitty," she chanted.

"Well, then, kids," Agnes was saying. "I have a sausage casserole, a pound cake, and some fresh fruit salad for us to eat now." She clapped her hands together. Her gardening gloves had disappeared. An noticed that her hands were rough-looking with very short nails that sported a good amount of dirt underneath. Agnes continued, "And for later on, I've got venison chili simmering in the pot. We'll enjoy that with homemade cornbread. I hope you brought your appetites!"

An looked over at Brad. *Venison?* Her eyes bulged out of their sockets. Then An looked at the kitchen table, full of… stuff, lots of stuff. Where would they eat? There was a large glass bowl with batter dripping everywhere, a thick open cookbook, eyeglasses, a stack of dishes, three stemmed wine glasses, an open box full of pictures, and some other items she couldn't identify… all atop the small kitchen table.

Brad walked over to An and kneeled down beside her chair and whispered, "Mama knows how to cook venison to perfection. Don't worry. You'll love it!"

Erica was pulling on An's sweater again. "Yap," she said.

"She can't quite get her Ls yet," Brad explained. "Yap means lap."

"Ah! But of course!" An scooped up Erica and unceremoniously placed the toddler on her lap. She smiled down at Erica, grateful for a distraction from the thought of eating Bambi. The little girl smelled of baby lotion and bananas. Strange combination, but on a baby, it worked somehow.

Hugging her close, An sniffed the little girl.

"You smell delicious!" An told Erica, who giggled and squirmed in her arms. The dogs had all three snouts now pressed against the sliding glass door, tails wagging furiously. An looked past the dogs, squinting at what she thought she was witnessing.

Cocking her head to one side, she said, "Um… Brad, honey." She cleared her throat before continuing. "There are chickens out there and… and are those goats?!"

"Yup, sure are. They don't have names 'cause we might have to eat 'em, the chickens that is. The goats are Cindy, Sandy, and Candy."

"Hm… yeah, that's what I was afraid of," An said, more to herself than anyone else. "But the goats have names, so we won't be eating them, right?"

"No, but they're mean as the devil, so we may have to shoot them," Brad responded with a chuckle.

"Oh," was about all An had to say on the matter. She didn't like the thought of shooting anything.

Agnes chuckled as if she had swallowed a squeaky dog toy, standing by the stove, stirring the large pot methodically.

An had a wonderful day, despite all the animals and Agnes's grating voice. Actually, once she had been there for a couple hours, she felt right at home. A number of times throughout the day, she found herself looking over at Brad, their eyes speaking a million words, conveying a thousand thoughts, and pronouncing a hundred I love yous.

She couldn't wait to be alone with him later. She planned to crush him with hugs and smother him with hot, passionate kisses. His adorable kids, the delicious foods—and yes, even the venison was superb—and the whole atmosphere intensified how she felt about him. It also highlighted her need to be a wife and a mother. She couldn't wait to walk down the aisle and say "I do" to the man she loved. She couldn't wait to build a warm, cozy home like this one—minus the chaotic clutter—and have her very own family that included two adorable little girls named Lynne and Erica.

At seven-thirty they put the girls down to bed. Brad tucked them in and sang them a lullaby that mesmerized

An. "Too-ra-loo-ra-loo-ral, too-ra-loo-ra-li…" he sang in a strong, deep voice. An stood outside the bedroom door listening, eyes closed, swaying a little. She was so much in awe of this man, who had a thousand facets and fascinated her to no end. After a while, she tiptoed away to join Agnes, who was now sitting at the kitchen table, a glass of red wine in front of her. Her cheeks were rosy-red, and her short, silver curls glinted under the kitchen light overhead. The bottle of wine she had finally polished off was having a calming effect on her.

"Oh, girl, you look like you need some wine!" Agnes got up and got another wine glass for An. "Let me get you a sip too."

"Oh, no, I'm not much of a drinker. But I will have another slice of that heavenly pound cake of yours. You'll have to share your recipe sometime."

Right then, someone began pounding on the door. Agnes ran toward the front door, shushing and saying, "They'll upset the girls for sure."

"I wanna see my girls," a female voice wailed. "I have the right, Agnes!"

"Alison, please, hush. They're sleeping." Agnes stepped outside, closing the door behind her. *She'll freeze out there in the cold*, An thought, as she got up to get a closer look from behind the window pane.

An could hear the voices of the two women outside—Alison's more shrill, and Agnes's more muffled—but she couldn't make out any coherent phrases. Agnes was doing a good job moving Alison away from the house.

Not quite sure what she should do, An watched and tried to make out what was being said out there. *Should I get Brad?*

At that very moment, Brad came out of the bedroom. "What's going on?" he asked An.

"Looks like Alison is here, and she's a little distraught?"

"Fuck! Double fucking fuck!" he exploded.

An was taken aback, startled. She had never heard him use profanity in front of her. She blinked at him. "Brad! My Lord!"

"Sorry, sorry…" He was running his hands through his wavy hair and seemed very agitated. She wasn't used to this Brad, and it unsettled her. Grabbing his coat off the back of one of the kitchen chairs, Brad carelessly put it on before stepping into his boots. He shuffled out into the cold too. Back behind the window, An watched the spectacle with growing curiosity.

Agnes and Alison had walked past the gate and were on the gravel area where the cars were parked. Agnes kept reaching to grab Alison, and Alison kept swatting her arms away, still shrieking her words, indiscernible to An now. Brad joined them, and An could see him waving his hands around and talking to Alison angrily. She couldn't make out any words, just sounds. Then he placed both hands firmly on Alison's shoulders and guided her toward her car, which was parked farther out, behind Brad's and Agnes's vehicles.

An didn't know what he had said to her, but Alison seemed suddenly drained and deflated. With her head down, she appeared to be crying now. Alison slumped against her car, her hands covering her face. An felt helpless and horrible. She felt sorry for Alison.

An had a sudden sinking feeling that something important was happening, something dark, but she was missing too many pieces to this puzzle, and this was probably one of those stories that could not be told from the surface—you had to peel some layers. Brad had said Alison was mentally ill, and An thought Alison appeared and sounded drunk now. Was she always like this? What exactly was happening? Confused and alarmed, An tried to bury her thoughts in some deep crevice of her mind. She didn't want this scene to cloud the beautiful memories, the hope for the future, the desire to be part of this man's world.

Alison had gotten in her car and was backing out now, gravel flying. Brad took a few steps back. An's heart was hammering in her chest. She remembered the story Brad had told her about Alison coming to Ohio and trying to run him over. Alison was acting like a crazed stalker, but what if there was more to this story?

Agnes had to be freezing out there with nothing but her T-shirt. Despite the chill, she and Brad remained outside for a bit, talking conspiratorially by Brad's truck. By the time Brad and Agnes came in and Brad and An got ready to leave, it was well past nine o'clock, and they had more than an hour's drive back to Vienna. Tomorrow morning would be a rough one. She couldn't be late either. With the holidays approaching, the psychiatrists' office was buzzing with activity. An was enjoying her job and the responsibility of running the office. Plus, the pay was good, and An liked her boss and coworkers and the interaction with the patients.

Brad was quiet and distant for most of the ride. Still, they held hands. He didn't bring the subject of Alison up, and An, trying to be thoughtful, didn't mention it either. She hoped in time he would tell her, but it would have to be on his terms.

"I wish you hadn't witnessed that," was all he said on the topic.

CHAPTER 10

THE METAMORPHOSIS

"Nothing really goes away—it just changes into something else."

> \- J.D. Vance

"We are all butterflies. Earth is our chrysalis."

> \- LeeAnn Taylor

An's head was filled with snippets of her time with Ben. Two full days had passed without seeing him, and she wanted to make contact but was unsure how she should go about it. She imagined he was engrossed in making plans for Lisa's service and funeral. For her part, An had been engulfed in old photo albums and more packing.

In between reliving old memories and truncating her belongings in neat packages, she ate popcorn doused in melted butter and generously sprinkled with sea salt and grated Parmesan cheese, while watching old *Space: 1999* episodes on DVD. As a child, she and CJ had watched the show together on television. The memory was bittersweet now that her brother had been gone from her for so long.

An imagined herself as the beautiful and exotic shape-changing Maya. She even wore her hair partially held back like Maya and attempted some smokey eye makeup as a young teenager to look like the character. Interestingly, An did have a strong resemblance to Catherine Schnell, the actress who played Maya in the show. An went as far as to say that if she ever had a baby girl, she would name her Maya.

After all the many stories An had recalled about *Space: 1999*, and the million and one memories she had shared about the show, Brad had finally bought her the entire series on DVD for her thirty-sixth birthday. She had loved it! Back then—had it really been twelve years ago?— the girls had still been home, and Brad was keeping up appearances enough to buy her a birthday gift. Time was, indeed, a strange phenomenon, elusive and mysterious, playing tricks on the mind.

The memories An had so treasured, with CJ at the core of her recollections, had to make room for Lynne and Erica. An and the girls had spent an entire weekend in their pajamas, in front of the big 60-inch screen downstairs watching the episodes. An had cried and laughed, sometimes animated with old stories, other times silently replaying the past in the quiet of her mind.

Now those memories were intertwined with An and CJ, and An and the girls, all tied together, forever connected in memories.

Back around 2004, Brad was gone a lot, working a new job, he had explained, a new job with a firearms advocacy group that had him traveling often. But An knew there was more to it than work. He had not shared the *Space: 1999* weekend with An and the girls. Having found the internet and MySpace, he had rekindled a number of old friendships and was consumed with rediscovering his own previous lives. He filled his weekends with hunting and fishing trips, sometimes shooting events, other times drinking and playing pool at old popular hangouts of his youth. His high school best friend, Miles, had returned by then and was becoming a constant fixture, sometimes even spending the night. The two men would drink and talk into the wee hours of pre-dawn, normally in the basement area of the house, or the garage, which Brad had turned into a nifty man cave—or they'd spend their time away from home altogether.

Some time ago, An had stopped trying to figure Brad out or inquire about his life. She simply let it be because quietly going along was simply easier. It kept arguments at bay and peace at home. Sometimes the two men would be gone the entire night—to where and doing what, An couldn't say for sure, even if she did have her suspicions.

Brad had cut way back on home and family so he could fit in more "life adventures," as he called them.

By this point, An and Brad had come to an agreement and no longer even shared the marital bed. An slept there alone. Brad had made the basement bedroom his personal lair.

Miles and Brad had been best friends all through high school and even into the time that An and Brad were dating and first were married. Then he had moved to Florida, according to Brad. While Miles was physically gone from their lives, Brad did make a couple of trips over the years to visit his friend. Then suddenly one day, more than a decade later, Miles came striding into their lives to resume his place as if he had never left. Brad was happy to resort back to the days of Miles.

"Life is much too short," he told An one day. "We need to seize the moment when we can. I'm done letting time pass me by. I think Miles takes the credit for reminding me of that."

"We could plan some trips. I have lots of vacation time accumulated!" An had volunteered enthusiastically. She learned quickly enough that Brad wasn't talking about enjoying time with her or the girls. Naming Miles in that sentence was the clue An had missed. Brad had no intention of filling his time with family. He had begun a travel journal a while back, a sort of bucket list detailing a number of places and activities he intended to turn into reality. Those, his "life adventures," did not include An or the girls.

One night, An had awoken from a bad dream, drenched in sweat, her bed covers twisted up so tight she had a hard time extricating herself from the tangled mess. She had tiptoed down the stairs into the kitchen to get a glass of water. Although the lights were off, sitting at the spacious kitchen island was Brad, dressed in an old discolored white t-shirt and his usual whitey tighties. He was eating potato chips and chuckling, his computer screen glowing, distorting his features.

"Hey," An had announced. "I didn't realize you were up too."

"Oh, just talking to Marcia, my old high school sweetheart," he had told her.

"I thought you lost track of her a long time ago," An had said. "Kind of an odd time to be talking to her."

"Well, the whole gang's together again. Technology is great."

"I didn't realize," An had said absentmindedly.

It seemed to An that now that Brad had found his old high school group of friends, he was choosing to spend countless hours talking with them on the phone or online. They were included in many events Brad and Miles planned, some which An had been aware of, but there were other outings and excursions she had not been privy to at all. She had not been part of the circle—not then and not now. It was disconcerting to her that day, finding Brad chatting online with old friends in the middle of the night. It seemed a little obsessive.

It didn't bother An early in their marriage that she was the one paying the mortgage, their bills, the girls' schooling, and funding most of their family vacations. But around this time in 2004, when Brad was so consumed with reconnecting with his old buddies, it had started to grate on An. Although her money funded most of Brad's excursions, he acted entitled to it. Brad only worked "projects" sporadically. He had stopped believing in full-time jobs.

"Having a 9-5 job just gets in the way of living life," he was fond of saying.

An had her suspicions about Brad's stifling closeness with Miles and the rest of the group, but she was growing accustomed to Brad's ways. It wasn't that she was oblivious; she simply pretended not to notice because it took too much out of her to question it or to care.

It was easier that way.

When Brad had a new person or venture to devote his attention to, he disappeared without explanations, reasons, or excuses. When there were no other seemingly interesting distractions in his world, Brad spent time at home and expected An to be there at his beck and call. For the most part, she obliged.

That was their dynamic.

On the other hand, An's life had shrunk down to a random activity here and there with the girls and establishing herself as a homebody with books, TV, and scrapbooking. She consoled herself with the thought that this was her true role in life, that she was actually happy with her home, her girls, and her solitary activities. But, if she was to be totally honest with herself, something major was missing. Something she was not prepared to face—not then, maybe not ever.

Sometimes she would let her mind wander back to the pre-Brad days when she would often dream about more, wanting more, expecting more, needing more. That feeling had been painted over, masked, buried for many years, but it had never been satisfied. Deep down, An was an unfulfilled woman. This, she would never reveal to her conscious self. Outwardly, she played the part of a dutiful wife, a loving mother, and a happy person.

An lied to herself that there was no reason to suspect anything nefarious from Brad's many escapades—and if a thought did by chance pop into her head, she quickly tucked it away and kept the waves calm. She chose to assume he craved time away and figured he needed his space and activities. She didn't begrudge him those things. She wanted him to be happy and to enjoy the small pleasures in life. Confronting reality was simply too laborious for An then. Complacency was a much more soothing and pleasant option.

The discovery of yet another woman who had come between them (someone in his intimate circle of old high school friends), was no big surprise. The womanizing An had grown accustomed to. It was expected and predictable. She could have overlooked it like the other times.

But then came the ultimate injury, the mother of all injuries. This, An could not avert her eyes from, and could not ever forgive. Because this injury was unspeakable. It could not be unseen or undone. It was either divorce or forever lose her mind. Losing her mind would have been a relief. She considered it. But losing her mind while in the presence of Brad would not wash away the disgust that coiled in her and rose up like bile, putrid and bitter, every time the images and the words came into her consciousness. Losing her mind would not blot away the fear running in her veins. Losing her mind would not resolve the problem at its root cause.

Losing her mind would have erased the girls and other positive things in her world. That was all she had. That was not acceptable.

An had looked the other way through many unspeakable deeds, womanizing the least of these offenses. Looking back, it was clear to An that the beginning of the end was introduced to her with Melodie. This was the vile affront that changed her perspective forever. Way before the last injury that catapulted her into action, it had all begun with Melodie. An winced at the remembrance. She should never have accepted a lot of things before Melodie, but this one clearly had been grounds for leaving. Yet she hadn't. If only she had, then the ending could have played out differently. Maybe.

She regretted not having taken action early on. She regretted a lot of things. An had tried unsuccessfully to divorce herself from regret, but it wasn't that easy a feat. It's not as if she could simply ask for a restraining order against it, or have a judge sign a divorce decree to make the union null and void. Regret was corrosive and all-consuming; it persisted, it lingered, it couldn't be destroyed, it couldn't be squashed like a pesky bug. She wanted it gone from her life, yet it stuck to her like glue.

Coming out of her reverie, back to the present of 2017—a whole world away from the recollections of more than a decade ago—An sipped her remaining green tea and honey, and munched on the last of the popcorn before steeling her nerves to pick up the phone. She dialed Ben's number. They had exchanged cell phone numbers during Ben's last visit.

His voice sounded groggy as he cleared his throat, then said, "Hello?"

"Hi, Ben? It's An? Just wanted to call and see how you are holding up?" She rolled her eyes at herself, feeling silly and thinking she sounded awkward ending her statements in question marks. *Old habits die hard,* she thought.

"Hi, An! I've been going through some things here at home, getting a little rest, and making arrangements with the girls. What's up with you?"

"Oh, just packing, watching episodes of an old favorite show… not much."

"Cool beans! What show?"

"Oh, you probably wouldn't know it. *Space: 1999?*"

"I used to watch that, many, many moons ago." He laughed as he said this.

"Well, I'm surprised you know what I'm talking about. Most people don't even remember it."

"Want to have dinner with me tonight?" Ben blurted out.

It took An by surprise, but a smile formed on her lips. After a brief silence, she said yes. "I would love it!"

They chitchatted for another minute or so, trying to decide whether to order in or go somewhere.

"I need some fresh air," Ben finally announced. "How about the little Italian place off of Main? The one on Lark Street," Ben said.

"Pane e Vino? I love that place!"

"That's it! I'll pick you up in a bit, say six-thirty? I want the chicken piccata piled high with capers and that delicious lemon sauce smothering everything." He chuckled.

An laughed. "I might copy you and have exactly that!"

Promptly at 6:29, Ben drove his car two doors down the street and beeped his horn to let An know he was there, just as they had planned. The air was cool and crisp as An stepped out of her front door and got into Ben's bright-red '67 Mustang.

"Cool car!" An told him, running her fingers along the shiny paint.

"I know. That's what my daughters say. They love to drive it when they're here. I dusted off the garage cobwebs and voila! Your chariot, milady!"

"Did they leave?" An asked, chuckling at Ben.

"Only for the day to take care of some things back home. They'll be back in the morning," Ben explained.

An nodded her head as she watched Ben's profile. He pulled away from the curb. She asked him if she could roll her window down to feel the breeze on her face. Her cheeks were naturally tinted pink. Her chest and ears felt hot too from the excitement of getting out of the house. She felt silly and giddy but waved those thoughts away. She was enjoying being right here in this place, at this moment, and that was that! She would simply embrace the silliness and giddiness and just be free.

"Penny for your thoughts," Ben said, breaking the silence.

"Oh, nothing really," she told him. "I am simply enjoying the night, sensing the world around me."

The light turned green, and they drove in silence before Ben pierced the quiet once more.

"You seem sad."

An sat motionless, thinking about what Ben had said.

They were silent for a beat; then Ben asked, "Could you be happy again, An?"

An pondered that question for a long while, feeling no rush to answer. The chains that bound her were starting to break away, and she could feel pent-up emotions dislodging and shifting. She wasn't sure what was happening, what metamorphosis was taking place within her, but she felt this strange sense of liberation. She could recreate herself into any shape; she could feel or say whatever she wanted. There was no Brad to think about and no judgment.

What is happiness, anyhow? Who defines it? She was thinking these thoughts as she finally answered Ben.

"I think I'm happy right now, this exact moment," she told him. "The evening air caressing me ever so tenderly, like a lover… the moon looking down on me as if to keep me safe in its halo… the sound of the tires on pavement whispering sweet nothings… and you, you keeping me company, indulging me, letting me be myself. It makes me happy to be right here, right now. I'm finally just being me."

"Well said, Miz Poet." Ben smiled, quickly glimpsing her profile.

In the silence that followed, Ben began chuckling softly, then more loudly. "'The wind caressing me like a lover…'" He was unable to finish as a burst of laughter rose up in his chest.

"The moon looking down on me…" An stopped in mid-sentence and burst out laughing, too, such a hearty, joyful laughter that Ben let himself go, laughing along with her, unabashedly. They laughed together until their eyes watered.

"Oh God, my cheeks," An managed to say. "Ouch, my stomach!" She snorted, and this brought about another fit of laughter from both of them.

Ben began wheezing and coughing. "Stop making me laugh!" he begged.

"I can't!" she wailed.

They managed to finally compose themselves by the time they reached the restaurant. An dabbed at her mascara-smudged eyes with the tips of a tissue she had dug out from her purse.

Ben cleared his throat, saying, "We needed that. Laughter is good for the soul, they say, and the heart too."

He was quiet for so long, his hands firmly on the steering wheel. An reached across to touch his arm lightly.

"You okay?" she asked him.

"Yeah, yeah. Let's go in."

They were seated near the fireplace. It was well stocked, the flames crackling and sparking. An inhaled the smoky scent of burning wood mingled with the crusty pizza dough baking in the brick oven, onions and garlic being sautéed in the kitchen, the olive oil and Italian spice flakes in front of them. She smiled across the table at Ben, her cheeks glowing in the firelight, her eyes twinkling with life.

"You look beautiful," he told her, smiling back.

"Not too shabby yourself, Mister." Their eyes held, as their smiles stretched wider.

The bread came, to be dipped generously in the olive oil mixture. They ordered a bottle of dry Riesling.

"I didn't realize I had been missing Lisa. Now more than ever, but for a long time, I've missed her... a very long time."

"What do you miss most about her?" An prodded.

"This," he said simply. "The laughter, the interaction, her beautiful smiling face, the closeness... you know, just being with each other like this."

"I understand," An said with a nostalgic look clouding her features now. "To say that I miss Brad would be such a despicable admission I could never utter it, even if the thought did sneak in. But I do miss the sense of family, home, gatherings... I miss my girls. Oh, how I miss our walks and talks, eating together, playing Monopoly and Bananagrams. watching *Space: 1999*." An looked away because her eyes were misting over, her voice cracking and her chest tightening.

"Are you okay talking about what happened with the girls, or do you need to change the subject?"

"They hate me." She looked across at Ben as if asking for understanding and forgiveness, fully knowing he did not hold the power to absolve her of her guilt or her sense of loss.

"They lost respect for me for not standing up to Brad," she continued. "They stopped trusting me for not better protecting them. They despise me for keeping his secrets. They abhor the fact that I stayed all those years." She bowed her head, shaking it from side to side. "I failed them, Ben. I totally failed them. I deserve their absence and their wrath."

Ben reached across the table, his fingers searching for her hand. She obligingly placed it on the table. He grabbed her hand in his bigger one, fiercely, reassuringly.

"Don't beat yourself up so hard, An. They are adults now. At some point they need to stop shifting blame and just accept whatever happened. Do you still talk to them at all?"

"No. I don't even know where they are. I haven't seen them in years, since Erica finished college. They made it clear that they never want to see me or talk to me again. Or be a part of my life."

"It may change one day. They just need to mature a bit."

"No, I doubt it. They have been very firm about wanting—needing—me completely out of their lives. I lost them because of my poor judgment. I have no one else to blame."

"I'm sorry," Ben whispered. "What exactly was it that caused them to turn on you?"

"I can't go into it just yet."

"It's okay," Ben told her.

Their entrees arrived, saving An from the discomfort of talking about the girls. Two chicken piccatas with sides of asparagus. They refilled their glasses and concentrated on eating and drinking for a minute, chewing and savoring the texture of the chicken, pounded thin, and the crunchiness of the al-dente asparagus, all mingled with the tartness of the sauce and fruity, crisp wine.

An was the first one to speak again. She needed to divert the conversation away from the topic of the girls and away from her.

"Do you know anything about multiple people coming and going to your house the day Lisa died?" she asked, diving right into the topic, headfirst. It took courage, but she was feeling bold.

Ben watched her, his glass lifted in front of his face, distorting the scowl that had appeared there. "I'm not sure what you are referring to. Did you witness it, or did someone else tell you something to that effect?"

An's face and neck grew hot. "I'm sure I heard one of the neighbors say something—something about more than one car in front of the house, people coming and going that very day."

"I don't know, but whoever told you that I'm sure mentioned it to the police, and they are likely investigating it."

"Do you have a guess as to what that may have been all about?" An pressed him.

Ben took a deep breath through his nose, then blew out of his mouth, making a warbling noise. "Whew! Well, assuming it's true, I suppose it could have been people that Lisa was working with to put her plan into action. Maybe an attorney, friends, or people she wanted to confer about something… I don't know who, really."

"Did she have many friends, people she trusted?"

"She had a few, despite having lost touch with many of her friends over the years. I know there was a priest she conferred with on occasion, a little like a mentor. There was a childhood girlfriend, Angela. But, now that I think about it, it's been many moons since I heard mention of her. One or two old colleagues from work she stayed in touch with."

An's breath caught at the mention of Angela, but she held her tongue. "What about your kids?" An asked. "Was Lisa close to them?"

"Lisa had grown so distant over the last few years. She didn't like company, and she didn't like going anywhere. It was difficult having a relationship of any kind with her. I don't know.

"She refused to get any type of counseling. She just shut herself away as if… as if to sort of erase herself, like she just wanted to fade away, disappear… I can't explain it well. It bothers me that I didn't do more. It bothers me that I let it happen."

"I'm not sure you had control, Ben," An told him in an attempt to assuage him. He seemed to have grown agitated the more he talked about it.

"The kids felt powerless and confused. Maybe even a little embarrassed by her behavior. Josh went away to college, then joined the military. The girls left home too, as soon as they could. Went to college and stayed down in the Hampton Roads area."

"I don't even remember seeing them out and about in the neighborhood, to be honest," An told Ben.

"I think as Lisa became more and more of a recluse, it had an impact on the kids. They, too, became more guarded, more detached, more loners. They steered clear of us."

The meal now eaten and the wine polished off, An felt drowsy and tired. She was ready to head back home and hide in the familiar rooms of her home, where she felt safer.

But Ben seemed to need more time. Maybe he had something he needed to say out loud. He asked if An would share a square of tiramisu. She was exhausted from the intense interaction and being out, but, sensing that Ben wanted to stay longer, she obliged.

As they dug into the layers of custard and ladyfingers, Ben blurted, "I have been so terribly lonely for so long."

An watched him closely. She felt too limp from all the wine to dissect this one. "I can relate," she told him at last. "Is that how the infidelity crept in?"

He stopped eating and tented his hands in front of him, pensive. "She didn't even care, nor did she try to stop my actions, when I confessed, trying to alleviate my own guilt."

"She didn't do anything?"

"She said she knew and didn't begrudge me."

"Wow, so she didn't react to it at all?"

"It was just her way. That's how she handled unpleasant things. But, later that night, I awoke with her sobbing. I tried consoling her, I tried talking, but nothing soothed her. I asked if she wanted a divorce, and she stopped sobbing long enough to give me a death stare.

"'Divorce will never be an option for me,' she told me. She said it with so much fierceness and conviction, it scared me."

An perked up a little, wondering if this last revelation had anything to do with Lisa's untimely death. She didn't say anything to Ben, but it was disconcerting to think that this could have been motive for both murder and suicide. If divorce would never be an alternative, suicide might have been Lisa's only option if Ben wanted out. As for Ben, if Lisa would not grant divorce, and he was desperate for freedom from this marriage, perhaps his options were narrowed down to one.

Murder.

An searched Ben's face, his eyes, his mannerisms for telltale signs of something dark and murderous, but only saw a handsome, mild-mannered man sitting across from her. She simply could not believe Ben was capable of killing, especially killing Lisa.

But what if he thought he was helping her? What if he saw himself as a facilitator, an angel of death? Maybe Lisa was so depressed that she wanted to take her own life but couldn't. Maybe Ben facilitated that deed. Maybe, just maybe. An shivered involuntarily.

"I didn't have anything to do with it, An," Ben said it so quietly that An almost didn't hear it in the din of the other diners and the hustle and bustle of the restaurant. "That's what you're thinking, isn't it?"

An's heart was thumping. Her face grew flushed again. "I'm not the only one wondering, Ben, you have to understand. People always suspect the spouse and those close to the—the... the victim."

"Yeah, of course. But, in this case, I had nothing to do with it. I know we had a strange relationship. Lisa refused to sleep with me, share our marital bed after that night, but I still cared about her. That would not be a motive for me at all."

"So, what about the other woman? What about your infidelity?"

"It's complicated," he said. "I ended it, of course. But Lisa left the door wide open for me. She paid me back by having her own affair, something online. It was never physical, you understand, but it still hurt. I guess you could say we had an open marriage of sorts."

"I don't get it at all. It boggles the mind why you two chose that arrangement." An wanted desperately to think of them as close, as being able to deal with their differences and then continue a happy life in a loving relationship that could withstand everything that was thrown at them. Why was their union not strong enough to brave the onslaught of whatever came their way? She had always seen herself as such: she and Brad standing on the bow of the *Titanic* taking on the world and coming out of it all stronger, their love deeper. What a dreamer!

Love was nothing like she had dreamed it would be, and life had not turned out as she had envisioned it, not at all.

But who should she blame for her disappointments and misfortunes in her life? Her parents? The evil lurking in the periphery of her life? The injustices perpetrated by unknown others? What or who should carry the brunt of her failures? Bad luck? A dark karma? Voodoo? God? Brad?

For her, she couldn't legitimately blame any one person or any one act or any one perception. It was all mired and entrenched in her own psyche, her own decisions and indecisions, her own mind gone rogue.

Back in the present, Ben was articulating. "Try not to judge, An. We each live with circumstances that perhaps may be unacceptable to someone else. It just became comfortable for us. It was a strange situation, for sure, but we chose to accept it and we lived with it."

An thought about this, knowing she had no authority to judge anyone for how they lived their lives. Her own life with Brad had been the epitome of strange and dysfunctional. *If you live in a glass house, you can't very well throw stones*, she thought. Yet the fact that Lisa was dead changed everything, shining a bright spotlight on her and Ben's marriage and their "arrangement." An was now convinced that Ben and Lisa's lifestyle had at least something to do with Lisa's demise. She just couldn't figure out how exactly it was connected. A strange feeling overtook her, as if she was just given the biggest clue and missed it.

Back in the safety of her own walls, tucked between her fluffy blankets and oversized pillows again, An felt exhausted, the mental kind that rendered someone completely numb. She wanted to sleep but couldn't. Her mind kept going back to Ben, back to their conversation. She tried to go over everything that had happened that night, desperately looking for that clue that had escaped her.

The following morning, An awoke with the sunlight tentatively stretching out across the horizon. It looked like it was going to be a muted blue day, no blinding sunlight. An tried to decide if she should just go back to the comfort and the nothingness of her black and dreamless sleep. She grunted and immediately regretted it. Her throat hurt, so scratchy and parched.

Finding the gumption to finally get up, An put her robe on and then wandered around the house aimlessly, shuffling her slippered feet. She made coffee, found an old paperback in the library, and sat in her comfy chaise, propping herself up to read a few chapters. Her thoughts wandered to Ben and the dinner the night before. The evening had started out so hopeful and carefree, but then the conversation had veered off into a dark alleyway with a gray thunder cloud overhead.

Suddenly, there was a loud knock. She jumped, startled. Immediately, her thoughts went to Ben. *God, my hair is a mess, and I must be quite the sight*, she thought, getting up from the chaise lounge. She licked her dry lips and ran her fingers through her thick hair. She hoped that she and Ben could sit at the kitchen table, have a hot cup of coffee, and talk about pleasant things that would replace the uncomfortable topic of the previous night.

She opened her front door and was immediately alarmed to see Detectives Connor and Conrad standing there. They weren't wet this time, but their appearances were otherwise similar to the last time she had seen them. *But why in the world are they back here again? What do they want with me?*

"Hello, An," Detective Connor said. "We were in the general area and thought we'd stop by rather than have you come to the station."

"Okay, how can I help you, Detectives? Are there new developments in the case next door?"

"We have obtained the telephone records for Lisa, home and cellular. We are puzzled about something and wanted to clarify. Can we come in for a minute?"

"Of course," said An, curious and a little puzzled herself. The detective's tone was different. Something had shifted.

The detectives walked in. An noticed that they both scanned the living room and adjacent library as if expecting to see something out of the ordinary. Detective Conrad walked to the edge of the stairwell and looked up, then looked down the hallway toward the kitchen and into the dining room. Detective Connor had been watching An intently. *Very curious, indeed.* Aware of the change in the detectives' manner since their last visit, An was uncomfortable. Goosebumps formed on her arms and scalp. She wanted them out of her house—now!

Should she not have let them inside? Should she ask for an attorney? This was an ongoing investigation, and they were not smiling or behaving in a very friendly way this time. What had the telephone records revealed? An wasn't sure how police work was conducted, but it seemed like things were moving rather quickly. After all, Lisa wasn't even buried yet, or scattered—whatever they did with cremations.

"Ms. Jordan—An—we're not going to beat around the bush. So, let me not waste your time unnecessarily and get right to it. We were not able to talk to your ex-husband in person, but we did speak by phone. He tells me you and he knew the Spencers, had been to their home, had a friendship in fact."

An frowned, looking at the detective with a stunned expression. "I mean, we were neighbors, but we didn't socialize? We were certainly NOT friends?"

"He said you did socialize, and you were, indeed, friends. One of your neighbors confirms it. Telephone records seem to suggest it. I'm trying to understand why you lied, why you would have us believe you were not friendly with the Spencers."

"What are you saying, Detective? I don't understand. I did not lie. I am not friends with the Spencers?" An broke eye contact when she told the detectives she had not lied because Angie came to mind. She felt duplicitous.

Detective Conrad had stopped perusing the home and now stood with hands on her hips, fingers facing back, as she watched and listened to An and Detective Connor go at it. An thought her posture suggested she was ready to reach for her handgun. She felt insulted and hurt by this realization.

"Why would your ex-husband say you knew Analise and Benjamin Spencer then? Clearly, someone is not telling the truth. And the other evidence doesn't seem to be on your side either."

"Other evidence?" An stared at the detective, wild-eyed. "Well, we were at their house at least once that I recall for a barbeque? I think? But it was a long time ago, in the first few months or so after they moved here. I didn't know them; I don't know them. I'm not sure why Brad would say that? But Brad always has some agenda? You'll have to ask him why he's saying what he's saying?"

An's voice had reached a high, shrill pitch. She was on the verge of tears.

"Sometimes the evidence is the best way to corroborate what witnesses—people involved—are telling us. In this case, An, we have telephone records showing calls from your home to the Spencers' home and vice versa. There are also calls made from Analise's cell phone to your home. Do you have an explanation?"

An was aghast. She blinked rapidly, repeatedly. None of this made any sense. She did not know Ben and Lisa enough to call them. She certainly had never had any telephone conversations with either of them. This was beyond bizarre! The thought that she was being framed for something clearly crossed her mind.

But who? Brad? And why? How?

"Detectives, I can't explain any of this, but I can assure you I never placed nor received any calls to or from the Spencers? I don't know what's going on here? It had to have been Brad then!" An felt utterly frantic, looking from one detective to the other. She blinked again, several times, trying to clear her vision and her mind.

"You have to believe me. There must be some way to clear this up," An continued, pleading.

"Am I under some kind of suspicion here?" she asked Detective Connor, looking straight at him, trying to keep her eye contact steady, but she felt her lids blink several times. The room seemed stuffy and hot to her; beads of sweat were forming under her breasts and along her temples.

"We are just trying to get some answers so we can get to the bottom of this. A woman is dead, An, do you understand? And things aren't quite lining up for me."

"No, they're not," An said in a near whisper.

"Are you being completely honest with me, An? Do you know something you're not sharing with me? If the answer is yes, you need to come clean, right now!"

An continued to stare at Detective Connor. *Had he spoken with Angela?* she wondered. Did the police know about Angela and her connection to both Lisa and An? What should she say if anything?

"I have told you all I know," An finally said. "I'm not sure how else I can help you? I don't know why Brad and the neighbor said what they said, and I can't explain the phone calls?" An tried in vain to keep the question marks out of her sentences but was finding it impossible. This entire sordid situation was confusing and disconcerting.

Was Brad somehow involved? But how? She no longer put anything past him, and frankly, she was feeling the tentacles of fear spreading across her heart and mind. And how did Angela fit into all this? She wanted to tell the detectives about her, but that would make An appear complicit somehow. *OHGODOHGODOHGOD!* she was screaming inside. *What is happening, and what do I do?*

"Which neighbor told you I know the Spencers?" An had found her voice again, and was desperately trying to regain her composure.

"That's not really relevant. However, let me say this. You have been seen with Benjamin Spencer… before and after Lisa's death. But you told me you didn't have a friendship with him. You told me you did not know him."

"That's the truth, Detective. I hardly had any contact with either of the Spencers, except to say hello from afar. I did go to Mr. Spencer's home after Lisa died to pay my condolences? And we had dinner last night. We're just trying to console each other, you know? My divorce, his loss?"

An broke eye contact, looking down at her hands as she twisted and rubbed them. She realized this might make her look nervous and even suspicious, so she stopped, dropping her arms to her side.

"I see," Detective Connor said. "Tell me something, An. Were you aware of a relationship between your ex-husband and either Benjamin Spencer or Analise Spencer? Did you know of any communication between them? Recently? We're talking real recent."

"What do you mean by 'real recent?' Brad moved out months ago. He does still have a key. I have not changed the locks because we're still dealing with the disposition of our belongings and such?"

"So he would have had ample opportunity to be in the home alone with you gone somewhere?"

"Well, if I knew he was coming, I would make myself scarce if you know what I mean? The less contact with him the better? He scares me sometimes." An stammered her words, lowering her gaze as she uttered the last sentence. She wasn't sure why she had divulged that. She just needed all this attention diverted elsewhere, away from her. This was just too much. How in the world was it that both she and Brad were now in the middle of a death investigation?

Detective Connor was scrutinizing her face intently, and Detective Conrad had walked closer, listening, watching. They were all still standing in the living room. An's legs felt wobbly. She wished she could reach one of the couches and sit without tumbling to the floor.

"Why are you afraid of him, An?" Detective Connor asked. "Did he do something to you?"

"No, not to me. Well, yes and no. I—I don't know!" An felt tears threatening to spill. Her throat was tight.

"You're not making sense. Who did he hurt, An?"

"I shouldn't have said anything. It's only a suspicion. No, I can't go into it. Please, just go."

"Okay," said Detective Connor. "But are you 100 percent sure you don't want to tell me something else before we go?"

An remained silent for a minute, eyes downcast. When she looked up again, she had made up her mind about something. "His ex-wife disappeared many years ago. He said he paid her to leave and never return, but some people think there's more to it. His wife, Alison, has never surfaced after she supposedly left, not even to try to communicate with her daughters. She is a missing person to this day."

"Did you withhold information you may have possessed at the time about Alison?" Detective Connor asked the question while Detective Conrad looked on.

"No, I don't think so, but the girls came to believe their mother was dead and Brad and I were involved somehow. That's why they don't want any contact, any relationship with either of us." An looked up at the detectives, tears now streaming down her face. Thinking about Erica and Lynne still hurt so darn much. "I didn't. I would never have hurt Alison. I love those girls."

An covered her face with her hands and sobbed; all her careful restraints were now broken. Deep wounds were suddenly exposed, opening the dam. She was embarrassed but did not know how to keep from crying, so she simply stopped caring. She already looked a mess anyhow.

Connor looked over at his partner, and, understanding the silent communication, Detective Conrad walked to An's side, putting her arms around the other woman and guiding her to the couch.

"Now, now, it's going to be alright, An." Detective Conrad patted An's leg as she sat next to her on the couch. "Just take a deep breath and relax."

An swiped at her tears and looked up at the detective, trying to focus her attention. Her face was red and blotchy from crying.

Detective Conrad took her opportunity. "An, think back; think hard. Is there anything that stands out in that old case that you think may have a connection? Just an opinion or a nagging feeling, anything?"

"I think he's trying to erase me just like he erased Alison once he was done with her," An declared.

The detectives stared at An.

"I see. So, how does Analise's death fit in, do you suppose? Think, An. Think carefully."

How could she possibly concentrate with this headache that constantly came and went? She tried to stay focused in the moment.

"He's making it complicated, going to all this trouble in a roundabout way, all to somehow frame me? I know it sounds totally crazy. I dunno. I just don't know anything anymore." Tears began to fill An's eyes again as she stared at Detective Conrad. "I feel totally crazy. I think that's what he wants. And it's working. He's gaslighting me, don't you see?"

Detective Conrad patted An on the knee, a sad, knowing look shadowing her features.

An was desperate as she continued to speak. "I think he used some type of mind game to manipulate Alison into either going crazy or committing suicide or both? And I think he's using some kind of mind game to manipulate me into doing the same? As far as Lisa, he could be using the same mind technique, only his goal with her is to get to me or frame me or hurt me somehow in an indirect way."

An felt crazy and knew she sounded crazy to the detectives. She looked from one to the other, frantic, pleading for understanding. But in her heart of hearts, she knew Brad was somehow involved. She was familiar with the term gaslighting from her days at the psychologists' office, and she had become convinced Brad was using it on her. This had to be all part of his plan to drive her mad.

Detective Connor sighed audibly. He paced the room, blowing air through his mouth.

"An, would you agree to go under hypnosis?" he finally said.

An immediately thought of Angie. *It will all come out,* she thought. *They'll know I've been withholding information. It will convince them that I'm involved for sure.*

An looked at him, bug-eyed, her lips trembling. "I'm afraid to do it," she finally admitted. "I'm so afraid of what I might discover there, hidden in the shadows of my own mind."

CHAPTER 11

TIES THAT BIND: 1991

"Families are like men; you can't live with them and you can't live without them."

— Unknown

"Family quarrels are bitter things. They don't go according to any rules. They're not like aches or wounds. They're more like splits in the skin that won't heal because there's not enough material."

- F. Scott Fitzgerald

An sometimes thought the idea of family was an intriguing puzzle; its definition was elusive, even contrived. Its members, relationships, composition, disposition were all intricate and interlinked. Whether a family consisted of two members or hundreds, its viability and vibrancy were dependent on all the members as a whole, operating as a unit.

With Juliet and Harrison gone, An's family of two was at grave risk of extinction with CJ reluctant to be an active participant. Perhaps An knew this in some obscure corner within her mind. Her need to hold on to this family was intense, but as it slipped away from her, her deep yearning to build a new one, or belong to another, was far beyond her realm of conscious thought. It was more of an instinctual urge to belong and survive.

As Thanksgiving 1991 approached, An became increasingly frustrated that she had not been able to coordinate a time for CJ and Brad to meet after these many weeks. Brad was quickly becoming a big part of her life, and with CJ already established there, she wanted the two men to know each other. Brad seemed eager to make CJ's acquaintance. He proposed dates and chimed in with ideas.

But CJ, for some odd reason, was resisting the inevitable meeting. In fact, now that An thought about it, CJ had been discreetly putting some distance between them. The weekly dinners they shared had all but stopped since Brad had come into An's life. CJ explained that things were hectic at work. "Don't you become like Ma and Pop," An had admonished. CJ had laughed it off. But An sensed something had shifted, and she couldn't put her finger on it.

CJ had always been somewhat private and quiet, but now he seemed downright withdrawn and sulking.

The daily phone calls had become a once-in-a-blue-moon occurrence, and that's only because An called him. CJ's distant behavior disturbed An. She couldn't pinpoint the place and time it had begun to change. Was it because of Brad? Perhaps CJ was uncomfortable and unsure about his sister finally seriously dating someone. He himself didn't date much; he'd never seriously dated anyone in fact.

Was he jealous of her happiness? Was it the loss of his parents still fresh in his mind? Were the struggles with the family business finally taking a toll? An was baffled, but she was persistent about the importance of staying connected.

An did not want CJ to spend Thanksgiving alone. With both parents now gone, it was important that they be together around the holidays to try to build some semblance of family and tradition. An was set to spend Thanksgiving with Brad and his family, but she was torn and anguished about not being able to include her brother. She finally talked it over with Brad, and they came to the conclusion that CJ needed to be part of the family festivities.

An called CJ and made the offer.

"I'm not comfortable with holidays to begin with, An, you know that. I'm especially not comfortable spending it with a bunch of strangers."

"We both need to get out of our comfort zones, Little Brother. I really need you there. It will be my first time meeting Brad's dad and that side of the family too. Please, CJ? I need you there."

The other end of the line was so quiet and still, An thought CJ had hung up on her.

"C? Are you there?"

"Yeah, yeah, I'm here. Just thinking. I dunno. I kinda had some other plans."

"What plans? Spending it alone? Wait. You have a girlfriend?" An teased him in a sing-song voice. "Aw, is that it?"

CJ chuckled. An could almost feel his face heating up on the other end of the line. "Nah, don't go there, nothing like that. I just really, really would rather not."

"What plans then? Why would you not want to be with your family? I'm all you've got. Come on, CJ!"

"Okay, fine, I'll go," he said with a touch of exasperation and a hint of resignation in his voice. "If it's really *that* important to you, I'll go."

"Brad is important to me, and you're important to me. I want you to meet him. And Thanksgiving is important to me too. I want you with me; we're family, remember?"

CJ sighed and started to say something, then stopped himself.

So it was settled.

An woke up with the jitters Thanksgiving morning. Outside, the wind whistled and hissed as it scattered yellow and brown leaves around in swirls that formed like mini tornadoes and then dissipated. The sky was pale blue. An touched the bedroom window to gauge the temperature outside. It was cold. Brad was there, slightly snoring on his side of the bed. He had recently hired a nanny for the girls, and Agnes had cut back on her work hours as manager at a local supermarket. This allowed Brad some extra freedom, which pretty much made him a semi-permanent presence at An's.

The night before, An had prepared a green bean casserole to bring and share with the others. She had doctored up the fresh green beans with a little extra sautéed sweet onions and garlic. Brad bought apple cider and a few bottles of wine to bring. They planned on leaving at eleven o'clock that morning to ensure they were there right around noon. Brad's dad and the rest of the family were scheduled to arrive a little later, driving from the farm in Ohio. They planned to camp out at Agnes's and return home sometime Saturday. An was feeling anxious about meeting them. She was also feeling anxious about Brad and CJ finally coming face-to-face.

That morning, CJ was to come to An's apartment for breakfast and leave his car there, and the three of them would drive together to Agnes's home. An was up early, showered, and dressed. She was wearing a long, brown, stretchy skirt with a bright orange knitted sweater. Coffee was brewing as she assembled the fixings for bagels and lox—one of CJ's favorite dishes. He was due to arrive any minute.

Brad had showered and shaved and was wearing faded blue jeans and an unbuttoned brown-and-orange plaid shirt over a plain brown T-shirt. He looked pretty dapper. He strode into the kitchen, putting his arms around An's waist and planting a wet kiss on her right cheek. She turned her face up at him just enough to give him a smile and comment on his outfit.

"We match!" she told him. There was a *rap-rap-rap* on the door just then.

An and Brad stood for a second, unsure of their next move. Finally, An pulled away from Brad's embrace and made a beeline to the front door, saying, "He's here!" Brad followed close on An's heels and hovered behind her as she opened the door.

She flung the door open, and there across the threshold stood CJ, an arrangement of fall flowers exploding in yellow, orange, and red in front of his face. He was also holding a rectangular white box—a pastry box it looked like—with a thin white-and-red string crisscrossed and tied on top. He slowly slid the bouquet down to reveal a smile from ear to ear, and his twinkling blue eyes were as alert and sparkling as ever. An loved those dimples! His normally longish hair was shorter than she remembered.

She threw her arms around her brother, not caring that she was crushing the flowers. He chuckled, trying to wrap his loaded arms around her. Brad stood back, quietly watching, hands stuffed in the pockets of his jeans.

"Come inside, you!" she finally choked out. "Meet Brad... at last!"

CJ had not looked at Brad since arriving, and he now seemed to visibly stiffen up, the smile vanishing. Brad looked him over with a slightly amused smile. Then he extended his right hand for a shake. CJ seemed to hesitate.

An watched, noticing CJ's strange demeanor. She was unsure why he was behaving so standoffish.

"Come on, guys," An said. "Here, let me take these and you two say hello or something." She took the flowers and pastry box from CJ and continued walking toward the kitchen, leaving the men to trail behind. Brad pulled CJ into him and slapped his back loudly.

"Come on in the kitchen. Let's get coffee and lox!" she called over her shoulder. The men followed as she bubbled over with enthusiasm. She had missed her brother more than she could express.

"You look awesome!" she told him, approvingly eyeing his khakis and eggplant-colored pullover. "Thank goodness you left the black behind," she continued, as they all stood around the kitchen table.

"Come on, CJ, have a seat and stop looking so uncomfortable and uptight," she said as she pulled a chair out for him. "You. Are. With. Family." By punctuating each word, An hoped CJ would get the picture.

An got the pot of coffee and cups to add to everything else laid out on the kitchen table. Brad sat at the head of the table as usual. An poured the steamy brew into each of their mugs, then sat down across from CJ. They sat admiring the spread before them.

"Eat, eat!" she told them.

Brad reached for the bagels slathered in cream cheese and piled high with smoked salmon, rings of thinly sliced red onions, cubed juicy red tomatoes, and sprinkled with capers. He offered the platter to CJ first.

"Mm mm mm!" Brad grunted with pleasure as they began eating. "Your sister is a keeper," Brad told CJ.

CJ looked over at An with a weak smile and then reached across the table for her hand, needing reassurance. Brad watched with curiosity, grinning. Then he made eye contact with An and winked at her. CJ quickly pulled his hand away, lowering his gaze to focus on the loaded bagel in front of him.

CJ's heart was heavy; An could tell. Was there something he wanted to tell her? It felt dark and important. She was trying to decipher his thoughts, but he kept breaking eye contact.

Then it seemed he had made a decision. Smiling at her reassuringly, he said, "I'm glad you're happy, Sis."

An felt a twinge of guilt for her absence at the bakery and all of the related business. Knowing that CJ had taken on the bulk of all the responsibilities of running the family business, An suspected that might have been why he seemed strange and withdrawn. He seemed tired. These were the thoughts running through An's mind as they all got in Brad's Ford pickup truck to drive to his mom's house.

An was riding shotgun, so CJ climbed in the backseat. The first few minutes everyone fell silent, taking in the scenery in the privacy of their own minds. An finally twisted herself in her seat to face CJ and asked for a rundown of the business activities, something that normally animated CJ. She hoped this was a topic that would get him talking since he had been unusually quiet even for him. But CJ aptly averted the conversation.

"More importantly and more pressing, I want to know about these people I'm about to meet and what to expect," CJ told An.

"Okay," An said. "I suppose we can talk shop later."

CJ seemed relieved.

An went on to describe the girls for him and told him a little about Agnes and her home, trying desperately to tell him about the clutter in a delicate way. Then Brad added short descriptions about the others. Seeming a little distracted and distant, CJ listened quietly in the back.

When An asked him what was new with him personally, he claimed not to have a whole lot going on and appeared to divert the conversation elsewhere whenever a personal question was thrown his way.

"Really, An, you know me. I'm a drama-free, simple guy. I work, I eat, I sleep; that's pretty much it. I don't have time for shenanigans."

"Living your life is not shenanigans, young man!" An teased. "Haven't you heard the old adage? All work and no play makes Jack a dull guy!"

They pulled into Agnes's private lane, and still, CJ had managed to share nothing about his life or give any updates on the business. An found it curious but chose to let it be for now. She would attempt to get to the bottom of it later.

Delicious aromas, the girls' giggles, and twangy country music with lots of banjo assaulted their senses as they neared Agnes's front door. Peeking through one of the side windows, they could see Agnes stirring something on the stove. The girls were chattering and playing on the living room carpet; Barbie dolls and their various outfits were scattered about. It appeared that the holiday, and entertaining company, had not prompted Agnes to clear the clutter in her home.

Brad rapped on the windowpane to get their attention, then twisted the doorknob to open it. The girls and Agnes looked up. The dogs in the backyard chimed in by barking in unison. Lynne came at them at the speed of lightning and knocked her father off balance. He stumbled, falling backwards with her onto one of the Adirondack chairs on the front porch. They giggled so everyone knew they were a-okay. Erica ran over to An and hugged her legs. Then Agnes arrived, throwing her arms around An, with Erica squeezed between them.

"And is this handsome creature CJ?" Agnes squeaked in her Mickey Mouse imitation, as she pulled away from the group hug. She approached CJ and gave him a bear hug, too, then stood back to eye him from head to toe. She smiled approvingly.

CJ stood cemented to the one spot, mouth agape, his eyes staring unblinking. Even though An had tried to prepare him, it appeared he was still a little stunned. He had returned the hug limply, arms up in the air, not quite knowing what to do with them.

Inside, Agnes handed them all glasses of sparkling wine. She poured herself the real deal. She was prattling away, the girls were babbling, the television set was on in the background, music was still blaring, the dogs continued their yapping, and no one could decipher a word that was being said.

An loved it.

Agnes raised her glass and made a toast to Thanksgiving and all the good cheer that was to come their way. The girls joined in with their sipping cups of apple juice. After some searching, An finally found a spot on one of the windowsills to park her glass. Then she joined the girls on the carpeted living room floor to play with the Barbies. She chuckled in awe of the tiny red stilettos and black-and-white polka-dotted dress she had chosen to dress one of the dolls. An never did have a Barbie growing up, but she remembered asking her mom for a Marie Osmond doll. She laughed out loud at the thought. The girls stopped what they were doing to look up at her in surprise.

"It's just all so cute!" she told them.

CJ came to join them on the carpet, a little awkward as he plopped down. "What's so funny?" he asked her.

"I was reminiscing about my Marie Osmond doll. Remember her?"

Now it was his turn to chuckle. "How could I *ever* forget?"

An's eagle eyes spotted Brad and his mom speaking in hushed tones by the stove, appearing oblivious to the rest of them. A sense of unease blanketed her as she wondered what they were talking about so seriously and surreptitiously.

A little later, Brad and CJ had gone back out to get the rest of the things they had left in Brad's truck. Agnes continued working on preparing the dinner feast, while everyone else joined forces to add the leaf to the kitchen table and set it for dinner—not an easy feat since they had to find temporary spots for all the many things that covered it.

While waiting for the rest to arrive, they munched on cream-cheese-stuffed celery sticks and black olives to keep the hunger at bay. The girls decorated their fingertips with the black olives and were eating them one by one off of their tiny fingers. An watched mesmerized by their creativity and cuteness.

Finally, the rest of the clan got there around three-thirty that afternoon. When they heard the van's tires crunching the gravel outside, everyone got up and made their way outside to greet the others.

Emma and Ethan were the first ones to come bounding out of the vehicle.

"Grandma!" cried Emma. She flew into Agnes's outstretched arms. Ethan followed suit, a little heavier and a little slower than his sister.

Brad had told An that Emma was eleven and Ethan nine. Emma was adorable with a thick, long braid down her back, the ends tied with a satin purple ribbon. Ethan wore thick black-rimmed glasses, and he had chubby dimpled cheeks. An watched in wonder. She loved the exuberant energy of children. Lynne and Erica joined in the hug pileup. They were all giggling at this point. Then

Agnes ended up on the ground, snort-laughing as she went down. Having polished off two bottles of Merlot already, she hardly cared.

In the din of laughter from Agnes and the kids, they heard, "Grandy, just gimme your hands! YOUR HANDS!"

An turned her attention to the spectacle by the van. A woman's very round buttocks were sticking out of the back, wearing a short, pleated black skirt, and equestrian-style boots. An realized it must be Brad's sister, Marlene—who had been named after Marlene Dietrich, Agnes's beloved movie star idol—trying to help their grandmother out of the vehicle. An, being ultra modest, was instantly embarrassed for Marlene, even though the other woman wore black leggings so everything was properly covered up.

An sensed CJ nearby. She turned to her right, and the two siblings made eye contact as laughter rose in their throats. CJ placed his hand over his mouth in an attempt to stifle his. It made An feel good to see him smiling. She, too, reined in the urge to laugh out loud.

She also spotted Brad, as he was making a beeline to his dad, who had come out of the driver's side and was walking toward the house. His young wife, Glory, had gotten out of the front seat and was trying to catch up to her husband, her ankles twisting in the four-inch heeled boots she wore. An knew that Don, Brad's father, and Glory had been married for about five years and that

Glory was twenty years younger than Don. In fact, Glory wasn't much older than Marlene.

Don was an affable guy with a permanent, jolly smile etched on his face. He had a long gray beard that almost reached the belly button of his wide girth and a shiny bald head. He and Brad embraced. Glory looked on, seeming out of place. She wore a bulky, tan-colored, faux-fur coat over something short that was barely visible past the coat's hemline. Her raven hair was piled up high on her head. A white sash decorated with little rust-colored, green and yellow leaves held the bun on top of her head together. Its long tails trailed to just above her shoulder blades.

Eventually, everyone said their hellos and made it in the house for the long-awaited Thanksgiving dinner. Like a sponge, An had been soaking everything in, trying to decipher the little subtleties of this family and the intricacies of their relationships. An instantly liked Marlene, sensing that they could bond as sisters in time. Little Erica looked a lot like her, with straight reddish-blonde hair, freckles dotting her perfect skin, and blue-green eyes.

"I can't believe Brad hasn't brought you to the farm yet," Marlene told An once dinner was over and the girls had gone down for a past-due nap. Most of the others were settling down too, the tryptophan coma taking hold. Or perhaps it was just the flip side of all the excitement and anticipation of the prior days. Agnes had started a pot of coffee brewing, and the aroma was divine!

The two women, sitting side by side on the piano bench, eyed Agnes, who was methodically slicing up the pies: two pumpkin, two pecan, two apple. A big bowl of freshly whipped cream was sitting smack-dab in the center of the table, along with a bowl of fresh cranberry chutney. A sugar trance was sure to follow this next round.

"He asked me to come next time he makes the trip. We just need to find the time," An explained to Marlene. "I'm sure he'll get around to it sometime soon."

"Well, you'll have to come and stay for a few days. Assuming the family secrets won't keep you away." They both laughed, but An wondered about this hint Marlene had dropped on her lap. But first she had a more pressing question to ask in order to assuage her curiosity.

"Marlene, I hope you don't mind me asking, but why do you call your mother by her first name?"

Marlene looked straight ahead, letting the silence fill the space between them for a second. "My mother and I have a complicated relationship," she finally answered. "We were never close growing up. I left home at sixteen and made some poor choices... drugs, wild lifestyle, you know? It wasn't until Emma was born that I tried to turn things around and sought family once more. I really didn't think I'd ever see anyone in my family again. My mother and I grew farther apart while I was away, and there was quite a lot of resentment on her part."

"Whaaat? You? Away from home, drugs, resentment? I would not have guessed it. Why did all this happen? Brad never said anything about it." An was honestly in shock by this blunt revelation. Her curiosity grew.

"I would not expect him to tell you. He doesn't like talking about this stuff. Besides, his version of events is different from mine—so is Agnes's by the way. I'm guessing that he never spoke of Gordon either. That's our brother, who happens to be incarcerated in Nevada."

An's eyes were big as saucers as she stared at Marlene, speechless for a moment.

"No! I had no idea—never even knew about a brother. Oh, my gosh, incarcerated what for? How long?"

"Life sentence. He murdered his best friend over a girl." Marlene uttered the words as she looked at her chipped, bitten-down nails, totally matter-of-fact and emotionless.

"Oh, wow, are you kidding? That's horrible!" An stared at Marlene's profile, her heart flip-flopping and her mind racing.

"I know," Marlene said. "And, to make matters worse, he has never repented and has continued to hurt us all from behind bars."

"Is this the family secret you were alluding to? And what do you mean by hurting the family from behind bars?" An couldn't believe what she was hearing, and the sordid tale got stranger by the second.

"Yeah, that's our big secret... Well, Gordon has tried on numerous occasions to reach out to the family, begging for money or whatever. At one point, he had been talking to Grandy, had her come visit him and all—this was a number of years ago, mind you. He almost had her sign away a bunch of her possessions, including some land she owns in Florida. Luckily, we found out about it before it was too late. He's very bright and very persuasive and manipulative. Bad juju, for sure, if you ask me. I could tell you stories about him that would make your jaw drop to the floor."

Well, my jaw is already on the floor, An thought. She was incredulous, at a total loss for words. She blinked several times trying to clear her vision and decide how best to react and respond to this barrage of strange news. She wanted to hear more but was overwhelmed at that moment.

Agnes saved the day when she announced, "Who wants pie?"

Marlene jumped out of her seat to join her mother in the kitchen and begin serving dessert.

"What in the world?" Marlene suddenly exclaimed.

Everyone turned to look. Ethan had a spoonful of the whipped cream halfway to his mouth. He dropped it back in the bowl and just stared at Marlene, his eyes big as two moons, his chipmunk cheeks streaked white.

"Caught you red-handed, buddy!" she told him.

"I didn't do anything!" he protested. "I was helping Grandma stir the whipped cream, that's all."

"Were not! You were eating it," his mother accused. "The evidence is all over your face, Mr. Man!"

"Pecan for me!" Don said, springing out of his seat on the couch next to Brad where they were trying to watch football. "My very favorite in the whole world. And Agnes's is the best of the best."

Glory rolled her eyes and made a face like she had eaten a sour lemon at Don's compliment of Agnes's baking.

An averted her eyes to search around the room for her brother. She caught him sitting atop the pile of old newspapers on the rocking chair. His head was bowed as he stroked the little gray kitten sitting on his lap, purring in contentment. He seemed far away and sad, but An couldn't quite see his face to be sure of his expression. Something seemed amiss with her brother.

On the other side of the room, little Ethan was still under the spotlight of his mother's gaze. Don had come to the rescue, now standing by his grandson to hook an arm around his neck, pulling him away as he said, "Let's go, tiger. Better get out of the kitchen before you get into more trouble."

Marlene shook her head from side to side at her dad's diversion to save Ethan.

"Fine!" she said. "But wipe your face though," she ordered Ethan, then turned in the direction of Grandma June. Cupping her mouth with both hands, she hurled a loud question at Grandma. "WANT PIE, GRANDY?"

Grandy had taken up residence on the far end of the big couch, swaying her upper body and tapping her feet as if listening to some catchy tune in her head. When she didn't answer, Emma—who was sitting by Grandy's feet on the carpet—tapped her on the leg to get her attention.

"SAY WHAT?" Grandy yelled back from across the room, seeming a little startled.

"Pie, Grandy! Do you want some pie?" Marlene repeated the question.

"WHAT?" Grandma screamed back at her.

Marlene sighed in exasperation. "Goodness gracious," she said under her breath. Then yelled louder, trying to penetrate Grandy's hearing range. "PIE, PIE!" The dogs began barking outside at this, joining in the noise and commotion.

"Oh," Grandma June said in a normal, inside voice. "Bye-bye, honey. You don't have to yell so loud, though. Where are you going on Thanksgiving and at this time of day?"

"Jesus, Mary, and Joseph!" Marlene exclaimed, rolling her eyes. "Agnes, just give her a piece of pumpkin with some of that homemade whipped cream of yours, Ethan's slobber and all. She'll never notice. I don't think her dentures can handle the pecan, and she's not crazy about cooked apples."

Pies made An think of her mother, but she tried not to let those thoughts mar this Thanksgiving memory as she appreciated the dynamics of this family, chuckling a little at Marlene and Grandma's exchange.

She had never even told Brad about the pies. Her mother was in a better place, for sure, maybe still enjoying her pies. She hoped anyway. She searched the room again for her brother, wanting his cool reassurance. CJ was still in the same spot, holding MeMe on his lap, but he was looking up now. When her eyes met his, they hugged and comforted each other with their gazes, smiling knowingly from a distance.

"None for me, thanks," she said, more to herself than anyone else.

An waited all evening to catch Marlene by herself again so they could resume their earlier conversation, but she never got the opportunity that day. She found it hard to believe that this fun-loving, down-to-earth family could have such scary skeletons in their closet. She thought she and Brad had opened up about the most important issues in their lives. She thought she knew him. *Why would he not have told me about Gordon?* It seemed like a big deal not to have shared sooner. *What else do I not know?*

They rode home that night in an unsettled quiet. As the day progressed, CJ had gotten more distant and nearly nonverbal by the time they left. An puzzled over it, but she, too, had some disturbing thoughts running through her head so she didn't probe her brother's moodiness. Lulled by the soft music playing in the background and the movement of the truck, An closed her eyes letting the day, snippets of her life, and her unrealized dreams for the future all mingle inside her mind.

When they finally reached the parking lot of her apartment building, CJ was quick to jump out of the car as if his bottom had caught on fire. He hugged his sister fiercely but hurriedly, then said he was tired. It had been a long day, and he was heading home. When they pulled away from the embrace, An watched his back as he walked away from her. She didn't want him to go and had the urge to run after him, but Brad had grabbed her arm and was already gently guiding her away.

That night, curiosity got the better of her. Lying in bed next to Brad, An broached the topic, as gently as she knew how.

"Why didn't you tell me about Gordon, hon? I promise not to judge, and I'm a good listener if you ever want to talk about it."

"I see you've been talking to Marlene. She has a big mouth, and she blows things out of proportion. Be careful talking to her, An. You're too naive sometimes and really need to learn to better discern things."

Brad's words and attitude stung her a little. With her feelings slightly bruised, An went silent, withdrawing within. She felt a small fracture form in the foundation of their still-budding relationship.

"But you do have a brother, Gordon, in prison, don't you?" An asked after a pause.

"Yes, and he was always a big bully, and that's why we've all ripped him out of our lives and never talk about that horrible chapter. Marlene should just keep her mouth shut." Brad turned the lamp off on his side of the bed and gave her his back. "Today was a really nice day. Can we please just focus on the good times and the good memories? Gordon doesn't exist to me. Night, sweetie."

Without answering Brad, An turned her night lamp off too and then slid under the covers. She lay in bed awake for a long time, staring at the dark ceiling as she pondered the day and tried to imagine the future.

An never again said a word about Gordon to Brad, afraid of opening up that can of worms. *Every family has a bad apple in their midst, don't they?* She tried to banish the prickly feeling of discomfort to the back of her mind. Brad was right. They—she—needed to focus on the new memories, on the good times, looking forward and not backwards. Gordon was a closed chapter that should remain just that, buried and closed forever.

Time whizzed by like a shooting star in the time between Thanksgiving and Christmas. Christmas Eve had always been magical in An's mind; it was the heart of Christmas for An and her family. This was the day they had their big dinner if there was one to be had, and the night they opened presents that had covertly appeared under the tree, or under their parents' bed if a tree had not materialized that year.

Their plans were always a little haphazard. It was not an easy feat to coordinate around the holidays, especially with Harrison's "other" family—an aside topic that was always a dicey proposition. The uncertainty and randomness of those days made An feel even more strongly about having a well-organized get-together now. Unfortunately, the stars were not lining up and allowing things to go as planned.

An had tried to reach CJ and coordinate with him their Christmas Eve plans, but he was simply unreachable. She had thought they made progress earlier in the day on Thanksgiving: the laughter, the joy, the sense of togetherness had been there between them as if it had never left. But now they were back to square one. An was worried that something was not well with her little brother, that some discord was percolating. The distance between them—not in time and not in miles, but in a jittery anxiousness churning inside her—was a gaping yawn in her heart.

Brad had been distracted too, needing to spend more time at home with Agnes and the girls. He had explained to An that Alison was drinking heavily again and was neglecting the girls when they were spending time with her. Sometimes, she would disappear for days, and other times, she would lose chunks of time in drunken stupors that lasted hours, days, weeks... who knew.

He was left with little recourse but to go back to court to fight for the girls by denying Alison time with Lynne and Erica every other weekend. The girls were acting out by misbehaving, and Alison had hired an attorney. Things were getting ugly, according to Brad, and he had his hands full.

An understood Brad's preoccupation and his desire to spend time with his daughters, away from her, but missing him spread before her like an eternal ocean she could not cross. She felt helpless and powerless to rescue anyone, including herself. The sense that *family* was slipping from her grasp was like a giant pair of hands wringing her heart until it bled dry.

She stayed busy at work. That wasn't too difficult with so many people suffering from anxiety and depression around the holidays. The little psychologists' office was humming with activity. Moments spent at home were more difficult to fill with thoughts other than Brad and the girls—and CJ. She went through the motions of decorating the little apartment with a Christmas tree and a wreath she made herself with pine branches and cones, and a big red velvet bow to tie it all together. She filled the place with red and green candles: pine-scented and pumpkin-spice-scented ones.

She was starting to wonder if this lonely state of being would throw her over the edge and make her a patient at her own clinic when she finally told herself she needed to snap out of this funk. She needed to take control of the situation, especially as Pop's death anniversary loomed closer. It was less than a week before Christmas, and a change was needed quickly.

She called CJ at the office and left a message with Millie, the receptionist, saying unless he called back, she was stopping by with presents, a Christmas tree, and a steak dinner on Christmas Eve regardless of whether or not she was welcome. She also resolved to tell Brad she wanted them to plan a family dinner with Agnes and the girls. She was simply not going to sit back and wait for him to decide what they were going to do, as was their established practice. She was taking the bull by the horns, and that was that!

That same night CJ called back. He and An had a long conversation that left An in a bigger fog. CJ announced that he was taking a trip to Europe at Christmas, just to get away from everything. He knew An would not have approved, so he had been avoiding her and avoiding the topic of Christmas altogether.

"I don't get it…" she had said, despondent. "Who's in Spain for you? Why Spain? How did you come to want to go there for Christmas? Did you just close your eyes and point at a spot on the map?"

"In a way it was random, yes, but we still have property there, from when Pop used to travel to Spain for business. We—I—still need to figure out what to do with it. A couple of my buddies are going too. I just need to get away. It will do me good."

"What exactly is going on, CJ? None of this makes sense. I thought you had sold that property already. And what buddies? Please talk to me."

"I have friends, An. You don't know every little detail about my life, and frankly, you shouldn't. You're my sister, not my mother or my wife!"

His explosion was a punch in the gut for An. She gasped, insulted. *What the heck is happening?*

"I just feel like we need to be together. It's all still so fresh," she whispered. "And you can't just throw something like this at me. It's not fair."

CJ's voice softened. "I'm sorry. Please don't feel sad, An, please. Just try to understand. I need some space right now, that's all. I'm not trying to be callous, but you have Brad and the girls. Ma and Pop are gone; things are not the same. And maybe I just don't want the same things you do, An. Please don't try to cage me; let me fly just this once."

"Cage you?!" She uttered the words, incredulous. Who was this CJ she didn't recognize? She felt herself slip down the rabbit hole into the topsy-turvy world of Alice again. "I cage you?" she asked no one in particular. Her lips felt cold and numb, her entire body buzzing with fury. The hurt had turned to anger now. "I'm trying to hold our family together, that's all! It's just us now, remember? Just us orphans!"

"Sweet Lord, An, don't be mad at me. I don't know what I'm saying. I'm doing a lousy job of explaining things. But can you please try to understand even if you don't understand it all right now? I'm dealing with some stuff too. I can't go into it just yet."

"What stuff?" she asked. "And why can't you talk about it? I'm your one and only sister, your only family member. You should be able to talk to me!"

"Look, why don't we get together before I leave," CJ told her, completely avoiding her questions. "I want to get a little something for you. We can have dinner and talk more. What do you say? In person, face-to-face, not on the phone."

When An remained silent, trying to process the information and the implication of CJ's words, CJ continued talking, trying to explain, "I'm leaving in a few days, on the twenty-third, day before Christmas Eve in fact, so maybe the day before I go, we can get together?"

An hardly heard what CJ was rattling on about. The buzzing in her ears had grown to a deafening decibel.

He continued, adding insult to injury, choking the air out of her lungs. "I know I'm probably not making a whole lot of sense to you right now, and I'm sorry about that. I know this is a lot to take in, An. But I've given things some thought, and I need a break. I thought I was strong enough to handle the business, but I'm not. I just need to get away. John Jacobs is very capable, and he'll be fine taking over the day-to-day running of the business while I'm gone. We can talk about it more when I see you, but I want to restructure the business some too. Think about location, direction, future..."

He let his words trail to take a breath, as if he had not intended to say so much just yet.

"What! Wait, wait, wait," An told him. "You're not even explaining anything, CJ. You're just talking nonsense."

An was overwhelmed with confusion and burning-hot anger, the cold hurt having left her. This whole conversation was getting stranger by the minute. She couldn't figure out what CJ was trying to tell her or do. This was all so uncharacteristic of him.

"To use one of Pop's favorite phrases, 'what in tarnation are you talking about, CJ?' Yes, Siree Bob, we do need to meet and talk. Let's hold off on this conversation before I lose my mind," she told her brother. "It's sounding to me like you are making long-term, life changing decisions in a way that's alarmingly too sudden. I need to know what's happening and why!"

"I'll try to explain a little better when I see you, but... An." CJ went silent for a long minute as An waited for another shoe to drop. "Let's just keep all this to ourselves. Meaning maybe Brad—or anyone else—doesn't need to know. Okay?"

"Okay," she responded, deflated. "Since I'm pretty lost as to what's going on, I don't think I would know how to talk about it or what to divulge about it anyhow."

After hanging up the telephone with CJ, An pondered their conversation for a long time, trying to get a handle on what might be happening with her little brother. Maybe she had been wrong by disengaging and distancing herself from the business as she had, letting CJ take charge and shoulder the weight. The truth was that she wasn't really interested in running it, and CJ had always seemed entangled in it. Even when Juliet and Harrison were alive and they were growing up, CJ had devoted a lot of time and energy to helping around the shop.

Once their parents died, he appeared to An to be consumed with continuing to grow and expand the bakery. She had wanted him to have it, to run with it, to make it his own dream. She had even forgotten the condo in Spain, which was used mostly for the business as their overseas headquarters or by employees as a getaway vacation home.

As they had expanded internationally into Western Europe, having a place there made sense as the trips there became more frequent. Harrison also used it as a place for him and Jill.

An hadn't given it a second thought as she relinquished her hold on the business to allow CJ more freedom to run it, but she still held an interest in it and retained a small percentage of the ownership. An had not doubted CJ would make it better, stronger, and more successful. But now, everything had changed in a blink of an eye. She had no inkling as to why.

But if CJ was suddenly disinterested, or not in a position to run the family business, then a restructuring had to be considered—maybe even a sale. After some thought, An felt she was open to the possibilities, but she would let CJ sort it out before having any discussions with Brad.

As luck would have it, Brad also called her that night.

"I wanted to surprise you, but then I started thinking that you might make other plans, so I figured I'd better call to tell you I made reservations for us at the Capital Grille at Tyson's for Christmas Eve. Dress up and be ready for an amazing night! What do you say, pretty lady of mine?"

An chuckled at Brad's enthusiasm. Thankful for this distraction, she mustered up every ounce of energy she had left and gathered up every speck of cheerfulness she could spare. "I had no doubt you would come up with something out of this world to make it a special Christmas. I love you so much, Brad."

So it was decided.

Christmas Eve, An dressed in a slick black velvet dress with a slit up one side, exposing her leg all the way to the thigh. Her hair was done, makeup perfectly applied, and a short, black wool coat covered her upper body. She grabbed on to Brad's arm as she carefully traveled the steps from the car to the entrance of Capital Grille.

She had decided to put on hold the entire lengthy conversation she had with CJ a couple days ago. It would have to wait until she could better inspect and deal with all of the implications. They had worked out the major details about the restructuring of the business, and An had made peace with the fact that they were not having a big family dinner on this special day.

She still didn't quite understand CJ's motivation, and she sensed she wasn't being shown the entire picture, but she had decided to try to make peace with it.

She tried to minimize the realization that her life was not going in the direction she had tried to steer it. With a smile planted on her lips and the determination of a bulldog, she tried to just enjoy this time with her beau. They were seated at their table. *I'm just too controlling*, she told herself. *Relax, just relax,* An reassured herself over and over. *It will be what it will be. Just lean into it.*

Her filet mignon was cooked to perfection. The mashed potatoes and sauteed spinach and mushrooms were bursts of yumminess making her taste buds dance. The entire experience took her breath away. Brad had done it again, turned her frown upside down—a phrase he was fond of saying. He was turning her bad memories of this time of year into a brand-new experience.

Creme brûlée arrived for dessert as she was dabbing the corner of her mouth with the black cloth napkin and thinking that her dress felt a bit snug around the waist after all that delicious, rich food.

Brad had planned the meal well, ordering it ahead of time. A bottle of champagne accompanied the dessert. She eyed Brad suspiciously as he fumbled with his inside jacket pocket. As she looked on, puzzled, he finally produced a little black box, which he opened before her.

She gasped.

The glint of the diamond temporarily dazzled and blinded her, or maybe it was the tears behind her eyelids.

"Oh. My. Gosh!" Her eyes were brimming over as she put a hand over her mouth to keep from screaming.

Brad got on one knee clumsily and popped the question without further ado, "My beautiful An, marry me."

She smiled at him, fanning herself.

It was so typical of Brad to frame the question with a period rather than a question mark. He was always so sure of himself. When it came to An, he could always predict her down to a science. And if she didn't react appropriately, he knew just how to mold that reaction into a whole new one. Obviously, he knew without a speck of doubt that her answer would be a resounding "yes!"

"Yes. YES, YES, YES!" The yeses kept tumbling out of her mouth as tears of happiness spilled from her eyes. Pop came to mind right then. She wished he was still there. She imagined him smiling down on her, a proud-Papa look in his eyes.

They both stood up, and An squeezed Brad until he screamed for air. The two waiters that had brought the desserts and champagne were still standing there, smiling from ear to ear. It seemed all eyes in the place were now on them—in a good way.

"Mrs. Antoinette Goode," Brad whispered in her ear. "I can't wait to make it official. You are mine. Forever."

An closed her eyes to savor those sweet words for eternity.

CHAPTER 12
MISSING PIECES: 1992-1993

*"I think perhaps I will always hold a candle
for you—even until it burns my hand. And
when the light has long since gone... I will be
there in the darkness holding what remains,
quite simply because I cannot let go."*
          - Ranata Suzuki

Between that Christmas of 1991 and the wedding in May
1992, An was consumed with planning the ceremony and
reception, buying their new home, and preparing to begin
her new phase in her brand-new life. She was going to be
a wife and a mother all at once! She was thrilled, she was
preoccupied, and she missed all the telltale signs.

CJ had traveled to Spain, fallen in love with it, and
now devoted a lot of his free time to that "paradise," as
he called it. He told An he was captivated by the beauty,
the people, the traditions, and for once in his life, he felt

accepted. An had a nagging feeling that there was a lot more to this story, but she chose to accept CJ's explanation for the time being, in part because she had much too much on her plate.

CJ begged An not to tell anyone where he was, not even Brad. They only communicated through email, through one of the bakery's email addresses. An did not like keeping things from Brad, but she rationalized that Brad had his own secrets. Plus, it wasn't like she was outright lying. She just chose not to talk about CJ to him.

By early spring, CJ was sure he wanted to buy a home in Europe, his own little villa. He seemed distant but content, so An looked no further than the surface. Although An felt estranged from her brother and harbored an intense need to reconcile and reconnect, time slipped away, and the daily grind of life marched on with the issue left unattended on the back burner.

Slowly, the emails became a rare occurrence. An concluded that their parents' deaths, so inopportune and close together, had a lot to do with CJ's behavior, and she was dragging herself—kicking and screaming—to a place of acceptance in her mind and heart. It would be what it would be. She had little to no control over it.

They had had a long productive conversation that Christmas and came to the conclusion that selling the business was probably inevitable, eventually. It appeared that CJ had given it a lot of thought and seemed to have everything under control. The attorneys were already involved to ensure a smooth transition and to be sure the family estate was protected. The properties and a lot of the wealth was controlled and covered under a trust, which Juliet and Harrison had put in motion many years ago.

An was uncomfortable with it, but had agreed to CJ's—as well as the attorneys involved—request that anything related to the business be kept between the two siblings. Not even Brad should be privy to what was happening. CJ had returned for a few days only to attend to business and then returned to Europe. An had been part of the initial meetings with the attorneys and John Jacobs—the longtime, trusted employee who was not only running the business but, along with an anonymous investor, was interested in purchasing the bakery.

It would likely be months in the making, but once the business transferred to its new owners, the proceeds would be divided up between An and CJ and the funds protected in a trust. An wanted to take some of the money to put toward her own family home she and Brad planned to buy, and CJ could use his share to build his new home in Spain and rebuild his life however he chose.

But the bulk of the money could only be pulled out under strict conditions. CJ was adamant about this, despite An's protests that it was not necessary. She trusted him, and so she went along. She hated not being able to get Brad's input and didn't feel good about keeping mum on the topic to him.

This wasn't what An had ever visualized, but it was her reality. She didn't want it, she didn't like it, and she certainly resented her brother for it, but she felt powerless to change it. And a small part of her told her this was how it should be done.

Plus, she was preoccupied elsewhere.

As their wedding day raced toward them, An and Brad had found their dream home; the wedding venue was rented and paid for; An's gown was ready for her last fitting; wedding bands were picked out; the girls were beside themselves with excitement; it was all coming together.

An paid for it all. She and Brad never even discussed it. It was a silent understanding neither dared to add voice to.

A few weeks before the wedding, An was dealt an unexpected blow. CJ told her he would not be returning to the United States for her wedding. She was stunned and hurt.

"Are you ever going to tell me what changed you, CJ?" An asked her brother.

"Maybe someday, An. I can't right now. I'm really sorry, but it has to be this way. Please trust me on this."

So, she did. She had to trust that there was something so dire going on that CJ had to turn his back on her and destroy the family tie there had been.

This forced her to turn to Brad. She didn't divulge where CJ was or any information about the situation with the business, only that CJ needed time away and would not be attending the wedding.

"I already know he's disappeared, An. I also think you have an inkling where he might be and why he hasn't been in the office."

"How do you know that?" she asked him. "I don't know where he is right now, only that he needed to get away for a while and now he says he can't attend the wedding."

"I tried calling a few times just to try to be a friend to him. I thought you might like that, but it seems no one knows where he is or when he'll come back."

An found this revelation strange. They had discussed CJ walking her down the aisle, but Brad had never mentioned any attempt at contacting CJ on his own. Of course, An had been keeping a secret, too, so she didn't push for answers or explanations. She hated being deceitful; it always spelled trouble.

"It breaks my heart that he won't make an attempt to be here to share our day," An told Brad, her voice shaky and tears threatening to spill.

Brad changed his tactics, attempting to reassure her. "Honey, just let him deal with his issues. He will be okay, and when he's ready, he will come back to the fold. We don't have to have him at the wedding. It will be okay. Trust me."

"I just want to understand," she cried. "It's as if I've done something to offend him or hurt him. I feel rejected and punished somehow."

"You're reading way too much into it. It's not about you at all."

But An would not let it go. "I feel there is more. My intuition tells me so."

An was on the verge of letting her emotions get the best of her and spilling the beans to Brad about the business transfer and all the secrecy involved.

But then Brad stopped her with a bombshell of his own. "Stop it, An! You're so innocent and naive sometimes. Just stop pining away over your brother. You really don't know?"

"Know what? What are you hinting at, Brad?"

"There's nothing going on with your brother, other than being a gay man in a scary time to be one."

"What are you talking about? My brother is definitely not gay!"

"Okay, and that is precisely why he would never talk to you about it. You're too prissy and old-fashioned and would judge him and reject him!"

An's indignation could be heard in her voice. "I would NEVER! He's my blood. I don't care about that. There are worse things in life. You are just wrong! WRONG! And I'm not a prissy, old-fashioned, close-minded—whatever you said!"

An's sobs made her appear weak and pathetic to Brad; she knew that. But he kept his thoughts hidden from her.

"An, your brother told me so. He confided in me. He trusted in *me*. You act like the two of you are so close, but you don't even know him!"

"Why the devil would he do that, huh, why?" An's face was splotchy, tears flowing unchecked.

"He needed a friend, and I happened to be there. I listened."

"When was this? Where? Why would he confide in you? He doesn't even know you!"

"I don't want to betray his trust, but I caught him in a rather compromising situation." Brad smiled at An, an insincere smile that wasn't a smile at all—nothing but bared teeth. He shrugged his shoulders for added emphasis, threw his arms up in the air, and gave her his back. "Whatever," he said. "You hear what you want to hear and see only what you want to see anyhow. So, have it your way."

An watched Brad closely. He actually seemed to be enjoying being the messenger of this news, delighting in the conflict, and reveling in the revelation. But why?

"You've already betrayed him," An told Brad, as she walked away from him to compose herself. She never asked him where he had been or prodded for details of the 'compromising situation.' She just wanted to run away and bury her head in the sand. This was too much to digest.

Later that evening, Brad went looking for An. He found her sitting on the living room couch in her pajamas, finalizing the order for the wedding menus and seating arrangement. They only had about fifty guests—mostly Brad's family and friends—so it wasn't much of a chore. He sat next to her, putting an arm around her shoulders, and then forcing her to face him by moving her chin toward him with his thumb and index finger.

"I told you all that about your brother not to hurt you but to protect you, sweetie."

She searched his eyes. "I understand," she told him, but it was a flat-out lie because she really didn't, and his eyes weren't telling her anything at the moment. She simply did not want to engage him. She just wanted to put the whole thing behind her.

"I didn't want you to think you were to blame somehow for his attitude, not coming to the wedding and all," he continued. "I hate to see you suffering. You're too good, and he's being selfish. I love you and don't want to see you sad. You're everything to me, An, everything."

This, An understood. She began crying tears of relief and happiness this time. She decided then that she was going to focus on her wedding, her life with Brad, her future. She would deal with CJ some other time perhaps. Not now.

She stood up in front of Brad to hold his face between her hands, then got on her knees on the couch, straddling Brad to better shower him with kisses. "I adore you, Bradley Goode."

He returned her kisses, fervently, passionately.

"You don't need him, An," Brad told her. "You have me, and you still have your inheritance, right? That's your money, baby. He can't touch it, and he can't take me from you either."

An frowned at this. *What a strange thing to say.* She hugged his neck and hoped he would think the crazy thumping of her heart was desire for him, nothing more.

CJ did not come to the wedding, and neither did Alison. CJ was invited and expected to be there as An's only surviving family member. Alison, however, was not invited but was expected to show up and disrupt this special day. It just seemed to be her way to show up without an invitation and cast shadows on happy gatherings.

Brad had told An not to worry, that he would be carrying his holstered gun. This did little to alleviate An's angst, but she did not voice her true feelings. She waited, crossed her fingers, and hoped all would turn out just fine. But An's worries were unfounded because the wedding day came and went, and there wasn't a hint of Alison. Everything went according to plan, without a hitch. Except that CJ wasn't a part of it.

The ceremony took place in a little historic chapel in Vienna. An looked stunning in her white, form-fitting dress with short sleeves and a heart-shaped bodice. The short train flowed behind her, making tiny ripples when she walked. Her tulle veil was held in place by a small crown of white-and-pink roses, and her hair was held back on the sides by little combs, with the natural waves bouncing down to the middle of her back. She held onto Brad's dad, who had volunteered to walk her down the aisle in the absence of a father or CJ. Despite not having her brother there, An was determined to make this the happiest day of her life. Joy filled her heart.

Peggy was her maid of honor, and Brad's best friend, Miles, was his best man. The girls walked down the church aisle in their pink satin dresses and crowns of baby's breath, a basket of pink rose petals held between them. They beamed at the guests as they threw the petals to the sides, slowly making their way down to the front of the pews.

The reception took place in a rustic and quaint restaurant in nearby Tyson's Corner. On the small dance floor, An—now Mrs. Bradley Goode—laughed until she cried doing the chicken dance. Brad watched and saluted her with his bottle of half-drunk beer. It had been a lovely wedding.

That night, the girls went home with Agnes so Brad and An could drive to the Ritz for the night. After the lovemaking, they cuddled, feeling warm and giddy. An was thankful it had all gone so well. Alison's absence was curious, but An wasn't complaining about missing out on that drama. She did, however, miss CJ like the dickens. She wondered where he was and what he might be doing. Was he thinking about her?

"I noticed Alison hasn't been bothering us for a while now," she said to Brad one day, a few weeks after the wedding. "No sign of her on our wedding day, and I don't think she's taken the girls for a while. You haven't talked about it, but you seem pretty calm."

"I know," Brad retorted. "And it's a good thing for us. I think the last time she had a weekend with the girls was around Easter. I believe she's back in rehab. Works for me."

"Have you talked to her at all? Shouldn't we know for sure?"

"Nope. I'm happy she's out of my hair, that's all. We would all be better off without her around. Plus, not seeing the girls when she's supposed to may be grounds for her to lose her visitation rights altogether."

"Well, I for one don't want to live in limbo, Brad. It's not good for the girls either to have their mother in and out of their lives like this, don't you agree?" An asked, starting to get a little peeved about his nonchalant reaction to the whole situation.

"Stop worrying about it. I'm taking care of it already." Brad seemed annoyed by her questions. "Just let it be," he told her.

In a way, An was relieved and happy to have the girls all to themselves, without Alison lurking in the shadows of their days. Having Alison as a constant threat was stressful. But the not knowing if or when she would return was nerve-racking too. It puzzled An.

Alison might have been an aimless, lost soul, but she did seem to care about the girls. Could she up and leave like that without even saying goodbye to her daughters? And if she went to rehab, why not let Brad know so he could explain it to the girls? Somebody had to know where she was.

As the days became weeks, and weeks turned into months, An pretty much put Alison out of her mind. But just as she had begun to relax, thinking maybe Alison had simply run off, leaving her daughters behind, Alison was back. And she was back with a vengeance. Claiming that Brad had been abusive to her and the girls—both physically and emotionally—and that he had tried to coerce her into giving up her own children.

For months, the fight continued, now with attorneys on both sides involved. Brad kept reassuring An that it was simply a matter of time before they regained full and complete custody of Lynne and Erica. Everyone knew about Alison's drinking and her neglect of the girls. No judge would award her custody. But An was worried sick. For the first six months of their marriage, the fight for the girls kept An and Brad closer than ever as they joined forces to battle a common cause.

Then the unthinkable happened. Alison was awarded joint custody: one week on, one week off. That meant that every other week, An and Brad would be without their girls. For An, this was devastating news. The bond she had formed with Lynne and Erica wasn't any different than if she were their biological mother. She didn't want to live half of her days without them. She was heartbroken.

Alison's family had rallied around her, and she was stronger with her family backing her. She had gotten a little apartment of her own and had found a part-time job at a call center. The hours were flexible and allowed her to spend time with the girls. Brad was paying Alison practically half of his wages in child support, which did not make him a happy camper.

Brad had approached An on a number of occasions to discuss money and how they needed to fund the fight for the girls. He argued that it was high time they take over some—or all—of the reins of the family business. Although tempted, An did not divulge the status of the business, simply offering to help with additional money, which she pulled from her personal funds. This seemed to aggravate Brad more than the actual fight for custody of the girls, but An remained firm on that front.

"I have plenty of money to cover all of our expenses, Brad. Plus, I have a job with a steady paycheck. I don't like to meddle in the affairs of the day-to-day business. That's more CJ's area," she had told him once.

"But CJ isn't around, An, is he?"

When An didn't respond, Brad had pushed, "Do you really know the status of the company?"

"I don't want to know."

"So, you'll just accept being robbed by your own brother or the vultures within the company?"

"Brad!" An had exclaimed. "Relax already! I'm getting my share fair and square."

"As your husband, I think we need to sit down and go over the numbers and the paperwork," Brad had told her. To this, An had given him her back, leaving the room.

"I'll get the money to the lawyers," she had told him as she went.

This conversation repeated itself more times than An liked, but Brad seemed to be appeased with An's ability to come up with large sums of money whenever he complained or flat-out asked for it. An just wanted to keep from a prolonged legal fight over the business her parents had built. She especially didn't want a legal fight with her baby brother.

Although puzzled and angered by Brad's apparent need to control her family business and profits, she was relieved that he was taking the legal fight for the girls better than expected, remaining calm. She was also glad he had his friend, Miles, to powwow with and keep his mind off the injustice of it all.

By all accounts, Alison had not been a good mother, had not even wanted to embrace motherhood, deserting the girls for months on end. She claimed she did it out of fear of Brad and to get counseling and help for her perceived abuse and her drinking problem, but An had her doubts. She simply could not see Brad hurting Alison in any way. *Alison did a good job playing the victim card, though*, An thought. She was extremely believable.

Then one summer day in late June, a little over a year following the wedding, when Alison was due to get the girls from their ballet class, she was a no-show. Being the backup, An got the call.

Weeks went by, and there was no word from Alison. No one had seen or heard from her. An worried, but Brad reassured her that Alison was just being Alison. She would turn up when it was convenient for her. As for their case, Brad told An this was perfect. Showing her true colors by disappearing and leaving the girls yet again, Alison had put a nail in her own coffin as far as custody of the girls was concerned.

Two months passed and still no word from Alison. She had not been seen at her apartment. She had not reported to work. Her family had no idea where she was. Her little beat-up Honda Civic sat in her apartment parking lot collecting dust, undisturbed.

Her pocketbook was left behind with all of her personal belongings, including cash and her driver's license. Nothing was disturbed. It was as if she just disappeared off the face of the earth without a trace.

Although disconcerting and troublesome, it was not totally unexpected when the authorities approached An one day. Two investigators cornered her as she was leaving work to pick up the girls from after-school camp. They had gymnastics classes that afternoon, so she was leaving early to get the girls there on time, then home for dinner. She was preoccupied with these thoughts as she was leaving her building.

"Mrs. Goode?" the man wearing khakis and a lavender dress shirt under a tweed jacket asked as he approached An's side just as she was about to reach her parked car in a spot directly in front of her office.

It was the end of October, and it had been raining most of the week; it felt more like winter already than early fall. Although the rain had finally subsided, it was overcast and dreary out. The clouds overhead were sometimes just wisps of cotton-candy swirls with spots of blue for a background, but then—like this moment—the sky would suddenly turn ominously dark with thick gray clouds heavily sitting overhead.

An turned abruptly to look at the gray-haired man who had so swiftly come to stand beside her like an apparition. His face was marked by acne scarring, and he had dark bags under his eyes as if sleep was a rare commodity in his world. He was tall and imposing, and his nose was a little red. On second examination, An concluded that he either had a cold or was hitting the bottle of bourbon a little too hard lately.

A second man was approaching. He was also tall, but thinner compared to the first man. He was as good-looking as a movie star—resembling Kevin Bacon, actually. He wore starched, creased blue jeans and a white dress shirt peeking under a lightweight jacket with the sleeves rolled up. He was younger and sported a goatee.

"Yes?" An answered with suspicion in her voice, her eyes guarded but alert. "Who wants to know?"

"Detective Burbage. This here is Detective Mantyka," he said, throwing his right thumb casually behind him. The detectives did not smile or offer any pleasantries. They got right to the point. "We're investigating a missing person's report and wondered if we could have a few minutes of your time."

"Of course, but I have to pick up my children from daycare shortly. A missing person, you say? Who's missing?" An asked the question, but of course, the image of Alison came to mind.

"We understand, ma'am. This should only take a few minutes. Otherwise, we'll have to inconvenience you further with a trip to the police station. I don't think you want that."

"Sure," An told him impatient but curious too. "I have a few minutes." She had hoped to make a quick stop at the supermarket, but now she would have to lug the girls with her or wait for tomorrow.

"This is in reference to Alison Goode, formerly Alison Kowinski."

"That's my husband's ex-wife."

"Yes, ma'am. Her family has been unable to locate her for the past couple months. Her mother reported her missing. We're looking into it."

An was shocked. "My understanding is that she just disappears every now and then but eventually comes back. Missing! No, I don't think so."

"We have heard that same sentiment from others, but her mother seems to think it's different this time, says her daughter was making real progress cleaning up her act. It may just mean she doesn't want to be found. Alison, that is, but we still have to do our due diligence."

"Yes, of course. But I don't think I can be of much help, Detectives? I didn't really know her? As far as I know my husband hasn't been in contact either? You should talk to him, not me, actually."

"We have already talked to him, Mrs. Goode. Your husband, that is. Just the other day," Detective Burbage told her.

"You have?" An was surprised at this nugget of information. It appeared Brad had kept this meeting a secret from her. An wondered why he didn't mention it. They had had a conversation about Alison a few days back when An questioned Brad why Alison wasn't getting her visits with the girls.

"Yes, indeed. We had a nice little chat. It seems he didn't share with you, huh?"

"No, he didn't," An said absently, chewing the inside of her right cheek.

"Tell us about the last time you saw Ms. Kowinski. Anything you can think of. Sometimes a detail that seems unimportant may actually be significant," Detective Burbage explained. He had a deep booming voice with a slight lisp. His Adam's apple bobbed up and down pronouncedly as he spoke.

An looked at him quizzically, making direct eye contact. She pondered what he had said before she found her voice to answer him.

"I don't really see her or interact with her unless it somehow relates to the girls? I wanna say I saw her last back in May or June? Yes, early June. The girls had a recital; they do ballet. I went. I saw Alison there, briefly."

"Did she talk to you?" Detective Burbage asked.

"No. It was our week to have the girls so we would be taking them home? I didn't see Alison at the end of the recital, so I assumed she just left early. The girls would have liked to see her, though."

"Did that seem unusual to you? The fact that she left early, that is."

"No, not really. Like I said, it wasn't her week."

"There were no other visits or phone calls with the children?" Detective Burbage asked.

An thought about it for a minute. "No. But, a few weeks later when she was supposed to pick up the girls, she was a no-show."

"So was that the last time she had contact with the children?" Detective Burbage had asked the question again, while Detective Mantyka listened with interest, but remained quiet.

"Well, she picked them up the following week when it was her week. Then we had them, but Alison did not get them that last week in June, when it would have been her turn with the girls. That's as far as I can recollect."

"So, how was the relationship between the three of you? Did you get along?" This time Detective Mantyka interjected. Detective Burbage had taken a break to sneeze multiple times. An counted five sneezes while trying to focus her attention on Detective Mantyka.

"Whew, excuse me!" Detective Burbage said. He pulled out a handkerchief from his pants pocket and blew his nose loudly.

"God bless you!" An told him before answering the other detective. "Like I said, Detective, I never really talked to her. There was virtually no relationship. My husband doesn't like that she neglects the girls, so he gets frustrated sometimes. He feels the girls would have better stability if Alison didn't have them half the time—and I tend to agree," An concluded.

"Allergies, Detective?" she said, looking in the direction of Detective Burbage.

"No, I think it's just a damn lingering cold," he told An. "This weird weather is causing havoc in my system."

"Okay," Detective Mantyka said, ignoring the comments on allergies, colds, and weather phenomena. "So, let me get this right. Your husband and his ex-wife are in a custody dispute, right? And you're not happy with the situation. Seems to me you both would be better off without Alison around. And so would the girls. Would you say that's accurate?"

An frowned at this, eyeing one and then the other detective. They didn't smile or show any outward emotion, just kept poker faces as they waited for her answer. She cleared her throat, uncomfortable with how the conversation had suddenly taken a turn. It felt as if they had twisted her words somehow.

"There's no dispute. We share the girls fifty-fifty," An told him, defensively. "Neither one of us are happy about Alison being in and out of the girls' lives. It's difficult for all of us."

The detectives continued to look at An as if expecting more even when she had gone silent. Then Detective Burbage decided to veer off onto a different tangent.

"Have you ever seen them interact? Ms. Kowinski and your husband, that is."

An had the image of Brad and Alison fighting outside Agnes's house the first time An had gone there to visit, but she didn't share that with the detectives. She had also listened in on one or two telephone conversations that ended with Brad calling Alison some rather unpleasant names that would make even these seasoned detectives' ears singe a little. An also chose to keep this to herself.

"Yes, I heard them talking once or twice. They seemed civil. I never heard anything too horrible from my husband. I mean, they are divorced and have kids together, so things can get nasty sometimes. But Brad always tries to take the high road. He always tries to put the girls first, you know?

"I also know that Alison was out of control a lot due to her drinking problem? Once she tried to run my husband over in Ohio at his dad's farm. I don't want to speak ill of her or anything, but she's just a little on the unstable side? That's just my opinion."

The detectives had been listening, nodding their heads, encouraging An to go on and allowing her to speak her mind. Detective Mantyka had pulled out a pen and small notepad and had been writing on it every now and then.

"Right, right," Detective Burbage said knowingly.

"Did you see this firsthand, Mrs. Goode? The incident in Ohio, I mean," Detective Burbage asked.

"Oh, no, no. Brad told me the sordid details."

"So, what do you believe happened to Alison?" Detective Mantyka asked An.

"I think she just left. She wanted a fresh start, maybe? She's done it before so it's not unthinkable."

"You think she would leave her girls after fighting so hard for custody?" Detective Burbage wanted to know.

"Well, my understanding is that she has a drug and alcohol problem. Maybe that's a stronger urge?" An shrugged her shoulders as she explained this, eyebrows raised in question. "It's just a guess."

"What does your husband think? About what happened to his ex-wife, I mean."

"He doesn't know but speculates something similar. But you talked to him already. What did he tell you?"

"He thinks she ran off or something bad happened related to her drinking," Detective Burbage shared.

"Do you think it's possible she met with foul play, An?" Detective Mantyka asked this time.

"I'd hate to think it, but maybe?" Although there was a little breeze in the air now, An felt sweat pricking on her scalp and heat rising to her upper body. Her mind was wandering to uncomfortable places. Why hadn't Brad mentioned an encounter with the police? Where was Alison? Did Brad know something, or worse, did he have something to do with her disappearance? This was unthinkable to her, yet the thought had taken shape in her mind.

"Would it be alright if we followed up with you in case we have more questions, Mrs. Goode?" Detective Burbage asked An.

"Yeah, sure. But I don't know what else I can tell you. I didn't know her, nor did I interact with her. The girls barely talk about her."

"Like Detective Burbage here said, sometimes you know more than you think you know, An," Detective Mantyka told her. "Bits of critical information sometimes hide in unknown little crevices in your mind. Eventually, it may come to you. And even if it's just a nagging feeling or an opinion, just give us a call. We want to know."

"Okay," An said. "I will certainly keep that in mind and call you if I think of something or remember something."

"As a mom yourself, I'm sure you can relate to how frantic Ms. Kowinski's mother is right now. And also, as a mom you must understand how this is affecting the children," Detective Burbage added. "If you know anything, Mrs. Goode, anything at all related to Alison's disappearance, you need to do the right thing."

"Yes, of course," An whispered, her head bowed and her eyes on the black pavement. *Do the right thing,* she thought.

The detectives handed An their cards. Detective Mantyka thanked her for her cooperation, and then they were gone. An got in her car but didn't drive off for a long few minutes. The detectives knew something she didn't. An sensed this very poignantly. And Brad was keeping secrets. Something wasn't right. She sensed this even more acutely, deep in her gut. What should she do? What should she say to Brad?

In the end, she did nothing, said nothing, other than addressing the topic with Brad very briefly.

At home that night, her thoughts were scattered. She watched Brad, waiting for him to say something, explain something, acknowledge something, darn it! She watched him at dinner as he chewed his chicken cutlet, mashed potatoes, and peas. He cut his meat in tiny, precise bites, stabbed two or three pieces with his fork before bringing it to his mouth. Then he chewed slowly and meticulously. Everything in her world that night had become magnified and played in slow motion.

Later, she watched Brad as he galloped on his knees around the spacious basement play area after dinner, giving the girls horsey-back rides. He heed and hawed, kicking his back leg every now and then. The girls giggled, begging for more. He ruffled their little heads and gave them raspberries on their smooth tummies. An watched, so enamored with the man, yet so puzzled by him. *He could never have hurt anyone,* she thought to herself. *He marches to his own drummer sometimes, but deep inside, he's just a gentle soul. He would not have touched a hair on Alison's head, never!*

An waited for him that night, staring at the ceiling, as he tucked the girls in. It had been her night to bathe them and his night to tuck them in, and then he was reading in the bathroom as part of his personal time routine. Normally, she would be fast asleep by the time he finished his daily readings in solitude and climbed into bed next to her, but tonight, she waited as sleep failed to arrive.

When he finally crept into bed, she immediately turned to him. "The police came to talk to me about

Alison's disappearance," she said, breathless as her heart hammered in her chest.

"Oh, really?" he said without emotion.

"Did they talk to you, too, Brad? Why didn't you tell me?"

"Oh, yeah, they did. It was just a few days ago. It must have slipped my mind. I don't like scaring you or bugging you about these things."

OH, REALLY? OH, REALLY? IT EFFING SLIPPED YOUR MIND? WHAT THE HELL! An was screaming in her mind, but outwardly she said, "How could you not have at least warned me, Brad? This is a big deal if Alison really is missing. Don't you care? Aren't you worried, scared out of your wits?"

"Why would I be? She does it all the time. She's unstable, she drinks, she does drugs. I'm glad she's away from my daughters!"

"But, Brad, what if something did happen to her this time? That's your daughters' *mother*!"

"No," Brad said, turning to her, propping himself on one elbow to face her. "*You* are my daughters' mother now," he said as he stabbed a finger on her chest. "Don't ever forget it, and don't ever let me down."

An was awake in the darkness for hours after that as her heart thumped away. *What had just happened, for the love of God?* she thought. She couldn't shake the conversation with the detectives, nor the conversation with Brad, out of her mind. Where was Alison, and did something bad happen to her?

Brad snored like a bear beside her, without a care or a fear in the world, while An lay in bed, her eyes burning a hole in the ceiling. Sleep eluded her. Her dream landscape was barren and desolate. She pictured Alison, who was gone. No one knew where. She pictured CJ, also gone. To Spain or somewhere far from her, who knew where exactly. She pictured Pop and Ma, even further away from her to the unknown land of the afterlife. She pictured Lynne and Erica's precious faces, who were still here. She loved them. She would be here for them; she would protect them and take care of them.

They belonged to her.

And she was their mother.

It was not clear to An what exactly happened to the closeness she and CJ had shared. It seemed that overnight everything changed; everything became nebulous and uncertain, as if while An slept, that detestable Christmas Grinch materialized and stole away all the laughter, the memories, the togetherness. *Poof!* It was gone. In its place, a foreign uncomfortableness, an awkward void settled in.

For years, An tried to wrap her brain around what happened, yet always felt blind and powerless to what should have been clear and indisputable before her.… Looking back, she would liken it to what happened between her and the girls later on. Except that with the girls, the same sense of incredulity and disbelief was there, but the why had been clear as day from the get-go. An knew what had happened, how it happened, what should have been done, what could have been done… She knew she had failed them horribly, and yet she felt ineffectual in patching up the damage. She had soothed herself with self-pity and guilt instead.

With CJ there was no understanding; therefore, no amount of guilt or regret could have assuaged the despair An felt. She had grieved for the loss of him, their shared history and togetherness. She grieved for the friend she had lost, the brother she loved, his presence in her life. But she could not, would not, accept his blatant rejection.

So, An had persisted in her attempt at communication with him while he persisted in pulling further and further away from her, until finally, he physically put distance between them by moving hundreds of miles away, to a whole other country, across a vast and bottomless ocean. How could she have competed with that? How could she have reeled him back in? While trying to build a home, get to know her new husband, raise two young daughters, her brother and stabilizer was abruptly gone from her.

It seemed to An that all had been well the day they went to Agnes's home for Thanksgiving. Whatever it was that happened or changed between her and CJ was born that day. An had relived it over and over in her mind, trying to find the clues that eluded her.

She had enjoyed the family banter that day: the chatter of the kids, the delicious food, the laughter, the sense of coziness, the feeling, the indescribable warmth inside of her… that this was what she had always wanted, what she was born for. She hungered for it. She reveled in it. She was happy that day. She felt complete.

An wanted to belong.

Had she missed a clue?

Throughout that time, whenever An had made eye contact with CJ, his eyes twinkled, and he smiled warmly back at her. He, too, had seemed happy, comfortable, at ease. Or did An just want to believe those things? Had she seen only what she wanted to see as Brad later accused?

At some point, all the men had gone outside—including Ethan. The women stayed in and tried to clean up, careful not to disturb the disorder that was Agnes's home. Don and Ethan were the first ones back inside. An remembered feeling giddy at the thought that Brad and CJ were still out there, bonding she had hoped. An wanted them to like each other, and she wanted them to be friends. She had visions of family gatherings with the two men in her life, always there, keeping things harmonious and balanced. Yet, if there was a moment in time when things shifted, it had to have been that very moment.

Because when Brad and CJ returned, CJ seemed perturbed, his eyes hooded.

An had noticed the difference and was quick to find a moment to ask CJ if everything was okay with him. Brad seemed unchanged, untouched, unruffled, so why was CJ the only one looking guarded and sad?

"Everything okay, Little Brother?" An had inquired in a near whisper.

"Yeah," he had answered flatly.

"You seem so serious suddenly," An had told him.

"Brad and I had a serious conversation about family and life. It tired me out a little, I guess," CJ had explained. "I'm fine. Everything's fine." CJ had reassured An.

At the time An had bought the explanation hook, line, and sinker and let it go with merely a shake of the head. It seemed to make sense to her. She had looked up from where she and CJ had been standing and noticed Brad watching them with a smirk. Brad had given An a little wave from across the room and winked at her, looking confident and pleased with himself. That cocky confidence had been one of the many things An found attractive about Brad. He was always so at ease with himself and his surroundings. An envied that control and assurance. She had waved back, feeling the warmth and love return. She was safe. This was a loving, fun family. They had their flaws and quirkiness, yes, but they were a good bunch. An was sure of it.

Looking back now, through the eyes of years of distance, she wondered how she could have gotten so much wrong. Through the lens of time, she found it hard to accept how she had ignored all that, letting the clues pass her by, looking with blind eyes, for the sake of what? The idea of love? The need for family?

What was reality and what was truth got so contorted and twisted out of shape at times. Sometimes An questioned whether truth and reality were even a thing. Perhaps, it was all just perception—her perception. And perception had no bounds and no shape; it took on a different form for each person.

The drive back home that Thanksgiving night had been eerily quiet. Brad had held An's hand, which rested on the middle console of his Ford pickup. His rubbing of the back of her hand had felt reassuring and lulling. The radio had been playing some country station in the background. An had closed her eyes and let go of the world around her. Aside from the music and Brad clearing his throat every now and then—a strange habit of his—there was no other sound inside the car. CJ was quiet and motionless in the backseat, already gone from An; she just hadn't quite known it yet.

When they had gotten back to Vienna, CJ was like a scalded animal jumping out of that backseat. He was quick to mumble a thank you and proclaim his exhaustion. With a hurried hug and no eye contact, he disappeared into the night, toward his own car. An was fairly certain that whatever changed happened that night because she couldn't remember anything being quite the same between them ever again.

An didn't know. She didn't know then what she came to know later. And the knowing deeply hurt and damaged her.

An had many favorite memories of CJ as they were growing up. One of those was the day An had carelessly picked up one of her mother's prized bowls brimming with fresh fruit to bring to the dinner table. She had been reading *Little Women* in the sunroom and was utterly annoyed when her mother had yelled for her to bring the bowl of fruit she had arranged earlier in the day, to the dining room where she and Harrison were sitting together discussing business. They had all finished polishing off a large pepperoni pizza they had brought home for a rare dinner together. Afterwards, An had escaped to pick up reading where she had left off.

An was thinking about why her mother didn't get the darn bowl herself. They were going to eat the fruit, not her! Why were they home and not at work this evening anyhow? She had grabbed the bowl and twirled out of the kitchen in a huff. Just as she crossed the threshold and turned into the butler's pantry leading into the dining room, the bowl slipped out of her hands and tumbled to the tiled floor. She blamed it on the weird energy, like a giant hand that had tapped that bowl right out of her hands. She watched in utter horror as a pink Gala apple and two tangerines rolled away to rest a couple of feet in front of her; fat, purple grapes bounced everywhere. And the shards of hand-painted pottery glared up at An, shiny broken pieces of glossy white with little bits of red and yellow.

Crap, crap, crap, I am so busted, she thought.

At that very moment, CJ had come running toward An from the sunroom, and Ma and Pop had stumbled out of the dining room to stand there watching An and the disaster she had created. Juliet glared at her daughter, slowly shaking her head and looking very displeased with the scene. Pop sported a well-well-well kind of smile.

"You okay, Sugar?" Pop had asked An. To which An had shaken her head yes, but continued to stare at her mother, fearing Jules's angry unspoken words. CJ stood by An's side.

Juliet's eyes were squeezed into little slits. "You, young lady…" she spat at An. An had gulped involuntarily.

"It was me, Ma! I bumped her!" CJ announced out of the blue.

Huh? An turned to him wondering what in tarnation he was saying. It most definitely was not him.

An had turned to watch CJ in awe and puzzlement. Her twelve-year-old mind reeled as her baby brother had just made himself a target of their mother's wrath, taking the proverbial sword for An.

Juliet had then turned her gaze slowly toward CJ, lips pursed. "Have you any idea how much that bowl cost? Do either one of you have an inkling of its sentimental value to me?" She said this in an alarmingly low and controlled voice, each word overly enunciated.

An gulped again and searched for Pop to intervene, quick! But Harrison had turned and was walking away from them because he knew Juliet's anger well, and he had never learned how to handle that side of her. An continued to stare at her mother's contorted expression, noting every little detail, afraid CJ would recant his proclamation of guilt at any moment now, out of fear, and then she'd be on the receiving end of Juliet's fury.

"You!" Juliet had turned to An. "Clean up this mess and stay out of my sight."

Juliet had then turned her attention back to CJ. "This is what carelessness gets you, Mister. Get the belt and wait for me in your room."

As soon as An could, she ran to find Pop and plead with him to stop the carnage that was surely taking place upstairs. "It was an accident, Pop. She's being totally unfair to CJ. Help him!"

Harrison had retreated to the safety of his office, crossed feet up on the edge of his desk as he reclined back. He held a Cohiba between his thumb, pointer, and middle finger. Rings of thin smoke danced around his head. He looked at An with knowing eyes as she stood there breathless, pleading her case or, more accurately, CJ's case.

"You want to discuss the merits of fairness in life, do you now, sweetie pie?" he said to his daughter. An stood rigid and mute, eyes bugged out of her head. An's cheeks grew suddenly hot. Her outrage and indignation walked right out the door at his tone of voice.

"You had the power to stop your brother's punishment in its tracks, and you chose silence," he continued. "*Someone* was careless and destroyed a valuable item that meant a great deal to your mother. *Someone* needs to be punished for it. Period, the end."

An quietly skulked away in shame, knowing her father knew that *she* had been despicable, which meant Juliet probably knew too. This was worse punishment for An than the belt. She detested Harrison's logic sometimes.

After taking the belt to CJ, Juliet had gone on to bed, exhausted, An imagined. An had snuck up to check on CJ later that night. He showed her the red welts on his back and smiled proudly.

"I will never let her see my tears," he told An. "But I did cry a little after she was gone because it hurt like heck."

"You are amazing," An whispered. "You didn't have to take the blame, you know. You did nothing wrong. I was the one who broke Ma's bowl. I deserved the belt."

"I'm just stronger than you," he told An simply. "You would have cried in front of her. Crying makes you weaker and her more powerful."

An didn't give CJ's words much thought or weight back then. She was twelve, and he was ten. What did they know about anything? What did *he* know about perceived weakness and sense of power? Much later, An came to admire her little brother's strength, how he refused to give their mother—or the world—the satisfaction of seeing him cry, denying anyone any vestige of power over him.

An admired how well CJ wore his tough-guy suit for the entire universe to see. Yet underneath it all, he was a gentle soul, a kind and sweet man she was proud to call her brother. An admired the fact that despite wearing that heavy tough-guy suit, he was still in touch with the man inside. As hard as she tried, she could never be the strong, wise, capable human being that CJ was.

That so-long-ago moment had survived the ravages of time for An because of the perceived act of heroism from her brother for her. It was possibly the first conscious memory that An had of CJ taking care of her and protecting her from harm. It would not be the last time he purposely put himself in harm's way to shield An. That was why it seemed so foreign and contradictory to An that he would reject her and distance himself from her without an utterance of explanation, right as she was embarking on one of her biggest life voyages.

Removing himself from An's life was the equivalent of removing a protective rampart from her world. She felt exposed, vulnerable, and defenseless to any attack.

Had CJ realized that?

It hurt An to think of CJ so far away. He was always a giver and a pleaser, his role one of reconciliation and consolation. He was strong, he was present, he was An's Superman. An had recounted every instance involving CJ from that Thanksgiving night to the day he left for Spain. For years she had relived and reinvestigated each moment but found nothing that explained his abrupt absence from her life. Not until so much later.

An recalled the night she and Brad fought over CJ, Brad insisting he had caught CJ in a compromising situation that appeared to suggest CJ had a gay lover. Could this be part of the puzzle? Why CJ felt he had to cut ties and leave like that? It would not have mattered to An. It would not have changed the fact that he was her baby brother, and she loved him to pieces. But An simply did not believe this was the case. Yet what reason did Brad have to make up such a story? Why Brad refused to elaborate on the "compromising situation" added yet another layer to the growing mystery.

Her brother had become a stranger overnight. Why had this happened? What had occurred to change CJ in such a way? He was mum on the topic, and An had been unable to decipher any of it on her own. At a loss,

An had tried to accept it, albeit not very gracefully. Like a stalker, she had hounded him. She called the office incessantly, she followed him, she made unexpected trips to his apartment to the business. She had begged and pleaded for an explanation. But, in his calm and collected voice, he kept explaining that this was his life, his choice, nothing more. He tried to keep An calm. He explained that he would return when he was ready. He told An to just give him his space for a while, that he would be in touch when he could or when it was necessary.

Lies. They were all lies, it turned out. He had no intention of coming back into An's world, and he certainly could not have An in his.

Right before Christmas, preceding CJ's departure to Spain—as it turned out, Spain was not his final destination at all, though at that point An didn't know this—An and CJ had gotten together for a pleasant meal. It turned into a long conversation that settled a lot in regards to the business, but did little to clarify the rest of the puzzle. An had no choice but to accept what she had no control over.

For that moment, "that last supper" as she often referred to it, An had her brother back. They talked about the old days and their childhood memories. An reminded CJ of the broken bowl incident, and they both had a good chuckle about it. It felt good to bask in CJ's light that last time.

They had hugged for a very long time, and CJ had kissed the top of An's head as they were saying goodbye.

"Be safe, Little Brother," An had said in a quiet voice to hide her emotions. Because talking in a normal voice would surely expose An's true feelings and possibly open up the gates of suppressed tears and raw emotions. He'd pulled away to look into An's eyes and seemed on the verge of some revelation, An had thought, *Say it, say it!* encouraging him from the private confines of her thoughts. But he hadn't. A dark, sad look had covered his features, and he broke eye contact.

The moment was lost.

"I can't protect you anymore, An," he told her.

"Do I need some kind of special protection?"

"This is it. This is the only way I know to keep us both safe," he'd declared ominously.

"What are you saying? Can we just speak English here?" She had felt a little frustrated with this code-speak of his.

"Nothing," he had said. "I'm sorry, just being dramatic. You know me."

And just like that, Little Brother was on his way to some new life, somewhere across the Atlantic. An had waved goodbye from inside her car and driven away choked up by the tears strangling her.

An hoped to see him again one day, but feared that was the last time they would lay eyes on each other.

CHAPTER 13

MY ALBATROSS: 1995

*"I might enjoy being an albatross, being
able to glide for days and daydream for
hundreds of miles along the thermals. And
then being able to hang like an affliction
round some people's necks."*

- Seamus Heaney

Looking back to the beginning, it was hard to remember
a time without Brad, a time An didn't feel compelled to
cherish him and put him on a pedestal, a time when she
didn't feel the need to protect him. An was absolutely
devoted to him. Whether he deserved her affection and
adoration was quite debatable. Funny, how time changed
one's perspective. Looking at her rearview mirror of time
with Brad, An questioned whether what she felt for him
was even love. In the beginning, she admired him and
looked up to him. His word was infallible, his character
unquestionable. To her, he was handsome, smart, strong,
and wise beyond imagination. He captivated her with his

words, his stories, the way he carried himself: so easygoing, so confident and fearless, so in control.

An often referred to him as her knight in shining armor. He took away her despair and turned it into hope, her doubts into trust. He made her feel safe, more confident, more in control of herself... or so she thought.

But did she really experience those things, or did she just pick and choose what she thought she should feel? Could feelings simply be fabricated? An's best friend, Peggy, was fond of saying, "You can't change what you feel!" An used to agree. Now she questioned it.

People sometimes convinced themselves they should feel a certain way because they really wanted to or because they thought they should. Perhaps An did feel love for Brad then, and now that their love was dead, she wanted to explain it away, pretend it never existed. It was a curious thing: love, memory, time, life, all of it.

You would think that once the truth came out of the shadows and into the light, An would see everything painted on a different palette, and then she'd be released from the shackles tying her to Brad. But it had the opposite effect. The more daring he got, the more destructive, the more outrageous he became... well, the more An wanted to hold on. More and more, she became mired in the yesterdays, what could have been, and what should have been. What she wanted it to be.

Oh, how she told people she had a special bond and a fairy-tale life. And, to think, she had actually believed it! She believed, even when it had become a complete open lie. When things began to change—or was it that An's vision began to clear?—she refused to accept the new faces of Brad that were being revealed to her. She couldn't, wouldn't, believe that this man, her husband, the love of her life, was not the man she thought he was. To believe would mean that her perfect home, her beautiful life, everything that was An herself, was a sham, a farce, a fake.

An was fond of saying that she loved Brad unconditionally. She adored his girls, adored his family. She adopted his way of life as her own. She basked in the sunshine that was Bradley Emerson Goode. As the essence of her very being shrank and shriveled, An became an extension of him. How did a seemingly normal, smart, educated woman disappear from herself to be engulfed and devoured by another? An had no good explanation as to why. Other than that she hungered for a life that was a figment in her own imagination, so she tried to force the pieces together even when they didn't fit.

On An's wedding day, as she and Brad were moving the last of their belongings into their new home on Orchard Lane, a dove so pristine and perfect—pure white—had landed between them. Its head had swiveled to look at An, then at Brad, then back to An. Was it questioning something? Was it delivering a warning of some kind? An had decided to interpret it as a good omen at the time.

"It's a sign of all the good things to come," she had said to Brad. He'd remained silent, his attention riveted on the piece of furniture he was carefully picking up from the back of his truck.

"Uh-huh," he had mumbled, eyeing the bird with suspicion, maybe even fear. "Just don't touch it. Birds are dirty. They carry all kinds of diseases."

Ignoring his admonition, An had said, "He's so beautiful. Look at him! I'm sure it's a sign of love, peace, and goodwill. You have to agree; he's beautiful!"

The dove then took flight and disappeared as swiftly as it had appeared between them. It had been a cloudless May morning. Birds chirped away, and An's new front yard had already begun to bloom: orange lilies and blue and purple chrysanthemums. Splotches of color framed their soon-to-be life, together as one. In about five hours, they would be Mr. and Mrs. Bradley Emerson Goode. An had felt shocks of happiness and awe radiate up and down her spine. She had only good expectations that day.

Without another word, Brad carried the rickety rocking chair, held together by some old twine, into the new home. His maternal grandfather—whom Brad had been named after—had made the chair. Brad's mother, Agnes, claimed it once the elder Brad had passed away. It had remained in Agnes's living room—from one home to another—for two decades, mostly serving as a perch for her many animals or as a repository for a potted plant or a stack of books. Brad had asked his mother for it so that he could refurbish it and bring it back to life to have it be one of his and An's cherished pieces of furniture in their new home.

He carried the chair gingerly, tenderly, in his arms, crossing the threshold into their lovely new home. He had chosen the library as its new residence. Typical of Brad, the chair would sit in its new corner, decrepit and lonely, awaiting its facelift, while he researched the best way to repair it. For nearly two years, it sat to the right of the fireplace, awaiting new nails, sandpaper, and paint. To show a little gratitude for the thing, An had bought a large bright yellow-orange-and-red striped pillow to be its companion. She had tucked it safely between one of its arms.

An and Brad had bought the house on Orchard Lane, and settled on it, three months prior to their wedding day, which was to be their official move-in date: May 21, 1992. It was certainly *their* house, their dream home, but An had paid for the large down payment with money she had inherited from her parents. She viewed their new home as a gift from them, and it made her feel closer to her parents and made the house extra special. She never envisioned living in any other place. This was her forever home. Her Pop would have approved, and Ma would have loved it.

Although it was not the intoxicating feeling of being in love An remembered most about Brad when she looked back, love him she did, with all of her heart. There were numerous times—even after the transformation had begun—when An would find herself watching Brad, admiring his profile. He might be reading, or working on a project, or watching television, unaware of her watchful eyes. She remembered thinking how lucky she was to be his wife. Most mornings, she awoke with the sense of having a blessed life.

The dichotomy that was Bradley Goode was one of the things that actually kept An by his side all those years. She was sure of it now. Because the darkness came in shades of gray, always interspersed with specks of gold. That's the story she liked to put forward anyhow. When it started to become clear to An that there was a different Brad underneath the façade, she fiercely held on to the Brad she thought she knew and had married.

One of her most endearing memories of Brad was the night she had fallen asleep on the couch downstairs in the den watching TV. An was notorious for falling asleep as soon as her head hit something, preferably—and normally—Brad's chest. A pillow was her second-best choice.

After eating dinner and putting the girls to bed, they had often headed downstairs to watch a movie. That particular night, Brad was sitting cross-legged on the floor to clean one of his handguns, and An had placed her head down on the arm of the couch, watching him and half watching television. With her head cradled, she was soon out like a light.

When her eyes had fluttered open and she surfaced to consciousness, it was just in time to see Brad carefully putting a pillow under her head and tucking a blanket around her. He then pulled a stray hair away from An's forehead and kissed it. He had turned the lights out as he went. It had been such a tender moment that An simply let the tears of joy flow once he was out of sight. *My sweet husband*, she had thought then.

But a mere few months after that intimate, loving gesture—and barely three years into the marriage—Brad had arrived home with a bombshell.

With raven-haired Melodie and her child in tow, Brad announced that they were currently homeless and needed a safe place to stay for a little while.

"She has nowhere to go, honey," he told An. "Please be understanding and let her and her boy stay with us. I promise it will be for just a short time."

An had a gazillion questions and was very unsettled. Although baffled and unsure of the whole situation, she was still trusting: trusting of Brad and trusting of the entire world. Despite An's trepidations, she agreed.

Melodie and her son moved into An's home.

Melodie was petite all over, with well-manicured tiny hands and feet. Wild dark hair flowed to her waist. Doe-eyed with honey-colored irises, she had a clean, no-makeup, kind of beauty. An was conflicted about Melodie. She wanted to hate her, yet she found herself liking the young woman. It was certainly strange having another female and her young son living in her home—a woman her own husband had brought home, no less. It was awkward at first, yet Melodie was so bubbly and pleasant, An soon found herself relaxing. She cooked, she cleaned, and she was an angel with Lynne and Erica. An was still working full-time then, so Melodie was a definite help around the house.

Melodie's name fit her well. She sang like a bird and even played the guitar. She told An she had met Brad when she came into his shop asking about self-defense classes and wanting to buy a gun for protection. Her ex-husband had been physically abusive, and she was apprehensive about what he was capable of doing, so she wanted a way to protect herself and her son. An found herself relating to Melodie and caring for her. An's home offered Melodie a safe place, where her ex could not find and hurt her.

But then came that fateful night.

An had not been feeling quite herself. She was tired and sluggish a lot then, even losing some time. She found herself in a heavy, dreamless sleep, when her cough woke her up.

Her throat was dry and scratchy, and her tongue felt like a piece of lead in her mouth. With a hint of a headache coming on and her head groggy from sleep, An got up to get some aspirin. She realized then that Brad was not in bed with her, which was not unusual. He often got up in the middle of the night when he couldn't sleep and headed down to the library to read or to the basement den to watch television. An tiptoed out of her bedroom, listening for the girls. All seemed well and quiet—maybe too quiet.

The stairs connecting the main level and the top level did double duty: one flight led down into the living room area; the other on the opposite side led into the kitchen area. It had been one of the architectural attractions for An. She loved the design and functionality of those stairs. Because An and Brad had planned on having a large family, the home was a good size, maybe 4,000 square feet of living space. They had the four bedrooms upstairs: the master bedroom and bath, three other smaller bedrooms, and an extra full bath.

The girls each had their own rooms, and they used the fourth bedroom as a spare guest room. That was the room Danny, Melodie's ten-year-old son, currently occupied. He was a quiet and bookish boy who seemed to need his own space. There was also the basement, which was finished. This included a large playroom for the girls, doubling as a den and game room, with a sixty-inch television taking up one wall, and a pool table in the center. There was also a large bedroom and full bath down there. Brad's thought was that one day, perhaps his mom would live with them and take the large lower area. Wanting to provide Melodie with some modicum of privacy, An had offered her the bedroom in the basement of the home.

An searched the entire main level for Brad, growing a little frantic as she went. The house was silent and dark, no sign of Brad anywhere. No television blaring, no voices, no lights on anywhere.

The only place left to look was the basement.

Apprehensive, An touched the doorknob to the lower level, needing to check, yet not wanting to know what she might find. Maybe it would be best to stay in the dark. But she dared to open the door a crack, trembling, knowing in some far-reaching recess of her mind what she was about to witness.

She crept down the steps stealthily in her bare feet and flimsy nightshirt. She felt chilled, vulnerable, exposed. An hoped this was nothing more than a dream, yet knew it wasn't. She knew but still needed the startling confirmation of a pinch.

She crossed the vast play area where, a mere few hours earlier, the family had all been playing Twister. The kids were laughing, bodies twisting and tumbling. Before Twister, they had made homemade pizzas in the kitchen upstairs, the girls giggling as they dug their little knuckles into the soft dough and squeezed some of it between their tiny fingers. Melodie had grabbed her guitar to play "Amazing Grace," of all songs. Her fingers so aptly and fluidly engaged the strings; her raspy, sultry soprano trilled through the kitchen walls, bouncing around the rest of the house, resonating in An's heart somewhere. Brad joined in, singing backup to Melodie in his strong, clear bass. An just hummed along, beaming with happy thoughts and good feelings.

Her crown might not have always been on straight, but An felt like the queen in her beautiful home. They were a big happy family, all of them.

Downstairs, the girls had been all giggles and squeals, with peals of laughter from the adults every so often. Even sulking Danny seemed to be having fun, smiling from ear to ear until someone looked his way. Then he'd plaster the serious face back on. He was slowly warming up to the rest of the clan, though.

This was not unusual for An. Life on the weekends those initial couple years was normally filled with games, laughter, and the pitter-patter of the girls, cooking and having fun together. Those first few years before Melodie had been magical, with a few exceptions. The occasional times of stress and discord were few, like when An learned that Alison had gone missing, but eventually, even that faded from mind.

By the time An reached Melodie's door, she was both shivering with cold and sweating with anxiousness, all at once. She put her ear against the door. Nothing but silence greeted her. For a split second, she almost fled back up the stairs, rationalizing that Melodie lay in bed peacefully sleeping, and Brad probably went out for a walk or was sitting in the backyard contemplating something. But An's curiosity got the better of her. She had to know. She had to see.

She cracked open the door, just to assuage her doubts, she told herself.

She looked.

Melodie was fast asleep on the left side of the bed, one pale naked leg carelessly flung over the side as she lay on her stomach.

Brad was on the other side, sleeping on his side, one leg on top of her and one arm encircling her small frame.

An's heart sank. Her breath suspended above her head somewhere.

An and Brad had an intimate joke they often referred to, about how Brad was like a boa constrictor when they slept. He would wrap his arms around An and throw a leg over her, totally holding her in place. If An tried to move or get out of the embrace, he would tighten the hold so that she couldn't escape. That's how he was sleeping now but with *her*!

It seemed like An stood there for an eternity, her feet rooted to that one spot, her heart thudding in her chest. An ocean buzzed in An's head like being inside a giant sea conch. She could almost feel her skin wrinkling up, her hair turning gray, her joints growing stiff. She tried to summon tears, but none came.

Planet Earth had stopped spinning on its axis. The world stood completely still.

Brad stirred just then. His eyes popped open, and he jumped up, making eye contact with An. Their gazes locked and held. An thought how she must have looked like wild-eyed death not quite warmed over.

And how did Brad react? Oh, Brad was cool as a cucumber. No shock, no fear in his gaze. He even smiled at An. Smiled for Pete's sake!

"Honey. Hey, everything okay?" He whispered it so nonchalantly.

Oh, everything is perfectly fine with me and the whole damn universe, An thought sarcastically. *My entire world just lost its bottom, but why should that be a problem? I'm fine. Everything is hunky-dory. Absolutely nothing to fret about!*

"What is happening?" An heard a hoarse voice say. It must have been her own, but it sounded nothing like her—just a haunted, ghost-like voice.

Brad had hopped out of bed, his nakedness startling and disconcerting. He came toward An, his index finger to his lips, indicating he wanted her to keep it down.

REALLY?! HONESTLY?! HE'S SHUSHING ME? An screamed inside her head. Just then An found her feet somehow, turned, and bolted up the stairs, gulping for air that failed to fill her lungs.

He reached her halfway up the bedroom stairs. He had found time to put his briefs back on, thank goodness.

"Don't make a scene, An," he hissed.

An turned to face him, feeling wild and crazy. Ready to chop him up into a million little pieces, then bulldoze the house to the ground and be done with it all.

"You are sleeping with her right under my nose?" she said softly, with a calm she did not feel. "WHAT THE HELL!" she screamed. She screamed so loud she scared the bejesus out of herself. The whole house would awaken now, the entire neighborhood would hear, and the FRIGGING UNIVERSE WOULD KNOW! She didn't give a hoot.

He grabbed her then, swiveling her around to face away from him. He had An in a chokehold, his left arm around her neck and his right hand over her mouth.

"Hush already," he hissed into her ear this time. "She needs comfort. What's so wrong about that? Where's your compassion? You are such a privileged bitch!" He spat the words, his spittle sticking to An's cheek. Her head was starting to go fuzzy at the edges, and her body felt limp. She fought for consciousness, blinking, blinking away the spreading black.

What the hell is happening? How did I become the bad guy here? COMPASSION? COMPASSION? she kept screaming inside her mind because he was blocking her words, strangling her rage and stifling her completely. An had her eyes squeezed shut, and tears were now threatening to spill in earnest. She couldn't breathe. Life was oozing out of her.

"Listen," he said, as he turned her around to face him, releasing his hold. An gasped, sucking air in as deeply as she could, trying not to tumble to her knees right in front of him. His eyes were full of love and concern suddenly. *How can he change like that?*

"Sorry. Did I hold you too tight?" he said, one hand reaching out toward her.

She backed away from him, all the while keeping her eyes fixed on him. She couldn't find the words for the jumbled confusion she was feeling and the rage roiling inside her.

"What the fuck?" she managed to say, hoarsely. An didn't think she had actually ever in her entire life uttered that profanity out loud, but it felt so darn good to say it.

He touched her cheek ever so tenderly with the back of his hand, before An could pull away. "I love you, An," he said with emotion. "You know I love you. I'm not trying to hurt you, baby."

"Then what are you trying to do to me? How is sleeping with her in my own home not hurtful? How is what you're doing not hurtful and despicable?" An spat the words at him. "You're disgusting! Oh, and don't ever call me 'baby' again."

"There is plenty of love to go around. You already have me. She is all alone, she has no one, and she's lost so much. I know you're a compassionate person. Do you not get it?" Brad said.

The air left An's lungs again, and she was without speech, uncomprehending. As always, Brad was able to rationalize the situation to his advantage. An was beginning to feel selfish and ungrateful and hateful. She was beginning to feel like a cold, unfeeling jerk. Yes, suddenly, *she* was the bad one.

"This is wrong," An told him. "You're wrong for tearing our family apart like this, and you know it. Don't turn this on me, Brad."

He smiled, seemingly oblivious to what An had just said. He swiftly grabbed her face, planting a kiss on her lips. His face was so close to hers, she could feel his foul breath, as she struggled to free herself.

"Only *you* have the power to destroy this family, honey. But I know you. I know you will come to your senses." He turned and began descending the steps. Then he stopped and turned back to An one last time to say, "It will be okay, darlin'. I love you, and you are my wife and the mother of those two beautiful girls. I promise you we will come out of this stronger and closer. We're helping someone in need, doing a good deed. We need more of that in the world. When she's good and strong, she'll be on her way, and we'll regain our old life, I promise."

An watched him descend the stairs, a swing in his step, feeling pretty good about himself by the looks of it. An kept asking herself over and over again, *What in the world just happened?*

And yet she was painfully aware of the notion in the back of her head that told her, despite what she had just witnessed and despite Brad's reaction, she would stay.

She was going nowhere. Where would she go? Who would she be? Who would come to the rescue? Brad would have his way because An would always stay put. A little more broken, a little less her, but she'd stay put nonetheless. Who would mother her precious girls? No, she was going nowhere. This was her family and her home!

Like a zombie, An stepped back in her bedroom, locked the door, and plopped back in bed. Brad did not come back to check on her, and his side of the bed stayed empty and cold. An lay in bed feeling betrayed, betrayed by Brad, but even more betrayed by her own self. *My life will never be whole again*, she thought. She felt as if she had fallen through that rabbit hole into another world where topsy-turvy was the norm.

In time, morning crept into An's consciousness, dazzling ribbons of light playing on the walls like a kaleidoscope. She listened to the birds singing outside the window without hearing; she watched the sun splashing across the sky without seeing. Blind, deaf, and mute to the world on a seemingly sunshiny Saturday summer morning. Eventually, sounds within the house reached An. When she heard Lynne and Erica calling for her, she had to muster the strength to get out of bed and fumble her way downstairs.

The aroma of bacon grease and syrup greeted An as she entered the kitchen. Her stomach recoiled. Brad, Melodie, and Danny were already dressed and seated at the table munching. *What a cheerful family picture they make.* An wanted to vomit from the smell and sight before her.

Lynne and Erica were chasing each other around the kitchen. Melodie smiled and asked if she should make something for the girls. An mumbled that she'd take care of it. An tried hard to block all of them out of her senses. Then Brad stood up and came to hug her from behind. He was chewing, and it suddenly hit An that he ate with his mouth open, and it annoyed the crap out of her. He kissed the side of her face and whispered *good morning.*

That irritated her too. But he smelled good and clean, looking newly showered and shaved, all bright-eyed and bushy-tailed.

Life went on as usual that day and the next day, and the days to follow. As Brad had predicted, Melodie eventually found more interesting greener pastures and moved on. One day, An came home, and she was gone, along with all vestiges of her, her son, and her belongings. As if she was never there. No note, no goodbye, no nothing.

Years later, that "Year of Melodie" would seem strange, far away, and tame by comparison. Looking back, An thought that was the beginning of the end, but in reality it should have been the end, period. She should have left, or, better yet, she should have kicked him out. Nothing of the sort happened until it was too late for everyone.

CHAPTER 14
TWO WORLDS COLLIDE: 2006

"In our ever-changing universe, lives collide, and, like runaway planets, we just keep going."
- Michael French, *Once Upon a Lie*
"Worlds will collide if love has anything to do with it."
- Anthony T. Hincks

From the moment An laid eyes on Lynne and Erica, the mother-daughter bond was instantly formed with both girls. An was in love and in awe of the two little angels that miraculously dropped into her life. There was little doubt the girls belonged to her; they were meant to be with her. She loved her role of caregiver and nurturer. She was beyond proud to have a hand in raising them. These were her children to love and protect for eternity.

The question surrounding what had happened to their biological mother had always been a dark cloud for An. Did she secretly want Alison out of the picture? Absolutely! She never voiced it to the world, and she had a hard time accepting it within her own mind. But if she were to be totally honest, An desperately wished and hoped Alison could disappear forever. And then one day, she did!

Alison was a nuisance, a sore spot, a thorn in the side of An and Brad's happy family. Although a bit perturbed when Alison actually did go missing, An privately saw it as a blessing, an answered prayer. And in the darkest, furthest reaches of her mind, she wished Alison would stay gone. *There must be a God*, An often pondered when the years came and went and Alison did in fact stay gone.

An and Brad had discussed An adopting Lynne and Erica, but that process was never finalized. It was complicated with Alison permanently missing. The fact that the mystery of what happened to Alison had never been solved kept that black cloud over An. She lived with the fear that Alison would turn up one day and reclaim her children. But as the years went by and Alison did not return, that fear became more and more a faded memory. Her mind even played tricks on her now and then, making her believe Alison had never existed and she, An, was the only mother Lynne and Erica had, and would ever have. Sometimes An fantasized that she, An, had actually birthed Lynne and Erica.

But the day of reckoning had been approaching, unbeknownst to An—the two realms of past and present on an unavoidable collision course.

It was August 3rd, a Sunday, possibly An's favorite day of the week for as long as she could remember.

Lynne had made An a proud mother, indeed, when she decided to attend James Madison University to study psychology, just as An had done twenty years earlier. And, now, Erica was poised to follow her sister, attending the same school to pursue a degree in political sciences. In just two weeks, the two girls would be loading up their car and making the trek to Harrisonburg to settle into their new apartment and attend college—Lynne, as a junior already, and Erica just starting as a freshman.

The excitement around the Goode household was palpable as the girls made their final plans to leave for school. Agnes had not been well the past couple years, first undergoing surgery for an issue with her colon, and then testing positive for skin cancer, which had resulted in the girls spending more time visiting her.

Meanwhile, An busied herself with gardening and cooking, creating amazing flower arrangements for their dinner tables and using some of her vegetables and herbs to concoct exquisite five-course meals for the whole family to enjoy—all while still working at the little psychologists' office, which had doubled in size since its earlier days.

An now did a lot of the work from home, mostly dealing with the medical coding and insurance side of business.

That Sunday had started out pretty much a mirror image of other Sundays. An was up early to have a cup of coffee with Brad before he left for his adventure with Miles—this time a big shooting event out in Leesburg. Then, when the girls were up, she had made bacon and French toast for them, joining in with another cup of coffee, a piece of buttered rye toast, and a couple slices of well-done bacon. She tried to stay away from the French toast as it didn't always agree with her stomach.

After helping the girls sort through some household items they wanted to take with them, Lynne had announced they were going to pick up some things at Agnes's house and visit for a bit. They made plans for dinner and a movie together later that evening. An did not easily give up her Sunday dinners and that precious time with her girls. If they wanted to be with friends or anyone else, An normally insisted it be at her home. Sometimes there would be groups of ten, twelve, even fifteen people gathered around the kitchen table. An loved every minute of it!

But the girls were only gone for a short couple hours before returning. An had immersed herself in doing some cleaning and baking. She thought she might even have time to play around in her garden before the girls were back. She had no inkling about what was to come.

"MOOOM!" Erica stormed into the house, noisily stomping down the lengthy hallway toward the kitchen in the back of the house. Long red hair flying behind her, she was on a mission to find An. "MOM!" she bellowed again.

"In here!" An answered.

Erica walked into the kitchen to find An down on her knees with her upper body inside one of the bottom cabinets. Rummaging inside, she finally pulled away, coming out for air.

"Got it!" she said. "I knew I had one of these jelly-roll pans somewhere." She stood up, pan in hand.

"We need to talk, pronto!" Erica yelled, her face glistening red from the anger and the heat outside.

"Okay, okay, but let's slow it down and lower our voices just a little. What's the matter now?" An wondered how her precious little ball of fire had in a flash grown into this self-assured, stomping young woman preparing to begin college in just a few short weeks.

"Lynne and I are just now coming back from Grandma's; she's still not well, and Dad hasn't even gone to see her, *by the way*. We found *this* in the box she gave us with old stuff belonging to Alison." She threw a newspaper clipping at An. The paper fluttered up in the air, slowly glided down, then settled on the floor by An's bare feet. Both women followed the trajectory of the floating piece of paper with their gazes.

Erica's face was bright crimson, and beads of sweat were visible on her forehead from the heat outside, her brisk walk inside, and the emotions roiling and coiling inside her. By contrast, An's face had turned ghostly white. She was pretty sure she knew what this was about. She had dreaded this day for years, hoping against hope the day would never arrive, and she would never have to explain. But she should have known the absurdity of that wish.

The girls didn't live in a bubble. With the leaps and bounds technology had taken, anything was easily searchable. It was only a matter of time before one, or both, girls came across something related to the period of time their mother disappeared. An hadn't considered, however, that the information could be leaked from someone in their midst. The catalyst coming from Agnes, of all people.

Erica, more than Lynne, had been curious about Alison. An assumed this was because she had little to no memory of her own mother, while Lynne had glimpses of memory here and there. An tried answering their questions as best she could. Everyone in the family had stayed on the same rehearsed script of telling them their mother had left of her own free will to start over somewhere.

"You never told us about this," Erica was now saying in a tight, quiet voice brimming with rage. Her eyes filled with tears. She tried in vain to hold back her emotions. Behind her, her sister appeared. Unlike Erica's red and enraged features, Lynne seemed calm and sedate, her coloring even. But that was just the difference between the two sisters. Even if they harbored the same volume of rage inside, they displayed it quite differently. Erica blew up like a volcano, spewing red-hot, loud lava. Lynne, on the other hand, contained the explosiveness within, showing only a well-controlled blank, cool exterior.

Lynne looked on at the spectacle in front of her with hooded, perturbed eyes, showing more sadness and somberness than anger. But beneath her composed expression another, more ominous emotion lay seething— one no one else could witness. She crossed her arms in front of her as if to brace herself for support, and stood on the kitchen threshold, watching and listening.

An turned away from her daughters' gazes slowly, buying time, furiously thinking, and trying her best to stay calm and collected. She placed the pan she held on the countertop. Then she bent down and picked up the scrap of old newspaper cutout.

"Okay, what is this, girls?" She looked at the scrap and came face-to-face with a faded black-and-white photo of a smiling, young Alison. A deluge of old memories and old feelings flooded back—memories and emotions she did not want to confront, not now, not ever. For a moment, An held her breath, her stomach gurgling and churning, turning to mush. The headline read: *Vienna Woman Missing—Investigation Underway.*

"You never told us she was *missing*, only that she had left, just walked out on us. Why did you and Dad lie, why?" Erica was now sobbing, making little gasping sounds. "There was an investigation? Police were involved? Did you think it would stay buried forever?"

Instinctively, An approached her daughter and tried putting her arms protectively around her. "Shh-shh-shh, baby."

But Erica shoved and pulled away from her.

"No, no, don't even try to touch me. You lied, you manipulated, you connived... Why? I want answers. I want answers NOW."

"No! That's not how it was. Maybe we should get your dad over here first," An suggested.

"No, I don't want to see him and hear more lies, more cover-ups, more deceit. No way, Jose! You tell us. You tell us what you know."

An looked past Erica at Lynne, her eyes begging the older sibling for assistance. "Lynne, I don't know what to say… I don't understand why your gran—"

"Never mind Grandma; she's a sick woman trying to make amends. She knows the truth should not stay buried. Just tell us what happened. Enough with the lies." Lynne cut An's words off, her eyes cold as the North Pole. Her words and her stare were an ice pick through An's heart. She had never seen Lynne look at her with such coldness and disdain. And now that the anger in Erica's face had been replaced with such a forlorn look, An just wanted to hold and comfort them both.

"Well, did she or did she not walk out on us?" Erica chimed in, wiping her face with the backs of her hands and trying to compose herself, keeping her wits about her so she could get the answers she needed.

An sighed. "Everyone believed she ran off; your father said she ran off. I had no reason to not believe him. The police couldn't find her or any evidence that something bad happened to her."

"Well, Grandma said we should use the brain the good Lord gave us and decide for ourselves," Erica told her. "Judging by that article, I would say something else happened to my mother; she didn't walk out on us. Don't play dumb!"

Referring to Alison as 'my mother' was another ice pick to An's heart, but she kept her composure, for now.

"Something else happened to her, *An*," Lynne said. "The way Grandma looked, I'm pretty sure Alison did not run off on her own. You must know something. You *have* to know something."

Lynne calling An by her name instead of Mom cut like a giant dagger. An swallowed audibly, finding it difficult to take a breath with the ice picks and dagger pinned to her heart.

An sighed again, feeling defeated.

"I, too, questioned it," she said in a quiet voice. There was no point in trying to put the genie back in the bottle, and An knew it. She resolved to at least tell the girls what she knew, even though this was going to make Brad the bad guy.

"You have to understand, girls. Everything we did was to try to protect you. Your dad paid Alison to leave and not ever come back. He said he paid her a large amount of money as inducement to stay out of your lives. You two needed better stability and—"

"And you went along with it?" Erica uttered incredulously. "You believed it?"

"And kept it a secret?" Lynn asked in disbelief. "You didn't question the investigation at all?"

"Of course I did! I did what I thought was best," An tried to explain.

"No, you did what Dad asked. You always cover for him. Did you not think of us?"

"I was thinking of you and your sister, Erica, yes. You have to believe that. I thought I was protecting you, keeping you safe, providing you with the nurturing you needed."

"By helping to keep our biological mother from us? We were just babies!" Lynn said this while shaking her head, her lips curling up in disgust.

"Girls, really, I barely knew Alison. Let's wait for your father and then have a sit down."

"Really, An, you think my father will have a sit down and explain it all and make it all okay?" Lynne asked.

"Stop it! It's MOM to you! I'm still your mother! Whether she left or was forced to leave doesn't change that!" An's voice was an octave higher as she glared at her eldest daughter. Her entire being shook with the injustice of it all. She couldn't bear the girls treating her this way, interrogating her like this. The only thing she was guilty of was wishing that Alison would stay away. She hadn't asked her to go, she hadn't paid her to go, she hadn't done anything to cause her to go or to stay away all these years.

"No, you're wrong. It changes everything!" Lynne spat out. "I have totally lost all respect for you. You would do anything for that man, cover up anything, stay with him no matter how unhappy or how badly he treats you. You are complicit!" Lynn's words tumbled out of her as if of their own volition. Then she turned and ran upstairs to her room, slamming her door behind her for good measure.

Erica stood there watching An for a minute. "She's right, you know," she told An. "Keeping his secrets makes you no better than him, guilt by association, *Mother*."

"I understand your wrath, but it's displaced a little. What was I supposed to do?"

"Did you think to call the police and tell them Dad had paid Alison to leave? That piece of information could have changed the investigation; it could have changed everything! Did you?"

"No," An told her truthfully. "I never called the investigators about it. Your father said he was handling it; he had told the investigators everything."

"Because you were only thinking of Dad and how furious he'd be if you did something to challenge him. You didn't think of us or Alison, and that's sad," Erica concluded, tears streaming down her cheeks.

"You're right," An told her. "I should have thought it out better. My judgment was clouded, and I'm sorry."

"Lynne and I are going to do all we can to reopen the investigation and see if we can get to the bottom of what happened to our mother so that we can make peace with it one way or another."

An remained silent, simply shaking her head in acknowledgement.

Erica turned to leave the room, then stopped and said to An, "Did you know Grandma has an entire box of pictures of Alison and us? Dad too. From back when we were babies. And all these many years, all we had to remember her by was the one picture you two let us have. That's a shame."

"I'm so sorry, Erica. I guess I was being selfish, wanting you and Lynne all to myself. I didn't think it all the way through." An was so choked up with emotion she could barely get the words out. How could she make the girls understand that in her heart of hearts, her decision to simply look away was what she thought was best? She didn't feel it was her place to question what was happening. She didn't think she could have influenced anything. She had been wrong, but it wasn't out of malice.

"I wish you would just stand up for yourself! Stand up for us, for Alison, for doing the right thing. When was the last time you stood up to *him* on anything?" Erica looked at An, anger and emotion making her chin quiver. "You know what I think?" Erica continued. "I think you and Dad together did something to Alison."

Erica turned away from her mother and followed her sister's footsteps up the stairs and into her own bedroom. The second door slammed, shutting An out. She stood rooted to the spot, unable to move or act. *What had just happened?*

Feeling utterly without words, sapped of energy, An was at a loss as to how best to handle this and how to comfort the girls. Maybe she shouldn't have kept the investigation a secret, but her motives were mostly about keeping the girls safe and protected from any unpleasantness. They were so young! She had come to believe—or perhaps she had *wanted* to believe—that Alison had left of her own accord. She did have a history of disappearing and reappearing as she pleased, without regard to anyone. An had even witnessed her unstable behavior once or twice. Alison was known for her drinking. The investigation had gone nowhere fast, stalling and then growing cold. There was never any evidence that Brad had anything to do with it, and certainly there was no evidence that she, An, had anything to do with it.

Disturbed about it, An had turned to Brad for answers and reassurance after it happened. Finally, one day, Brad confessed that he had paid Alison to go and not come back. An had believed it, her mind at ease. It made sense to her then because she had needed a straw to grasp. But now she questioned Brad's explanation and her own need to believe. In the past she had questioned it only in passing because it made things easier to turn a blind eye. Except this time, there was more at stake. This time, she could lose the girls. She couldn't bear that thought.

Did Alison really walk away? Did Brad pay her to disappear? Or did something else happen? Was foul play afoot? An had enough pieces to the puzzle to put it all together, yet she was incapable of facing that dark hole, so she carefully concealed the clues in her subconscious mind. She simply could not, would not, look the demon in the eyes. Were the girls right? Was she complicit by turning a blind eye? The fact that she cowardly looked the other way?

Plopping down at the kitchen table, An took stock of the situation. She examined more closely the newspaper clipping, staring at Alison's smiling face, which seemed to look back at An accusingly. An's anguish bubbled up to the surface, and the tears finally overcame her.

"What have I done?" she whispered to no one in particular.

Deep in her gut she knew. Her intuition told her all along Alison had not walked away from her young daughters, of her own will. She also suspected Brad knew something more about her disappearance. In fact, the clues to what had happened to Alison had been in the house with An all along. The truth was demanding to be heard. Had she really been that naïve to think that the Then and Now would never meet? Time had lulled her into thinking that maybe, just maybe, Alison's fate would lie dormant for eternity, and everyone involved would live happily ever after. *But this is no fairy tale*, she thought helplessly.

Raising the girls wasn't always a smooth ride, but it had been An's greatest accomplishment in life. As the sisters grew into beautiful, well-adjusted, smart, and happy young adults, An looked on with pride and joy. She had done this! Many times, single-handedly. Although appearing to be an engaged father early on, Brad was often distracted by one thing or another that seemed to somehow consume his time and thoughts.

He would pick and choose moments with the girls, then plumb disappear, leaving An "in charge." An had been the constant rock standing strong for the girls. It was An who worried while staying up with them when they were ill. It was An who dropped them off and picked them up from school and An who went to the parent/teacher conferences and school events. They were her world, and losing them was an unbearable thought.

An did the only thing she knew how to do to deal with the pain and uncertainty that had suddenly become her reality. She immersed herself in her culinary activities. She made a roast and baby potatoes for dinner. She broiled asparagus and stir-fried portabella mushrooms. She baked fresh rolls and made a mixed green salad. She made a pineapple upside-down cake—the girls loved her version. The house was full of the delicious aromas of An's cooking and baking. While the frenzied activity kept the dark thoughts away for An, the aromas eventually brought the girls downstairs. They had composed themselves and told her they were ready to have a discussion. An sighed in relief, hoping against hope that they would rethink their position, and maybe things could eventually go back to normal.

"Let's eat something first," An told them.

They worked in silence setting the kitchen table and getting the food ready to be served. An sliced up the roast, which was so tender, it was practically falling apart. The vegetables were fresh and crisp. They began eating, and An nearly forgot the girls' earlier anger. She prayed they would forgive her.

But her relief was short-lived. The girls were not interested in taking back anything they had said, and they made it clear that nothing was ever going to be as it once was. They told An they were going to talk to the authorities and try to reopen the case into their mother's disappearance now that they were confident she didn't walk out on them. Something happened to her, something that kept her from them all these many years.

"What exactly are you hoping to accomplish after all this time?" An asked them.

"Maybe nothing," Lynne confided. "Maybe it's too late, and any evidence that may have existed is gone. But we have to try to find the truth. We need to know whether she left us or she went against her will. And if she's still out there, we want to find her and get to know her. We hope she is out there somewhere, alive and well."

"We don't want Dad to know what we're up to," Erica said. "He will not only try to stop us, but he will throw roadblocks our way as much as possible. I'm sure he has something to hide about all this, and I'm not standing for it anymore."

An knew it would be totally futile to stop any of this, so she simply nodded her head and went along with it. She did not want to jeopardize any vestige of a relationship that might still be possible with the girls.

Finally, An told them, "I have to tell your father the issue at least came up. I'm in your corner as much as I can be. I will never stop being your mother, and I will always love you with all my heart."

Lynne answered for herself and Erica when she told An, "We know you're going to talk to Dad about it, and we do understand to some degree. But because we will absolutely not be derailed, we're not sure how our family life will look going forward. We plan on looking up Alison's side of the family to try to put pieces of the puzzle together. We don't really know what we're going to find and how it will impact our emotions, but at least for the time being, we want contact with you and Dad kept to a minimum."

An became agitated all over again, tears stinging her eyes. "Girls, please, that feels like punishment to me. I am trying to understand and remain on your side, and I do want to try to make amends for my silence, but you're not making any of this easy. Please don't shut me out."

But at the end of that conversation, An became painfully aware that the girls were now grown, young women on a mission, and she had lost her place and influence… at least for now. They were hurt and angry. Most importantly, they did not trust. They didn't trust the people in their lives nor the stories they were told. They didn't even trust what they believed anymore.

Nothing was going to soothe their pain but finding out what happened to Alison. In order to make sense of their world and heal, they needed time and space from An and Brad.

Another loss, An thought bitterly. *How much more loss can I possibly take and still keep breathing?* This realization made her grow outwardly stoic and cool. She was going to bear through this too and hopefully come out stronger. She had loved them with all her might, the best she knew how. She had given it her all. She hoped it was enough to bring them back one day.

That night when Brad arrived home, in the wee hours of Monday morning really, An met him outside by the garage where he normally parked. She told him the short version of what had transpired. She left the part about telling the girls that Brad had paid Alison to leave and never return. Brad seemed distracted, only half listening to her, something else occupying his mental power.

"I'll talk to them," Brad said. He walked away from the conversation and An. Inside the house, he headed to the kitchen, following the aromas. Once in the kitchen, he rummaged in the refrigerator, bringing containers of food out. He loaded up a plate of roast, potatoes, and vegetables to warm up in the microwave. An followed his movements for a while, but it was the middle of the night, and she was mentally and emotionally drained. She told Brad she was going to sleep and climbed the stairs to her bedroom, looking forward to the comfort and warmth of her bed.

She never heard Brad come up. In fact, he didn't, choosing the basement couch or extra bed instead. That had become the norm a long time ago.

The next morning, she awoke with the sound of murmuring downstairs. She grabbed her robe and was making her way down when she heard Brad raise his voice. "I'm telling you to let this go, or you'll be sorry! Alison was a rotten wife, a worse mother, and I don't want either one of you in contact with her or her family. Do you hear me?"

"We're both old enough—"

She heard Erica's brave voice. Then both girls were silenced when Brad slammed his fist on the kitchen table just as An walked in. The lid of the sugar bowl, which had been left on the table, flew into the air, and sugar spilled out onto An's pristine tablecloth.

The girls looked white as a sheet, sitting at the table, still in their pajamas. Brad was now right next to Erica's chair, where she sat stiffly, looking straight ahead.

"I don't give a crap! Do you hear me?"

"BRAD!" An yelled, indignant and scared for the girls. She had never seen Brad talk like that to them. He was totally out of control, and Brad was rarely out of control. An was shaking by the time she reached the girls.

"Stop it, just stop!" she told Brad, coming to stand behind the girls on their side of the table.

"I want them gone when I come back!" he spat as he walked past An. She could feel the heat from his anger emanating from him.

"They're your kids. Where do you expect them to go?" she asked his back. He just kept on going. An turned to the girls. They looked terrified.

"I don't want to stay here," Erica said to her. "I won't stay here a single day longer."

"She's right," Lynne agreed. "We'll stay with Grandma until we have to leave for school."

"No, you won't," An told them. "This is your home."

"No," Lynne said. "This no longer feels like home. We don't belong here."

"Let's just sit, have a cup of coffee, and think this through." An tried to sound reassuring, but she was still shaking.

"He told us if we don't stop with the questions about Alison, he'll make sure we disappear too," Lynne told An, her voice shaky.

"I don't believe that," An answered. "They are just words. Obviously, he didn't mean it literally."

"Are you sure about that?" Erica asked.

"Did you not see the devil in his eyes just now?" This time, it was Lynne's turn to ask. "Maybe you, too, should find another place to stay."

Lynne's ominous statement was jarring to An. She was baffled by how, just like that, her entire world toppled.

No one was acting like they should. She felt her own face begin to slide off, a slow melting from the top down and ever so slightly sideways. She was unsure who these people—her family—truly were, and she was afraid to learn what other face was beneath her own. Her center had shifted. Nothing was right. Nothing.

CHAPTER 15

AWAKE IN SLUMBER

"I don't paint dreams or nightmares. I paint my own reality."

> \- Frida Kahlo

"A sword is never a killer; it is a tool in the killer's hand."

> \- Maggie Stiefvater, *The Dream Thieves*

Nearly ended, this fall day had been a perfect one, over-flooded with the sun's brilliance raining down. As twilight set in, the last rays of light put on an unforgettable show of color: swirls of orange and pink, followed by a blending of purple swaths, and finally scarlet bleeding through. Inside the intensive care unit, the display in the sky went undetected. Standing vigil, it was now the curly-haired woman's turn to sit and watch "Sleeping Beauty," as some of the nurses had dubbed her. Later, the woman would be replaced by the tall, dark man with the haunted eyes.

Others came to visit too, but more sporadically. The first week, they all came, sometimes multiple times in a day. They watched Sleeping Beauty with guarded sad eyes, whispering hushed words in stilted tones, hoping and anticipating her eventual return. Curly Hair and Haunted Eyes were regulars at Sleeping Beauty's side, one coming in the evening and the other in the wee hours before the morning's arrival. They knew the authorities had taken extra security measures, but they wanted to make doubly sure Sleeping Beauty knew she was loved, and that she was safe.

Time crept by, transforming night into day, nightmares into day-scares.

In the pre-dawn silence, the cardiac monitor whizzed and whirred in a low monotone, beeping every so often. Eventually, all the colors outside coalesced into a deep dark blue, followed by a silky-smooth blackness marked only by a spattering of twinkling silver dots. In the hospital bed, Sleeping Beauty lay very still with her arms now outside the white sheet that draped across her body. Haunted Eyes wanted to see her hands, her fingers, just in case they twitched or moved. A blanket lay on the foot of the bed to be used to cover her arms if she felt cold.

Her chest rose in an abrupt and unnatural way, held for a second, then fell again. The gasp and sigh it made continued in even intervals. A tube protruded grotesquely out of her neck from the tracheostomy, which was attached to the mechanical ventilator. This contraction was juxtaposed by the woman's angelic pale face poking underneath the white bandage wrapped around her head. Her hands lay flat beside her, palms down, the nails on her hands long and uniform in size, perfectly shaped.

It was now Haunted Eyes's turn to stand vigil at Sleeping Beauty's side. He sat on the chair next to her bed, head bowed. He appeared to be asleep and oblivious to the hustle and bustle in the corridor outside the room, except his lips moved tirelessly in quiet prayer. Hours passed, and the man eventually slipped into actual slumber. He missed the doctor's assessment of the patient and the nurse's vigilant checking of vital signs. Eventually, night reversed itself once more. Everyone had become accustomed to this choreographed dance.

The heavy curtains of the hospital window were ever so slightly apart, letting a thin ribbon of weak sunlight in as the sun slowly lumbered up in the horizon, breaking through the haze of dawn. The man was barely visible in the shadowed corner of the room. His hand had been holding hers at times, but now it lay limply over the sides of the chair as he lightly snored, his chin lolling on his chest. The slow rise and fall of his breathing was in noticeable contrast to the woman's severe up-and-down chest movements.

The room was sterile, medical equipment its only décor, except for a colorful bouquet of fresh-cut flowers in a clear vase on the cabinet opposite where the man sat. Outside the room, in the nurses' quarters and hallway, activity was beginning to emerge from sleep.

A young nurse in dark blue scrubs peeked in the room, pulling the bed curtains to the side for a better view. She had just arrived for her shift and was making her rounds. She checked the cardiac monitor, reading the peaks and valleys the colored lights made, assessing the various numbers it displayed. Then she examined the tube and wires connected to the woman, as well as the IV sack. She moved to the foot of the bed, where she picked up the chart and scribbled on it. Pleased that all seemed as it should be, she took a quick look at the slumped-over man, shook her head, sighed audibly, and made a sad grimace before tiptoeing out again.

Outside, the piercing whine of an ambulance's siren could be heard approaching. It became more and more ear-splitting the closer it got to the hospital's emergency entrance, right below the room's window. The man jumped up, arms flailing. He blinked several times before sitting up straighter in the chair, then bending down to look at the woman's face. Her eyes were closed, but they were moving from side to side as if watching a tennis match. He blinked several times, then placed his warm hand on her arm as he continued to closely watch her face.

Abruptly, he stood up, scraping the oversized chair back. He put his own face right up on top of the woman's and blinked several times to clear his vision. Appearing suddenly disoriented, he looked about, then bellowed for the nurse.

"NURSE! NURSE! COME!"

The same young nurse came running in, her rubber soles squeaking to a halt.

"What is it?" she asked the man, who was now wild-eyed and breathless.

"I think she blinked! She twitched! I really think she's waking up. Today might be the day!" he announced.

She eyed him quizzically, skepticism marking her features. His assertion that she was waking up had become more and more frequent in the last day or two. "We've gone through this before, Father," she admonished. "Step back, please. Let me take a look," the nurse said in an even, calm voice, trying to move him out of her way. She would indulge him once again, doubting Sleeping Beauty was ready to wake up. She had been showing signs, though, and doctors were encouraged by her progress, so it would be wrong to dismiss him. They all believed she would eventually resurface. It was only a matter of time.

When exactly, no one knew.

The nurse went from one side of the bed to the other, assessing and reading the monitor, then checking the patient for vitals. Her face was unreadable until she looked up at Haunted Eyes and announced, "I'm not sure there's any real change, but I'll get the doctor."

"Thank God!" Haunted Eyes exclaimed. "She's coming back. I feel today is the day."

The nurse scurried out of the room. The man went back to holding the woman's hand. He stroked her cheek with his knuckles.

"I knew you'd come back to us. I knew it!"

Sleeping Beauty's eyes fluttered again ever so slightly.

"That's it, that's it. It's safe now, you can come back, you can return now, it's been long enough," Haunted Eyes chanted.

Sleeping Beauty had awakened at last, and she was attempting to communicate, but it wasn't simply a matter of waking up and picking up where she had left off. Her injuries were significant, and the road ahead would not be easy. That entire day, doctors had come and gone, talking in hushed voices, examining charts and folders. They took her pulse and shone pinpricks of light into her eyes. They ran tests and checked the bandages on her head.

Indeed, she had awakened!

Now, the road to recovery had to be assessed and mapped out, her brain function placed under a microscope and tests to be done. Would she be the same woman? Only time could tell.

Sleeping Beauty seemed disoriented, making whimpering noises and trying to form words that wouldn't come out.

"Daaay," the woman croaked. She tried to clear her voice. It felt as if her mouth and throat were full of sand. Nothing worked. She could not form the words and say what she so desperately wanted to say.

"Nooo…" she cried as tears pooled and spilled from her eyes.

"It's alright. Just hold my hand. You're safe," Haunted Eyes said. "You don't need to say anything just yet."

She clutched his arm so fiercely, it surprised him that she had that much strength in her after all she had gone through and then being asleep for so long.

"Oooh!" she told him, panic in her voice. She kept swallowing, trying to moisten her lips with her tongue as she scanned the room, her eyes trying to focus. The nurse brought ice water and paper towels to dab her lips.

"Slow it down, nice and easy," the nurse cautioned Sleeping Beauty.

Tired of the sounds that simply would not come out, Sleeping Beauty sobbed at times, her fingers trembling as if trying to type on a keyboard. At times, she would get visibly agitated, shaking her head from side to side in frustration.

"Shh-shh-shh. Don't stress yourself out. You're doing good. There's plenty of time for talking. We know. We know what happened, and you're safe now," the curly-haired woman told her when she came to visit once she found out Sleeping Beauty was waking up from her long slumber.

"Nooooo," Sleeping Beauty moaned. She began whimpering, the tears spilling again.

"Father, what is she babbling about, do you suppose? Have you made out anything?" the nurse asked the tall man at one point, her voice hushed, her cheeks nearly touching his shirt lapel. "The police want to question her; they are itching to come in, but the doctors have to say yes first," the nurse whispered conspiratorially to him.

Haunted Eyes simply smiled at her, accepting that he would always be "Father" to her despite his having corrected her numerous times. He decided to just let it be.

In answer to her questions, he whispered back to her, "She's just scared, that's all. Her thoughts are jumbled up. As far as the police, they'll have to wait however long it takes her to be coherent again."

The nurse looked at the woman and frowned. She patted her arm. "You're okay, sweetie. We're taking good care of you."

CHAPTER 16

PLAYING WITH FIRE: 1992

"Expect anything from anyone; the devil was once an angel."

- Unknown

Miles was an odd sort of fella, but he could be likable when he was not being annoying. An took an immediate liking to him for some inexplicable reason. The first time she met him, he had been invited to the apartment for dinner on a Saturday evening in early November of that first year An and Brad met. Where Brad was tall, pale skin, blue eyes, and reddish-brown hair, Miles was short and thin and had a tan complexion and dark eyes and hair.

He arrived in black jeans, charcoal T-shirt, and a black bomber leather jacket. His hair was swept back in a pompadour. An had chuckled to herself as she admired the whole Fonz look he had going on. She imagined a cigarette tucked behind one of his ears too, although she came to realize he wasn't a smoker, had never smoked actually. But, hey, she loved *Happy Days* and watched the show every now and then. Fonzie was one of her beloved characters. Maybe this was the reason she liked Miles right away, or maybe it was the brotherly bond he had with Brad that made him immediately special in An's eyes. Or was it the bad guy image he tried to portray? Who knew?

Miles strode in, looked at An a little sideways and cockeyed, his big brown eyes shaded by unusually long, thick eyelashes. He offered his right hand to her, saying in a surprisingly deep voice, "I'm Miles Dorsey. I'm sure Brad has mentioned me."

"Yes, of course he has," An told him, extending her own right hand. His hands were small and soft. He held on a little too long, causing An to pull away slightly. The lingering handshake had been a little creepy to An, but it was all part of his persona, and An accepted it.

He smiled at her sheepishly. "You're prettier in person," he told her.

An smiled back at him, feeling warm inside, pretty on the outside, and accepted all around. Maybe she liked Miles instantly because of his flattery; she was a sucker for it. Whatever it was, it didn't quite matter. The important thing about this encounter was that An was already piecing together in her mind visions of the three of them being best buddies, going river tubing (one of her favorite pastimes) or target shooting (one of Brad's favorites).

A day at the nearby Kings Dominion amusement park would be nice too. They could include CJ since this was one of his favorite things to do. Oh, how she wished Brad and CJ would eventually have the same kind of friendship Brad seemed to have with Miles. Perhaps in time. A girl could dream, couldn't she?

An and Brad had worked on making dinner together that day. Brad told An that Miles's family originally came from Sicily, Italy and that his grandma—or "Nona" as Miles called her—influenced by those Italian roots, made the best pasta dishes: lasagna, gnocchi, ravioli, tortellini, and, of course, spaghetti and meatballs to die for!

It so happened that Brad had a "secret" spaghetti sauce recipe, so they decided to make spaghetti with homemade meat sauce. The secret ingredient, Brad confided, were the chopped sweet onions and freshly sliced garlic sautéed in olive oil, then lots of fresh ripe tomatoes thrown in—skin and all. It didn't matter because it was all going to disintegrate in the simmering process. The ground beef needed to be browned separately, drained, and then added to the sautéed mixture to slowly simmer for a couple hours. Everything would be generously sprinkled with thin ribbons of fresh basil and slivers of Parmesan cheese before serving.

Plating was crucial, he had said, because the art of eating involved the sense of taste, as well as smell and sight, sight being a pretty important one. The colors and how the food looked had to be just so. All the senses were stimulated in unison for the most amazing eating experience.

Brad explained that there was a science to cooking good spaghetti too, of course. The spaghetti was the base or the foundation that showcased the entire dish. The water had to be at a rapid boil when the spaghetti was dropped in, and it absolutely could not be overdone. It had to be al dente and then lightly tossed in olive oil, with a pinch each of salt and pepper.

An enjoyed listening to Brad as they worked together in the cozy kitchen. She loved the sense of teamwork as they prepared the meal together. She felt her heart swell with love, for the man, the home they were creating together, the sense of family and togetherness. She was bursting with happiness in those early days. She could hardly believe that this perfect life was truly hers.

Miles sniffed the air and smiled approvingly, kissing the tips of his fingers loudly, then splaying his fingertips out in an exaggerated way.

"I love the smell of sautéed garlic and onions," he announced. "It's making my mouth water."

An had appreciated Miles's easy way, sauntering around the apartment as if he lived there. He seemed at home, smiling approvingly and buttering An up with pretty words. He opened the fridge and retrieved a can of beer.

"I knew he would have what I like," Miles said, popping the top off the beer can and tipping it to his mouth, taking a big swallow. "Mm-mm… so good."

"You two have done well, kiddos. I love this little place," Miles told them. It made An beam from head to toe.

Miles opened up drawers and peeked in cabinets; he even tested doorknobs and window locks. He was incapable of sitting still, constantly moving around, touching one thing or another and talking incessantly. It made An a little dizzy watching him, especially when her own personality was one of calm sedateness. But, nonetheless, she liked him. She liked his constant smile and perfect white teeth, and she liked his easy banter.

Most of all, she enjoyed watching Miles and Brad interact. Brad seemed to come alive, talking more easily, smiling more quickly, and just more animated and witty than normal. Interestingly, the bond between the two men, that seemed so attractive to An initially, was what she came to resent and detest the most later on.

Those first few months and shortly after An and Brad were married, Miles and Brad were inseparable. Brad always made time for his friend, and often, they seemed to be in cahoots with each other, working on a project together, appearing to be up to something no one else was privy to. They seemed so close that An was not surprised— perhaps a little taken aback, but not surprised—that the first time she had the opportunity to step into Brad's little closet of an office in the back of the gun shop where he worked, she noticed that it was Miles's photo that sat prominently on Brad's desk.

Pictures of the girls and a family group picture, that included Agnes as well as the Ohio clan, sat on a filing metal cabinet in the corner of the room, behind the desk, but Miles was the only face on Brad's desk. That Christmas, An had made a point of framing a picture of herself and a more recent one of Lynne and Erica, suggesting to Brad that they should go in his office, in a place he could easily see their smiling faces. Her own desk at work was by now crowded with pictures of Brad, she and Brad together, Brad alone, and the girls in different poses.

When An had the chance to go into Brad's little office again—they were married by then, and she had been meeting him for lunch—he happened to be tied up with a difficult customer at the shop and was running late. She simply told him she would wait in his office. She was a touch dismayed to see the new photos hanging on the wall above the metal filing cabinet. Miles still sat on Brad's desk, the sole smile perched there.

She let it go, but there were other odd happenings that began to pull and fray the edges of the picture-perfect three-way friendship she had initially visualized. Just little things that nagged her.

There was the time An questioned Brad about a charge on their joint bank account for flowers. When confronted, Brad admitted he had bought flowers for Miles to cheer him up.

"You bought flowers for a guy friend?" An had asked, her lips curling upwards in a scowl. "That's just weird."

"Yeah, so what? I don't care if it's weird. He likes them!" Brad had explained, a little indignant. "Why do you question everything I do with Miles, An? Huh? Are you jealous because you've never had that kind of a close friendship?"

"No, I'm jealous because I don't get flowers from you; you said it's a waste of money because they just die. But *he* gets them?"

He waved her concerns away, laughing at her. "Listen to yourself, An. You just need to grow up a little, honey. You get plenty more from me. You have all of me already. There's no need to worry. Just be happy with what you have, okay?"

An let it go but thought Brad's reaction was condescending and inconsiderate. She tucked her uncomfortableness away because she didn't want to create waves, and maybe Brad did have a point—it wasn't such a big deal after all. She could get herself flowers if she really wanted them; Brad had no obligation to send her flowers even if he was her husband. Besides, she never wanted to be the jealous, needy type.

Yet another time, An had arrived home and parked her car behind Brad's pickup since Miles's car was beside Brad's car where An normally parked. The two friends were sitting in lawn chairs in front of the garage, beer cans in hand. They were laughing heartily as An approached.

Brad slapped his knee and bellowed, "That was kind of gross, you have to admit, Miles, buddy."

"What was gross?" An inquired as she reached the two men.

Brad took a swallow of beer, peering at An from behind the can. Miles just looked away, not really embarrassed, but more like a dismissal of her.

"We were reminiscing about how Miles drank beer from my boot once," Brad told her, then watched her with an amused expression stamped on his face, waiting for her response.

He's taunting me, she thought. *He wants a reaction.* An was uncomfortable, as if she was being ganged up on, like she was the outsider in an intimate replay of events. Feeling like an intruder, she wanted more than anything to bolt out of this situation.

Miles continued to look away, a smirk on his face now, while An squirmed in her own skin.

"Oh," she said because it had been a strange revelation, and she wasn't sure what to say, and she certainly didn't want them to know that the tiny tentacles of discomfort were crawling all over her.

Over time, these little awkward snippets of information and strange occurrences caused An to begin to not just squirm with discomfort in the presence of Miles, but to resent him—or even fear him a little. She dreaded seeing the two men together, although Miles was at An's home nearly every weekend back in those days.

She tried to swat the uneasiness away, telling herself she needed to find some friends of her own to spend time with and stop being so critical and possessive. Those were not attractive traits she wanted to have. She decided she would look into developing some type of personal hobby to keep herself occupied when Brad and Miles were hanging out. In the meantime, she focused the center of her attention on the girls instead of dwelling on the two men.

Then there was the snake incident, which topped it all and changed everything for An. That was the straw that broke the camel's back. It turned her discomfort into distrust, and the resentment and fear became even more pronounced. An made a concerted effort to stay away from Miles as much as possible; she even begged Brad to not take the girls anywhere near Miles's home and Monty. The thought of Monty terrified her.

Brad told her she was overreacting, but An was adamant that she and the girls needed to keep their distance. The whole snake thing was creepy to her.

An had overheard the two men talk about Monty—a python Miles owned and loved like a pet—on a number of occasions. An had never had the pleasure of meeting Monty, nor had she ever been to Miles's home, thank goodness. Because that's where Monty lived in one of the bedroom suites. Monty shared the home with Miles, and sometimes Abigail, Miles's girlfriend. According to Brad, Monty was a handful, so Abigail—who adored all animals, tame and wild—often helped out.

An also knew from Brad that Miles's family was well off—not that she personally had ever met any of them or talked to them or gone to their homes either. Supposedly, Miles had been living at home with his parents his entire life. The family home was large, but Miles's parents had grown tired of him and his shenanigans… and Monty.

They decided it was time for Miles to move out and fend for himself like the adult he now was. Their solution was simple and obvious to them: set their son up for success by purchasing him a rather large country home out in the boondocks of Loudoun County, where Miles had always dreamed of living. He was convinced that real estate expansion was going to skyrocket, and in about twenty years, the homes there would be coveted, and their value would increase many times over.

Along with the home came more than twenty acres of land—mostly wooded and undeveloped. Miles planned to one day build all sorts of outdoor entertainment spaces: a shooting range, a zoo/safari-type area, a dirt bike track, a pool and hot tub, even a paintball scenario area. But, for the time being, sitting around drinking beer with Brad seemed to be enough. They had ample time to dream about all the things they were going to build in those acres of land; they sketched their plans on paper, or they hatched and schemed ideas right there in An's kitchen or in the garage.

An learned to let them be but kept her guard up and her ears open. On the Sunday of the snake incident, An was baking Valentine's Day cupcakes with the girls in the oversized kitchen of the new house on Orchard Lane. The day had arrived frigidly cold for northern Virginia. At about ten o'clock that morning, Miles had come in rubbing his cold hands together and looking for a hot cup of coffee. The two men were enjoying their mugs of coffee and talking about going to a movie and then to a local bar to play pool, all indoor activities to help them stay warm.

An had a mental list going of all the errands she still needed to run for the upcoming week. She needed groceries, she realized. Not to mention the laundry hadn't been started yet. On top of it all, she had all the housework. She surveyed the mess in front of her where the girls had poured batter into the tinfoil as well as all over the table, and drops were visible on the tiled floor. She had to clean that up before it hardened.

The phone rang just then, jarring her out of her thoughts. Brad hopped up to pick it up from the kitchen counter as if this was an important call he had been waiting for all morning.

"Hey, Abby… Wait, what? Hold on a minute, sweetie." Brad handed the cordless phone to Miles. An was puzzled. First of all, this was probably the first time Abigail had ever called the house; she hadn't even realized Abby had their number. Second, why would she call here? Third, what had happened? Something was going on because Miles was screaming into the phone.

"Abby. Abby. ABBY! Listen to me carefully," Miles was saying, talking fast but overly enunciated. Brad was reaching up on top of one of the tall kitchen cabinets by climbing on a chair to retrieve the .45 he kept there.

Oh, this is bad.

An's heart began pounding. She instructed the girls to quickly head downstairs and turn the television on for a while. Lynne had turned seven and Erica four in the ten months or so they had lived in the big house. Being the older sister, and sensing something was afoot, but also thrilled at the idea of watching television on their own, Lynne grabbed Erica's hand and pulled her along. "Yay, let's see if *Tom and Jerry* is on, Erica!"

"Yipyipyipyip!" Erica sang as she followed her sister into the hallway, then down the stairs, their little feet stomping on the wooden steps.

"No, no, sweetie… I'm telling you, GET THE GUN IN THAT CABINET IN THERE like I showed you before. NO! I MAY NOT GET THERE IN TIME," Miles was screaming, going from a level voice to a frantic back-and-forth.

"What's happening?" An asked Brad, her own voice panicky, both hands on her head as if to hold it in place, just in case it decided to roll off.

"I think Monty has Abby."

"WHAT? The snake? What does that mean he *has* her? He has her how exactly?"

"I mean, he has wrapped himself around her, and she can't get him off. We may have to shoot him to save her." Brad enunciated the words in a stilted way as if talking to a hard-of-hearing child.

"WHAT! But how?" An asked desperately. "How big is this thing? How could this happen?"

"Stop saying what," Brad told her. "Monty is huge, probably six or seven feet long. Abby is tiny and—"

"Are you coming with me, Brad?" Miles said as he ran to the back door, flung it open, and jumped down the entire three steps of the deck in one swoop. He lurched forward as if he was about to fall on his face, then caught himself and picked up speed running toward the front of the house where his Corvette was parked.

Brad ran after him at full tilt.

"I'M CALLING 911!" An yelled after the men as they fled.

"NO!" Brad yelled back. "Just stay put!"

An ran back inside and grabbed the cordless phone, which Miles had dropped on the kitchen table. *The heck with Brad and his orders!* She was calling the police and that was that! She pushed 9, then 1 and stopped. She didn't even know the address. She cradled the phone back on its usual stand on the countertop and stood there, thinking of what she should do to help. What *could* she do?

In the dark again, she thought. *How did Abby even know our number?*

She closed the back door absentmindedly. The heated air was escaping, and the cold was sneaking in. She sat down at the table and audibly blew air out of her mouth. There was nothing to do but wait. She might as well call the girls back and finish the cupcakes. Valentine's Day was Friday, but they would not have time for baking during the week.

The shopping list was created, but the shopping did not get done that day. An let the girls sit in front of the television as she worried and did housework. By dinner time, the entire house sparkled, laundry was done, and she had made mac and cheese, chicken cutlets, and broccoli for dinner. There had been not a single peep from Brad or Miles. She was on pins and needles as she waited.

At eight o'clock, An put the girls to bed. They were asleep almost immediately, their little bellies full of cupcakes and cartoons swimming in their heads. An had to work the next morning, and the girls had school and daycare, then ballet classes. In September—*Oh, Lord, that will arrive in no time at all!*—little Erica would start kindergarten. Lynne would start second grade already. *Wow, time is zipping right by.*

How was it possible for time to speed by now that she had a family? As a child and even a young, single adult, time dragged on as if loaded down with weights. Birthdays, Christmases, and other holidays took years to arrive each year. An would grow impatient and bored waiting for time to pass. Now, it felt like time was on speed, never willing to wait for things to get accomplished or savored.

But on this day, An felt like a child again as she waited impatiently for Father Time to drag its lead feet and bring her news of Abby and Monty. *Why haven't they called or returned home?* She was ready to jump out of her own skin.

Still, An had not heard from Brad by nine o'clock, as she finished tidying up the kitchen from dinner with the girls. Lunches had been made and packed for the next day, outfits picked out, and chore lists completed.

By ten o'clock, An was too exhausted to wait up any longer. She went to bed. But about an hour into her slumber, she was awakened by an unidentifiable noise. She opened her eyes groggily and listened. There were voices coming from downstairs. She got out of bed and tiptoed to the top of the stairs, listening. She could hear voices but could not make out the words from this distance. Brad and Miles were back, and it sounded like they were warming up something to eat in the middle of the night, as they chitchatted. She could smell the chicken and broccoli.

She made her way down quietly, listening, careful not to step on the creaky spots or bump anything in the dark.

She turned right when the stairwell split. Left led directly to the kitchen door, and right went the opposite way toward the library and the hallway that doubled back toward the dining room and kitchen. This way was longer, but she had the cover of the long hallway wall and more shadows for concealment.

She was about halfway down the hall when she heard Miles, the words now coming to her clear as day.

"If truth be told, I'd probably be more upset if we had to shoot and kill Monty than if Monty swallowed her up. Damn girl drives me crazy with her whining."

They both chuckled and chewed loudly.

Then it was Brad's turn to speak. "Tell you what—I'm happy we didn't have to kill Monty, but I gotta tell you, that was clever on Abby's part to have the presence of mind to stuff the sheets in Monty's mouth and save herself."

They laughed again. They chewed some more, open-mouthed. An hated that sound.

"Clever. Yeah, I guess so, but dumb to try to feed a python that size while on her period and wearing next to nothing. Monty smelled blood and that's all she wrote!"

They laughed again in between the talking and the chewing. While Brad's laugh was hearty and deep in the chest, Miles's was a wheezy, phlegmy guttural noise. An grimaced.

She felt sick to her stomach listening to this conversation. She stifled a burp and covered her tummy with her hands as her stomach began making gurgling sounds in protest of the situation. But the men were still laughing. She didn't think they could hear her.

"All's well that ends well, my friend," Brad told Miles.

"Yeah, well, maybe this time I got rid of good ol' Abby for real. She was pretty shaken up."

"Plenty of fish in the sea, buddy," Brad told his friend.

At this, they laughed again. *Probably drunk too*, An thought. *Pathetic men*. They had worried her half to death, and now they were talking about Abby and her predicament in such a cavalier way.

"Good thing she remembered my number is programmed in your phone, though," Brad said.

An didn't hear Miles's response because she had decided then to tiptoe back up the stairs, hoping they would not hear a creak or squeak that could give her away. She didn't want to face the two men, and she now knew that at least Abby was okay. She was disturbed about how they were discussing poor Abby and minimizing the tragedy that had been avoided.

Why does Miles feel the need to have a snake that size in his home anyhow? She shook her head. She was tired. She supposed Miles needed a snake for the same reasons Brad carried a gun with him most of the time: to feel powerful, in control, in charge… and maybe to keep their own fears and cowardice at bay.

Going back to bed felt like the right thing to do right about then. Her mind was wandering down a slippery slope, and she didn't particularly like the tone of her own thoughts.

As An lay in bed, her eyelids drooping, her mind beginning to go fuzzy around the edges, she realized the power of eavesdropping. She had dropped in and dropped out without detection, having gathered the intelligence she needed. Now she could use that knowledge, mull it over, digest it (*Sorry about the pun, Abby*), and do with it as she pleased without a confrontation, without suffering any unwanted consequences, without the information being filtered.

She would give this eavesdropping business a second try at some other point in time. It was a safer way to gain entry to a potentially dangerous territory. *Staying safe is critical.* She yawned and flipped onto her other side.

Eavesdropping could keep her miles from Miles and yet afford her some insight into the strange world of Brad and Miles. She smiled at her cleverness as she drifted off to sleep. She smiled even wider at Abby's own brand of cleverness. Without resorting to guns and bloodshed, she had averted disaster with a simple plan of action. *Very clever, Abby. My hat's off to you. Now you need to run and stay gone,* An thought as she finally nodded off to sleep.

After the snake incident, An was hypervigilant of the girls and their activities. Like a hovering mother hen, she kept a close eye on them wherever they went and wanted to be nearby as much as possible. She even began thinking about cutting back her work hours to be home with them more often. When Brad announced that Alison was starting another round of court battles to get full custody of the girls, An was frantic with worry.

"Again? But how can she do that, Brad? She pretty much gave you custody for almost a year—an entire year! She doesn't have a job and no home to speak of."

"That's just it. She thinks she can take the girls and take me to the cleaners. She sees how we are living and wants a piece of it. That's just how she is."

An mulled that over. She didn't want Alison to take the girls, but at the same time, Alison *was* their mother; she had rights, no?

"We have to do what's best for Lynne and Erica," An told Brad.

"Right! And her getting any more custody is not in their best interest. She's a drunk for God's sake!" Brad had exploded. "But she got a judge to side with her, so it looks like beginning next month, we are one week on and one week off," Brad announced.

"What! No!" An said. She began wringing her hands together. "So, we won't see them for a whole week at a time?"

"We don't have a choice," Brad told her. "She went to rehab, and she's been attending AA meetings, and she says she's cleaned up her act. Total nonsense!"

"Well, there's got to be a way to stop it, fight it somehow," An told Brad.

"That's not how these things work, An. She had the supervised visits, then the every-other-weekend visits, and now she's having her rights restored—such bullshit!"

"But I'm their mother too," An said, almost in tears. *What about me?*

That Easter proved to be a trying time for the entire family. The month of March began with Lynne and Erica being taken by Alison for that entire first week, as she asserted herself as Lynne and Erica's "legitimate" mother. An cried a lot over this and agonized over losing her place in the girls' lives, upbringing, and future.

As a month of this arrangement passed, ever so slowly, An recognized the signs of depression in herself: the lethargy, loss of appetite, inability to concentrate, the sense of hopelessness. She wanted CJ. She longed to see her brother again, talk to him about everything going on in her life right now. She wondered where he was, why he had chosen to disappear from her the way he had. Since his leaving, An had gotten a postcard postmarked Barcelona, Spain, and an email. They had been lacking any real information and intimacy, sharing only that he was well.

She wanted answers, she wanted stability, she wanted normalcy... she wanted happiness and sunshine. She missed Ma and Pop so much.

After the snake incident, it seemed everything was topsy-turvy. Brad was gone a lot, saying he was helping Miles coordinate some of the work at his farmhouse; when home, the girls appeared moody and distant; and An was consumed with thoughts of loss—her parents, her brother, her miscarriage... now her girls.

Taking care of the girls and making them her own had been a kind of salve An had put over the wound her lost baby, and CJ getting rid of his life and moving so far away, had left. She felt that wound yawning and stretching, pulling her raw skin apart all over again.

It hurt. It hurt like hell.

That Easter was surreal. Agnes had been feeling slightly better and had wanted to have dinner at her home and invite the Ohio clan, but she had a relapse—doctors hadn't quite figured out what was wrong with her—and simply could not take on the task.

Normally, An would have snatched up that baton and ran with it, but she too was not feeling up to it. The Ohio people had weakly suggested they should do it, but they were too disorganized, and, frankly, An was not up for the drive or seeing any of them. That first Thanksgiving, meeting everyone had been a little bit magical for An (albeit with some weirdness thrown in), but since then, in the two times they had visited Ohio, both occasions had been sad and somber: the first for Don's heart surgery that almost took his life and the other for Grandy June's funeral.

An looked back in time, that nagging, uneasy feeling returning in waves. She remembered sitting next to Marlene in the little chapel for Grandy's service. The older woman had clutched An's hand so fiercely, it startled her. Marlene had turned her teary eyes to An.

"Life is so tragic," she'd mouthed, almost inaudible.

An simply nodded her head in agreement, not able to find any words of comfort and wisdom.

"Sometimes, I just want to close my eyes and never open them again," Marlene had continued.

"Don't say that," An had whispered back. "Your kids are right there. It may scare them."

"An, are you happy? Really, truly happy?"

"Well, yeah—"

"Is my brother a decent guy?" she had interrupted.

An had simply looked at Marlene, speechless.

"Once," Marlene had continued quietly. "I looked at him, and suddenly, his face was different," she whispered, her lips now close to An's ear. "It was as if it blurred, and a devil's red face could be seen just under his own real face, horns and all."

An placed both arms around Marlene, hugging her close and tight, both to comfort her and to silence her, because Marlene's words had frightened An. Marlene's heart was beating fast and irregularly. An's own heart was thumping away with fear and some other emotion she couldn't quite identify.

"Shhh," she crooned, rocking Marlene back and forth. "Grief is a strange and powerful emotion."

"How do we know them for sure, An?"

"What do you mean, Marlene?"

"I mean how do you know the people close to you? How do you know for sure who they are?"

The two women held on to each other for a long time in silence. An didn't have the answer.

That April, very reminiscent of Harrison and Juliet, the entire brood—An, Brad, Agnes, and the girls—had gone to dinner at a Japanese steakhouse for Easter. An had bought baskets for the girls, but there were no treasure hunts or egg coloring. Her mind was already filling with images of next week being without Lynne and Erica. She tried to smile through it all.

If only she could have glimpsed ahead to two short months into the future, then she wouldn't have to cry. She would have seen that her situation would have reversed itself, and life would have returned to the way it had been before Alison decided to assert her parental rights.

If she could have peered into the future, she would also have seen that Miles would be gone, and Brad would be hers again—at least for a time, at least until the next shiny object presented itself.

CHAPTER 17

IN THE HAZE OF CLARITY

"Who you were, who you are, and who you will be are three different people."

- Unknown

After the Detectives Connor and Conrad left, An was restless and anxious, unable to concentrate on anything. She tried baking a cake layered with fresh strawberries, thinking she would go see Ben and bring an offering of moist morsels, fresh fruit, and homemade butter frosting. She quickly lost interest when she realized all she had was canned fruit, and going out searching for fresh strawberries—or any other fruit—was out of the question.

She tried going back to packing, but this task seemed now too daunting and pointless. Should she call Brad and ask what the heck he was up to? Should she search for a criminal attorney? Should she consider seeing a psychiatrist? Could Brad really be trying to harm her somehow, or was it all in her head? She was befuddled and anxious, unable to focus on much of anything.

She finally picked up the phone and dialed Tina, who answered on the first ring as if she had been expecting the call. "Tina, it's An. Can we talk?"

"Sure, I'll be right over," Tina answered without hesitation. *Once friends, always friends,* An supposed, even after so many years of slowly but surely reverting back to being just waving neighbors. An marveled at how friends could be distant, and then, when one needed the other, they picked up right where they had left off. *Friendship is a beautiful thing.* She smiled to herself.

An stood by the door, looking through the side glass panel, itching to have her friend in view. She hadn't fully realized how alone and lonely she had become. It occurred to her, in a moment of clarity, that she was becoming a bit of a recluse like Lisa. She shivered.

An immediately opened the door when she saw Cristina jogging up the driveway, in black tights and a long, oversized, oatmeal-colored sweater. Her feet were stuffed in fluffy, bright red ladybug slippers; on one foot she had a bright pink sock and, on the other, a highlighter-green sock. An smiled at the other woman's ensemble. Tina was well known for her splotches of colorfulness. Always a bright spot in an otherwise blah place.

When Tina reached the door, An opened it and then reached up and embraced her friend with a fierceness neither woman expected. When they began pulling away, Tina held on to An's shoulders and studied her face with concern.

"You okay, hon? What's happened?"

"I've missed you," An said. "…and I'm kinda lost. In a bind, I think."

Tina guided An inside the doorway. They walked into the living room, sitting on one of the sofas, staying close to each other. "I've missed you too, sweetie. What kind of bind? What's going on? Tell me everything."

"I don't know. I'm scared. I'm confused. I can't make sense of things." An stopped her rambling and looked at Tina helplessly, smiling a weak little smile that ended halfway to the eyes, just a tentative twitch of the corners of her lips.

"I saw those detectives walking around. Does it have to do with that?" Tina asked knowingly.

"Yes, and more."

"I have time. I'm working from home, but my project isn't due for days," Tina told her. "Let's go into the kitchen, make some tea, and talk just like old times. What do you say?"

Sitting at An's kitchen table, a pot of tea in front of them and a platter of assorted crackers and cheese, An felt comfortable enough to start the conversation in a roundabout way by asking a complicated question.

"I miss you, and I miss our time together, the four of us, card night. Laughing, talking… How do you do it?"

"Do what?"

"How do you hold it all together—your husband, your kids, your home? How do you hold on to it all and get to keep it? Why did it work for you and not for me?"

The two women stared at one another for a long second, each lost in her private thoughts, running unchecked yet unshared. Tina finally broke the silence, seeming to choose her words carefully.

"Mostly luck, I suppose. There's no rhyme or reason to it. It certainly hasn't been a smooth trip without its bumps along the way. And it's not over just yet. We are not guaranteed anything in this life, An. Most of the time we are simply feeling our way in the dark, trying not to bump into something, and hoping for the best outcome."

"I never looked for guarantees," An responded. "All I ever wanted was to be a good mother, a loving wife, and live my life. I expected turbulence along the way. I thought Brad and I could conquer anything that came our way… I don't understand how it went so wrong when I tried so hard. I did everything I knew how to keep it together." An's eyes were pleading and anguished.

"Because you don't control someone else's actions, An," Tina told her. "You don't control the universe. Sometimes it just is what it is."

"I don't understand why it couldn't have worked… it's not even that I miss him. I'm actually relieved he is elsewhere. I'd be happy to never see him again, and I don't want the life of lies we ended up with. But I miss like crazy what could have been, the potential, the possibility of being with one person for a lifetime, sharing a lifetime… you know? Home, family, kids, grandkids… But now I have no time for a do-over, Tina. What's going to happen to me? I have nothing but… I dunno what… ashes."

Cristina got up and came to stand behind her friend, placing her arms protectively around An's shoulders, squeezing her tight.

"You did all you could to be the best mother, the best wife, the best person within your power. You are not responsible for Brad or his actions. Sometimes God tests us. Sometimes life deals us punches to the gut and heart. You carry on. You're a good soldier—you're a fighter! You just carry on like a good soldier!"

Cristina's words echoed in An's head, *you carry on like a good soldier*. But she didn't feel like a soldier; she felt more like a casualty of war, defeated and broken.

"If there is a God—and I'm not convinced at this point—he is a cruel one. He excessively doles out good fortune to some who don't even deserve it and leaves others to suffer for no apparent reason." An spat the words out with evident disgust. She had never been religious and rarely went to church, but she prayed every chance she got. She had never read the Bible from cover to cover and didn't have a strong grasp on her Christian roots, but she believed in a higher power; she had believed in God, in Jesus Christ as savior, once upon a time. Now she found it hard to believe in anything, let alone some elusive God up there in the vast and distant sky.

An felt alone in the world with only broken pieces of memories, snippets of a life gone awry. All the people she had fought so hard to keep had deserted her anyhow. All the many faithful prayers—where had they gone? Who had heard? She had prayed to keep her family together. She had prayed for Christmas dinners, Thanksgiving feasts, weeklong beach trips, sitting on Adirondack chairs in the backyard watching sunsets with Brad, the squeals of grandbabies splashing in the pool. No one heard, and no one had answered. No one cared.

No one. Not a soul.

"You are blaming God for Brad's actions and your own inaction, I think," Tina answered. "You should not have stayed as long as you did. There were other options. You know there were. But it's not too late to reclaim what is yours, An. And it's never too late to start over either."

"Were there other options, or was it just my fate?" An asked, not really expecting an answer.

"Yes, there were. Plus, God has been sending you gentle alerts all along. You just chose not to heed them until now. Now you pick up the pieces and march on.

Fate or not, you have some control over it. You have some power. Just believe and continue to be strong."

"There was nothing gentle about those so-called alerts. They left me battered and bruised," An told Tina with a sigh.

"It will get easier. Just hang in there," Tina told her. "Now tell me about the detectives. Why were they here? Are there any new developments?"

An wanted to tell Tina about Angie and her conversations with Ben, but something stopped her. It was crazy, but she felt paranoid, not sure who to fully trust. She decided to wait for now, but she did tell Tina about the detectives' visit and how they told An about the telephone calls back and forth between the two houses.

"I'm frightened, Tina, frightened that they think I may have something to do with Lisa's death somehow."

"That's crazy talk," Tina told her. "How could you possibly be involved? They're just saying things to scare you, thinking you might come up with some information. Don't let them get to you."

"But what if Brad is involved and he is going to drag me down with him?"

"How do you suppose he's involved?"

"I don't know, Tina. It's just a nagging feeling. Looking back now with more clarity, I see all the things Brad has done to me and been involved with. I see how he's hurt me without regard to anything. I just can't put it past him. I wish I knew how to better protect myself from whatever he's planning. I wish I knew how to protect myself from him."

"But you don't know if he's planning anything. You're giving him undue credit for masterminding something that may not even exist. These are simply suspicions, right?"

"Right… but there are things… there are things I haven't told you," An said absentmindedly, suddenly looking around. A somber thought had suddenly crossed her mind. She put a finger to her lips, shushing Tina as the other woman opened her mouth to say something.

"I want to show you something," An told her, getting up and motioning Tina to follow her. They went through the kitchen and out the back door. An motioned Tina to follow. "Come on," she said.

They went down the back steps and to the patio that spread from the side into the back of the house. The sun was shining, but it was brisk out, the wind whipping at them playfully. An wrapped her arms around herself. They huddled close. Tina looked at An with a frown.

"What the heck is going on?"

"It suddenly occurred to me—what if there are listening devices in there?" An told her, pointing with her thumb back at the house. "What if Brad can hear us?"

"Have you totally lost your mind?"

"No, I think I'm finally getting it."

"An, please listen to yourself, sweetie. You're not making sense." Tina looked concerned. She placed a hand on her friend's arm. "Let's head back inside; it's cold out here."

"I'm going to confront him, Tina. I'm going to see him and get this all over with. I'm done with it. I'm done walking on eggshells, feeling like I have no control."

"No, no, no! Absolutely do not go to see him! That's crazy! If you believe he's trying to hurt you, that's out of the question even more so."

"Okay, then I'll just call him."

"No! And, set him off? No, An! Just share with the detectives your suspicions. Ask for help or something."

But An was determined; she was not going to back away, not anymore. The time had come for her to redeem herself, try to mend what she had helped to break, and reclaim her life. She needed to fix the broken ties with her girls, with CJ, with Jimmy, with all the people in her life she had let down. She realized all at once what a coward she had been. What did life matter if she didn't— couldn't—stand for something?

"Come on, An, let's go inside. It's cold and windy out here. If you want, we can go to my house and finish this conversation. But, whatever you do, *do not* contact Brad. You hear me? Whether you talk to him or see him, you will need an army of people with you, not alone. Promise me!"

An looked at her friend, feeling a calm descend over her. She knew what had to be done; she needed to trap Brad and end her own captivity. She didn't even care anymore what happened to her.

She needed to find that video.

The video which would supply the authorities with the evidence to confront Brad and stop him from whatever he was doing. Simply having a divorce would not stop the evil. It was her responsibility to act in a way she had never done before. This was her fate. She was done being a victim and a coward.

"I promise, Tina," she lied. *I promise to be extra careful.*

Tina put an arm around her friend and began guiding her back toward the house.

"Okay, but just one more thing before we head inside," An announced. "What do you believe happened to Lisa? Do you really think her own husband, Ben, killed her?"

"Yes, I believe he did have some involvement. Even if he didn't actually physically kill her with his own two hands, he drove her to it. There was always something not right about them, just strange, both of them."

"We went out to dinner last night, Ben and I did," An blurted.

"Be careful, An. You're playing with fire, do you realize it? And I mean with both Ben and Brad. You're too naïve and too trusting. Please watch out. Promise me you won't do anything stupid."

"I promise," An reassured Tina as they reached the top of the stairs leading back into the house. The welcoming warmth of the kitchen wrapped itself around them. An hugged Tina. "Thank you. Thank you for coming and for listening. I'm going to take a nice long bath and relax my mind for a bit. I'm fine. Sorry about all the mumbo-jumbo talk."

"Okay, but will you give everything I said some thought? And call or stop by later. I have a really nice bottle of Riesling if you want to stop by for an early dinner maybe. I can make salmon. I know you love salmon!"

They both laughed, some of the tension evaporating.

"Okay then. You got me, but only if you make your amazing cheesy polenta to go with it," An told her.

"Done!" Tina said with a smile. "Give me a couple hours to finish some work stuff and get dinner started, then come on over. Ed will be delighted to see you!"

They said goodbye at the front door, and An promised to come by as soon as she got cleaned up. But her mind was already elsewhere.

An's thinking seemed clearer than it had in a very long time. She was on a mission now—thoughts and ideas tumbling to the forefront of her mind. Once Tina had left, An quickly made her way downstairs to a small shelter room between the storage area and bathroom. Something had occurred to her, something she should have thought of a long time ago. Why hadn't she thought to check the large safe Brad had left behind in that room? He said it was too heavy to lift, and he needed to find the right person to move it.

That video had to be somewhere. She was going to find it. She was almost certain—knowing Brad as she did—that he would have kept it.

Brad felt safe and secure in his home. As for An, he would not have thought her bold enough to go through his things nor smart enough to find anything of importance. An was sure of this. If he had something to hide, surely he would have left it in the house, believing it to be the safest place. An would use this to her advantage. If there was something to find, she was going to find it.

Trying the shelter room door, she found it was locked. He always hid the key to that room. It was possible he had taken it, but perhaps there was a spare somewhere. That was Brad, always had a backup to the backup.

It was not the kind of lock that could easily be picked; she knew that. Brad would have made sure of it. And, it was a heavy-duty door, not some flimsy wood she could easily break. She tested the door once more, leaning into it, then hitting it as hard as she could with her shoulder, putting her full weight behind it.

It didn't budge.

For the next hour or so, An searched the entire house for the spare key she believed existed. While at it, she also looked for any listening devices. She wasn't sure what a listening bug would look like but assumed she would know if she saw one. Since a lot of things had been packed, it made it less difficult to search. In the main level and upstairs, she searched drawers and nooks and crannies. However, it was a fairly large home, still holding a great deal of furniture and other possessions. She was running out of ideas and patience.

In a frenzy now, An felt savage and crazy and could not stop herself from this wild goose chase. She was on the verge of something—madness or insight, she couldn't quite decide which. Something, something on the verge of discovery. She could feel it, she could taste it… and yet it eluded her somehow.

Her mind raced frantically, and she was overtaken by this unsettled and deep sense of urgency. There was no time to waste. She felt she needed to act now! She needed evidence that could show the police who Brad truly was, and she needed to somehow exonerate herself. Not just in what was happening with the investigation into Lisa's death, but in all of it. She had been complicit, yes, absolutely. But she had to somehow mend what she could. She wasn't sure what exactly that entailed. She was simply going on instinct.

Going back downstairs, An tried to think like Brad. She stood in the middle of the space, eyes closed, trying to focus, and it came to her all at once.

Yes! The lip over the door—that's it! She felt for the key over the door in the tiny space made by the door trim.

Nothing. *Think, think, think.*

She went around the entire basement feeling with her fingers above all the doors but found nothing other than dust bunnies. She stood thinking, sensing a frantic hopelessness taking hold of her.

When nature called, she stepped into the large basement bathroom to use the toilet there, feeling tired and discouraged. Other than cleaning the area, she hadn't spent time down here since the girls had left nearly ten years ago. She looked around, admiring the white tiled floor, the shower curtain with the little black bears all over it, the antique dresser she had found in a shop outside Charlottesville, on Route 15, way back when.

She traveled back in time to that beautiful summer day: it had been mid-morning, and they were on their way to James River, where the following day they would spend time tubing, swimming, and enjoying a picnic. That night they would leisurely make their way to Charlottesville, stay at a quaint bed and breakfast, and then mosey on to the river to begin their river tubing adventure at daybreak.

The little antique shop had caught An's eye a while back. She had always wanted to stop there and peruse. It was the day! The crooked sign above the door said "*Treasure Trove.*" She loved that name!

They'd all jumped out of the car in anticipation of treasures to be had—she, Brad, and the two girls. Inside, the girls had found a section of the store that sold all sorts of old-fashioned candy. Brad had found four John Wayne tin wall art pieces—which still hung in the downstairs den.

And An had laid eyes on the dresser and just melted. "I love it, Brad!"

"Where will you put it?" he had asked. "We've pretty much furnished the house with Amish pieces. You know I don't like clutter, and it's dark and bulky. Probably heavy as crap too."

"I know just the place," she had informed him, only half listening to his words.

The dresser had fit perfectly in that nook between the shower and the closet in the large bathroom. When An and Brad finished the basement, they had built the bathroom specifically for the event that Agnes would someday live with them in her old age, so it was spacious enough to accommodate even a wheelchair if necessary. The piece of furniture, with its dark stain and intricate woodwork, had fit right in with the wooden bear toilet paper stand and magazine holder. In fact, the woodwork seemed to have been carved by the same artist. An had been impressed with herself and her knack for picking out unusual pieces of furniture here and there.

Back in the present, An admired the tall dresser with its three large drawers and the mirror on top, as if floating, held together on both sides by an intricate wood pattern that attached to four small drawers recessed back, leaving a nice space in the front half of the top of the dresser for knickknacks. It was quite a stunning piece of furniture. She would need to find it a good new home at some point. She walked over to touch the fine porcelain bowl on top of the dresser. She had filled it with little samples of soaps: lavender, fuchsia, wild berries, ocean breeze. She sniffed with her eyes closed, relaxing as the mixed scents filled her senses.

Turning her attention to the double doors leading into a small walk-in closet, An eyed the door, trying to remember what was stored inside. She had forgotten about this closet. Brad had put a few shelves inside, and she vaguely recollected storing some old blankets and comforters there.

She opened the closed door to look inside. Like she had done with the rest of the area, she reached up to feel inside the lip of the trim.

And, in the inside part, there was a key! *The* key, she suspected. With trembling hands, she took it to the shelter room door and tried it.

It fit perfectly, The lock turned and disengaged.

She tried not to scream with excitement and anticipation as she pulled the door open and stepped inside. She looked around, taking in a pungent, ammonia-like smell. To the left were two shelves stocked with MREs and various paper towels in bulk, medical gloves—so many boxes of latex gloves!—feminine napkins, gallons of water, myriad green military metal boxes, and old cardboard boxes of various sizes.

A strange feeling came over An just then, as she stood looking into the room, a sharp awareness she wasn't fully cognizant of, like a recollection on the tip of her tongue. It made the edges of her mind blurry and confused yet fully alert to the present. Dizziness overcame her, and she had to lean against the cool wall.

She wanted to explore and learn what else was contained in this room, but her mind screamed that she should bolt out of there. Yet her legs were frozen in place. She turned to the right where a shiny dark brown safe stood ominously waiting for her acknowledgement. Something inside the safe beckoned to her, whispering, taunting, daring her to approach. She had to know; she had to look. But she resisted, paralyzed by fear.

As if guided by an unknown force, An slowly made her way toward the safe, each step weighed down with trepidation and fear. *You shouldn't be here*, she told herself. *Nothing good will come of this. Run!* But she had to know. She reached for the handle and yanked hard.

It snagged, bouncing her forward. It would not open.

In her eagerness to see what might be inside, she had forgotten this safe needed a key or combination code. She then noticed the combination dial and realized she did not know it—had never known it. Her heart was pounding in her chest. She was on the verge of something big, something momentous, yet couldn't open her mind or the safe to retrieve it.

What the heck! There must be a way. Think, think!
She tried Erica's birthday.

Nothing.

She tried Lynne's birthday.

No go.

She tried Brad's birthday, his mom's, her own, their wedding anniversary, their phone number.

Nothing worked. Nothing!

In a panic, she racked her brain thinking of other phone numbers, house numbers, Social Security numbers… Any and all numbers that might be a possible combination.

Nothing.

Nada.

Zero.

Zilch. Ugh!

A thump upstairs brought her out of her trance.

What was that? Who's there? She ran out, testing the door first to be sure it would not lock before she pulled it shut behind her. She left the key inside, on top of the safe. She tried to slow her breathing down, quietly creeping up the stairs, listening and being careful not to make any noise herself.

Maybe Brad *was* listening somehow and had figured out what she was up to. He had come for her. It was all over now. He would never forgive her for going through his personal belongings.

She searched the entire house, moving all the way to the top floor, but found nothing. Back down in the library, An opened the drapes and pulled the window shades up. The sun was hiding its face behind some flimsy clouds as it descended on its usual westward trek. Gosh, she had been engrossed in her search for hours!

An perused the area again with fresh eyes this time. That's when she saw it. Her wedding picture, which An had moved from its prominent place on the mantle to a dark spot on one of the bookshelves, was face down. She picked it up carefully to examine it. The glass had splintered, leaving a jagged line running from top to bottom between the image of Brad and An.

"If this isn't a sign, I don't know what is," she murmured to herself. She set it back face down on the shelf where it had been residing and walked out. She needed a break to let her mind relax and do its work.

With the jittery feeling now gone, she decided she would get ready to go to Tina's in a bit; she would get there early enough to help her cook the meal. She missed having a cooking partner in the kitchen—Brad, the girls, Tina, even Agnes a time or two. She simply needed to get out of this haunted house, haunted not by actual ghosts but the past, the memories that festered. If she didn't get out, she was going to go stir crazy for sure.

Sitting at Tina's kitchen table, glass of wine in hand, An watched Tina chop vegetables for a salad. They talked like old friends. The salmon was in the oven, and the polenta was already done and cooling to the side.

Tina's children were a bit younger than Lynne and Erica. The girl was recently wed and settling in the Seattle, Washington area after she and her hubby made the move. Tina was explaining to An that she planned a visit there in the upcoming months. She had always wanted to travel west; besides, she loved a good cup of coffee and didn't mind the rain. An laughed out loud at this.

The boy had finished college in May and was contemplating getting his master's in forensic science. Meanwhile, he was working in a lab in nearby Woodbridge and sharing an apartment with a friend and coworker. Tina's children had grown up to become well-adjusted, stable adults. An smiled at the thought.

"Where's your hubby?" An asked Tina.

"Oh, out and about. I told him you were stopping by for some girl time and that he should take his time coming home," Tina chuckled. "He's a good guy, my Ed," she confided.

In the silence that followed Tina's comment, An looked a little sad, but she was happy for her friend. She was pretty sure Ed was a good guy, and she believed he and Tina would be together in marital bliss for their entire lifetime. She was sure of it. And that was a beautiful thing indeed.

When the meal was complete and Ed had made it home, they sat down at the kitchen table, which was now set with Tina's good china. At first they took a few bites in silence, enjoying the delicious morsels. Dinner was simple, yet amazing as always. Tina was a superb cook. The salmon was crispy on the outside and falling-apart flaky on the inside, juicy with a hint of teriyaki and ginger. The polenta was cheesy and gooey, just like An liked it. Tina had tossed the butterhead lettuce, thinly sliced sweet onions, cherry tomatoes, and diced English cucumbers with olive oil and a touch of balsamic.

They had little jagged chunks of Parmesan cheese and fig compote for dessert, which made An reminisce about her childhood. That was one of her mother's favorite desserts, or snacks. It was so European and so Juliet. An smiled at the memory, picturing her mother young and elegant, painted red lips and painted red nails, her short, cropped blonde hair framing her smooth-as-porcelain pretty face, daintily placing a dab of compote on top of her chunk of cheese, then bringing it to her lips. An was amazed sometimes at how many of these little snippets she remembered in such vivid detail.

It was just Tina and An left sitting at the kitchen table. Ed had excused himself to watch a car race he had previously recorded.

"Oh, life," An said to no one in particular, a dreamy look in her eyes. "Where does it all go, and what does it all mean?" She took a sip of her wine, her head swimming a little.

"No need to overthink it too deeply, my friend," Tina informed her. "Just sit back and enjoy what you can and what you have. The rest eventually falls into place, one way or the other."

"Yes indeed," An said pensively as two sets of numbers popped into her head: 10-3-62 and 3-10-62.

"That's it!" she blurted, jumping out of her seat and knocking her glass of wine. Tina was quick to grab some napkins sitting on the table to soak up the spilled Riesling.

"What's it?" Tina asked, startled by the outburst and the spilled wine.

"I hate to rush this moment. Sorry about the wine," An said hurriedly. "But I just remembered something, and I have to run home. Forgive me, Tina. We'll have to do this again soon. Tell Ed I said bye. I'll be back, but I gotta go now!"

"Okay…um," Tina said, seeming a little puzzled. "Just please stay in touch and don't do anything dumb, and you know what I mean by that, *Antoinette*!"

"Yes, Mom!" An said, smiling as she ran out of the kitchen, blowing an air kiss to Tina. The women laughed. "You are a blessing, Tina. I'll see you soon! *Ciao!*" An walked out the front door and was swallowed up by the night outside.

She ran to her own home, bursting inside, out of breath from the short run and from the excitement she felt. She stomped down the basement steps three at a time. Reaching the shelter room, An paused as her hands trembled. She knew the code; she knew it!

Brad used to joke about his birthday and Miles's being the same, only backwards. Brad's was October 3rd, 1962 and Miles's March 10th, 1962. But translated into code, it was 10-3-62 and 3-10-62. She had tried Brad's birthday already, and it hadn't been the right code for the safe, but she had not remembered Miles's. She was confident this was it. She had it. *This had to be it!*

She tried the code with shaky hands, rotating the dial left, right, left, then right again.

Click!

It opened. It actually opened!

The heavy door swung away, like a giant mouth yawning. She looked inside and was immediately dismayed. It was empty save for a banker's box on the bottom shelf. She pulled it out just enough to wedge its top off and peer inside.

It was empty! *What the heck!* she thought. Why would Brad leave an empty box inside a locked safe? It made absolutely no sense.

She pulled the box toward her, and as she did, it tipped to the floor due to the weight. Puzzled, An looked at the empty box. It should not be this heavy for an empty box. She stared at it quizzically. What was she missing here?

She moved the box out and flat onto the cold cement floor and kneeled down next to it. With slightly cold and shaky fingertips, she felt inside, on all sides, and then the bottom. That's when she felt a kind of "lip" that should not have been there. She examined it further and realized there was a box lid jammed inside, the top down and the inside of the lid facing up. It created a perfect "hiding" area, making the box look empty when it was not.

"Very clever, Brad," she whispered out loud. *Very devious but should not surprise me. It's very predictable of you, dear husband.* She shook her head with disgust but feeling victorious. The question was—what was he hiding in that secret compartment?

She pulled and pulled and could not get the lid to dislodge. It was as if it had been glued into place. But An persisted. She looked around until she found some sharp metal pieces in a bucket and a box cutter. She picked up the box cutter and carefully worked on the box until she got the lid to budge. Underneath, she discovered various typed pages, some stapled. She began pulling these out of their hiding place. Lists of things, sketches… a large manila envelope. An moved the papers aside. She was more interested in that large manila envelope at the moment.

She undid the little metal hasp in the back and looked inside. The envelope was full of old photos, some faded Polaroids. Her hands began shaking so violently, it made her entire body buzz like electricity.

I shouldn't be here. RUN!

But she couldn't run. She already knew the ending. There was no running.

Beads of sweat on her temples were threatening to drip. Her nose felt drippy too, and her eyesight clouded over. Her trembling fingers were so cold. Whatever was inside urgently beckoned to her, pleaded to be seen, noticed, acknowledged. But the tendrils of fear wrapped around her mind. She felt goosebumps form on her scalp and arms. The room felt suddenly small. Claustrophobia was setting in.

A little voice inside got louder and louder telling her to run, that danger awaited nearby. She desperately wanted to get up and leave, but she found she couldn't.

She had to know. There was no going back now. She *had* to know. Too late to turn back.

She saw the ending. She knew!

Too late, she thought. *Too late for me.*

She dumped the photos onto the floor.

And began examining them, one by one, spreading the collection on the floor of the shelter room.

OHGODOHGODOHGOD! her mind screamed. *Not again, not again!* Outwardly, she only whimpered like a small, wounded animal. She then turned her attention to some of the pages, blinking to read the typed words.

NO!NO!NO!NO!NO! What have you done! What have I done! Her mind could not hold these images, her psyche splintering. It was too much.

Too much to bear.

Too much to see.

Too much to know.

Shrieking in horror, An stood up and turned to bolt out of that hellish inferno, knowing there was no escape. Her foot caught on something by the door, and her ankle twisted. Losing her balance, she stumbled. She grasped for something to hold on to.

There was nothing.

She heard a pop, then a crack. Everything went dark. She felt—more than heard—a faint rustling; something touched her face. Her head felt hot but her body cold. She fought against the black hole that threatened to swallow her up…

…and lost.

CHAPTER 18

DIVORCING THE DARKNESS

"Deep into that darkness peering, long I stood there, wondering, fearing, doubting…"

\- Edgar Allan Poe

When the girls left for college that summer of Erica's freshman year, vowing never to return home, An's precariously constructed world came crashing down like a Jenga tower. The blocks of the puzzle had been neatly tucked and wedged into their rightful places. The knowledge that the whole construct could tumble down at any point if the wrong chunk was taken maintained a constant state of anticipation and suspense.

If the wrong piece was removed and the puzzle toppled, pieces scattering every which way, participants invariably looked on in shock and disbelief. It was not as if the outcome was a puzzle in and of itself; there was no mystery. Everyone knew that it was only a matter of time before the tower would eventually fall. Yet, when it did collapse, the reaction was one of incredulity. They gasped and shuddered, shocked at what the players already knew would be the result.

Similarly for An, the possibility of things going wrong, especially where the girls were concerned, was always a real and present threat dangling in front of her. She was highly aware that if the wrong piece was removed, it could spell disaster and upheaval in her life. Yet she experienced a crushing sense of astonishment all the same when her world collapsed.

She looked on in amazement, wondering how life would ever be the same again. How could she put all the pieces back together? How would she ever survive this turn of events? She assuaged her bruised heart by convincing herself that in time, everything would go back in place. She had raised these girls. Together, they had a long, shared history of love and affection. They had created strong bonds and beautiful memories that could not be destroyed.

Could they?

They were family. The ties that bound them to one another were not so easily snapped; they might tatter and fray, but the struggles they encountered together, and the joy and love they had experienced as a unit, added strength to that bond. They would certainly get through this eventually.

Wouldn't they?

For the four years that followed, An was able to keep tabs on the girls. An did, after all, pay their college tuition. She knew exactly where they were. The girls even allowed for a visit once in a blue moon. But they remained closed-lipped about their activities and life, especially as it related to developments about Alison and her family.

During that time, a strange phenomenon was taking place with Brad. He totally dissociated and disengaged himself from his own daughters. Yet he became the caring, loving husband An had once known early in their relationship. He doted on her, lavishing her with gifts: flowers, jewelry, lingerie.

He treated her to expensive dinners and planned weekend trips to places she always wanted to visit. They traveled to Savannah, Georgia; Sedona, Arizona; Santa Fe, New Mexico; and Reno, Nevada. They went skiing at Deep Creek Lake; river tubing on the James River, followed by shopping at nearby, quaint Charlottesville; and spent leisurely weekends at Rehoboth Beach.

It was a strange and disembodied feeling for An. On the one hand, she put a big chunk of the blame on Brad's shoulders for the girls' absence. She wanted him to fix the problem, talk to the girls, anything to bring them back home. She wanted him to take some kind of action, ownership, responsibility. She could not stand the way he was dealing with the problem so cavalierly.

Initially, as she waded up to her eyeballs in misery and anguish at losing her daughters, An wanted nothing to do with Brad. She felt disdain and anger toward him for his inability to take charge of the issue. She looked for something to finally convince herself that it was time to end the marriage. She plotted in her mind how she would once and for all put a stake through the heart of her holy matrimony and end it all for good. She could not stand the sight of Brad. She could not stomach the smell of her own husband. She wanted him to simply leave, die, whatever.

As if reading her thoughts, her emotions, and her intentions, Brad was by her side, answering her every need, at her beck and call to do whatever was necessary. He even had Miles stay away. He had recast himself into the man, the lover, the husband An had fallen in love with. She found herself coming around, softening her position. She just wanted it to work; she wanted to believe her life hadn't been a total sham. She prayed he would in time work on bringing the girls back around.

She eventually caved in to his charms, thinking this time he had really changed for the better and was working hard to make amends with her. An never looked deeper, never questioned why his behavior could go from indifferent to indulging, from good to bad at will, never suspected that he had an entirely different agenda. She simply trusted that Brad was who he portrayed himself to be and the world was what it showed itself to be. Her trusting nature became a dangerous flaw for An, bringing her eye to eye with disaster.

It was her nature to be supportive to an extreme; understanding beyond reason; giving and caring for others, to her own detriment. She supported Brad when he didn't deserve it and turned a blind eye. She tried to understand his motives when understanding had no place. Her blind love for Brad was self-destructive. It was as if by standing by him and claiming to love him despite his mistreatment of her and despite his unacceptable behavior, she proved to herself and to the world that love could conquer all. She wanted love to claim victory over all odds.

Oh, what atrocities were committed in the name of love—toward others and one's own person. In her blind quest for the perfect, everlasting love, An had made a mockery of the very thing she sought to admire and behold. Unknowingly, she had fed a monster she should have sought only to destroy. Those wily and sneaky shape-changing monsters inside even those we loved, inside ourselves.

Once Lynne and Erica finished their studies at James Madison, An eventually lost all track of them. She gave up her search simply because she grew tired and hopeless. The postcards and emails from CJ eventually stopped arriving in the mail as well. An was done chasing after people that shunned her. It was not that she stopped loving them or thinking about them. She simply grew cold—became numb to the people and the things she couldn't have or had no control over.

The last time she had seen her daughters was when she and Agnes drove to James Madison to attend Erica's graduation. The girls were polite but seemed anxious and withdrawn around An and Agnes. They never mentioned Alison, but their mother's family was there as a stark reminder of Alison. Although their presence made An uncomfortable, Alison's family were nothing but gracious. No one spoke a word of Alison or showed any anger or disrespect.

After that encounter, the two girls vanished from An's world without a trace. She even hired a private detective to locate them and still got nowhere. Agnes claimed not to know anything about their whereabouts, and Brad was mum on the topic.

"I know those girls, An. They'll come back when they're ready or need something," was all he said.

Brad had reverted back to his old self and his previous tricks, spending a lot of time with Miles upon his move back from Florida. Back in late 1992, Miles had relocated to Florida. Although he wasn't around as before, Brad traveled to visit him often. Then, right around the time the girls finished college and Brad was back to his old self, Miles returned to living in his Loudoun County property. The men were once more inseparable.

This time, the two men were spending more time at Miles's place, claiming to be putting some of their vision for the land into reality. An didn't know for certain since she was never interested in going there—especially after the Monty incident—and, in any event, she was never invited to set foot there.

An was left to find her way, alone, and heartbroken all over again. She went back to work full-time; she grew her garden even more grand and wild; she took gardening lessons and pottery lessons. She took up yoga and enjoyed her cooking and baking at home. Brad moved to the basement, and she knew deep down that he was womanizing, right under her nose. *The gall!*

None of her activities gave her the meaning she craved: the meaning she had always wanted from family. They filled her time somewhat, but still left her aimless and without purpose. She had a lot of extra time. Time she had difficulty filling even with all her various activities. She and Brad went on an occasional dinner out or to a movie, but she soon realized this was usually when he needed a favor, particularly money to fund one project or another.

She wasn't completely blind and deaf to his tactics. His rage over An allowing CJ to "escape," as he often referred to it, had died down some. He could not understand or forgive An for not fighting harder to keep her share of the family fortune. However, Brad eventually warmed up to the idea that he could still benefit from what had been handed down to An and were held in protected accounts. He played her and manipulated her to get what he wanted. It worked. Not because An was oblivious to his antics; she simply chose to indulge him.

An had accepted her fate, knowing Brad could be appeased and manipulated in turn, especially when it came to money. And so a strange dance continued back and forth. He still got the better end of that stick, though. He could play with her heart and her emotions in a way she could not reciprocate. She asked herself often why she chose this life. Why stay and take the injuries? Was she simply addicted to the emotional pain? Was that it?

The years passed.

Her life transformed into one of solitude and contemplation. She became adept at listening in on Brad and Miles and picking up little bits of information. She was hurt but not surprised to find paperwork that indicated Brad and Miles had bought other properties together and were in the process of developing them. She didn't think it could sting her anymore, yet when she turned up clear evidence of yet another affair, she was upset and hurt.

She had followed him one evening and watched as the two lovers met, went to dinner, then to the lover's home, squeezing through the door in a steamy embrace.

An wasn't living anymore. She tolerated her days quietly, enjoying a smile or a laugh every now and again, taking small pleasure in her activities, but becoming more and more secluded.

One Friday evening, her yoga class was canceled due to the instructor being ill. She drove straight home, thinking she might order some Chinese and plop down in front of the television to lose herself in something totally mundane and pointless.

She didn't expect to see Brad and wasn't surprised when his truck was not in front of the garage where he normally parked. She left her own car next to where his would have been and went in through the front door. The month of October had rolled around again, and it was about six-thirty in the evening. There was still weak sunlight filtering through the windows of the house, but when she walked in, she was surprised to see that the lights were ablaze in the kitchen, and the television could be heard blaring downstairs in the basement den.

She threw her handbag on the oversized chair at the entrance to the library and called down to see if Brad was there. No one responded.

When she walked in the kitchen, she noticed Brad's laptop on the kitchen table. That was highly unusual. He normally took his laptop wherever he went or locked it away. A ribbon of light oozed out, tempting her to look closer. He would never be so careless as to leave it cracked open like that; plus, she was sure it was password-coded. She would never be able to get into it.

But that stream of light beckoned her, dared her to touch it, take a look. *Come on,* it whispered to her seductively, *touch me, open me, take a look inside.*

She walked away, taking the time to search the entire house to be sure no one was there, hoping her thoughts would turn pure again. She peered out windows to see if Brad was back, almost wishing he was so she wouldn't do what she was about to do. The urge to look in his laptop could only spell trouble she didn't need.

She returned to the kitchen.

The light still spilled out from the laptop's opening. She listened carefully for any noise. Concentrating as best she could, she reached the laptop and pried it open with a shaky but determined hand. Lo and behold, it came to life right away. A CD had been inserted, and it instantly made a whirring noise, and an image came to life. An took half a step back but didn't avert her eyes. She couldn't even blink.

She watched, riveted.

An continued to stare at the screen, eyes bugging out of their sockets. Her hands flew to cover her mouth, one on top of the other, stifling a scream of horror. Along with the image, a voice had also come to life. An watched a young woman lying in a king-sized bed with black silk sheets. She did not recognize the room, the bed, or the sheets. Although the young woman's eyes were open, she seemed unable to move. The look on her face was one of absolute terror. The woman was naked, her arms and legs splayed out to her sides, her limbs pulled apart and away from her in a severe and grotesque way, tied to the foot and head of the large bed.

An recognized the voice instantly.

She watched as the voice got on the bed, crawled to where the woman was, and placed himself on top of her, beginning to kiss her mouth, making disgusting sounds, squirming around on top of her. The voice was totally naked like the woman on the bed.

An was glued to the spot, unable to move, watching with fear and disgust.

Outside, a car door slammed shut, then another. She couldn't look away. Her life depended on it, yet she couldn't move. She was in total paralysis.

The voice turned slightly, his profile identifiable and familiar to An.

"Are you coming?" it crooned, grinning clownishly.

Into view, An saw her own husband's back walk into the frame and begin to climb the bed on all fours. Lucky for An, he was still wearing his whitey tighties.

An slammed the top of the laptop down just as the front door swung open and Brad's voice could be heard.

Then footsteps approached.

In the nick of time, An escaped out the back door fluidly, flying as fast as she could down the steps, onto her patio, across the still-lush backyard, disappearing into the woods behind her lane.

Finding the walking trail there, she ran. She ran for her life. She ran as hard and as fast as her legs would take her. She had to escape her reality. She didn't care where she was going or who she encountered. All she could handle was her feet on the ground, pounding, pounding, pounding.

Twigs caught on her hair, leaves crunched under her soles, and little pieces of debris and pebbles flew around her. She was the bionic woman on a mission. Her legs pumped her away from that monstrous atrocity that had singed her eyes, destroyed her mind, and broken her heart.

She ran past some stunned walkers and joggers. Dogs barked at her, and squirrels scurried up trees. Her tears poured down her face, and her sobs were loud and hoarse in her throat. Her mascara smudged her eyes and her cheeks black, somewhat camouflaging her. Sweat matted her hair onto her scalp, forehead, and the sides of her face. She didn't care about any of it, not even the snot running out of her nostrils that she kept wiping with the back of her hand.

Eventually, exhausted, she circled back around and reappeared at the top of the circle, jaywalking like a drunken and crazed person. She saw a neighbor leaning on one of the pillars on his front porch, a cigar in hand. Such a serene scene did not seem right to An. The man pulled away from the pillar, the smoke drifting out of his slackened mouth. He might have said hello, but An was already veering away from him, going diagonally across the street.

She wasn't sure what time it was, but by now she was operating under cover of darkness and felt safer in its shadow. She found herself across the street—at Tina's house, her neighbor and friend—pounding on the back door, which was right inside the garage to the left of the house. She was thankful the garage door had been left open, so she was able to come in that way and not around to the front of the house where she could be seen from her own house. She didn't want Brad or anyone to glimpse her.

Tina's husband appeared in the mudroom that connected to the garage. He was barefoot, in baggy jeans and a faded T-shirt. He looked surprised to see An. He was a stout man, with broad shoulders and chest, and large biceps and hands. A tattoo that spelled "Tina" was visible just under the sleeve of his T-shirt, on the left upper arm.

Without a word to her, or even looking away, Ed bellowed, "TINA! Come quick!"

Then, without waiting, he grabbed both of An's hands by the wrists and pulled her gently into the small vestibule—their mud room—that led into the foyer and then opened up into the living room.

Tina appeared then. Her face went instantly white. "An?" she whispered. "Oh, my God! What has happened, sweetie?"

An could not find words to describe what she had seen or what she was feeling. She fell into her friend's arms, sobbing loudly. When Tina asked if they should contact Brad, An shook her head so violently it seemed it might fly right off her neck.

In the spare bedroom, An lay in a fetal position, crying. Tina just stroked her hair and rubbed her back.

"What can I do, An? Do you need a doctor? Should I call anyone?"

"No, no, please, no. I just need to stay here for a little while."

"You stay as long as you need to, sweetie. I just wish you'd let us help you."

An spent that night there, but the next day, she eventually returned home after showering at Tina's home and borrowing a pair of her leggings and an oversized T-shirt. She had brushed her hair and held it away from her face with a hair tie. Tina made coffee. An had a cup but was not able to eat anything her friend offered.

"You have to talk about it, An," Tina told her. "You know you can trust me."

"I can't talk. Not yet," was all she said.

As An crossed the lane haltingly, she turned back to wave, instinctively knowing that Tina would be watching her and feeling helpless about not being able to help. As predicted, Tina stood at the window, a worried frown on her face. Her husband came to stand behind her. He circled her in his strong arms, kissing her neck.

An felt a tiny twinge of jealousy that she didn't have strong arms encircling her nor feathery kisses planted on her neck.

Turning back again toward her own home, An imagined Ed saying, "I feel so bad for her, poor thing."

Tina would have agreed with her husband. "I'm worried about her. Something is not right in that house."

They would have been correct in their assessment.

In the backyard, An found the spare key in its secret hiding spot and let herself in through the back door. Inside, she tried to stay calm and figure out what to do. *This is it.* She had to get out of this crazy mess. She was finding it hard to breathe, to think, to do anything. The image of the young woman haunted An; it had, in fact, haunted her all night long. She couldn't get her out of her head.

She was so pretty… so young. It could have been Lynne or Erica. That thought made An sick.

What had happened to her? What had Brad and Miles done to her? Did they rape her? Did they kill her?

She could go to the authorities, but what would she tell them? She needed to find more evidence to back up her story. Knowing Brad, he would make sense of everything and convince the police that he was an upstanding citizen and An was the crazy one. She had seen it before, where Brad rationalized and explained away his actions—in a very convincing way—about something that was so clearly NOT rational or even normal.

An thought back to Melodie. When she had finally discovered that Brad was sleeping with her right there in her own home, he made the entire thing appear as if it was the most normal thing in the world. He was the virtuous, chivalrous one trying to help a lonely, down-on-her-luck young mother. An was the jealous, selfish wife, thinking only of herself. Then she had forgiven him, and they went on with life, because that was An's way—understanding and kind to the point of madness. She had empowered him to continue his abhorrent behavior with her own passive behavior. She should have acted then. She should have put an end to the insanity a long time ago. Her silence made her complicit in all of this.

"Oh, my Lord," she whispered. "This has to stop."

But, as time went on, An had almost completely put the Melodie incident behind her. She had forgiven Brad in her heart because she wanted to hold on to her young family, and she did love him. She told herself it was just a stupid mistake on his part, thinking his actions were misguided but maybe still virtuous. An had failed to realize that forgiveness without accountability was simply irresponsible.

Her unconditional forgiveness had absolved Brad of all responsibility, allowing him to continue his reign of power and control undeterred. And that unquestioned forgiveness had made An a slave to Brad's abuse. With that one act alone, she unknowingly had contributed to her own condition, compounding her captivity in his twisted world. Her inaction had now snowballed to a terrifying momentum.

This is all crazy!

Maybe the girls were right all along, and An should be fearful of Brad. An should have heeded their warning. Their biggest complaint about An—the thing they couldn't forgive—was her passive condoning of Brad's actions, which did equal damage. An had understood this on its surface when the girls tried to explain it to her, but she had failed then to grasp the depth of its implication. Whatever happened to Alison was a big deal to those that loved her. People didn't simply fall off the face of the earth. An had tried to look the other way. She had pretended it wasn't really her business. But Brad had been too calm; he had been too unaffected. It wasn't normal, was it? Now, she was sure he had something to do with her disappearance.

What had he done to her?

As she sat on her bed examining everything in this new light, she became more and more terrified. She had to leave; she had to escape this hell hole! She had to go right now before she lost her mind completely! *Who can I trust? Who can I turn to? Where can I go? There is no one left.*

Over the years, all the people in her life had one by one left, disappeared.

"I don't know what to do. I don't know what to do," An chanted to herself. She sat on the edge of her bed contemplating all this, her mind in a fog. Where could she find more evidence? What exactly was she looking for? Nothing made sense.

Could she trust Tina and Ed with this?

She couldn't involve Tina anymore. She couldn't involve anyone really. She didn't know what exactly she was dealing with. She couldn't get anyone else mixed up in this mess. But she had to do something. She had to get away somehow. All these years of looking away and pretending not to see; she had dug herself into this hole so deep. There might not be a way out for her.

Getting up, An locked her bedroom door and picked up her laptop. She sat in the middle of her bed, crossed her legs Indian-style, and balanced her laptop on her knees.

There must be someone out there; there has to be some place to get help. She had to find some type of protection, maybe legal protection. Or someone very powerful.

"Please, Lord, help me," she whispered, closing her eyes. "That's it!" she said, her eyes popping open again. "That's it, that's it! A house of worship, a holy place."

An began searching the internet for churches in her area. There were so many denominations, so many options. It was a little overwhelming. Then a name caught her attention, a name she knew well but hadn't thought of in years.

"Oh. My. God!" She couldn't believe her eyes. Could it really be the same James Turner? *Pastor* James Turner.

Jimmy!

It had to be. This was a sign. An began laughing and crying at the same time.

"I can't believe it. This is insane! What are the odds? I can't believe it!"

Could it really be true that this was in fact *her* Jimmy? An couldn't imagine it being anyone else. Their paths were meant to cross again. There had been a reason for their meeting all those years ago. She had to call and find out for certain. It was a Saturday. What were the odds someone would answer? She would call anyhow and find out, but she wouldn't use the house phone, though. She looked around the room. Then she remembered the previous day, running out the back door, leaving her bag with her keys and cell phone inside on the chair in the library where she normally put it.

She tiptoed out the door and down the stairs. She didn't want to see Brad. His car hadn't been there when she returned home, but that didn't mean he wasn't there. All she wanted was to reach her phone, snatch it up, and run back upstairs.

She didn't want to end up like Alison.

She reached the bottom of the steps and saw her bag sitting where she had left it. She reached for it eagerly. She just wanted to grab it and return to the safety of her room, lock the door, and make her call.

"Where have you been?"

An jumped. Brad had snuck up behind her, so stealthy she never heard him. She hadn't seen his car outside, and she had not heard anyone in the home.

"Golly, you startled me," she said, turning to face Brad. The terrified eyes of the young woman in the video came to her mind. She hoped her face looked normal to Brad. She hoped her thumping heart and shaky hands didn't give her away. She hoped her disgust stayed in check and didn't instead ooze out of her pores.

Brad looked at her curiously. "Where have you been? You were gone all night. I tried calling you, but you left your phone behind, and your purse, your car… strange, I must say."

When did he begin to take notice? An wondered. *When did he start to care where I am? He must suspect something.*

"I hadn't seen Tina in ages. I saw her outside when I got home from work, and we started talking, and one thing led to another, and I went in, and… well, we talked and talked, catching up, and I just stayed the night."

An knew she was rambling, but she was also astonished at how level and normal her voice sounded to her own ears. Turned out she could lie really well.

"You know how it goes," she continued. "We ate dinner together, had a couple glasses of wine, and what can I say? You know how I can't hold my liquor." An chuckled.

Brad had been studying her face the entire time, as if trying to read her expression. "You couldn't have called at least? You always cook dinner."

"I guess the wine went to my head. Sorry, I didn't even think to call. I had intended to order out anyway."

Brad continued to look at her in silence. Then he said, "You must have gotten here a lot earlier than normal for a Friday. Don't you take that stretching class or something?"

"Yeah, my yoga class was canceled."

"So, did you happen to go in the kitchen before you left? Did you touch my laptop? It didn't seem quite the way I had left it."

An's heart began racing more furiously. She was sure he could see the hammering of her heart through her shirt. It thumped so hard that her chest actually hurt.

"You know I never touch your stuff," she lied straight to his face without flinching. "And, yes, I went in the kitchen, looked out, and saw how pretty it is out there this time of year, so I went out the back door to admire it. That's when I realized I had forgotten the mail, so I walked to the front, and that's when I saw Tina."

"Where's the mail?"

"What?" An asked.

"You said you went to get the mail yesterday. Did you get it? Where is it?"

"Oh, I guess I got distracted and went to Tina's before getting it. Sorry."

An was astounded at her ability to lie like that. She held eye contact with Brad the whole time. He continued looking at her, his head tilted to the right. He did not seem convinced by what she was saying, but she didn't care. When he finally broke away, heading to the kitchen, she took a deep breath of relief and held on to the chair's arm for support.

"I'm gonna make something to eat," he told her as he walked away.

An grabbed her bag and went upstairs, back to her cocoon of safety. Years earlier, Brad had begun to, little by little, move all his things downstairs to the spare bedroom in the basement of the home. At first An was hurt that he didn't want to share their marital bedroom anymore. She found it strange for a husband and wife to sleep apart, but then she realized she felt relief more than anything. She had even found some literature that suggested married couples that slept apart were happier. They got more sleep and were better rested, which made them more productive. Sleeping in separate beds did not necessarily mean eliminating other activities, although for Brad and An, those activities did stop. A long, long time ago.

For years, their lovemaking had become a "once or twice a year" event, and it wasn't loving and warm any longer. His snoring sometimes kept her awake for hours. Additionally, she wasn't too crazy about his drooling, which made the pillowcases smell foul. So, all in all, his decision had benefited them both. She knew he preferred to stay up late, sometimes into the wee hours of the morning, doing whatever he did. Then he'd sleep in and go to work later in the day. An, on the other hand, was more of a morning person. It had worked out for the best.

Now, as she locked herself in her bedroom with her laptop and cell, she thanked her lucky stars she had this privacy. She was afraid that Brad would overhear her, so she waited impatiently for a few hours. Most Saturdays these days, he went to work for a bit in the afternoons. Or he and Miles got together. She wanted to throw up thinking of Miles. The young woman's terrified eyes returned to An's memory, along with the distinct taste of disgust. An gagged as she tried to swallow back the vomit in the back of her throat.

Hours elapsed as she sat caged in her own room, her own house, afraid to leave its confines. She heard a car approach. She heard voices. She heard things being moved around.

She recognized Miles's voice—that voice threatened to make the vomit resurface in her throat—and, peeking out the bedroom window that faced the front of the house, An could see the back of Brad's truck. It wasn't there earlier, so Miles or someone must have been driving it. There was another voice she didn't recognize. She heard movement in and out of the house and was curious to know what Brad was up to.

Finally, she heard Brad's car leave. Looking out the window, she saw it drive out of the driveway. She waited, listening for any noise inside the house. When she felt confident no one was there, she got ready to make her call.

Someone picked up almost immediately. "Yeeellow!" the male voice said.

It was him! An would have recognized it anywhere. Her breath caught. She hadn't expected him to be the one answering the church phone line, but she thought it was just another sign that this was meant to be.

"Is this Pastor Turner?"

"In the flesh," he said with a chuckle as if he had amused himself to no end.

"Jimmy?" An asked.

The phone went silent.

"Um… who's this?"

"It's An, Jimmy. Do you still remember me?"

"An," he said in a whisper. "You've been on my mind a lot lately."

CHAPTER 19
REVELATIONS RECAST

"The belief in a supernatural source of evil is not necessary. Men alone are quite capable of every wickedness."

- Joseph Conrad

There came a point, as An was driving like a woman possessed, when ideas began to solidify in her mind. Playing back the images in her mind's eye: the terror in the young woman's eyes... the nakedness of the *men* (she couldn't even bring herself to give them names because that would highlight her relationship to them and she wanted distance)... their voices... the act of filming their deed... Their actions!

It was all so terribly despicable and evil.

And these were men she knew! One was her own husband! *How does this happen?* She felt as if she were trapped in a never-ending nightmare.

Escaping into the comfort of oblivion was not an option any longer. An had to take action. This woman could still be in danger… or she could already be dead! The thought was unbearable. But, regardless, Brad and Miles had to face whatever they had done.

What would they do if they found out that she knew? What would they do to her?

Earlier in the day, after all these years and at such a crucial moment in An's life, Jimmy had once more appeared in her life. She tried not to question it too hard because it seemed to her she was on the verge of something fantastical that was beyond her control or conscious awareness. Events in her life were being directed as if controlled by an unknown force toward something not yet revealed.

Just a few hours ago, in her desperation, An's internet search of churches within a fifty-mile radius of her home had uncovered Jimmy. What were the odds? Like a long-ago memory that had suddenly been restored, it struck her that everything that had come before in her life was meant to happen in that exact order so that she arrived at this precise juncture, at this particular moment in time, for a specific purpose. Her life had not been in vain, and her days had not been for nothing; her purpose and destiny had collided, and she was on the path of discovering exactly what she was meant to be and do in this universe.

But why did it take so long?

Talking to Jimmy, An had done her best to give him some details of what was happening in her life. She told him she had seen something unspeakable in Brad's computer, and she feared for the young woman's life as well as her own. She needed help but didn't know who to trust or where to turn. They decided they needed to meet right away and come up with a plan of action. More importantly, An needed to leave the home as soon as possible.

Jimmy wanted to drive to An, but she insisted on needing to be the one to put distance between herself and the events of the previous night. She liked the idea of meeting at the church where Jimmy was the pastor. She would have to drive an hour away, but that would give her time to think.

An had looked evil in the eye, had cohabitated with it, and had somehow survived thus far. Not that she had deciphered the code of darkness, not that she had grasped the cold heart of the man she thought she knew, but she did understand and accept the existence of such things as evil in the world.

An had also come to realize there were two types of evil. There was evil that lurked in dark corners and stayed hidden in its proper place of gloom; it could be identified, and it could be kept at arm's length and dealt with accordingly. Then there was evil that dared to live in plain sight, right along unsuspecting people of all walks of life. This kind of evil was difficult to recognize and nearly impossible to capture because it had the face of the man next door. This was the evil that An had encountered, married, enabled, and loved.

She had provided him with the cover and protection he required to continue his dark deeds. She had taken care of his every need; she had allowed him ample time and resources to put into action his diabolical plans. She had even provided him with opportunities for his repulsive exploits. The thought made her sick.

She wanted to vomit.

She knew she had to do something, yet ridding herself of evil would not be as easy as leaving it behind. She was shackled and suffocating from the knowledge. She felt grimy and soiled. Not simply from the knowledge, but the fact that she had nested with the devil.

As An drove down the lanes of Route 66 pondering these thoughts, she felt more and more disgust with each mile, more and more dread with each minute that passed. But she also knew she was driving toward light and hope.

But was it in time? Could she still escape intact? Was she simply fooling herself that help was attainable?

If only she could have known then that what she had uncovered was just the tip of the iceberg, her revulsion and fear would have been multiplied many times over, and her mind would have surely splintered. The full knowledge would eventually come, but for now, a glimmer of hope still shone for her, and she was grasping it with all her might.

An was almost to Jimmy now. Her senses had become hyper-alert. Like a long-lost realization, she was open and aware, sensing in a way she had never before sensed. She was awake and alive! She had no doubt that the mission she was to embark on was meant to include Jimmy. They were placed together all those years ago for the purpose of meeting today. The excitement of this realization grew as she got closer to Jimmy.

On the phone, Jimmy had told An, "This is divinity at work, An. Do you understand the magnitude of what's happening?"

Jimmy's words had confirmed to An that something momentous was happening and that she was smack-dab in the middle of it. She wasn't sure yet what it all entailed, but she felt she would soon know.

The church building was a quaint, white structure, likely built in the seventies. The black-colored roof rose up into the heavens like three peaks, growing in size from smallest over the doorway to largest in the back. The steeple stood in the center roof's peak. The landscaping around it was immaculately maintained. An parked her car close to the entrance where there was an abundance of parking spots. As she reached the imposing front door, she noticed two large pots of fall flowers that were positioned at the entrance to the vestibule, one at each side of the door.

The door was unlocked as Jimmy had said it would be. The choir members were expected to come in for practice in the nave itself, Jimmy had explained. He would wait for her there, and then they could go to his office or the kitchen, where they could make a steamy pot of coffee and talk.

She walked in and instantly saw him. He had been sitting in the front pew. He looked back when she came in. Placing the book he had been holding down on the pew, Jimmy began walking toward An. He looked almost the same as he had nearly thirty years ago when they had first laid eyes on each other. His gait was energetic and purposeful to her small, tentative steps. His dimpled smile was as wide and friendly as ever. The only truly noticeable difference was his gray hair—what was left of it—and the tiny wrinkles around his eyes once he got close enough for her to see them.

Standing face-to-face and smiling at each other, they stood admiring one another, their eyes feasting on every detail of the other's face.

Jimmy was the first to break the sweet sound of the silence that stretched between them.

"You look even more stunning than in your youth." He opened up his arms to her.

She easily tucked herself there, between his arms, her face against his chest. "You look the same, Jimmy, and I have missed you," she told him, her voice muffled by the embrace.

They pulled away and looked at each other again, smiling and admiring the mysterious ways of the universe that had brought them together again, all these many years later.

"Wow, An. I'm so glad you're here! Shall we go make a pot of coffee and sit a while?"

"Yes, yes, please. I'll follow you," she told him.

"Come on then." He led the way, and she followed, toward a side door. Before leaving home, she had changed into a pleated gray skirt that covered the tops of her knees with a long crocheted black sweater over it. She had worn her hair loose, and the abundant waves bounced around her head and shoulder blades now as she followed Jimmy.

As Jimmy worked the coffee machine and put some pretzels in a bowl for them to munch on, they tried to catch up on the years that had filled the time between them. An wanted to know more about his life. He had shared on the phone that his wife had passed away about five years ago, and he had then taken a job in Virginia to be closer to his sisters and family. His son had been just fifteen when his wife passed away from cancer.

"It's a long, sad story," Jimmy was now saying. "She was a beautiful person with a bright soul. We had a wonderful life together, but she battled breast cancer for many years and finally succumbed. She initially did chemotherapy and was in remission, but when the cancer returned, she did not want to deal with the sickness from chemo, which she said was worse than the cancer itself. She just wanted to live her life and let the Lord do what he thought was best. She was a courageous soldier of God up until the end."

"Wow!" An exclaimed. "I'm so sorry, Jimmy. How old was she? And how are you and your son dealing with the loss now?"

"She was a bit older than me, a young fifty-five when she passed away. John had a rough time then, but he is in college now and adjusting as well as can be expected. He's doing great so far with his studies. He wants to be an architect," Jimmy concluded with a chuckle. "He's a wonderful young man, but enough about that. There will be plenty of time for catching up. Right now, we have more pressing issues at hand."

They sat down at one of the round tables in the vast kitchen. An looked around. Someone had done a nice job of decorating the space. Each table had a white doily in the center with a glass vase of fresh-cut flowers. It looked like the kitchen had been upgraded fairly recently with modern appliances and tiled countertops. There were lots of cabinets too.

"Now, tell me everything and anything you think might be pertinent to your present problem. You've told me the details of finding that dreadful video. And, before we go any further, I have to disclose something to you, An."

An was silent, her ears perking up for what Jimmy was about to say.

"I did contact a law enforcement friend of mine and told him about the incident, leaving out the real people, of course, in order to protect you. I described the woman to him and asked if he could poke around and see if he might find anything, like a missing person's report or complaint of violence of some type, you know. I just want to be sure that, if this person is still in danger, we are trying to do what we can to help."

"I understand and thank you. Yes, I totally agree." An grimaced just then and looked at Jimmy, unable to speak.

"What's wrong? What are you thinking?" Jimmy asked her, curious and concerned.

"It just occurred to me when you mentioned a missing person's report…"

"What?" Jimmy asked, seemingly trying to encourage her.

"Well, it's just that… you know how I told you I helped raise Brad's girls? And that their mother was pretty much out of the picture?"

"Yes, and you said there were some issues, and your relationship with the girls was damaged, and you haven't seen them in some years…"

"But I left out the part about their mother going missing back in 1992. She had won a major custody battle with Brad, and then she plumb disappeared. Brad told me he paid her to leave town and never come back. Her family was convinced she met with foul play—so are the girls, by the way. Do you suppose Brad or Brad and Miles had something to do with her disappearance? It's always nagged me, all these years."

"Whew!" Jimmy blew air out of his mouth and placed both arms behind his head. "Wow, that has an entirely new implication!"

"I think this is bigger than we can handle, Jimmy. But we don't have enough to motivate law enforcement to investigate, do we?"

"I'm worried about you, An," Jimmy told her. "I think the first thing we need to do is get you out of that house."

"But I think that would enrage him and make everything more unstable. I'm thinking I need to stay and help find evidence to corroborate things."

"I guess we need to find a way to protect you there if you stay. I would prefer it if you simply didn't go back today and then we'll work on figuring out everything else."

"No," An argued. "That would not stop him. That would allow him time to clean up the mess, fix things so he'll never get caught, and continue whatever evil he's doing!"

"An, you have to save yourself first before you can save anyone else. You have to take yourself out of harm's way. You have no idea what will set him off. We don't even really know the extent of what he's doing or has done."

"I think I can handle him. I just need a little time. Then what I really would like to do is get a restraining order, file for divorce, get him out of that house while I pack my things and figure out what to do with my life."

"Then that's what we should work on," Jimmy told her.

"But that's not realistic if we are to catch him in the act, try to gather some kind of evidence that he is involved in harming that other woman in the video, or maybe even Alison. What if there are others? I can't stand the thought! I can't stand it that I may have helped him hurt people!"

An's voice had turned into a shriek. She was frantic. Jimmy pulled her out of her chair to hold her close to him. She trembled uncontrollably in his embrace. He tried to steady her, holding her close to him.

"Let's pray about this; let's just get on our knees and pray," Jimmy finally told her.

For a long time, Jimmy prayed with An. He asked God for strength and courage, for wisdom and clarity. He asked for guidance to move forward with a solid plan of action. Afterwards, they sat side by side at the table.

Jimmy held An's hand in his, both of them looking straight ahead, at the wall in front of them.

She was the first to speak. "How do you know if your prayers will be answered? How do we know if we will be given strength, courage, clarity, wisdom to do the right thing? I don't hear anything, Jimmy. With all the praying I've done over the years, I have never heard anything. What does it sound like to have your prayers answered?"

Jimmy turned his body to fully face An. She turned her face to him, expectantly. Planting his elbows on his knees for support, he then held her small hand in his two strong ones and looked her straight in the eyes, almost searching her soul.

"You have to first believe with all your might. Then you open yourself up to God. You invite Him in. You don't always hear words or see images. Sometimes the answers come in other forms—it may be a smell or a taste or a memory or a dream. Sometimes it's just a feeling deep in your gut or a sense like déjà vu. Sometimes you think there's nothing, but you act in a way that you didn't expect, surprising yourself…"

She listened carefully. Then she whispered, "I was meant to bring him to justice, and the time has come, but I need your help. I have to find what we need in order to prove what he's done. I have to know what happened to Alison and to that young woman."

"Okay, I understand," Jimmy told her. "I have some connections as far as getting you physical protection. Even if we have to pay for a private person or company, we have to ensure you are safe."

"I know. Thank you. I know neighbors that I would like to confide in—not all of it, but to some degree. They may be able to help too."

"Okay, good," Jimmy told her. "Now, we're working on a plan of action. We just have to be very, very careful. You told me Brad asked you today if you had touched his laptop. That suggests to me he either suspects you of something or is paranoid. I'm worried about you going back there."

"I will be fine. He needs me still. He needs my cover, my protection, my money… he's not done yet."

"Yes, but it may be you next. And, An, at some point, and you don't know when, you may become too much of a liability for him, and it will outweigh what you can provide him… I don't like not knowing what exactly is motivating him."

"We'll simply have to keep praying and trusting, Jimmy."

Jimmy smiled at her. "Yes, we will," he said.

They talked for a while longer, making plans about their next conversation and meeting if necessary. If they could meet, they would, but otherwise, An would make contact by phone. An also gave Jimmy Tina and Ed's contact information. Jimmy promised to find someone that could offer some protection for An, maybe an off-duty police officer.

"I just want to be done. I want my divorce to be final right now. I want to pack my things and go. I can't stand it one more minute, but I know I have a job to do yet."

It was already dark by the time An drove back home. Her head was spinning, but she had found hope somehow. She was on a mission. She had waved to Jimmy as he stood at the entrance to the church, her heels clicking and her silk scarf waving in the wind.

She did not feel afraid as she walked up the steps of her house and unlocked the front door. She was no longer a woman captive: she was a woman of action. The house was in darkness, even though Brad's truck was parked outside.

Turning light switches on as she went, An headed to the kitchen. She eyed everything, carefully trying to pick up on any subtleties. She scanned the large kitchen, then turned to head back upstairs to her room, and that's when she bumped into Brad.

"Brad, you startled me! Geez!"

"You've been awfully jumpy lately, sweetie. Where have you been all day?"

"Just out. Window shopping, went for a ride to the countryside," she told him.

Brad stared at An for a long second. "Dressed like that?"

An was silent, choosing not to answer.

Brad looked at her with hard, piercing eyes. "I'm going away for a few days," he announced.

"Really? Where and why?" An amazed herself that her voice was so calm and level. She watched Brad as he watched her. He seemed his usual self, so handsome… he did not look like the devil. In that split second, she wanted to believe the video had been a dream, and her life was restored to the minute before she saw what she saw. In fact, she wanted the clock to go back to the day she met Brad and relive everything with the man she had fallen in love with. Could he really be the monster she saw on that video? Could he have hurt Alison? Others?

"Just some business for the work I'm doing," he told her. "I should only be gone for a few days, three, four maybe. Miles is helping me move some things."

"Okay," she told him. In her head, An was already devising a plan to search the basement and garage. This was her chance. She needed to find something, some evidence, some clue to show the police.

"We'll head out early tomorrow morning."

"Sure," An told him, turning to head up the stairs. She was worried that they might remove some evidence from the house. It was odd that he was moving things out suddenly and going away for a few days. *Did he know something was up?*

"Oh, and An…" Brad stopped in mid-sentence until An turned around to face him again. "I noticed you haven't been taking your pills, your Prozac."

"What? I don't take it anymore. That was a long time ago." She eyed him, puzzled and suspicious.

"Really? Are you sure?"

"What are you getting at, Brad?"

"I took a call from your pharmacy recently about your order. I'd be careful if I were you. That stuff can have some hallucinogenic effects on the brain."

"It must be a mistake," she told him and turned to continue up the stairs. She tried not to let the conversation rattle her, but it had clearly frazzled her nerves. She got in her bedroom and locked her door, then stood with her back pressed against it, eyes closed, breathing through her mouth, as her heart thumped loudly.

After Alison started taking the girls every other weekend, and after her miscarriage, An had gone into a deep and bottomless depression. She had been prescribed Prozac for a while, but it was a long time ago. *Why is Brad bringing this up now? What is he up to?*

Trying to bury that entire conversation in the back of her memory, An changed into her comfy pajamas and waited. It wasn't long before she heard scraping noises and voices coming from downstairs. Hours went by. She was tired and groggy but couldn't sleep.

Around four in the morning, darkness still reigning, An heard Brad's engine start and drive off. Restless, she put her slippers on and headed down to begin her search.

CHAPTER 20

THE DREAMER

"And people who don't dream, who don't have any kind of imaginative life, they must... they must go nuts. I can't imagine that."

- Stephen King

"No one tires of dreaming, because to dream is to forget, and forgetting does not weigh on us..."
- Fernando Pessoa, *The Book of Disquiet*

An was trying to surface to consciousness, but she found she could not move. Nothing worked. Her eyes were glued shut, her lips so dry and cracked like a desert floor, and she couldn't dislodge her tongue to moisten them. Her limbs would not budge either. Fighting to reach the light, An tried in vain to leave the depths of her dark abyss for a breath of air. Everything was stiflingly hot. The pounding in her head would not quit.

"An, wake up," she heard a female voice whisper close to her right ear. "Wake up. WAKE UP!"

The voice was soothing and reassuring. Such a sweet, sing-song voice at first. Then it turned angry in the blink of an eye. Loud, so loud and angry!

But I can't open my eyes. I can't move. She thought she had uttered those words, but they had only been in her mind. *Who's there?* she wondered, unable to ask out loud.

"You have to try and open your eyes, An," another female voice said, close to An's face. Her hot breath was like a puff of peppermint.

An tried to whimper, to say something, but nothing would come out. Her limbs were way too heavy to lift.

"She won't acknowledge us," a male voice said this time. "She's afraid of the consequences of conscious life, afraid of what she's done. She's just going to keep pretending she's asleep."

No, I'm NOT pretending! An tried to explain. She strained and strained her eyesight, trying to peek from underneath her eyelids and lashes. She wanted to open her eyes; she wanted to explain to them that she simply could not wake up. Her lips would not part. Her eyelids were glued shut. Her body was not responding to any command she gave it.

"Why did you do it, An? Why did you kill her?" the second female voice asked accusingly.

I DIDN'T KILL ANYONE! An screamed in her head. *I'm not a killer. I didn't do it! Not me, not me, NOT ME!*

"Wake up right now and face the music. Why did you do it, An?" the first female voice hissed.

"It's totally useless. She's not talking," the male voice added.

What are you guys talking about? I haven't killed anyone! I didn't do anything! Who are you all anyway?

An was so enraged at this point, she was finally able to open her eyes just a slit, out of sheer stubbornness and anger. She saw only undefined shapes and color swimming around. Her lips finally came unglued. A set of eyeballs were right in front of her eyes—hazel eyes framed by long dark lashes.

"Why did you have to do it?" the second female voice asked, her breath on An's chin and neck, almost a kiss.

"You best believe it won't happen again. Not to me. You will never be able to destroy me, to kill me," the first female voice told her, as she hovered right above the other woman, only her eyes and forehead visible.

Their two faces swirled and clouded over, mingling, becoming one face, as An's eyes fluttered and began to close again.

The male voice's source came into view. They all glared down at her. She knew those three pairs of eyes. She knew them! She knew them! But their identities eluded her broken mind.

"Lisa?" An finally whispered, confusion overtaking her. "Is this a dream?" But her eyes were already closed and her mind hiding, hiding deep. She was so tired, so, so very weary.

"She needs her rest," the nurse whispered to Cristina. "She'll be fine, but it's going to take some time. Those detectives are already hovering, waiting to talk to her. I don't know how long we can keep them at bay. What a horrible situation."

Tina shook her head, tears blurring her pretty brown eyes, threatening to smudge her dark mascara. Jimmy patted her shoulder in a reassuring way.

"She's strong," Jimmy said to no one in particular. "She's a strong lady." He sat down on the armchair at the foot of the bed, Tina now to his left. He put both elbows on his knees and lowered his forehead on the heels of his palms.

Sleeping Beauty rested on the hospital bed, now breathing on her own.

CHAPTER 21
RECOGNITION

"Love is no inoculation against murder."
\- N.K. Jemisin, *The Obelisk Gate*

"Lies are convenient when the truth is unfathomable."

\- Courtney M. Privett

Light streams in like ribbons of color in a kaleidoscope, shimmering crystals dancing on the walls. An peeks out from behind her pinched lids... slowly, tentative, afraid of what might be there, who might be lurking in her periphery. In place of the shades of dark and gray, shadows and haze, there is breathtaking, beautiful color! At last!

She is alive! She doesn't know how exactly, but she is alive.

The first face she sees is Jimmy's.

Her hand flies to her neck to feel the necklace that no longer resides there, dangling on her chest. Except her hand doesn't quite fly, it is just her brain imagining it. Her limbs feel like they are weighed down with a hundred pounds of pressure, her eyes are groggy, and her tongue is like a piece of sandpaper in her mouth. An's head feels like a giant balloon, floating, floating.

Jimmy, you're here! she tries to say, but her throat won't work. Jimmy keeps smiling from ear to ear. His eyes are moist with tears. He keeps telling An that everything is going to be okay, that he always knew she would come back.

Back from where? An wonders. *Where have I been?*

That's when she sees Tina behind Jimmy. Tina is sobbing and laughing at the same time.

An closes her eyes because this is all so disorienting and overwhelming. She needs to think, but her brain feels lazy and fogged up.

Then she remembers.

As her eyes droop and the familiar darkness brings her comfort, An feels safe enough to remember those last moments before it all went pitch dark.

Dark knowledge seeps into her mind, but she cannot face it just yet.

Too frightened to come out of the dark, An stays there just a while longer.

She stays inside the fear.

She wishes it would be forever night so the dark thoughts would stay hidden from light, in the shadow of her consciousness.

An can feel Jimmy's hand on hers. She hears voices. She instinctively knows that the doctors are trying to put her back together, but there is no way to fix her. They don't know what she knows. There is no escape.

Can I hide here forever? It feels safer in the dark. Is this what it feels like to die? she wonders.

She knows she has to face the light and the atrocities Brad has committed. Maybe he will come back for her to finish the job he started, but An is sure she has already died once. She knows what to expect.

Like a salve on her wounds, time is An's friend for once. It never was before, always in a hurry. But now An needs time to mend her broken mind and her broken body and her broken soul.

So, she sleeps.

Not the deep bottomless sleep she had been experiencing for the last few months.

Just regular REM sleep.

It isn't until she goes to visit Dr. Rudolph that she is able to release some of the images and try to make sense of what had happened to her.

An admires Dr. Cecilia Rudolph. Her hair is pure white, cropped short, and curly. Her entire face lit up into a generous smile when An is wheeled into her office. Wheeled in because her legs are still too wobbly to walk on her own and she doesn't trust her sense of direction anyhow.

Dr. Rudolph has kind yet piercing eyes that seem to miss nothing. Her lips are painted bright red, and the outer corners of her eyes crinkle when she smiles.

She welcomes An in, then sits on an oversized, teal-colored chair, across from her. The doctor's arms jingle whimsically with gold bangles—maybe half a dozen draped around each wrist.

"Those are beautiful," An tells her. "Both to the eyes and to the ears. I used to have a set of three a long time ago. A gift from my daughters."

An bows her head then, remembering Lynne and Erica. *My beautiful girls,* she thinks as she examines her nails. She used to grow them long and shape them blunt on top with an emery board, she remembers. But now they are short and dull-looking. Feeling like a new person, she resolves to paint them pink. Hot pink!

"Tell me about your bangles and your girls, An. If you'd like," Dr. Rudolph says.

An is mesmerized by the doctor's gentle and soothing voice. She looks up as two fat tears slip and track down her cheeks.

"Will I ever see their faces without associating them to the other images in my head?"

"Give yourself time, An. Don't rush the memories."

It takes An a few visits to the psychiatrist's office, but then she is at last able to face the darkness.

Like a movie in her mind, the images begin replaying. *Those ugly pictures… Oh, my God! Horrible acts… Dead people, dead girls. In the safe where Brad's things were, there were pictures of death.* It all comes tumbling into An's consciousness, and she knows she is not safe.

Not safe at all.

Never going to be safe.

Brad is coming for her, to do to her what was done to those other girls.

"OHMYGODOHMYGODOHMYGOD," she screams, but the words are trapped inside her head.

Outwardly, she crosses her hands over her throat as if to choke herself, choke the words away. Desperately, she tries to catch her breath, sucking in air in gulps too big to process.

Dr. Rudolph is instantly on her knees in front of An.

"Look at me, An. You are safe. Brad and Miles are locked away. They can't hurt you. Look around you. You're in the turquoise room. Here, you are safe."

An wants to scream out loud. She wants to tell Dr. Rudolph—Jimmy and Tina too—that she is so afraid. She does not feel safe. None of them are safe. But she can't speak. Her mouth won't work; her words won't materialize.

She tries to focus on the cozy turquoise room—she really does.

After waking up from her coma, it had taken An some time before she was able to speak again. Jimmy and Tina had been there. They had reassured her that she didn't have to fear Brad for now, that she just needed to get strong enough to talk to the doctors and the detectives to try to put all the pieces of the puzzle together.

But now, sitting in front of Dr. Rudolph, An feels a strong desire to run back into the comforting darkness. She could live there forever and feel safer. She feels like she has suddenly taken a million steps backwards in her progress.

She doesn't want the turquoise room; she wants the comfort of the darkness.

She can only cry and gasp for air.

No words.

Words make it all reality, wouldn't they? Words would make the horror true. Words would give voice to the unspeakable acts.

Dr. Rudolph's touch is what finally calms An. That magical, feather-soft touch as the doctor takes An's hand in her own hands.

"You're not alone anymore, An. We are all here to help. But only when you're ready. Give those images words only when you're ready. Face the light only when you're ready. No rush."

It takes time, but An finally find her words.

Words could free her, she realizes, if she could string them together properly. Yes, words would give voice to the atrocities, but they could also free her from the constricting bonds of secrets and dark thoughts.

Once her mind begins to heal, An finds the will and courage to help solve some of the mystery surrounding what had happened to her. She and Doctor Rudolph finally agree that An is strong enough to try speaking with the eager detectives.

When at last the day arrives and the detectives come into An's room, she gasps in recognition.

"Detective Connor! And Conrad!" An smiles at them weakly, a little relieved and a little confused.

"Hi, An," Detective Conrad says. The detective's eyes are kind and her voice gentle. She is taking the lead in this case, An notices.

"An…" Detective Conrad begins. "I am so glad you are out of your coma. I hope you feel well enough for us to talk about what happened to you. But first… An, how do you know who we are?"

Detective Connor stands behind his counterpart, looking expectant. He hasn't said anything, has just looked at An with a mixture of pity and awe. It seems it was a miracle An had survived her attack. But now it seems that An's acknowledgment of the detectives is creating a new kind of awe.

"Um… from meeting at my house?" An tells them. They stare at An, and the silence stretches a mile.

"An…" Detective Connor has said her name this time. "An… when did we meet at your house? Do you remember?"

An gulps, beginning to feel a strange sensation building from her toes and up to her face. She blinks and blinks, trying to remember, and not understanding why *they* don't seem to remember.

"You were investigating Lisa's suicide," An tells them in a near whisper. It is now her turn to look at them expectantly. *Surely, they remember.* But their puzzled, confused stares, squinty eyes and all, tell An they haven't a clue.

"Lisa?" Detective Conrad asks, shaking her head as she says it.

"None of it happened? Wow!" An says, more to herself than to the detectives. "My neighbors, the Spencers. Analise, the wife, she—she committed suicide," An tells them. But now that she is saying it, she isn't so sure of the events that took place, or didn't take place.

It appears that An has dreamed it up while in her comatose state.

"But you know our names…" Detective Connor says in wonderment. "How can you know our names?

We never told you our names. In fact, this is the first time we're meeting, An."

"It is?" An asks, trying to understand where those other memories are coming from. It would be easy to justify that her frayed mind had made up the remembrance, that she had simply dreamed about meeting the detectives, but how did she get their names right?

The meeting with Dr. Rudolph had not prepared An for this encounter with the detectives. This is one of the first clues that her jumbled memories are fact and fiction mixed together. But which is which?

There are a few times—like that first interaction with the detectives—when she experiences her mind so jumbled and fragile, she almost believes she is still trapped inside the dark corners of her thoughts.

Another time comes after, when she is being wheeled to Dr. Rudolph's office.

"Stop!" she tells the nurse. "Who's that woman in the white lab coat?"

"There are a gazillion of those, Ms. Jordan! Which one?"

"Right over there," she points. "With the reddish-brown hair, shoulder-length, petite, pretty nails painted red. Is it Angela? Is her name Angela or Angie something?"

The nurse frowns and squints, trying to identify the person in the direction of An's gaze. "I don't see her," the nurse said.

The nurse begins wheeling An again before saying to her, "I don't think we have a doctor by that name. But maybe she's new. Do you know the last name?"

"No," An tells her, feeling frazzled, agitated, disturbed. She is almost certain she has seen Angie in the flesh, talking to another doctor. She even laughed like Angie. But suddenly, An doesn't trust her memory or vision. She can't even trust her own thoughts.

She can't be sure of anything.

Jimmy prays with An in the days to come, reassuring her that her memories will be her own again some day. She needs to be patient with herself. But the truth is that maybe An doesn't want some of her recollections back. *Let them hide in the darkness.*

She wonders if her memories are being truthful to her. All the meetings with Dr. Rudolph have not brought to light or provided explanations for a lot of the jumbled recollections, like knowing the detectives and seeing Angie.

Why?

"Be patient, An," Jimmy had told her.

"Don't rush it, An," Dr. Rudolph had said.

"Go easy on yourself," Tina agreed with the others.

The doctors run a battery of psychological tests, trying to identify the root cause of An's jumbled memories. It is natural to have some temporary—or even permanent—memory loss due to her months in a coma, but it seems her particular case is a little different. She is a bit of a phenomenon.

Science, technology, psychology, these studies have advanced in quantum leaps. Yet not everything can be explained. Not all questions produce answers. The mind is a vast, complicated, mysterious galaxy.

An had no neighbors named Benjamin and Analise Spencer. There was no report of a suicide on her street, ever. Which means that her recollection of those events and her time with Ben never happened, save in her mind. So why does she have those vivid memories? Why does she keep replaying them in her memory? Why does An know Detectives Connor's and Conrad's names?

Did she really see Angie?

An doesn't know the answer. The doctors don't know; Jimmy doesn't know. No one knows.

What they all do understand, however, is that An had been viciously attacked and almost died. She had lain in a coma for nearly three months! She was not expected to come out of it. Her head injuries were serious and complicated and required multiple surgeries.

Tina is real, and Jimmy is real. They had been by An's side the entire time she was dead to the world. CJ is real, and Erica and Lynne are real. The deaths of An's parents were real. And Brad, oh, yes, Brad is very much real.

But, according to everyone, there isn't—and never was—an Angie or a Lisa. An is told those were figments of her imagination, as real as they seemed to her. The best An can come up with is that they were all pieces of herself. They had existed, and then they didn't. As An changed or her circumstances changed, a new An had emerged.

More than a year has passed, and An is still trying to figure it all out. Winter faded away; spring and summer came and went. Then winter reappeared, only to make way for another spring. An is grateful that she's still here, in this world. She's so glad she somehow found her family again in the midst and aftermath of chaos, pain, and so much destruction.

An is slowly rebuilding her life, one baby step at a time.

And with as much as An's mind had played with her, it is sad to admit that Brad is real. Unfortunately, the atrocities he committed were also very painfully real. Miles and Agnes are real. An wishes they weren't; she wishes she had never met them. But then again, if that were the case, she would never have had Erica and Lynne in her world… or Tina and Ed… and maybe Jimmy would not have returned to her.

Who knows?

Who knows the true secrets of life? Who knows why things happen the way they do?

Why did An's life turn out this way? Why her? Why did she love and marry a serial killer?

CHAPTER 22

REFLECTIONS

"Memory is deceptive because it is colored by today's events."

\- Albert Einstein

An reflects on the past like a Peeping Tom looking in through a hole in the wall. On the other side, the images playing out fascinate her, and the words being exchanged enthrall her, yet she is able to experience it with the emotional distance of an outsider. She's not living that life; she's simply witnessing it being lived.

An admits to herself that sometimes she takes certain liberties with her remembering of events. She might change a detail or two here and there because, well, she can! Who's to stop her? She is the sole creator, actor, and spectator of these reflections. Her adjustments don't actually change the outcome of things, and they don't sting anyone; they simply distort perceptions ever so slightly, making the memory sweeter, or easier to accept.

Otherwise, she would have to drive off a cliff or choose a padded cell for a home.

But the here and now is a different story altogether. Oftentimes, An lives it on the edge of her seat, never quite knowing when a monkey wrench might be thrown into the works. In this realm, she's not the sole anything; she's only a small-time actor playing a bit-part. But having been on this earth now for half a century, An is finally becoming better at discerning her roles and more adept at reciting her lines.

Coming out of her ordeal opened An's eyes to a lot of discoveries about herself and the world around her. She can't change what happened. That door has closed shut, and it has all been written in stone. She can only choose how to go forward, one tiny step at a time.

Some life mysteries not even An is privy to and will never unravel—like knowing those detectives' names after coming out of her coma. Or the fact that she married a killer.

An found out how her ordeal helped detectives put a bow on a number of missing person's cases in her area and beyond. She learned that Brad was not alone in his life of murder. Miles was his accomplice, and even Agnes was a partner in crime.

What are the odds that in one family alone, a son goes to prison for murder, another son is a serial killer, and their mother an accomplice to murder?

Agnes's involvement was a shocker for An. She knew Agnes doted on Brad. An herself blindly believed in Brad for a very long time, unknowingly providing the cover and funds needed for a lot of his murderous deeds. So, from this perspective, it wasn't difficult to understand Agnes's motivations. It wasn't that she physically participated in the horrors that Brad and Miles committed, but she kept quiet about a lot of things she came to know, and provided cover and protection, mostly out of fear of losing her youngest son the way she had lost her older son to a life in prison.

Agnes had known that Brad and Miles were involved in Alison's disappearance and then had "disposed" of her, but she didn't know the details. In a way, Agnes was a lot like An. The difference was that Agnes had been willing and aware of her participation and involvement. An had been in the dark.

An felt a heavy sense of responsibility for the missing and murdered girls. Maybe she could have helped some of them, like Alison and Melodie.

Yes, Melodie was one of Brad's victims. So was her young son. It seems strange that Brad and Miles would murder little Danny, even incomprehensible. He was just an innocent child. Yet Brad did not want to leave any loose ends hanging around to create his own noose.

An's anguish that she should have seen the signs still torments her sometimes. She should have been able to help somehow, been smarter… the guilt suffocates her out of sleep some nights. How could she have been so blind? She is paranoid, sensing all eyes on her, accusing her of being a lame fool, maybe even an accomplice to the horrors.

It took seeing the despicable video. It took the mind-shattering images to make her act. And even then, it was too late. Too late for the girls who disappeared and met a horrible end. Almost too late for An herself. If Tina hadn't suspected something was wrong and gotten the police to check her house that night, they might have come too late to save her from Miles.

It was Miles who, doing Brad's bidding, came to An's home that fateful night and attacked her with a bat—just as An had discovered the box of evidence in the bomb shelter in her basement.

An had reason to fear Miles all those years. She had reason to protect her girls from him. Too bad she didn't have that same instinct to protect them from their own father. The same father who murdered their mother and fed her to Miles's python, Monty!

Oh God! That thought still horrifies her!

The horror of it haunts An every day. But Miles cracked and spilled the beans, all of it. An can only imagine what this knowledge is doing to the girls.

To think that their own grandmother knew and helped to hide the evidence, protect the lies, and bury the memories. To think that the person who acted as their second mother, who was supposed to shield them from such ugliness, helped their father commit his despicable deeds. Albeit unknowingly, An had played a role. She idolized Brad wholeheartedly; she acted as a cover for him and had funded a lot of his activities. How stupid had she been!

An had driven the girls away from her. She had driven her own brother away too. She so single-mindedly wanted the life she thought was hers. She wanted the family, the normalcy—the dream she thought she was creating with Brad. She wanted it all so badly that she put it above all else. That construct, that dream, that *thing!* Her ideal life turned out to be anything but.

The detectives told her that Brad and Miles were tied to dozens of cases of missing girls—people. There were males too. The investigation is ongoing, but thankfully, Brad and Miles are now in prison, where they belong. No parole, ever! They will never get out.

CJ was a victim as well. It breaks An's heart to think what he went through. The investigators hope to find him alive. He is not in Spain, but he did go there for a period of time. He changed his identity and went into hiding. Investigators suspect he was a victim of extortion. He was also beaten and sexually assaulted as a form of intimidation and torture. An had seen the pictures with her own two eyes.

An can't stand the image, but she also can't erase it away. Those images torture her during sleep and when she's awake too.

An's little brother didn't go to the authorities, didn't go to An, didn't speak out. Simply gave in to what they wanted: money, power, control of the business. Always the clever one, he had figured out a way to hand over to Brad and Miles what they were stealing, yet was able to retain some of it for An and for himself. He had given the business away to save it.

It was never clear to An when exactly the torment of her little brother first began. But she was flabbergasted to find—when discussing with the investigators—that there was speculation that CJ and Brad might have met before Brad and An had ever met.

Just a freak coincidence. What were the odds?

It had been during the time that An had returned to James Madison to finish her senior year. Harrison had passed away, and Juliet was still alive but barely hanging in there. CJ was going through a rough time and confided his troubles in a friend, who happened to be a gay man. CJ and Nathan ended up at a gay bar in Georgetown.

They had struck up a conversation with two other men, who later turned out to be Brad and Miles.

Detectives had interviewed Nathan while trying to locate CJ, and that's how they came to know the story. This tale shed some light on the long-ago conversation with Brad about CJ's sexuality.

An is still confident that neither Brad nor CJ are gay. She feels that CJ would not have cared about appearances and would have gone to a gay bar just because that's where his friend wanted to go. And Brad had always had a strange fascination with those he believed to be on the "fringes of society"—one of his overused, politically incorrect phrases.

Once, while vacationing in Las Vegas, Brad had struck up a conversion with a woman he believed was a prostitute to "pick her brain." When An had questioned the strange exchange, he had told her that he was intrigued by prostitutes and homosexuals and wanted to "study" them and understand them, maybe even fix them.

"Like playing God or something?" An had asked.

"I guess," he had said.

"You liken yourself to God?" An had asked, a little incredulous.

"Well, why not?" he had said. "God was just a man. We are the ones glorifying him to epic proportions."

She had found this fascinating that he actually thought himself an equal to God.

Pairing this previous knowledge with the information she learned from the police investigation helped An to recognize some of the dynamics that had played out between CJ and Brad. Being the predator that he was, Brad would have felt emboldened—justified even—to bully CJ.

Afraid for his life and An's, poor CJ would have thought that the only way to keep both himself and An alive was for him to leave without a trace. He managed to save them by transferring the ownership of the business, yet keeping the proceeds of other properties in trusts and transfer funds to offshore accounts in order to protect their inheritance, which Juliet and Harrison had worked so hard to build.

Maybe An will never heal. But she's thankful every day for Jimmy. He is her rock, and An gives him a lot of credit for the progress she's made in the last eighteen months. Still, An knows she has a ways to go. She sees Jimmy at church on Sundays, and they try to get together multiple times a week. An needs him in her life to keep her stable, to keep her sane, to help her put one foot in front of the other.

An decided to keep her house. There are so many ghosts there and so many dark memories, but there are many wonderful, touching memories too. An loves her home like an old, trusted friend. It has comforted her, and it holds the echoes of Erica's and Lynne's laughter within its walls. An treasures and loves those moments with her girls. Here, she is trapped in time with them, and right now, that's exactly where she wants to be.

An has spoken with the girls on occasion, and they visited her twice while An was recovering in the hospital, after her long sleep. It was emotional and awkward seeing them. Knowing what their father did is a huge dark cloud that hangs over them. In An's heart she still thinks they blame her, in part, for Alison.

Brad sang like a canary when he felt the jig was up. He confessed to a lot, putting the brunt of the blame on Miles. He told the police he and Miles went to Alison's apartment. They incapacitated her by strangling her. Then they carried her out of the apartment in the cover of night. They kept her at Miles's house, they did despicable things to her body, and then they dismembered her and fed her to Monty over time to get rid of the evidence.

How does a human being do that to another?

An played back the echoes of that conversation so many years ago when Brad made it clear that he felt he was on the same footing as God. Brad had also displayed a desire to orchestrate and control those he saw as weaker or inferior to him. When you have an ego the size of the universe and an attitude of omnipotence, perhaps that's how a human being does that to another.

How is it that An didn't meet the same fate as the other women? Why was she spared?

"There's always a reason, An," Jimmy tells her. "God has a plan for all of us. You have to believe that.

"But those victims didn't have a chance," An reminds him.

To this, neither one has an answer.

An hopes and prays that God's plans include her regaining a relationship with her girls and finding CJ out there somewhere. An has lost so much; it takes her breath away. She wants some of it back.

She wants her brother and her girls back.

Until then, she has her giant house to roam in with her doctored memories.

CHAPTER 23

RESURRECTION

"I believe that the greatest truths of the universe don't lie outside, in the study of the stars and the planets. They lie deep within us, in the magnificence of our heart, mind, and soul. Until we understand what is within, we can't understand what is without."
- Anita Moorjani, *Dying to Be Me: My Journey from Cancer, to Near Death, to True Healing*

An had made direct eye contact with death and still had been allowed to come back to the living. It is a mystery and a miracle.

She still has strange dreams now and again, and she still thinks about Lisa and how her life was cut short. In therapy, An has come to see Lisa as her other self, the one she had eradicated in order to fit her new life as Brad's wife and the mother of his children. She had discarded Lisa like an old skin and grown another in its place.

Same with Angie. An always wanted to be a professional woman, smart and in control of her own destiny. And although she had kept some of those traits, it was in subterfuge. Brad could not know; it simply didn't fit his idea of her.

Her memories are still muddled, but she is slowly making sense of things. Her body is healing too. Her hair has grown to shoulder length after being completely shaved so doctors could tend to her head wounds. She has begun to put on a little weight, which is good.

An spends long hours in her yard. She pulls weeds, she mows, she plants, she waters. As spring grows closer, the perennials are making a comeback, and soon, it will be a jungle of color out there. She feels more alive than ever.

Life is good.

She will once more enjoy her basil in pasta dishes and salads, fresh mint in her tea, and bouquets of flowers tied with yellow-and-blue ribbon will decorate the kitchen table again.

Last weekend, she had ventured out for dinner with Tina. They ate teriyaki salmon, shrimp stuffed with crab meat, and loaded baked potatoes. They drank cheap white wine and ate chocolate cake for dessert. It was lovely. An's cheeks grew rosy as she talked and laughed. She told Tina how alive and carefree she felt. A weight had lifted off her chest, knowing Brad was behind bars.

"But I don't want to talk about him tonight. I want to enjoy this moment without Brad always hanging around my neck."

"I love that you're finding your smile again," Tina told her. "I admire your strength, An. You have gone to hell and back, girl!"

"You and Jimmy are a big reason I'm here today and can smile again," An told Tina, her eyes growing misty with emotion—good emotion this time.

The two friends looked at each other, their eyes dancing in the candlelight.

Tina broke the silence first. "Hey, we are finally getting new neighbors. The house two doors from you finally sold, did you know?"

"No, but I did notice the for-sale sign was gone. It sure is a pretty home. They did a good job updating it," An told Tina.

"I can't wait to meet our new neighbors."

That night, An goes to bed smiling, thinking about new beginnings. She feels good about these new neighbors. She mentally catalogs what she has in the fridge and the pantry. Maybe she will bake her famous raisin-oatmeal cookies. A casserole, even.

Life isn't so bad. She is lonely, yes, but she has plenty to fill her time, including continuing the search for CJ and how to win the girls over. In fact, An has been in contact with a private investigator that seems promising. He seems to be making headway in finding CJ and has hatched a plan to hopefully get him back safe.

An falls asleep wrapped in her fluffy comforter, her head full of warm thoughts.

The following day, An makes a cup of coffee while waiting for daybreak to arrive and then curls up with a stack of books she wants to read. The day drags on lazy and uninspired. Finally, talking herself off the library chaise, she stretches and hops up the steps to her bedroom to put some clothes on.

She turns her radio on and searches for a soft rock station. She hums to herself as she put on tights and an oversized T-shirt.

"I don't want clever con-oon-versation... I love you just the way youuu are..." An sings to a Billy Joel tune as she put her hair in a ponytail and dabs Chapstick on her lips to complete her ensemble.

At last, An laces up her old sneakers by the kitchen door and heads out for a run. She goes out the back door and through her yard until she joins the path back there.

She begins to jog. She swats a low-hanging branch that catches her hair, and keeps on jogging, a smile on her face.

But she can't swat away the images that flash her back to the day she found the video of Miles… and Brad… and the girl.

She tries to blink the tears and the images away.

"Not today, darkness," she whispers. "Not today."

This is my home, my path, my life… I am becoming whole again. Not today, she tells herself firmly.

At the fork at the end of the path, An rounds the corner to the left and doubles back toward home. She continues her jog, now pretty much speed-walking. Back in her neck of the woods, she emerges on her lane, on the other end of the circle as she makes her way home.

She slows her pace as she nears the house that was just sold. In the driveway is a dark blue Chevy Tahoe. She stops to study the house and its surroundings. She is thinking how pretty and serene it looks. Ben and Lisa Spencer flash before her mind's eye.

"Pretty, isn't it?" a deep male voice announces.

Startled, An jumps and turns to the voice. She gasps and stares at the man.

"I just bought her. You must be one of my new neighbors, I presume?" the man says.

An stares at him with a dropped jaw. He is tall and lean. His bald head glistens in the afternoon sunshine. He smiles, and she catches a glimpse of straight, pearly-white teeth. His chin sports a jazz spot.

She can't find her words. *What in the world!*

"I went on a walk around the neighborhood, just getting a feel for things, you know," the man tells her. "I'm Ben, by the way." The man extends his right hand. "Benjamin Spencer. And you are?"

An feels the world do a crazy spin. She fumbles, her hands outstretched, trying to grab at something. The man reaches to hold her, propping her up. She feels woozy all over.

What is happening? She is standing in front of Benjamin Spencer. The man who is supposed to exist only in her mind!

"I'm sorry," she finally manages to say. "It's just that you look exactly like someone."

He chuckles, his manner so at ease, relaxed, comfortable in his own skin. "I get that a lot," he tells her. "But I assure you that I am just me, and there's only one of me."

An is not sure of this at all. She swallows and stares at him some more.

"I'm An, An Jordan. I live two doors down, number 28?"

"Oh, cool. That's the second-prettiest house on the block, after mine, of course," Ben tells her.

"This is a pretty and quiet street. You and your family made a good choice. You'll like it here," An tells Ben.

"Yeah, I'm looking forward to it."

"So, it's just you and Li—your wife?" An asks, holding her breath.

"No, just me and my son some weekends, actually. I see some of my patients at my home office sometimes, so I need a good amount of space. I know it seems silly to have so much house for one-and-a-half people. I just fell in love with—"

"So you only have the one son?"

"Yeah, that's it. He's in college and probably joining the military after that. He splits his time between me and his mom right now."

"I see," An tells him. "His mom, right…"

The man looks at her, puzzled.

This whole exchange totally perplexes her. How can her real world and subconscious world be interacting in such a way? What is the explanation for it?

Back in the safety of her own walls, An ponders what just happened. She calls Jimmy to discuss it at length.

"The Lord works in mysterious ways, An. The answers will reveal themselves to you eventually, if it's meant to be."

"And if it's not meant to be?" An asks. "What if I can't solve the puzzle?"

"Then it wasn't meant for you to know."

"Why would God reveal one piece of it but not the end piece of it?" An prods.

Jimmy sighs. "An, I'm just a man. I don't have all the answers. We are not meant to have all the answers. We just have to trust that there's a greater force at play."

Exasperated with Jimmy's lack of answers, An finally ends their conversation and calls Tina to share with her the encounter with Ben, the new neighbor, whom An had previously met while in a coma.

"I think you hold all the answers inside of you, An," Tina tells her. "You just have to keep working with your therapist to uncover them. Just stick with Dr. Rudolph. Make sure you bring this all up during your next session."

"Am I going crazy, Tina? Be honest with me. Do you think my head injuries caused some psychological imbalance, combined with the discovery that I married and enabled a psychopathic murderer for nearly three decades of my life?"

"Sweet Lord, no, An! You're not crazy. You are smart and intuitive and on the verge of something… some spiritual or existential something. I dunno what. Stay calm and you'll put the pieces together."

Tina sounds worried as she asks if she should stop by, or if An wants to spend the night at her house.

"No, no, I'm fine, really," An reassures Tina. "I'm tired. I'm going to take a nice long bubble bath and go to bed early. I'll call you if I need anything. I'm seeing Dr. Rudolph on Thursday. I'm good, really."

At about eleven o'clock that night, An lies in bed, dozing off to the muted sounds of her television. Suddenly, her cell phone buzzes on her nightstand. She jumps at the sound, her heart pounding in her chest. *Who could be calling me this late?*

She picks up the phone and reads *Unknown Caller* on her screen. She lets it ring until it stops, only to begin ringing again. *What the heck!*

She picks it up, annoyed. "Hello?" she asks, a little on the brusque side.

"An! Thank God you picked up. We really need to talk. The sooner the better!"

An sits up in bed, her breathing ragged, her eyes popping out of her head.

"An, are you there? Listen, meet me at the bookstore tomorrow morning. It's urgent," Angie instructs. "We have a lot to talk about."

"Um… Okay? I'll be there," An whispers.

ACKNOWLEDGEMENTS

Writing was my first love and is my constant companion. It truly is a life energy for me. There are a number of people that have shaped and nurtured this passion. Many others have been instrumental in the process of writing this novel. Without them, I would simply have words on the pages of a Word document, in the dark of my computer's hard drive.

Mary Morrissey, my journey to publish my first novel was ignited by your message to take a blind step toward my dream and let the universe care of the rest. I took a leap of faith the very next day when I saw an advertisement for Paper Raven Books. I am so happy and grateful for you and your work.

NOVA Ladies! I adore you for your mission and purpose to bolster other women with camaraderie, solid advice, eye-popping events and trips, and good eats! I discovered you during a dark spot in my life, and you became a guiding light, including providing me with ideas and words for my storyline. When I needed a friend, I got more than 400 of you! When I didn't have money to buy the twins Christmas gifts, lo and behold, bags of presents "magically" appeared. During the early phase of my novel, you were there, helping to keep the dark at a distance and my manuscript from collecting dust.

To my friends and supporters who inspired many scenes and helped to untangle a few complicated issues. You are a powerful force, always motivating me to reach my potential and beyond. Mom, you believe in me when I don't. Peggy for saving me—mostly my sanity—when things looked bleak back then. Teresa for all the shenanigans that kept the tears away with laughter and mischief—you made me do it! Ed, thank you for helping me figure out some tricky chapters. So many others contributed to this story, some without even realizing it! There are too many names to list here, but I know who you are, and you know who you are.

To my siblings, Paul, Sandra, and John. Yes, I've always been older, extremely bossy, and wiser, but you always had my back. I appreciate that. Our childhood provided me with plenty of ideas for quite a few scenes in this book. I'm sorry for blaming you for the broken bowl, Polly! Sorry for feeding you flaming-hot peppers, Sis, and sending you to the emergency room when you were one, I think. John, I'm sorry I let you ride your tricycle around the kitchen table, crashing and breaking your clavicle. I was a horrible babysitter. I'm not sorry, however, for all the childhood mischief that fueled scenes and ideas for this book.

A special thanks to my cousin Ana, who provided hours of before-bed reading and storytelling. One of my most vivid childhood recollections is listening to you read your own stories and poetry to me as I drifted to sleep. You sparked my love of words. Without you, this book would not have had its inception.

To my beloved aunt and uncle (Ana's parents), who helped to shape me into the person I am today. You taught me painful life lessons, nurtured my thoughts, ideas, and aspirations, and made it all—fun! Also, to the rest of my immense extended family—there are 48 first cousins on my mother's side alone! We are spread out but always connected in thought. You make life so much more interesting and colorful. If not for you, the characters in this novel would not be as real and believable.

To all my coworkers and residents at HWTE and my friends at McEnearny. You add sparkle and meaning to my days and keep me curious, always curious about all sorts of things. Some of you have provided guidance through many life and work challenges. Others have offered friendship and encouragement to help me soar. Plus, you read what I write and give me feedback.

Last but not least, in memory of my dad, who left this earth much too soon. I have missed you since, but you live on in my memories, my heart, and in my writing.

Your energy and your life's purpose continues on in this novel too because you are a part of me. I am so blessed to have been born your daughter.